More Praise for

ELKHORN TAVERN

"*Elkhorn Tavern* has the beauty of *Shane* and the elegiac dignity of *Red River* without the false glamour or sentimentality of those classic Western films. Unquestionably it has the makings of a classic Western. Mr. Jones is at home among the ridges and hardwoods of a frontier valley: He knows what moves in its forests, how the land changes under the seasons. He holds us still and compels us to notice what we live in. . . . Mr. Jones lets us hear the terrible drums of war, the thrashing horses, and wounded boy soldiers squealing on hands and knees. He can paint a panorama of troops uncoiling out of the scatter of deserted camps onto roads of dirty snow strewn with corpses. But his story is not about the fighters; it is about their victims, those who try to survive the fight. . . . [Mr. Jones] makes heroic the unheralded pioneers homesteading in the Missouri territories during the Civil War."

—*The New York Times*

"Douglas C. Jones writes what might be called historical novels, but they are much more than that. They are stirring word pictures of the way things really were in this country not so long ago. . . . *Elkhorn Tavern* is even better than the books that preceded it."

—The Associated Press

"Jones is a meticulous craftsman whose dialects, dialogues, settings, and sayings seem so right and natural that one has the satisfying feeling of having read a novel without one false note."

—*San Francisco Sunday Examiner & Chronicle*

continued . . .

"In this stunning historical novel, Jones re-creates place, people, and events brilliantly . . . a fine, strong, affecting saga."

—*Publishers Weekly*

"A fine, uncompromising, unusually angled piece of Civil War fiction—from a master of gritty historical[s]." —*Kirkus Reviews*

"Jones may do for the historical novel what John Ford did for the Western film." —*Library Journal*

ELKHORN TAVERN

DOUGLAS C. JONES

 NEW AMERICAN LIBRARY

NEW AMERICAN LIBRARY
Published by New American Library, a division of
Penguin Group (USA) Inc., 375 Hudson Street,
New York, New York 10014, USA
Penguin Group (Canada), 90 Eglinton Avenue East, Suite 700, Toronto,
Ontario M4P 2Y3, Canada (a division of Pearson Penguin Canada Inc.)
Penguin Books Ltd., 80 Strand, London WC2R 0RL, England
Penguin Ireland, 25 St. Stephen's Green, Dublin 2,
Ireland (a division of Penguin Books Ltd.)
Penguin Group (Australia), 250 Camberwell Road, Camberwell, Victoria 3124,
Australia (a division of Pearson Australia Group Pty. Ltd.)
Penguin Books India Pvt. Ltd., 11 Community Centre, Panchsheel Park,
New Delhi - 110 017, India
Penguin Group (NZ), 67 Apollo Drive, Rosedale, North Shore 0632,
New Zealand (a division of Pearson New Zealand Ltd.)
Penguin Books (South Africa) (Pty.) Ltd., 24 Sturdee Avenue,
Rosebank, Johannesburg 2196, South Africa

Penguin Books Ltd., Registered Offices:
80 Strand, London WC2R 0RL, England

Published by New American Library, a division of Penguin Group (USA) Inc. Previously published in a
Holt, Rinehart and Winston edition.

First New American Library Printing, November 2010
10 9 8 7 6 5 4 3 2 1

Copyright © Kemm, Incorporated, 1980
Map design by Judy Howard
All rights reserved

 REGISTERED TRADEMARK—MARCA REGISTRADA

New American Library Trade Paperback ISBN: 978-0-451-23185-7

The Library of Congress has cataloged the hardcover edition of this title as follows:

Jones, Douglas C.
Elkhorn Tavern.
1. United States—History—Civil War, 1861–1865—
Fiction.   I. Title
PZ4.J7534Ei   [PS3560.0478]   813'.54   79-27818

Set in Adobe Caslon Pro
Designed by Alissa Amell

Printed in the United States of America

This book is dedicated to the memory of those women, no matter whether their loyalties were North or South, who tried to survive in the savage vacuum left after a seldom recalled battle of 1862. The fact that they lived at all is marked only in tiny, forgotten clusters of scarred headstones scattered among the hickory groves and oak ridges of that land, but their progeny are still there.

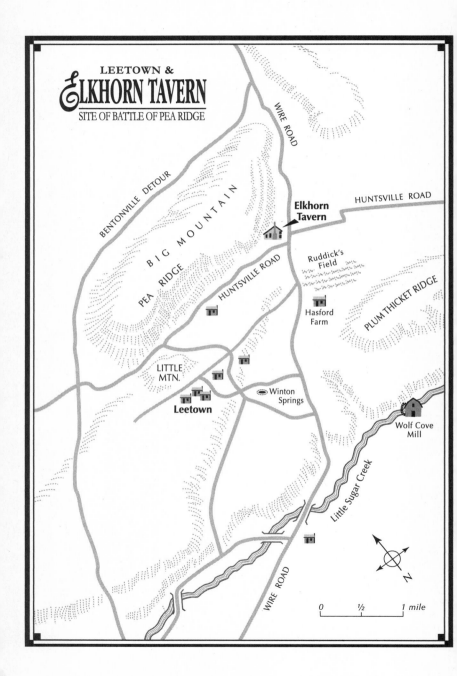

PART ONE

H e saw them coming along Wire Road, could almost hear the steel-shod hooves on the frozen ground, although they were at least a mile away and all he could actually hear was the wind in the black locusts around him. They came in column, the riders bundled against the late-February cold under slate gray clouds. The breathing of their horses created a milky vapor around them, whiter than the few remaining drifts of snow lying in shadowed places and clinging to the bark on oak and walnut trees.

They had first come into view beyond Elkhorn Tavern, bunching and stretching out again on the road through the thick timber. It was an undisciplined movement but certain in its progress, much as a copperhead snake goes across a woodlot in winter, sluggish but deadly. They were armed. He could see rifles across saddle horns or thrusting up like Indian lances, butts held on thighs. It was a formless group, smoke-colored, yet the guns were clear to him, as were the horses' legs moving and the heads of the riders. He marked the variety of their headgear—wide-brimmed hats and fur caps with flaps hanging out to either side like the helmet horns of raiding Norsemen. Even at a distance, he knew they wore no regular uniforms. He guessed there were about forty of them.

Across the wide, flat valley where dry cornstalks rattled in fields between woodlots, he watched the leaders turn into the yard of the tavern. Through bare branches of intervening trees, he could see the long white structure that sat against the wall of limestone high ground called Pea Ridge.

The riders surrounded the building, engulfing it, some of them running their horses into the rear yard. There was a tiny balloon of smoke from the hand of one who sat his mount before the tavern's front gallery. It took a long time for the report of the shot to reach him, and then the distance and wind turned it soft—the sound of a finger thumped against the side of a hickory barrel.

Riders were dismounting at the barns and the smokehouse, disappearing inside. For an instant he saw the white shirtwaisted figure of a woman in the tavern doorway, but then she was gone, the dark figures running along the gallery and going in after her. Untended horses milled about the grounds, no apparent effort being made to control them as their riders scavenged through the buildings.

This was no regular cavalry unit of either army operating in the area. He knew without having seen such things that these were guerrillas, partisans of one side or the other, and he turned and started running up the slope.

His long legs stretched out easily and his boots made sharp cracking sounds as they smashed the frozen leaves of autumn still on the ground. The muzzle-loading shotgun he carried swung back and forth loosely at his side. He ran with mouth open, his lips pulled back across his teeth. His angular face was just beginning to show signs of a fuzzy growth of whiskers, and at his ears and neck straight, straw-colored hair fanned back beneath a narrow-brimmed hat. He picked his way through the trees without thinking how, running full out, for this was home ground where he had lived all his life. It was his fifteenth winter, in the first year of the war, and his name was Roman Hasford.

A long way from the road, he broke from the trees and into the farmyard. At one of the windows in front of the long, high-gabled house, he could see the solid form of his mother holding back the curtain and watching him coming. Then there was a sudden knot of apprehension in his belly, because he was the only man left on this farm, and with him, the two women—his mother and his sister, Calpurnia, just turned seventeen and come to womanhood in such obvious fashion it embarrassed him to think about it.

By the time Roman Hasford reached the house, bounding across the covered porch in one stride, his mother was holding the door open. He burst inside, bringing with him a puff of chilling air. She closed the door quickly, looking up at him because already he was a full head taller than she. Waiting for him to catch his breath, she moved to the center of the small room. A fireplace stood at one end, the door to the kitchen at the other. There were a few upholstered chairs, a china closet, a polished library table, and a daybed in the room, which they called the parlor. Sometimes Roman's mother decorated the whitewashed slab pine walls with wildflowers, and hanging above the table was a watercolor portrait of a man in the uniform of a Prussian infantryman, with long, drooping mustache.

At the rear, a steep staircase led up to where Roman and his sister had their rooms, one at either end of the long structure. They called that the loft, and his sister, Calpurnia, had been watching him run up the slope from a small window there. Now she was coming down, moving quickly but carefully on the narrow stairs that were little more than a ladder.

"They've come," he said, his words rushing out with his breathing. "They're at the tavern, and look to be headed south. This way."

His mother touched his arm, watching his face with the same sharp blue eyes she had given both her children. His excitement seemed not to affect her, and that irritated him.

"Who's come? Slow down and tell me who's come?"

"A bunch of those bushwhackers, or whatever they are we've been hearing about."

Calpurnia had moved close behind her mother, and both

women stood immobile, watching his face. This irritated him even more, that they both seemed to think of him still as a wild-eyed boy, were reluctant to take his word for any calamity, large or small.

"It's likely just some army people," Calpurnia said.

"No, it's not just some army people," Roman said harshly, mimicking his sister's voice. "It's bushwhackers. Don't you think I'd know army people if I saw them? There's been enough of them around to know what they look like. These are bushwhackers."

"Are they horseback?" his mother asked.

"Sure they're horseback, and they've got guns. One of them fired a shot in the yard over there. They look like a posse," he said.

"What are they doing?" Calpurnia asked.

"Runnin' around like crazy men, into all the buildings," he said, exasperation growing with the questions.

"If they're bushwhackers, why would they bother anything at the tavern? Everybody knows the tavern people are for the South."

"It don't matter who people are for," Roman almost shouted. "They don't care who people are for."

"All right, all right," his mother said, touching his arm again. "Whoever they are, they're likely hungry and hunting grub." She held one hand to her face, tapping her lips with a finger as she always did when she was thinking. While Roman fidgeted and Calpurnia watched him, still with no concern in her eyes, they could hear the wind gusting under the eaves and, behind the house, the soft tones of a cowbell.

2   They had talked of this day coming. They had made plans for it since Martin Hasford had left to join the Confederates recruiting to the south. It was then the stories had begun to cir-

culate about partisans loose in the countryside, bands of armed men called bushwhackers or jayhawkers who claimed they rode for one cause or the other but who actually rode only for themselves. These men stayed clear of the real armies, for capture by either would likely mean hanging forthwith. There had been tales of looting and burning, of killings and worse in this part of the state where sympathy was equally divided between Union and secession.

Where the three now stood was five miles from the border of Missouri, a state torn from the beginning in its loyalties. They were only a little over forty miles from Kansas, a day's ride. Due west, less than twenty-five miles, was the eastern edge of Indian Territory, where everyone knew the owlhooters and night riders took refuge from white man's law. Perhaps worst of all, because passions here ran so hot over the issues that had ripped the country apart, almost all able-bodied men had dashed off at the first flash of war to join one color or the other, leaving it a place of women, children, and the old.

"How many are there?" Calpurnia asked, breaking the silence. It touched the quick of Roman's thinking, coming exactly to the thing that worried him most. His sister had a talent for doing that, as though she were a part of his mind. It confused and infuriated him because he could never fathom her thoughts. Looking into his sister's eyes was always like standing before a mirror, seeing only reflections and nothing from within.

"A lot. Maybe fifty," he said, stretching it to lend credence to his own urgency. He shifted from one foot to the other, still swinging the shotgun at his side. "We better do something. We better do something right now."

"Yes, I guess we had," his mother said. "All right. Do it the way we've talked about and get back to the house as soon as you can."

The woman moved quickly, once the decision was made. It

always surprised Roman, seeing his mother move like this when the need arose. She was a stout woman, only in her midthirties but already grown fat from too much flour gravy and pork. She looked like any good German hausfrau, which she was. Her features retained something of a delicate beauty, though gone puffy, and her hair, done back in a severe bun, was beginning to streak with gray. Her hands were small but tough from years of work, and Roman knew she was a powerful woman. Once, when a half-wild cow had cornered her in a milking stall, she had struck the brute between the eyes with her fist, and Roman had always imagined the cow had staggered a little with the blow.

What neither of the children knew, because she had never told anyone, was that after these flurries of quick action sharp pains would run along her left arm and into her shoulder. To Roman and Calpurnia she looked as she always had because they had grown up with her changing. Had they been able to look back and see their mother slender and graceful as she once had been, they would not have recognized her.

To people in this valley, she was Mrs. Hasford. To her children and husband, she was Mama. Her name was Ora.

They hurried out through the kitchen past the hot cookstove, the wind huffing noisily in the flue above it. The women took men's heavy winter overcoats from rear wall pegs.

"Get those dogs caught up first, Roman, and pen them in the barn," Ora said. "We don't want them yapping around the place now."

The dogs had somehow sensed excitement and begun to chase chickens about the yard. They were bluetick coon dogs, heavy of bone and good for bear hunting as well. They charged about the yard, scattering chickens and feathers until Roman caught up one and carried it to the barn like a squirming sack of cornmeal.

"You'd do better to put that gun down," his mother called,

fanning her apron at a swaggering flock of guinea hens, herding them toward a wooded draw south of the farmyard. The churn house was there, built of native stone over a spring that issued clear water the year around. "Put the gun down, Roman," she shouted again. He left the shotgun leaning against the barn wall and ran after the other dogs.

At the rear of the barn, Calpurnia had a halter on the cow, a small blue roan of undetermined ancestry. She unbuckled the leather strap around the cow's neck, threw the bell aside, and started from the barn lot up the gentle slope east of the farmstead, pushing at the cow's warm flank, coaxing in a gentle voice as they went. She knew exactly where she was going, having thought about it a great deal since they'd first planned this hiding of live-stock. There was a wild plum thicket sheltered by rock outcrops about a quarter mile from the barn. Calpurnia knew it would take a long time to get there with the slow-moving cow, but it didn't matter. This was her only job.

She always enjoyed going to the plum thicket, even in winter. And she was enjoying it now, feeling no sense of fear. In all her life she had never seen a brutal act of violence. There had been the schoolyard fights among the boys, but these were more sporting romps than viciousness, as had been her own sometimes physical disagreements with Roman when they were younger. And each year at butchering time she had worked with her mother in the kitchen, away from the killing. Besides, killing hogs and cattle was a part of making life work, like plowing corn or harvesting barley. It was impossible for her to imagine that across the valley were those who would do them harm. Wars were stories told in the books her father had given her, stories that had happened a long time ago. She went up the slope with the cow without ap-prehension, even a little amused at her brother's anxiety.

Roman's major task was the draft animals. There were two horses, both mares and easy to manage, and the mule. The mule, for once, submitted to the hackamore without fuss and went along quietly with its mother and the other horse as Roman led them from the barn lot. Soon, he was pulling them past Calpurnia.

"You better get that cow hid," he said. "You better hurry up."

"If you're in such a rush, why don't you ride one and lead the others?" she asked, and he thought she was laughing at him. But he did as she suggested, although it galled him. She was always like that, poking fun at serious business. Even now, with bushwhackers likely on their way. Girls were not supposed to be like that. They were supposed to be flighty and afraid. But Cal was like their mother, tough as slab hickory.

He thought it might be a flaw in his heritage, what with the family womenfolk always calm when the men were running around impetuously, grabbing guns at the slightest provocation. But at least he liked his own womenfolk better than most. He thought of Lucinda Cox, who was married to the young Joseph Cox at Elkhorn Tavern. Lucinda never knew what she was about, night or day. She hung on to Joseph like ivy to an oak, and likely had to ask her way to the privy. Joseph was the only man left at the tavern now, and him just two years Roman's senior. Old man Cox and the two older boys had driven their cattle over into Indian Territory to keep them away from the armies and were still gone. Then Roman remembered the five black slaves Mr. Cox had brought up from Mississippi, but he didn't know whether to count them as men on the place. He had no experience with coloreds, slave or free.

He wondered why he was thinking about the Cox family when he had troubles of his own. Perhaps because he could still see in his mind those dark riders closing around the place across the valley. And nobody there except the old lady, five slaves, Joseph, and Lucinda—herself a bride of less than a year and already pregnant. And fourteen years old.

Roman was in an uncut stand of hickory when he heard another shot from across the valley. He pulled the horses in and tried to quiet the mule enough to listen. He wasn't sure because of the wind, but he thought he counted three more shots. They must be killing the hogs over there, he thought, and decided he'd gone far enough. He wondered whether the mule wouldn't smell horses in the farmyard below from this distance and set up a racket if the bushwhackers came. If it did, then Roman doubted even bush-whackers would go stumbling around in the woods looking for one mule. He tethered all the animals to a tree on a short lead, and hobbled the mule besides. He wasn't concerned about them taking distemper from the cold. They had thick winter coats and, besides, they spent most of their time outside. As he bent to check the mule's hobbles, the animal nipped him on the butt. He slammed the flat of his hand against the mule's face but there was no fire in either bite or slap. This was a routine thing that happened each time they came near one another.

In the farmyard below, Ora Hasford had managed to drive all the guinea hens into the woods. The chickens were a different proposition. Some of the old setting hens followed the guineas meekly enough, but the younger birds fluttered around the yard, avoiding Ora's rushes, making a terrible squawking and loosing feathers on the wind. Finally she gave it up, but at least most of the flock had taken to the woods. The rest remained stubbornly in the yard, defying her.

"Damned chickens," she muttered aloud, that being the only swearing she ever did, and usually to herself. Since her Martin had been gone she found herself saying it more frequently. She wondered if perhaps her chance of entry into heaven was jeopardized by it.

She ran to the barn with short, rapid strides, her legs stretching the gingham dress under her man's coat. It was the only kind of dress she ever wore, buttoned down the front, flared in the blouse but cut to hang straight to the tops of her high-button shoes. Except for church and visiting, or trips to the mill on Wolf Cove of Little Sugar Creek, she always wore a white half-apron. The only color about her was the thick golden wedding band on her left hand.

From the barn she brought a pitchfork and ran to the pigsty. There had been two shoats left after fall butchering, but they had rooted out of the pen and gone wild in the woods. Now there was only the sow, a huge saddle-colored brute that eyed Ora with malevolent distrust. The sow had been taken to boar at Wolf Cove sometime before and was coming down early, already vicious. As Ora approached, the pink-rimmed little eyes glinted and the sow charged, but came up short with a tang of the fork in her nose. After that one thrust, the big beast allowed herself to be prodded toward the churn-house hollow. Watching her disappear into the woods, Ora hoped the guineas and chickens would have the sense to stay away from her.

"Damned guineas," she said aloud. They were still making their loud clatter in the hollow. If anyone came, the guineas would set up a bedlam of noise, being better watchdogs than any dog. And they laid eggs big as hen eggs. Martin Hasford's people had brought the ancestors of these birds from Georgia because they kept snakes away. In all the time she could remember, Ora had never seen a rattler or even a copperhead in their dooryard.

But they are no protection against men on horseback, she thought, except to warn of their coming. She sighed heavily and turned to the house, looking once up the slope, but seeing no sign yet of either of her children she went inside.

3 Calpurnia was back first and the two women set about making the evening meal. It was growing dark when Roman came off the hill and reported that he'd heard more shots from the direc-

tion of the tavern. Calpurnia glanced quickly at her mother, but Ora's expression did not change. She continued to move about the room deliberately, showing none of her dread or uncertainty. She knew it was her duty to reassure the children, and being stoic was the only way she knew how.

No lamp was lit. The two women worked silently, each knowing exactly what the other was about. This was a large room, and in addition to the stove there was a cabinet where dishes were kept, called the safe. In one corner of the room were a double bed and wardrobe, for this served as the master bedroom. Over the room hung the scent of bacon rind and sassafras because these things were always here—the rind to grease metal pots, and the sassafras for tea.

They sat at the round oak table, lighted in their meal only by the red glow from the lower open door of the stove. There was corn bread with butter and the last of summer's black-eyed peas, and milk brought from the churn house in an earthen crock. Most of it seemed to hang in Roman's throat, and he observed with disgust that his sister ate with her usual huge appetite.

"Well?" Roman asked finally. "What do we do now?"

"We just wait and see," his mother said.

"Aw, hell's fire—"

"Don't talk ugly," she said sharply. "We'll just wait and see."

Roman started to rise from the table, pushing back the chair, cane-bottomed like all the others that his father had made before Roman was born.

"I better get the shotgun. I forgot and left it at the barn."

"Leave it where it's at," Ora said.

"Aw, Mama . . ."

"It'll make more trouble than it can get you out of if those people come here tonight."

"Oh Lord, I forgot in all the running around, the cow hasn't been milked," Calpurnia said.

"I'll do it," Roman said, half out of his seat again.

"You're the worst milker in the family," Calpurnia said. "Besides, you don't know where I hid her."

"Well, I'm not gonna just sit here like a bump with you out there thrashing around in the woods."

His sister was grinning at him as she fetched a milk pail from its peg on the rear wall. A lantern hung there, too, but she made no move to take it. That gave Roman some satisfaction anyway, that at least she was beginning to realize there could be some peril in this night. But it meant she would be out on the ridge alone in the dark, and this disturbed him in a way that made his voice break when he spoke: "I'll go with you."

"Stay with Mama," Calpurnia said. "Just sit here like a bump." She laughed and, pulling on one of the men's coats, went out into the darkness. Roman fumed, his lips moving silently as he made some rejoinder to himself.

"Eat some more peas," Ora said.

"I ain't hungry no more," he said.

She knew this habit he had of falling into loose language, no matter how well his father had taught him. She understood it was a way of rebelling a little, a part of his impatience with these awkward years when manhood seemed to come so slowly.

"She makes me mad," he muttered.

"She just likes to tease. Now listen, Roman, I want you to go down to the road again and watch for a while. So you can tell us if anything comes down the road."

"Well . . ." He hesitated, knowing this was only a thing to placate him. "All right. If you need me, blow the horn."

Years before, Martin Hasford had whittled a hunter's horn taken from a dehorned bull, and it hung now from a peg on the back porch. The elder Hasford had used it to call in the dogs after a hunt, and Ora used it as a summons to dinner. The mellow tone of that horn would carry for miles through woods and into the hollows of this country, and as soon as Roman mentioned it he realized neither of them wanted to attract such attention to themselves.

"Never mind the horn," he said. "If you need me, I'll know it."

She smiled as he went out, swaggering a little. She knew he would detour by the barn and pick up the shotgun, but it was better now to let him have his way. After he was gone, she rubbed her shoulder, where the stabbing pain lingered. And now her hand hurt, the one she had used to hit the cow.

Ora Hasford wasn't concerned about her children being out in the night woods. They knew these fields and forests, and were likely safer there than in the house. Maybe I should send them out to sleep in the woods tonight, she thought, but knew they would rebel at any such suggestion.

She moved to the window and saw that the clouds were breaking up and the moon coming on full. She watched her son moving toward the road, the shotgun in one hand, and she smiled. But there was a sadness in her each time she looked at Roman now. She had watched with considerable dismay as this boy grew to the urgings of a man. She had seen his terrible embarrassment whenever Calpurnia came into the room with nothing on but her chemise. He spent a lot of time now at the mirror over the back porch washstand, feeling the new growth of downy whiskers with his fingertips. Or chewing cuds of his father's tobacco furtively, and swearing when he thought no one was around. She knew all this, and it somehow touched her as nothing else about him ever had.

It seemed to Ora Hasford that her daughter had been a woman since long before the girl had shown any outward signs of it, full of more wisdom and love of life than her years should have allowed. But Roman was coming on more slowly, and there was still much wide-eyed wonder and amazement in his face as he watched his world spreading out before him. Many boys his age were married and had started families, but he was a long way from that, still to Ora her towhead baby.

More disturbing than all of that was Roman's recent cautious comments that able-bodied men should be in the army. She knew he was itching to follow his father off to war before he missed any of it.

"There is a generation whose teeth are swords," she muttered aloud, misquoting the line from Proverbs.

Depressed, she turned back from the window to wash the dishes in the dark.

4   Roman went down the slope quickly, through the oaks to the tangle of black locusts that bordered the road. The wind was dead, but it was colder, and with the cloud cover moving off, the air had a brittle snap. He pulled his coat tight around his neck and stood against the snake-rail fence, looking along Wire Road toward Elkhorn Tavern.

There were fires in the yard. Even with the moonlight he could not see the tavern building, but he knew exactly where to look. The blazes, about a half dozen of them, made tiny pinpoints of red in the night. Now and again one would flare up, as though someone were throwing on fresh wood.

Behind him, in the spring hollow, he heard a horned owl call. He wondered about the livestock, back in the timber. He worried about the chickens especially, and the guineas, having seen tracks of a weasel near the churn house just the day before. And there were the foxes, too. Of course, there were no wolves so close to Wire Road. It had been years since he'd heard or seen one. They had gone back toward the east, into the rough country around White River. They had been pushed back by the farms and settlements growing along this eastern edge of Indian Territory between

Missouri and the Boston Mountains. It was becoming a civilized place, and all in his lifetime. Along this very road where he stood, Butterfield had run his stagecoach line from Saint Louis to Fort Smith and on beyond to California. And along here, too, they had built a telegraph line from Missouri to the south. Hence the name Wire Road.

But there was no stage line now; it had come to an abrupt stop because of the war. And the telegraph line, although still standing, was seldom used, because at one end of it was the Yankee army and at the other the Confederates.

Then he thought about his sister, back on the ridge in her wild plum thicket, milking the cow in the moonlight. He'd known all along she'd hide the cow there. It was her favorite place. They called it Cal's plum thicket, and from that even named the high ground behind the house Plum Thicket Ridge, although it was not a ridge at all actually, only a wooded ground higher than the flat land where Wire Road passed. Calpurnia would go there in the summer with a book, or sometimes just to sit and think. About what, Roman had no idea. She had gathered the fruit from those stunted trees since she'd been a little girl, and helped her mother make the thick red jelly. Well, he thought, she's sure as hell's fire the best cook along the valley, except for Mama. And smart, too! Smarter than I'll ever be. She always learned quickly the things their father tried to teach them. Although he had gone four years to school, and she only two, he had come out of the Leetown two-room academy knowing less than she had when she went in.

But she was hardheaded. And pretty, too, a lot prettier than Lucinda Cox or any of the other town or farm girls he had begun to notice lately. Light brown hair falling down her back, a valentine face with a sprinkle of freckles across a small nose. And growing tight into all her clothes, though as soon as he thought about that, he tried to think of something else.

Somewhere along the valley a dog barked. Yard dog, he

thought. Nothing like the baying of coon dogs or the music of foxhounds running. Just an old yard dog. But it was almost the time of year for good fox hunting, with spring only a few weeks off. The reds and grays would be out, teasing the dogs like Cal teased him, letting the dogs run them until they tired of the game and denned. But then, he realized, except for hounds that went off on their own, there wouldn't be much fox-racing in this valley for a long time to come.

He looked down the valley toward Leetown, where the family went to church and where he and Cal had gone to school. He saw no single light there, as if the people had denned like foxes, waiting for the hounds to give up and go home. He swept the valley with his eyes, back to the north where the fires winked around Elkhorn Tavern. He was a little surprised at himself, and proud, too, that he could think of weasels and foxes and Calpurnia's freckles with that unknown threat lying just across the valley, warming itself before the fires.

The cold was seeping through his clothes and his feet were going numb. For a while he stamped about in the dead leaves, but the noise seemed overwhelming in the cold air and he stopped. It was well on to ten o'clock when he gave up his watch. Going back through the oaks, he thought they might turn around and go back to wherever they came from. He had known this valley all his days, each stand of trees, each spring and creek, each house and barn and lime-rock ridge. Now there was an unfamiliar presence here, one that had no place in the valley, and all he understood was his fear of it. Once more he felt the knot in his belly that had come after seeing those riders moving along the road from Missouri, their rifles up like lances and their cap flaps like horns.

II

Bare branches created a black lacework across the face of the lowering moon, and the slope before the house was like a white blanket patterned with the shadow stripes of trees. At the kitchen window, the curtain drawn back to give her a full view of the yard, Ora Hasford recalled the times she and her Martin had sat here, watching the last light of a spring day fade in the west, smelling the perfume of blooming locusts and wild honeysuckle.

For as long as she could remember, one of her great delights had been to see this land change under the seasons, its sounds and scents and substance. But always the spring had been her favorite, when the hills began to grow their puffs of color and the far ridges cut a sharp green edge against the sky. Those had been the times she and her husband would enjoy together, at the end of the day, sitting at this window and watching the west go dark.

They seldom spoke then. But finally, with the evening star sharp over the valley, he would touch her shoulder.

"Time for sleep now, Mama," he would say, and pat her rump as she turned toward the bed.

With Martin gone, she missed nothing so much as those moments with him after the children were safe in the loft. It was even possible to imagine that such tender moments had happened more often than they actually had, for Martin Hasford had never been a demonstrative man. Their relationship was almost matter-of-fact. The touch of his fingers came infrequently. Yet she knew a gentleness in him, even though his expression of it was so disguised that few others recognized it, not even his own children.

There had been two letters from him, written in a place called Russelville, somewhere along the Arkansas River, where he was drilling with a newly formed company of infantry. That was better than she had expected, because although Martin could sometimes be expansive, he could, in his usual mood, be taciturn. And besides, there was no mail service that deserved the name, so she supposed that perhaps he had written often, without the letters ever having arrived.

Now there was no odor of locusts, nor any sound of the chuck-will's-widow that fluted across the valley during those warm months. There was only the cold, and the emptiness of her bed and the hooting owl in the spring hollow. She counted the bird's calls. There were always eight, then a long pause, and then eight more.

There had been considerable fuss getting Roman up to bed. He had wanted to stay with her for whatever might come. But finally, with his early apprehension and excitement diminished like the heat coming from the cookstove, sleep had become impossible to resist, and he had gone up to his feather tick. Calpurnia had been sleeping long since.

Ora Hasford held a heavy comforter about her neck, folded around her body to her knees. She tried to ignore the cold on her ankles, listening to the owl hooting from the spring hollow. She wondered how the crows knew that this old owl roosted in a hollow hickory snag there. Each day they came to scold him. Sometimes Roman ran out in exasperation at their infernal racket and fired at them with his shotgun. He never hit one, of course, because, as is the nature of crows, they always saw him and recognized the gun and took flight before he could take aim.

She thought for a while of lighting a small candle and reading the Hasford Bible. She read badly, at least not nearly so well as the children, but sometimes she found comfort in the poetry of Psalms. She had read many of the passages so often they came to her mind unbidden, especially when she was alone.

When she had the massive book, she thought better of the candle and just sat with the Bible clasped in both hands in her lap, taking some solace from that anyway. She seldom prayed, at least not in words, because unlike her husband she was self-conscious about such things. She had never called on Divine Providence to assist her in any trial, depending instead on an earthly determination. And she did not pray now, but sat in the dark, holding the Book.

As she began to doze, a line from the Bible came to her. "I open to my beloved but my beloved had withdrawn himself and was gone. . . ." It was a verse she had read often, but secretly. She knew her husband considered all such references base and vulgar, like most of the entire book of Solomon, even if it did come from the Bible.

At first, she had no idea what startled her. She sat up stiffly, coming out of a light sleep, knowing only that something had changed. For a moment she tried to understand it, and then she knew. The owl had stopped his calling, the night was completely still. She lifted the window sash a few inches and the bite of the night air stung her face as she bent to the opening. She heard nothing at first. Then there was a whisper, more an impression of sound than sound itself. She listened for a long time before she recognized it.

A column of horses was passing along Wire Road directly below the house.

She had hardly digested this when the guinea hens in the spring hollow began their clamorous warning, shattering the silence. The sound sent her rushing across the kitchen, dropping the Bible and kicking the comforter from around her feet. There was a wild instant of panic as she bumped hard against the cold stove, but she quickly controlled it. Without any plan, she found her way to the safe and drew from a drawer the meat cleaver used at butchering time. She ran across the dark kitchen to the parlor and, opening the front door, stepped out into the cold.

She waited in the shadows of the porch roof, damning the guineas' abrupt chattering but thankful for it, too. Then she saw them, coming up the slope from the road, the horses picking their way between the trees. There were four riders, and for an instant she wondered why so few had split off from the column. She knew there were a great many more below, else she never would have heard the horses. As they drew near the house, her fear was gone, for now she could see what was to be dealt with; her jaw set and she was icy calm. She gripped the meat cleaver, able to feel the sharp fourteen-inch blade tight against her leg.

The lead rider came directly toward the front of the house. He was wearing a wide-brimmed hat with a plume, and a long cape that flowed back across the croup of the horse like an afghan spread over a footstool. His figure was rotund, a welding of dark circles, each set partly inside the next. His eyes, as he drew near, shone in the moonlight reflected from the front wall of the house. They were round and somehow furious, set above apple cheeks disappearing into a flowing black beard that spread across his chest like a tangle of barbed wire. The hat brim, the curving plume, the melon-shaped face, all showed above a bulbous body that seemed to strain out against the saddle pommel.

Ora Hasford knew when she saw the saddle that Roman had been right. This was no army man, because neither army used work saddles with high horns, almost Spanish. These were partisans.

The other three angled off to one side, toward the corner of the house. One stood out for her at once. He wore a slouch hat that hung down behind, concealing the shape of his head in the dark. Still, she felt some vague sense of recognition when she looked at him. He was tall and slender, and rode awkwardly. There was a formless quality about him, lacking depth, like flat pieces cut from a cardboard box and pasted together. Of the three, he was the only one not carrying a rifle.

She had no time to ponder who this man might be. The leader had pulled up near the porch, swaying in the saddle, held there by the weight of his body. She could smell liquor, for which she had always had a sensitive nose, and knew that these men had been heavily into the whiskey stocks at the tavern. As the leader reined in, so did the other three, off to one side, and above the racket of the still-chattering guinea hens, she heard one of them snickering.

The bearded man fumbled for the flap of a saddle holster, but before he could draw the pistol, Ora stepped out into the moonlight. He gave a little start that quivered through his bulky frame, and his hand paused on the half-drawn weapon. Then he straightened in the saddle, a wide grin across his mat of beard, leaving the pistol in its holster. At first effort, his words were nothing more than a deep gurgle, unintelligible to her.

"What is it you want?" she asked, and there was no tremor in her voice, rather a harshness that made the horse shy back away from the porch.

"I see you have harkened, madam. You have harkened to our coming," the man bellowed, swaying in the saddle. He touched the brim of his hat and she could see the long fringes on his elbow-length gauntlets. "I am Colonel Clarence Caudell, madam, of Kansas, commander of Caudell's light irregular cavalry." He appeared pleased with the sound of his name and let it roll off his tongue like thick syrup.

"What is it you want?"

"We ride for the Union, madam . . . and with the spirit of John Brown," he added, as though shouting a command.

Ora knew then these were not bushwhackers but jayhawkers, although the distinction was of little consequence. Bushwhackers were southern sympathizers, so they claimed, while *jayhawker* was a euphemism for free-soiler. Had she been allowed to choose, she would have preferred night riders for the South, because of her husband's loyalties. But she had no choice.

"You've heard of the magnificent John Brown, I assume," Caudell was saying.

"I heard he was some crazy man hanged for treason someplace in the East," she said, and knew as soon as it was out that the words were the wrong ones to use. Caudell seemed to puff up, his body bulging out like the feathers on a fighting bantam rooster. He felt for his saber, the chain rattling, but he did not draw it.

"You speak of treason? You, with your secessionist blasphemy, speak of treason?" he shouted. "We've come to buy horses for the Union army even now marching south into this place. Marching here to free it of all taint of rebellion. If you don't watch your tongue, madam, I will confiscate your stock and give you no hand receipt for their value."

"I haven't got any stock for sale, or for stealing, either, and no place to spend your hand receipts," she said stubbornly, knowing that was the wrong thing to say, too. But she was unable to control the rising bile of anger.

With a sudden lurching movement, Caudell raised one gauntleted hand, and with that signal the other three rode around the house toward the rear. Ora ran along the porch, although they were quickly gone, and now she was waving the meat cleaver and knew Caudell could see it. She could hear the muted sounds of the dogs barking from the barn.

"You keep those men out of my yard," Ora shouted. "All of you, stay out of my yard."

Although he seemed ready to fall from his mount, Caudell quickly reined the horse around to the end of the porch, confronting her again.

"Don't interfere," he roared. "We'll have those two horses. Be thankful we leave you the mule."

It came like a blow to her, that this man whom she had never seen nor heard of knew about the horses and the mule. And, what was worse, if he knew that, then he must have been aware that her husband had gone off south.

"My husband—"

From behind the house came one sharp sound, quickly cut off, and she knew that one of the men there had caught a chicken from its roost in the coop. She could hear them calling to one another drunkenly, and the barn door slam. And from the hollow, still, the guinea hens racketed.

"My husband—"

"Your husband, madam, is off to the south, leaving you here alone to learn how dangerous it is to stand for evil, how dangerous it is to stand for human slavery."

"Nobody stands for slavery."

"Your husband is off to fight in its behalf."

"Nobody has gone off to fight for slavery."

"Then why is your man not here to greet us, to assist us in our struggle?"

"He's gone off to Wolf Cove. He'll be back directly."

Caudell laughed explosively. "You lie, madam. You lie to me. Don't you know there are eyes, loyal-to-the-Union eyes, that watch you constantly? You cannot deceive us."

Her fury at his words came so violently, she took a step forward, the cleaver up. But he was laughing at her, pulling his horse just beyond her reach.

"You are in danger here, madam, serious danger."

"You take your men off my place, or I'll have the sheriff after you for stealing chickens."

"Your sheriff is an old man, with no authority over me," Caudell said. He reached behind him in a saddlebag and held up a coil of baling wire, the metallic strands gleaming silver in the moonlight. "If your sheriff tried to oppose me, I would hang him with this. I will hang anyone who stands in my way, madam."

Caudell stopped and looked back down the slope. She could see another rider coming, kicking his horse along, and she drew back into the shadows again, edging toward the door. The oncoming horseman pulled up a short distance off, and when he spoke she caught the burr of hill-country speech, so unlike that of Caudell.

"The boys has moved on, Colonel. We'd best get ourselfs out of here now."

Caudell made a grumbling sound in his throat, still holding the coil of wire against one thigh like a loop of rope. Before he could speak, the man in the slouch hat appeared at the corner of the house. In his hands were two chickens, heads-down, and Ora Hasford knew he had wrung their necks.

"They've hid the stock," he said in guarded tones she could barely hear, then spurred off toward the road.

Caudell glared at her, his eyes shining in the reflected moonlight like boiled eggs ready to pop from his head.

"You take warning, woman," he said. "I will not tolerate your resistance, nor anyone else's who comes before me. Only my compassion for you and your family keeps me from razing this farm. But I will not always be so lenient. You will find this valley a terrible place to live, you and your cubs, secessionists among our loyal Union citizens."

"You can burn in hell's fire," she said and, taking a step forward, spat at him. Bit chains rattled as he wheeled away and rode back through the trees, still unsteady in the saddle, clutching at the horn with both hands.

The final two came around from the rear, each carrying something she could not at first identify. Then she saw it was a ham and two sides of bacon, the last of their meat from the smoke-house.

Furious, she ran to the end of the porch, waving the cleaver and trying to shout, but unable in her rage to make a sound. Watching them disappear into the trees, she stood panting, trembling so badly the cleaver almost slipped from her hand. Then suddenly she was chilled to the bone, and she shuddered violently.

"Damned Yankee pigs," she sobbed, turning back to the door.

Just inside, she leaned against the wall, waiting for her breathing to slow. Her heart was pounding and her hands trembled. It was a shock that her temper had flared so fiercely, and a surprise that she had uttered the word *Yankee*. She had never said that word before, despite hearing it often. She had no notion what Yankees were, but she supposed them to be a people from some far-off place, a strange and different breed. The free-soilers in the valley she did not consider in the same class. She had watched from a distance the Union patrols along Wire Road, but she had never spoken to any of these men, nor even been close to them. But this night she had been near enough one to smell him. And though these guerrillas were no part of any Union force, and she knew it, in her rage and despair she had no inclination to separate the two.

There was a movement across the room, and with a sharp intake of breath Ora lifted the cleaver. Crossing to her mother, Calpurnia came into the light of the moon slanting through the window. She was holding Roman's shotgun clumsily in both hands.

"For Lord's sake, Cal, you scared me half to death."

"I thought you knew I was here, Mama," the girl said. Ora could hear the soft click as her daughter let down both hammers of the gun. "The guineas woke me up."

Ora Hasford was no more demonstrative a person than her

husband, but she had the urge now to take Calpurnia in her arms and hold her close. Yet she made no move to do it as the girl came near.

"They stole some chickens," Calpurnia said, her voice low but steady. Pride swelled up in Ora for this girl, standing in the house with a shotgun she had never fired, and knowing how only from watching her brother.

"I know it. And everything in the smokehouse. I should have thought about that and hid the meat, too."

"A body can't think of everything, Mama."

Ora reached out to touch Calpurnia's shoulder and felt the flannel nightgown.

"Are you barefooted?"

"Yes, but I'm not cold."

"You'll catch your death. Get back to bed. We'll talk about it in the morning. They've gone now."

"Why were they in such a hurry?"

"I don't know, but thank God for it. Is Roman awake?"

"Lord, no. If he was, he'd be down here. He can sleep through anything."

"All right. Get back to bed now. We'll talk about it in the morning."

"They knew who we were, Mama," Calpurnia said. Ora started to say one of the riders was a man she knew, although she could not call his name. But she thought better of it. She had never believed in concerning her children with things they could do nothing about.

"I know," she said. "But let's talk about it tomorrow."

"I thought they'd come in the house," the girl said.

"No, they weren't hungry enough." Not yet, Ora thought, but someday, maybe. She kept that to herself as well. "I guess they fed well at the tavern. Now, get back to bed, and put that shotgun away before you shoot somebody."

Calpurnia slipped across the room without a sound, and Ora sighed and turned to the kitchen and her own bed. The flannel sheets were cold at first, but soon they began to warm. At last the guinea hens ceased their clattering from the spring hollow. After a while the owl began his hooting once more, the moon went down, and she lay in darkness. But she did not sleep.

Slowly the fear and anger subsided. Her mind retraced each thing she could remember, each movement and word, as though trying to recall the images of a nightmare. Not all of these men had been strangers, even though she could call no names. Else that Colonel Caudell would not have known so much about this farmstead. It left her stunned, not because of anger or fear, but because she could not comprehend it.

2   Before the hill country of northwest Arkansas had become the ground of contention between Osage and Cherokee, the families of Martin and Ora Hasford had been small farmers in the rich valley of the Regnitz River in Bavaria. But because they had long been uncomfortable Protestants in a Catholic land, they emigrated to America in the first year after Waterloo. Martin's grandfather Hasford—only they spelled it Hassfurt then—had been a victim of that bloody Sunday fight. Or at least, they all supposed that was the case, since he never returned to them after going off to enlist in a Prussian infantry regiment for the last campaign against the French that ended on the rain-soaked fields of Belgium. They came to call him Picture Grandpapa, for at some point before completely disappearing he had commissioned a watercolor portrait of himself, and sent it home.

It had been a shocking experience for the family Hasford, one of their menfolk voluntarily becoming a member of Frederick William's army. Like most of their neighbors, they had a traditional distrust of the Prussians and the threat of domination the north German armies represented. And in a home-loving people, it seemed incomprehensible that a head of family would simply march off to war in an impetuous moment, adventuring across Europe while his womenfolk and sons were left behind to plant rye and hoe sugar beets.

Picture Grandpapa's contradiction in principle was a legacy he apparently passed along, for it would reappear. At least, his defenders pointed out, he had gone off to a crusade against Napoleon, whom they hated even more than the Prussians.

The westering Hasfords represented an early trickle of the later flood of Germans who would crowd the ships leaving the old country in the decade before the Civil War. Unlike most of those who followed, they brought with them an abiding repugnance toward cities and a hatred of strong central governments.

They established a community in north Georgia, where many of their descendants still prosper. But to some, it was not a hospitable land. From the start, it was clear the hill people would have little to say in the destiny of their adopted country or state, political power being concentrated almost wholly among the lowland cotton barons, slave owners, and aristocrats who were militant and arrogant, reminiscent of the Prussians. Then, too, there were outbreaks of measles and typhoid and other maladies. Ora's parents both died during one of these recurrent epidemics only four years after she was born in 1826. She had been taken in by the Hasfords, for after all, she was related, a second cousin to the eleven-year-old Martin, who was already a stalwart young man with ambition, and handsome besides.

After a spate of bitter disputes over land titles with certain of their Georgia neighbors, many of the Hasfords moved west. They had little notion as they departed that the few Cherokees they had met in the mountains would soon be making the same trek, many at bayonet point. In 1836, they passed across the Mississippi at

Chickasaw Bluffs, soon to become Memphis. They traveled west overland to the Arkansas River, took keelboats to Van Buren, and thence overland once more through the Ozarks, heading north. They came to Dutch Mills, Cane Hill, Fayetteville, and settled finally in the valley of Little Sugar Creek.

The hardwood forests and rocky hills of this new land were even more demanding than the mountains of north Georgia had been. Within a year of their coming, Martin's father died. They buried him on the edge of an oak grove near the house he and his sons were still in the process of building. It was of logs, but would later be covered inside and out with clapboard cut at the Wolf Cove mill. But already, it had begun to take on the appearance of solid permanence.

Others of the Hasford clan had developed a greater land hunger than the Ozarks could satisfy. Many of them moved on to Texas in 1840, drawn by the promise of the republic's vast western land open to anyone willing to hold it against Comanches. Martin had no fear of Comanches, never having seen one, but by then there was too much of the farm in him to let it go. He and his brother Oscar stayed on, with their mother and the girl Ora.

Martin had been twenty-five when his mother took a blood infection from the scratch of a black locust thorn and died. They buried her beside her husband, and the same day Martin married the girl—not because there had been any agreement that he should, and not because either of them had ever thought of it, much less mentioned it aloud, but because it would be untoward having an eighteen-year-old girl living alone with two grown men, wife to neither of them.

The decision was as matter-of-fact as spring planting. Who would take Ora to his bed was determined by the flip of a twenty-dollar gold piece as the brothers stood face-to-face behind the pigsty. Martin lost.

Ora did not know until her second child was a decade into his life that her husband came by way of a losing coin toss. Then, when he finally told her one night in their bed, they laughed because by then it no longer mattered how she had come to him, only that she had come.

Martin, like his father before him, had been an ardent Lutheran, much taken to reading the Scriptures and other books. After the move to Arkansas, the family had become Methodists, the only other choice being Baptists. It did not diminish Martin's interest in the written word. He taught his wife and children to read, mostly from the Bible and Gibbon's history of Rome. His fascination with ancient cultures showed in the naming of his son and daughter, which he did without reference to Ora. It didn't matter. She deferred to him in all things he thought important.

It was Martin who insisted the children attend the Leetown school. To Ora, it seemed a waste of time. Calpurnia could learn all a woman needed to know in Ora's kitchen. Roman could take his lessons from his father in the fields and woods. Ora was not unique in this. In the decade before the war, only about one in ten white persons in that section of the country could read or write. But no matter what others did, the Hasford children went to school, because Martin said they would.

They had a good farm by then. There were a number of valley fields for corn and barley, and a cleared patch just north of the house where Ora grew her garden truck in summer. There was a good spring that never went dry, a forty-foot well that seldom did, plenty of timber and cattle and hogs for butchering each fall. They sold hardwood logs to the mill at Wolf Cove, and usually had enough grain to market some at Elkhorn Tavern, which by then had been established to accommodate travelers along Wire Road.

Martin's brother Oscar had gone off to Indian Territory before the war, claiming his intention of finding a squaw and raising a houseful of red young'uns. On the day he left, he told Ora as

Martin stood by scowling that his greatest disappointment in life had been winning that coin toss at the pigsty. They'd never heard from him since.

Like his forebears, Martin believed in hard work and minding his own business and conducting it without slaves, even though he could afford them. No one in the family had ever owned a slave, most of them holding that slavery and indentured servants were for the lazy, and because of that, morally wrong.

Then came the terrible days in Kansas. Barns burning, livestock slaughtered, neighbors ambushing one another over the issue of free soil or slave. The abolitionist drums had begun their thunderous roll in many northern newspapers. When Martin came by one of these at Leetown or at the tavern, he would read the editorial rantings against all white southerners and go into a rage. He was still steadfast against human bondage, yet he saw a bitter wickedness in outsiders trying to tell anyone how they should run their affairs. Although he would never own a slave himself, neither would he ever think of dictating his views to another man. Picture Grandpapa's incongruity was boiling up again.

After South Carolina and the Deep South left the Union and Lincoln called for volunteers, Martin began to compare the Yankees to the French. Their massive armies, he said, would march across honest farmers' fields, defiling everything they couldn't eat or carry off. Of course, all he knew of French armies was what he had heard of European wars two generations ago, and what he knew of Yankees was confined entirely to his imagination.

When Arkansas finally seceded, Martin brooded for a long time. He would take long walks through the woods, muttering to himself and slashing at the tree trunks with a hickory switch. Finally, he announced his intention of going off to join the Confederates.

Now, Ora was alone. She took it fatalistically, and kept her loneliness to herself.

There was nothing unusual about Martin and Ora Hasford. They were so like others of this hill country, they might have been interchangeable, like the parts of Colt revolvers. They had become a part of the land, of this particular land with all its peculiarities. They were a new race, come from many races. They had cut a culture from a country others did not want and seldom even passed through.

Two generations before, this had been Osage land, where painted warriors traveled the wooded ridges and hunted the stream lines, building their semipermanent villages, making their bows from the tree that French traders came to call the Osage orangewood. Now, those warriors were gone, and had left no lineage.

But when the Removal Cherokees had come through, camping along the rivers to fish until forced on by the army, many white men in the area had married their women. By the time of the war, there was hardly a community without its black-haired, black-eyed children who had the blood of chiefs flowing in their veins, and who bore such names as Brown or Coxie or Quinton or Carney. They, with all the others—the Germans and Welsh and Irish and English—had become a God-fearing, tough-living society.

They were a fiercely self-sufficient people—hardheaded, hardworking. They chopped out an existence from the hardwood forest and grubbed the rocky soil for meager crops; they grew their pigs and brewed their cellar beer or sour-mash corn in valley stills and drank it neat. They were a people who soon came to take for granted the stunning beauty of their hills, the bewildering profusion of birds and game and wildflowers, of rock-bottom streams flowing beneath limestone cliffs where eagles nested.

But who never took for granted their independence.

There had always been a difference of opinion about the reality of independence, a difference having little relation to one's political party—Democrat, new Republican, or old Whig. For those who came from Missouri and Illinois, it meant a strong federal government. For the others, it meant as little government as possible. To them, the growing conflict had only to do with self-determination and how best to achieve it.

The Hasfords had always been among those who wanted to be left alone, to manage their own affairs in their own way. Perhaps it had something to do with the long-forgotten dread, when they were rooting beets from the soil of the Regnitz River Valley and feared more than anything the domination of some outside force—whether Napoleon or the Junkers. Or perhaps it had to do with their living in this isolated place for almost a generation, becoming so provincial that even a visitor from nearby Missouri was considered a foreigner and not to be trusted.

Lying in her bed that night after the jayhawkers came, Ora Hasford thought of these things only insofar as she was capable. She had never been required to understand them, because it was all men's business. But if she could comprehend it only vaguely, of one thing she was certain. In these hills, the home was a family's sanctuary. Yet, on this night, she had been called liar by a stranger. Of course she had lied, to protect her children and home, which was not only acceptable but commendable. And for that, she had been shamed by a drunken man, on her own porch with a meat cleaver against guns.

Of politics, she had none. Her idea of a state was the land that nurtured her family, and her idea of morality was keeping her children clean in mind. But she had been called to account for her politics, a thing she had no way of accounting, nor did she have any defenses against such a thing.

This will soon pass, she thought, like a quick and terrible summer storm. But she knew at once that was wishful thinking.

It was dark still when she heard above her the sounds of her son stamping into his boots. With a sigh, and holding her arm, she rose to lay a fire in the cookstove.

3   In the growing dawn that was not yet light but only a gray smudge, the buildings of Leetown stood in scattered disarray, low and dilapidated. Somewhere west of town, near Wire Road, a rooster crowed. The lone rider drawing near the outskirts of the village cursed when a dog ran out and barked viciously for a moment, then, satisfied that this was no stranger, turned back and skulked away, still grumbling. The man rode to one of the structures that stood along the only street and dismounted at a small shed behind. He could see a yellow light in the kitchen window and knew his mother was up and making breakfast.

In the shed, he quickly unsaddled. With a handful of straw, he wiped down the horse's flanks, feeling the bony ribs beneath. He spent only a few minutes at the job, leaving it half-done, and turned back into the yard and walked toward the house, his long coat bulging with what he carried underneath.

He went through a side door, where a sign, hung facing the street, announced this as the Epp Shoe Shop. It was a small windowed room, where strips of cured leather were suspended from the ceiling all around, giving off an oily cowhide smell. It was here his father had taught him the cobbler's trade, and here on the husk-mattress bunk along one wall where the senior Epp had died only two years before, first extracting the promise that he would stay on in this shop and keep his mother for as long as she might live. He had since come to regret that promise, but he had no intention of breaking it. He threw his long coat over a worktable, knocking a leather knife off onto the floor with a loud clatter, and he cursed again.

"Is that you, Crawford?" a harsh, thin voice called from the kitchen. He said nothing, but walked into the lighted room.

The woman was standing at the kitchen table, her hands white with flour as she rolled biscuit dough. She stared at him through a tangle of disheveled hair. Above her raw leather brogans, her legs were bare. She wore a flannel nightgown and over that a heavy cloth coat.

He slipped a side of bacon from his waistband and threw it on the table, then pulled the two dead chickens from his belt and dropped them in the woodbox behind the stove.

"Where'd you get that stuff?" his mother asked.

"You can make some dumplings after a while," he said, sitting at the table across from where she worked, rubbing his face with bony hands.

"Well, I don't even want to know where it come from."

"No, but you'll eat it, all right."

"Take your hat off at the table."

He dropped the slouch hat on the floor, and she kneaded the dough, not looking at him again. They seemed stamped from the same mold, with wide, flat lips over teeth, none of which touched any other. The noses were long and straight, with pinched nostrils and a perpetual frown crease above the bridge. Her hair was a tattered gray, his a rumpled brown. There was a yellow cast to their skin, and their eyes were yellow, too, like a wolf's.

"Hand me that butcher knife," he said. "I want some of this meat."

He sliced along the rind, then cut thick slabs across the grain of lean strips in the tallow-colored fat. At the stove, he threw the chunks of bacon into a cast-iron skillet, his hair falling across his forehead as he looked down at the meat beginning to hiss and curl.

"Ain't there any coffee?"

"No."

"Well, we'll have coffee aplenty before long now, you can count on that."

"I don't want to hear nothin' about it."

The room filled with the heavy scent of the meat. He took it from the skillet half-cooked, greasy and with the fat just beginning to turn gray and translucent. She had her biscuits finished by then and put them in the oven and made white flour gravy in the skillet where he'd cooked the meat. Once more he sat waiting, rubbing his face with hands scarred by the cutting knives and callused by the needles he used to sew the tough cowhide to the soles. His own shoes were like his mother's, made in the shop under his hand, laced along the front and gaped open at the top like a brown paper sack only half full of potatoes. He wore homespun, a short coat and trousers patched at the knees and seat.

He was a stringy man, from the top of his narrow head to his protruding ankles, again like his mother. His arms and legs were long and gangling, and his skin stretched across the bones like an old linen sheet thrown carelessly over bare bedsprings. From the time he had first come to this valley from Illinois with his parents, he had been called Spider by the hill people. Only his mother could still remember his given name Crawford, and she was the only person who ever used it.

Spider Epp was twenty-four years old, in that time and place almost a confirmed bachelor, and he knew it was one of his mother's many despairs that he had not taken a wife and started raising a family. He knew because she constantly nagged him about it.

"You'll get yourself in trouble one of these nights, and that sheriff over in Bentonville will be here to arrest you and take you off to jail and nobody left to take care of me. Your father turns in his grave. Me with no daughter-in-law ner grandchildren either to call my own."

"That sheriff ain't gonna do nothin' to nobody. How many times I have to tell you that? Things has changed now."

"Things don't never change enough for the law not to get you."

"That secesh sheriff won't bother me. He ain't gonna do nothin'."

"You're in for trouble, riding out all hours, and now with them men."

"Nobody saw me tonight. Nobody around here. I ain't all that dumb. Besides, it's part of the war. If I can't go off and join the federal army up north and get me a uniform and all, then let me alone about ridin' with men around here, and doin' my part."

"It ain't no part of the war," she said. "I ain't all that dumb, either. Even if you think so. And them men, they ain't from around here."

"You been listenin' to that old secesh jackass Tulip Crozier over at the Wolf Cove mill. All he does is spread secesh trash."

She thumped the pan of gravy on the table before him, and then the steaming biscuits. He covered half a dozen open biscuits with the gravy and fingered slabs of the bacon onto his plate and started eating. She watched him, wiping her hands on her gown, and finally sat down and filled her own plate.

"Tulip Crozier may be a secesh, but he's had more schoolin' than you and me put together," she said. "And he's got him a good mill and a store and besides that, he doctors people and makes good money for it. More than your daddy was ever able to do. Make good money."

"He's a secesh trashmouth."

"Well, anyway, you best stay clear of these night riders. You'll end up on a rope someday."

"They're on army business," he said, his mouth full. "I knew they'd come someday, and last night I joined up with 'em at the tavern. After dark. Nobody saw me."

"I don't want to hear about it," she said.

"Well, then, why don't you let up on me, Ma?"

He bent over the plate, shoveling food into his mouth with a large spoon. His fingers were shining with grease from the meat, and now and again he wiped them on his trousers.

"Stealin' chickens don't seem like no army work to me."

"The colonel says we got to have our subsistence, too," Spider said dully, no longer capable of being irritated with her scolding.

"I don't want to know nothin' about it, nor hear anybody's name."

"Well, the federal army's coming. It's all part of the same war, ain't it?"

"Who told you the federal army was comin'?"

"They're coming. The rebels have started up here from down in the mountains to the south. They aim to take another try at Missouri, and the federal army's coming down to meet 'em."

"Who told you that?" she repeated. He made no reply, sopping up the last of the gravy in his plate with a biscuit. He was finished, then, and wiped his mouth with the palm of one hand.

"The federals got theirselves a new general named Sam Curtis, and he's comin' down to whup hell out of the rebels," Spider Epp said. "And I know a lot more. The rebels got theirselves a new man, too, a dandy called Van Dorn from someplace or another. They'll have at each other right around here, it looks like."

"Them friends of yourn knows a lot about it, I'd bet," she said. She picked at her food with a fork, eating little. "I'll bet they tell you all about it, don't they? Like they really knew and like they was part of the federal army, and you worth tellin' all of it."

He moved back into the shoe shop, leaving his mother sitting there picking at her gravy and still nagging him, calling after him about how important he was to have those men tell him so many things that likely weren't true at all.

In the darkness, he groped his way to the husk-mattress bunk, where he'd slept since his father died, and flopped down with a long sigh. The window was showing light now, and he could hear sounds of the village coming awake. Down the street, a cow bawled, and he thought, I'll have me a cow before long and we can have milk gravy instead of that soapy paste she makes with water.

From beneath his coat, he pulled a revolver. In the gloom, his fingers traced the long octagonal barrel and the smooth cylinder. It was a .36-caliber Navy Colt his father had bought the year before he died, the first such weapon owned by anyone in the community. To his father, it had been a special symbol, of status and power. To Spider, it had been a special prize held out on this same bed the night his father died. A part of Spider Epp's promise to keep his mother had been purchased with the gun. Had it come to his mother's hand, she would have sold it before the old man was cold in the grave. It had cost seventeen dollars, almost enough to buy a cow and any number of other things, which his mother had let no one forget from the moment the pistol had been purchased.

For as long as he could remember, it had been hardscrabble, his father trying to feed the family on the little or nothing he made in the cobbler's shop. Living hand to mouth, month to month. Even though the old man had all the appearances of a good Yankee, the free-soil people in this valley had never taken to him or his wolflike son. They looked down on the Epps as they would total strangers, although they had come from Illinois over ten years ago.

They all treat us like we was red Indians or white trash, he thought. They argue over the few pennies we make stitching the tears in their boots or nailing on lost heels. We don't live as good as the niggers at Elkhorn Tavern. Not near so good, with their ham and cold buttermilk each night at supper, and white bread on Sunday and their wool caps and flannel underwear. And their toilet, built specially for them with the back boarded up so the winter wind don't blow in from underneath when a man's sitting there and freeze his ass before his business is finished. And if they ever put in a hard day of work at the last and the cutting table like I do, they'd likely skip out for Missouri. And likely steal everything they could carry besides.

But now, a different time had come. He would have cured bacon and coffee and livestock of his own, a Jersey cow, and wear patented shoes bought in Bentonville, or even Cassville in Missouri, and wear trousers made in Saint Louis and not the homespun that took no color except gray or dirty brown. He wasn't sure how this would come, but with the war there would be a way to take it all.

He could still taste the raw whiskey Colonel Caudell had given him, store-bought and as red as a bay horse. Colonel Caudell and his boys, they didn't have to drink the clear corn liquor made in some valley still. They knew about the good things and how to have them. And now, he was part of the colonel's irregular cavalry, Spider Epp a part of the war. The colonel had said, We'll be back. You can expect us. And Spider Epp had said, I'll be ready. Then the boys, with the colonel leading them, had disappeared down the road Spider Epp had shown them, a road that led west toward the Indian Nations.

He thought about the Hasford farmstead, the best in this valley. He thought of Calpurnia Hasford and smiled, rubbing the long pistol barrel with his fingers. Calpurnia Hasford, always thinking she was better than town people, always looking at him as though he was a hill-country wild hog wandered in from the woods. Now, he thought, we'll just see about her.

The federal army was coming, right through this valley, to drive away the rebels, to drive them all the way south and then take over the whole of western Arkansas. Then we'll see, he thought— after they've done that, we'll see who is the boss hog around here.

He had gone to school less than two years, back in Illinois, and he could barely read and write his own name. What he knew, he had learned from his father, and that was mostly bitterness. The old man had come south with his family to make his fortune, and when that never came to fruition, he soured on everything South and Southern and became his own particular kind of free-soiler; in him there was no idealism. Nor in his son, Spider. Both were interested only in what they could hold in their hand, like the Colt pistol, or what they could chew with their ragged teeth, like the sugar-cured Hasford bacon.

Without even being aware of it, Spider Epp knew better than anyone in this valley what was about to take place. He smelled the turmoil and violence, and knew without being able to put it into words the changes that would come and the opportunities it would present. He was like a gray squirrel boar, sensing somehow the coming tornado and taking to den without knowing why until the slashing winds came. But Spider Epp had no intention of taking to den.

III

Sometimes, in late February, the skies would clear and the sun would come, warming and bright. These were pleasant days, a harbinger of spring before the last blustering days of winter. Cardinals in flocks would flash through the low plum and hornbeam, feeding on the ground, still two months from the time they would pair and take up nesting territories. A solitary hermit thrush might be heard from one of the wooded lots alongside the old cornfields, its *tuk-tuk-tuk* coming clear across the windless air. For the first time in weeks, the distant hills would stand out sharply, their shapes no longer misted and vague under heavy cloud. There would be the scent of fresh earth as last summer's plowed ground thawed and warmed. Those who lived there knew these were small respites before March winds that sometimes brought more ice and snow.

The day after the jayhawkers came was such a day.

With dawn, Ora Hasford understood the jayhawkers' abrupt departure. A number of Union cavalry patrols were moving south along Wire Road toward Little Sugar Creek. She knew that so long as the blue-clad troopers were in the vicinity there would be no trouble from guerrillas.

Roman was allowed little time to watch the soldiers, nor wonder at their presence in such numbers. Since breakfast he had been furiously sullen, having been allowed to sleep through everything that had happened during the night, and smarting, too, from Calpurnia's teasing that he would sleep beyond judgment day unless the horn was blown directly into his ear.

It was a humiliation that he had been the first to see danger, first to warn of it, and then had slept soundly through the racket of guinea hens, barking dogs, and the talk and giggling of drunken men. Worst of all, it had been Calpurnia standing with his own shotgun against marauders instead of himself, a fact she was gleeful to explain to him in great detail.

It came as no surprise that his sister would oppose night riders or anybody else. He had learned long ago that she could hold her own in the farmyard squabbles that sometimes erupted between them, even when it came to kicking, scratching, or gouging. The only time he had ever been whipped by his father was after one of these, and it still tormented him when he thought about it. Calpurnia had not been whipped at all, though she had started the fight and got the better of it besides.

Ora Hasford did not need to sense her son's discomfort. He made no bones about it. So she put him to work as soon as he finished breakfast. While he ran in the stock from the woods, she and Calpurnia took inventory. Although the meat was gone, there were still the sow and chickens and guinea hens, two gallons of sorghum molasses, a bushel of dried apples, a crock of hominy, another of kraut, a keg of salt, two combs of honey, a few odds and ends, and a considerable amount of shucked corn. Ora measured some of this into a flour sack and sent Roman off to the mill to have it ground.

"But ride the woods," she said. "Stay away from Wire Road and those soldiers. And saddle me a horse. I'm going over to see if those folks at the tavern are all right."

Roman threw a sidesaddle on Bess, the gentler of the two mares, although he knew his mother was capable of handling any horse as well as a man. The mule he saddled for himself, and was twice bitten in the effort.

They rode off their separate ways with the sun just coming into the valley from the ridge behind the house. Ora would find at Elkhorn Tavern that all the horses had been taken, some of the pigs killed and roasted, and a great deal of store whiskey consumed. The Coxes had been locked in one of the guest rooms all the while and were frightened but unhurt.

No second thought was given to leaving Calpurnia alone on the place. There returned with daylight that long-established notion that home was safe haven, as though the sun drove away not only the reality of the night before, but any memory of it. As for the Yankee soldiers, they had never bothered anyone in the valley, and Roman was part inclined to wish some of them would drag his sister off to Missouri where she would be made to cook and wash clothes for them. He stopped short of thinking what else they might do.

Roman took his own sweet time, riding east from the farm, then angling southward. He could be as casual as anybody else. He could act as though visiting night riders were an everyday occurence. He could show them all that he didn't give a good goddamn!

Gray squirrels were out enjoying the sunlight, fluffing their tails and playing tag in the treetops. Roman stopped a number of times and watched them, making the chucking sound with his tongue that was supposed to imitate their barking. In a grove of young sycamores, he made a detailed inspection of tree trunks where deer had been feeding.

On the high ground above Wolf Cove mill, he could see the narrow ravine of Little Sugar Creek as it cut sharply eastward into the high plateau. Beyond that was the valley of White River, and beyond that the wilderness mountains that marched on for 150 miles toward the Mississippi River flats. All of this was an ancient seabed, thrust up almost two thousand feet at some point in the dim prehistory of the continent. Roman had often seen the fossil remains of ocean life in limestone outcrops. As time passed, the rivers and streams gashed deep cuts into the tableland. And although people called them mountains, the Ozarks were actually a valley topography. Even in the wildest, most tumbled terrain, in every direction the horizon was flat, marking the original outline of the old plateau. But close in, hundreds of hogbacks and ridges and spurs were clearly defined above the valley floors, especially in winter when the gray bare branches of the hardwoods etched each contour like suddenly suspended smoke.

Roman reined in the mule and sat enjoying the warmth, pushing back his narrow-brimmed hat so the sun flooded across his face. He watched a flight of crows over the far ridge, their calls coming to him faintly. The mule shifted his feet impatiently on ground that had gone soft. Although most of the snow had burned off across the valley, Roman could see patches of white on the shaded slopes.

"Wolf Cove," Roman said aloud, and thought of Indians as he always did when he came here. Legend had it the name came from the Osage. There was no way of knowing if such a thing were true, the English-speaking whites seldom bothering to translate Indian names as the French had done. Some said it was called Wolf Cove by the Cherokees when they came through, but Roman knew that wasn't true. It had been Wolf Cove long before the Removals.

The mill itself was a patchwork of rough-cut lumber, logs, and native rock, mortared together with homemade limestone cement. Upstream from the mill, Tulip Crozier had filled the creek with large stones, creating a small pond. Water rushing over these and on toward Grand River in the Indian Territory turned the undershot wheel. In the narrow valley behind the mill was Crozier's living quarters, a log cabin, and beside that his steam-powered sawmill. There were a number of outbuildings, a pigpen, and a horse paddock. There was a small clapboard building he used for a store, and downstream a few hundred feet stood the sorghum mill, where a large steel pot sat under the grinding apparatus attached to a long pole. Farmers from all over the valley brought in their timber to be cut, their grain to be milled, their sorghum to be ground and boiled into molasses, and Tulip Crozier charged them ten percent of the result.

As Roman forded the stream below the millpond, Tulip Crozier came from his cabin, two foxhounds at his heels wagging buggy-whip tails and grinning. Skinny as a beanstalk, his neighbors said of him, and the ankle-length coat he wore now did not disguise his gaunt frame. It was hardly remarkable in a country where there were few fat men. He wore his hair long, below what had once been a rather stylish high beaver hat, and from the rear thrust a turkey vulture feather. His beard was white, like his hair, but stained around the mouth with tobacco juice, unlike his teeth, which he kept clean with a studied application of frayed willow twigs and baking soda. He wore boots from his Mexican War days, and in his waistband was a horse pistol of the same vintage. He kept the gun loaded with birdshot, which he used to pepper the rats and shrews that appeared from time to time around the mill.

"So. Roman," Crozier said, speaking as he always did in slow, measured cadence. "And your mama?"

"Howdy, Uncle Tulip," Roman said, handing down the sack of corn, then dismounting. "Mama's fine."

Crozier turned to the mill, speaking over his shoulder as he went, the boy following.

"And the soldiers? I reckon you've seen them."

"On Wire Road."

"They came here, too. Looking at my trail, between the mill and the road. A strange people, soldiers. I know, boy. I've been one myself."

It was cold inside the mill among the polished wooden shafts and beneath the solid oak rafter beams dusted with the powder of many years' grinding under the wheel. Crozier poured the corn into the hopper and yanked the lever that engaged the gears with the drive shaft from the waterwheel. Roman could hear his corn being crushed by the great flat disk turning on the netherstone. The place smelled of flour and meal, and of tobacco juice that was splattered in brown stains across the floor. It was an odor that Roman had come to associate with the man as well.

In this land where minding one's own business was preached like a religion, but where nonetheless everyone was intensely curious about everyone else, Tulip Crozier was an enigma. All they knew of his past was that he had served in the Mexican War and had been on Little Sugar Creek since before that. Some said he had bought from the Osages the land where the mill stood, but that was likely not true.

One summer he had disappeared for almost two months and returned with a wife, as beautiful as any woman who had ever been in the valley and at least twenty years Crozier's junior. Nobody ever came to know anything about her, either, because after a few weeks she was gone. Crozier never said where. There were rumors she had run away with some Frenchman—a favorite story, for among the German and English settlers along Little Sugar Creek the French were more despised than anyone, including Indians.

Whatever had happened, a great many people agreed that Tulip Crozier would be impossible to live with for long. He drank too much hard whiskey and usually smelled bad, and it was whispered that he could make strange demands of a woman during the night.

During the time the Butterfield stage was still operating, Crozier would often take trips to Springfield or Fort Smith. He would appear at the tavern to buy his ticket wearing city clothes, with patent leather shoes and a cane. All spiffed up, the people called it. When he returned after two weeks or more, he would be rumpled and bleary-eyed, as though he had spent his time drunk in some big-town whorehouse.

Or sometimes, he would disappear into the woods for a week, coming back finally to some kitchen door for breakfast, his clothes dusted with crumpled leaves and twigs, his eyes bloodshot and his breath smelling of sour mash.

"Your appetite? It's good?" Crozier asked, disengaging the drive shaft and bending to scoop the meal into the sack. Roman knew now he would get the usual examination of his health. Tulip Crozier was not a doctor, but he had been an enlisted man in the medical department during the Mexican War and had accumulated some expertise in the use of medicines, nostrums, and poultices, as well as in the setting of broken bones and the treatment of gunshot wounds and dog bites.

"It's all right," Roman said.

"And your bowels?"

"All right, I guess," Roman said, the question embarrassing him, even though he had known it was coming.

"So. We've finished here. I'll give you a nice bottle of tonic. I got it from a man out of Springfield. Good for the blood and for the movements."

Crozier could hardly let a visit pass without distributing a bottle of his favorite tonic. Roman recalled one such instance years ago. He had taken a sip on the way back to the farm, and liked the taste. Before he arrived home, the bottle was empty and he was a little drunk. He spent the next three days mostly sitting in the privy. Calpurnia had thought it hilarious but Ora was furious, insisting that someone should go to Wolf Cove and take a barrel stave to Crozier's back. Nothing came of it, but Roman learned to take Tulip Crozier's remedies in small doses, and then only under the direction of his mother. Roman always suspected that his father thought the affair was funny, too.

They walked to the shack store, Crozier asking if they had heard from Martin.

"Not for a spell. But Mama's expecting another letter any time now."

Martin Hasford was Crozier's closest friend in this valley.

Some said his only friend. They enjoyed talking together over the checkerboard in the Hasford kitchen, or standing around a ridge-line fire listening to fox dogs run. They spoke of history and philosophy and of the Old Testament—never the New. Nor did they speak of politics. Taciturn as he often was, Tulip Crozier had made it known that he detested politics and politicians, with the misery they brought on common people. Most of all, he detested the present war. When some unfortunate citizen brought up the subject in his hearing, he would fall into a purple rage. Roman had seen Crozier angry, and it frightened him. But he and Calpurnia had always called the old man Uncle Tulip.

Most of the people in the valley realized Tulip Crozier came from Jewish stock. This was not held against him. Among the majority of these hill settlers, anti-Semitism had never been an issue, or if it had been once, they'd since put it aside. They simply said that here was a shrewd old man who knew how to make ends meet and who was sometimes a little strange. They generally admired him for the former and overlooked the latter.

Crozier brought out a small bottle filled with brown liquid and Roman slipped it into an overcoat pocket. There was a spool of thread as well.

"So take this to your mama," Crozier said. "Good silk. Your mama can make those little crotchets with it."

"We had visitors last night," Roman blurted. He had not intended to say anything about the incident because of his embarrassment at having slept through the best of it. Crozier stiffened, his eyes going wide to show the whites where there was a network of tiny brown veins.

"Soldiers? The soldiers came there?"

"No. Mama said they were jayhawkers," Roman said, and went on to tell how he had watched them come to the tavern, and late in the night stop at the farm. He did not mention that he had failed to see this part.

Crozier grabbed one of Roman's arms with a suddenness that startled him, gripping so hard it hurt.

"You said your mama was all right? She's all right?"

"Sure, she's all right. She rode over to the tavern this morning to see what happened."

"She rode out into the valley, away from home, with all these soldiers around. . . ." He stopped, sputtering, his eyes bulging and his cheeks above the beard going red.

"Well, it's only a mile. She said she'd be safe."

Crozier whirled and started for the horse paddock, his long coat flapping out behind and his arms pumping like a paddle-wheeler. Roman ran to catch up to him.

"What's the matter? Where are you going, Uncle Tulip?"

"Where am I going? you say. I'm going over there."

He turned back to Roman again, glaring, his eyes hot.

"I'm going over there. Your mother is a good and decent woman, out in the valley with all these soldiers. I'm going to find her and bring her home and stay with you at your farm, to see no harm comes."

Roman almost laughed, thinking of his mother's reaction to a man not a member of the family coming to camp under her kitchen window. But then a kind of panic seized him because if such a thing were forced on her, he'd be the one who'd brought it about with his jayhawkers story. He clutched at Crozier's sleeve.

"Listen, Uncle Tulip, she wouldn't like that at all," he said. "Besides, by now she's back home already, and she says the jay-hawkers have gone."

"And why have they gone?" Crozier shouted, the brown spittle coming from his lips. Roman realized for the first time that the old man had a small soggy cud of tobacco in his cheek. "Why? Because of those soldiers. And do you understand about soldiers, boy, or does your mother? No, you do not. Soldiers can be worse than the night riders—did you know that?"

"But, Uncle Tulip—"

"So, listen to me, boy. This army over in the valley is looking for our people—you know that? Looking for the army your papa may be with. And our army is looking for them—you want to bet? And if they find each other around here, you know what will happen? They will go at each other and grind everything down, just like that wheel in there." He waved a hand frantically toward the mill. But then the fire seemed to go out of him as quickly as it had come, and he stood before the boy shaking his head and panting, his jaw working feverishly now on the cud.

"But, Uncle Tulip, Mama says—"

"Mama says, Mama says," Crozier cut in, but not so hotly now. "What does that dear mama of yours know about such things? Armies are like millstones, you see? Those night riders, they are a personal thing. A bunch of outlaws you can shoot, and the people will say, Good, good, you shot some of the bastards. But you can't do that with armies. They are impersonal, and shooting at them does no good and will get you hanged besides."

"They don't look like they mean us harm, even if they are Yankees."

"Harm? Of course, they don't mean harm maybe. But they will grind everything down, and you will be sand under their boots. I know, don't I? I was in an army once."

"That was a long time ago, Uncle Tulip."

"Long ago, was it? Hell, boy, armies do not change—don't you understand that?"

"No, I don't. All I know is, Mama said it would be all right now, and besides, she'd throw a fit if you came over there, or anybody else did either, to save her from night riders or the army. I understand that."

"My God, boy," Crozier said with dismay, and then abruptly threw his arms around the boy and hugged him. It was over quickly as Crozier stepped back, both of them a little embarrassed. Roman had not been hugged since he was a little boy, and Crozier knew it. "So, maybe your mama is right. A man is helpless, sometimes. Wait here a minute."

He disappeared inside the shack store once more, and when he came out he held a sack of parsnips, shriveled from winter storing, a bag of salt, and two dressed squirrels. Their meat was dark red and Roman knew they would turn brown and crisp in the frying pan.

"Here. Your mama can make a nice stew. I shot them this morning in one of the sycamores along the creek." As Roman pocketed these things, doubling the squirrel carcasses and shoving them in on top of all the rest, Crozier took his arm again. "But you tell that mama of yours, if she needs me, she send you for me. You hear that, boy?"

"Yes, Uncle Tulip," Roman said, relieved now that the old man was not coming with him back to the farm. "I'll tell her."

Crozier moved toward him, and Roman was afraid he was about to be hugged again. He moved quickly to the mule and mounted. The old man was at his knee, looking up, and Roman saw tears in his eyes.

"I love you and all your people, Roman. All you Hasfords. So I do."

"Good-bye, Uncle Tulip," Roman said, and pulled the mule around and toward the creek. "Come on, mule, let's get home."

Climbing steeply up the slope to the high ground again, Roman was deeply distressed. He set a great store in this old man. Since as far back as he could recall, Tulip Crozier had been every part the uncle to him. He had taught Roman how to make rabbit traps, how to chuck like a barking squirrel so that one would pause with curiosity long enough to be shot. He had pointed out the marks wild turkey and deer made in the woods, and which plants could be boiled to make salad greens. One Christmas, when Roman was barely able to talk, Crozier had given him a cast-iron toy locomotive and then tried to explain what a locomotive was because Roman had never seen one. And this man, whom Roman trusted next only to his father, was fearful for Ora Hasford.

Roman had always imagined that anyone who knew his mother could see that she was equal to any situation. But it was obvious now that Tulip Crozier did not have such confidence.

If someone had the power to cause Roman Hasford to make a choice, he would have said he loved his father more than his mother. But there had never been, since he could remember, any doubt about where the family strength lay. Roman knew his mother's traditional province was the house, extending out as far as chicken coop and spring, but stopping short of pigpen, barn, and field. He was well aware, too, that although his father was ignorant of what happened in Ora's domain to make it work, she knew what happened in his—and after his father left, was capable of running that also, perhaps even better than he ever had.

At the top of the rise, Roman paused and looked back into the valley. Tulip Crozier was nowhere in sight around his buildings. Roman looked beyond the valley of Little Sugar Creek, toward the south, where he knew the Boston Mountains stood. He could not see them, for they were no higher than the point where Roman sat the mule, but there the valleys were deeper. Somewhere, beyond the haze of distance, was the southern army, and recalling what Crozier had said, Roman wondered if his father was with it. He suddenly wanted very badly to see his father, to walk with him along the fence rows as they had done so often and speak of crops and rainfall and temperature.

Crozier had said, "I love you and all your people." It was a word strange to Roman's ears, *love*. He could not recall ever having heard it spoken in his home. He wondered, now, if Martin

Hasford were to stand before him, would he say it to his father? It began to trouble him that he never had.

"Come on, mule," he said finally, because that was the mule's only name. Even though the day was still bright, it had turned gray for Roman, as though his sun had burned out.

IV

The Confederate army lay encamped some eighty-five miles south of the Little Sugar Creek fords, where they had been trying since mid-February to avoid frostbite and starvation. They were Missourians, Texans, Arkansans, Louisianians, and a few from Indian Territory. Some had fought in Missouri and been driven out, some had fought in other places, and some had never fought at all. They had yet to face an enemy together as one army.

But all of them had spent many months in the field, never having supposed when they started that campaigning would take such a toll on cloth and leather. They were a tattered group, with little evidence of uniforms except for the officers and among a few units provided with such niceties by the communities where they had been recruited. Trousers and jackets were beginning to display a wild profusion of colorful patches. Shoes were wearing out, and many of the men were barefooted.

Weapons were as dissimilar as clothing. There were soldiers armed with ancient flintlocks, and among the percussion rifles and muskets calibers were so varied that resupply of ammunition was a nightmare for ordnance officers. There were a few batteries of Napoleon guns in the artillery units, but most were equipped with whatever could be provided from Union arsenals captured in Texas at the war's outbreak.

Draft animals were as ragged as the men. There was little forage, and grain purchased from local farmers had almost run out. In this mountain camp, there were few farmsteads about, and those few adequate only for victualing small families and not armies. Most of the horses looked like wild prairie mustangs with their heavy winter coats, shaggy and unkempt. And even of these, there were not enough. Cavalry units were sometimes partly afoot, and in the artillery horses came only four to a gun and limber, rather than the usual six.

The troops were billeted in ramshackle lumber huts or under tentage worn threadbare in the winter winds. They ate parched corn and sowbelly, seven days a week, and many a rebel soldier waited anxiously for spring when polk greens would sprout along the roads and pathways of the hills. There was no coffee and little tea, and white flour was almost unknown.

Major General Earl Van Dorn, just appointed commander of the trans-Mississippi, arrived in the manner which had characterized his entire life, with exuberance and dashing charm. If the condition of the army dismayed him, he gave no show of it. He announced their mission at once: to attack northeast and secure Missouri and Saint Louis. There was scarcely anyone who did not realize that if he were successful, Missouri would be lost to the Union and the South would have an excellent base for attacks into the Ohio Valley. It was an ambitious plan for an ambitious man. And Van Dorn would initiate it with a bold strike into Missouri's southern flank by way of the old Butterfield stagecoach line.

Chief among his problems were ammunition supply and the constant bickering of his subordinates. His appreciation of logistics was faulty from the start, and would get worse. But by his personality and force of character, the second problem was soon solved. Or at least suppressed. He had always been a man willing to listen, and perhaps this helped endear him to generals now serving under him who previously had spent much of their time arguing about who ranked whom.

On his second day in camp, Van Dorn toured the regiments of his army. There was no parading or pomp. The troops simply came out of their tents and huts and stood in ranks. They watched Van Dorn pass, none of them showing any emotion, except perhaps disdain for this dandy who had yet to prove himself. Their faces turned toward him as he rode among them on a splendid sorrel gelding, their eyes staring unabashed into his own, without flinching.

What the troops saw could not help but impress them one way or another. Van Dorn was a darkly handsome soldier, a Mississippi aristocrat with well-trimmed mustache and chin whiskers, in every way the picture of antebellum manhood. The troops knew, too, that here rode the grandnephew of former president Andy Jackson, whom many of their fathers had voted for even after he was dead.

They knew his record, too. He had fought in the Mexican War and since then had been wounded four times in skirmishes with Comanches. Now he rode past his men, pausing here and there to chat with them. Their calculating eyes measured him, lingering on the polished buttons, the gleaming saber chain, the insignia of rank—stars inside a wreath of laurel—and the waves of golden braid on his sleeves.

First, the troops of Sterling Price, former governor of Missouri, the clean-shaven, cherub-faced general who had started a staunch Union man and who had disagreed so violently with federal intervention in his state that he had become a dedicated southerner.

Some of the best artillery units in the army were Price's, and Van Dorn looked at the guns with appreciation. At one battery, he stopped and addressed a tall sergeant of section.

"Were you at the battle of Wilson's Creek, Sergeant?"

"Yes, sir, I was," the sergeant said, coming to what he supposed was an attitude of attention and doffing his cap.

"Next time, we can perhaps change the outcome."

"Yes, General, I allow we could."

"Are rations for your section adequate?"

"If adequate means a lot of salt hog and ramrod corn bread, then they are, General."

"Where is your home, Sergeant?"

"Rolla, sir."

"Good. We will be seeing that fine little city again soon."

Then the men of General Ben McCulloch, dour and frowning former Texas Ranger, California-gold-rush-days sheriff, and veteran of the war for Lone Star independence, where he had served with Sam Houston. The two generals presented a startling contrast in styles. Van Dorn was the embodiment of cottonland aristocracy, McCulloch equally representative of the stubborn breed who had carved out a white Protestant culture among the Spanish on the Indian frontiers of Texas.

They rode slowly past an infantry regiment, where the men stood without an overcoat among them. They were clad mostly in butternut and shoddy, the shredded wool and water material that made profiteers millions during the war and fell apart in the first rainfall. Van Dorn could see bare toes, the long nails like acorn hulls, peeking through the folds of burlap or canvas wrappings. Hands scarred and toughened with hoe and plow gripped .577-caliber Enfield rifles, their brass fittings polished. From beneath the brims of floppy hats, their defiant pale eyes followed the generals and staff officers.

"The Sixteenth Arkansas," McCulloch snapped. "One of the fine regiments in your army, General."

They had no appearance of a fine regiment, except for the condition of their weapons. To Van Dorn they looked like a rabble of farmers out on a prolonged bear hunt, and poverty-stricken farmers at that. He could not help overhearing some of their remarks.

"Lookee there," one rawboned soldier muttered, his cheek bulging with the one commodity this army had in abundance. He spat a stream of tobacco juice off to one side, never taking his eyes off the general. "Ain't he a caution?"

"Old Earl," another murmured, himself old enough to be Van Dorn's father. "Take us all the way to the Mississip', plumb to Saint Louie."

"Lookee that gold braid," said the first. "You could reckon it'd come to about ten dollars to the ounce."

"Ain't he a stud horse?"

"They say he sure as hell is, a real caution with the ladies."

"Take us all the way to the Mississip'. Or square on to hell!"

There was the rustle of mirthless laughter in the rear ranks. Passing, Van Dorn turned to his subordinate.

"That is one of your best regiments?"

McCulloch flushed and scowled.

"I judge not by their shoes or talk, but how well they shoot."

"An excellent yardstick, my dear general, an excellent yardstick."

The third of Van Dorn's lieutenants was Albert Pike, Harvard graduate, admitted to the federal bar along with Abe Lincoln, an explorer, scholar, and author of books and tracts. One of the more famous Masons since George Washington, with his long, flowing hair and beard, he might have passed for a warrior from the Old Testament. But Van Dorn reviewed none of Pike's troops in this Boston Mountain camp, for most of them had not yet joined the main body. They would march from the Indian Territory to catch up to the main body of the army en route to Missouri. Among them would be Cherokees and Choctaws, and a scattering of Creeks.

His cursory inspection complete, Van Dorn turned to the task of writing march orders. There was some wrangling among his general officers about who should lead, but he quickly suppressed it. He exhorted each to his own mission, and reminded them of their high purpose, his dark eyes snapping all the while. Afterward, nobody could recall that he had said anything dealing with resupply of ammunition once the army was engaged with the Yankees.

Van Dorn's impatience infected the entire army. Men began to pack kits with corn and the few other items they would take along, throwing away the accumulated excess. Soon, the camps were trash dumps of discarded pots and pans, dishes and crocks, woven straw sleeping mats too cumbersome to carry, bits and pieces of furniture stolen at various times from surrounding farmyards. And playing cards, worn thin and spongy from use, scattered over the ground like the fallen foliage of some strange square-leafed plant. And among these, the bottles and jugs, quickly emptied of what little was left in them.

What extra ammunition was issued the men exchanged among themselves, until each had enough for his own particular weapon to last through a good skirmish, at least, if not a full-out battle. Charges that had been in rifle and musket chambers since mid-February were drawn and replaced by new powder. Percussion caps were carefully packed in their leather belt pouches. Harness was set in place and cleaned, saddles oiled, and the artillery blacksmiths were busy at their forges till all hours, shoeing the horses that needed it most.

The last supply train arrived, the wagons having wound their tortuous way up the mountain road from Fort Smith. Three days' ration of fairly fresh salt pork was issued, along with more corn and a quart of molasses for each six-man mess unit—a sure sign the army was about to go into action. Letters were hastily written on any scrap of paper available and given to local farmers in hope they would eventually reach their destination. As the order of march came down through each echelon of the army, excitement grew to such a pitch that on the last night even old soldiers found it hard to sleep. They were eager to be away from this place, out of the clinging mud and still-half-frozen meadows, out of camp and inactivity. And into action, any kind of action. Away from boredom and the bloody flux.

During a cold dawn, the army began to uncoil from its camp and onto the roads leading north. Somewhere a band was playing, and in many regiments the drummer boys beat out their rolls. There were even a few cheers when Van Dorn or McCulloch or one of the other generals rode past. The horses of the army sensed the exhilaration, too, prancing and pawing or pulling hard into the limber harness, their breath exploding out in white bursts of vapor.

Uncased now were the battle flags, emblems of their young republic, presented to them months past by the ladies of their respective regions, with appropriate impassioned speeches, not a word of which they could now remember.

First came the best of the army's cavalry squadrons, supported by two light batteries of artillery and followed closely by the infantry under Price. The Missourians stepped out smartly, raising their battle cry, for they were finally going home. The mass of men and horses flowed slowly into the roads, bending always north, and it was noon before the last units of the army left their camps. Along the way, farmers and their womenfolk stood well back on the hillsides and watched, and a few of them waved. The troops responded with cheers and waving hats.

Through Cane Hill and Prairie Grove and Fayetteville, they could hear ahead the scattered firing as the cavalry drove Union detachments out of each succeeding town and village. There were long waits, then sudden bursts of rapid step to catch up again. Soon, there was no more cheering, and the band and drums stopped. Each soldier plowed along through his own growing fatigue, pressed by the mounted officers. Those in the rear stumbled and cursed as they passed over the road cut to deep ruts by the artillery and wagons that had gone before. The slashed surface was becoming crusty and hard as the temperature fell. And soon, too, the ditches alongside the road became cluttered with discarded blankets, canteens, knapsacks, and other gear suddenly grown too heavy to carry.

The army's leading units were still thirty miles from Leetown when Van Dorn came down with a severe cold. He took to his bed, the cot of an army ambulance wagon. His men staggered on toward Elkhorn Tavern and the fords along Little Sugar Creek, sixteen thousand souls. And the western sky had begun to grow dark, the wind colder, the elements gathering for the last storm of March 1862.

2   The Union army of southwest Missouri began to concentrate along Wire Road between Little Sugar Creek and Elkhorn Tavern in that first week of March. Since the rebels had retreated south to the Boston Mountains, there had been federal troops in the area, though wildly scattered. Now they came in force, along all the roads in their dark columns, flowing like a blue river.

The most direct route from the south to the cities of central and eastern Missouri was Wire Road. The federals began to fortify the bluffs along the north bank of Little Sugar Creek where the road crossed the stream. There, the infantry entrenched in the rocky ground and artillery sited their batteries to cover all the crossings. Great breastworks of oak, cut from the surrounding woods, frowned down on the shallow fords. From that line north to Elkhorn Tavern, the army established itself, along Wire Road and around Leetown, spreading across the cornfields and through the woodlots.

Tentage sprang up overnight, sometimes in measured rows, sometimes scattered among the baggage trains, the cavalry pickets, the reserve infantry regiments and ammunition parks. Across the valley, in daylight their fires sent up thin columns of gray smoke, and after dark they shone like chimney sparks suspended motionless in the blackness of the night.

Spider Epp watched them come. He had seen the Confederates who had marched through this valley toward the south, their lack of discipline and uniform, their sorry-looking horses. This was a different kind of army. Their uniforms looked fresh, straight out of Saint Louis depots, and their horses were grain-fed, sleek, and well muscled. He gloated over this and, talking to himself, called it his own army.

The mounted troopers who rode through Leetown displayed a casual arrogance, the self-importance of all cavalry in all armies stamped on their faces. But although he admired the horseflesh, even more fascinating to Spider Epp were the infantry formations, marching behind their colors, a hedge of metal above their heads as they carried Springfield .58-caliber rifles as shoulder arms. When some of them passed, he could hear the soft guttural sounds of their speech, for these were soldiers of Franz Sigel's corps, Germans only recently emigrated to the farmlands of Illinois and Iowa, or the cities that stood beside the Great Lakes or the Mississippi. They were from a later movement of Germans from the old country and had little in common with those in this valley who had arrived three decades before.

On the first night, Spider Epp stood at the shoe-shop window, watching the passing artillery, limbers, and caissons making a hollow sound on the hard-packed streets. Battery after battery passed, moving toward the south and Little Sugar Creek. He marveled at the heavy horses and their shining coats. First came the six-horse team drawing limber and gun, usually a twelve-pounder Napoleon but sometimes a rifled Whitworth or Parrot. Behind each gun came another team of six, drawing the caisson. The crewmen sat on the ammunition boxes, hanging on grimly as the drivers—one riding the left animal of each team—urged the horses on.

After the rest of the battery came the battery wagon and the traveling forge. One battery would hardly be gone before the next appeared—six guns, eighty horses, and almost a hundred men.

"By God, look at them guns," Spider Epp said. "My army, by God, my own army!"

As the units moved into the woods and fields around Leetown, he became aware that the town was emptying. People were throwing baggage into carts and wagons, onto mules and horses, and leaving hurriedly toward the west. His mother began to complain that they should be packing, but he told her to make a pallet in the root cellar and, if she was frightened, to go there and stay.

Standing at his last, he watched the passing troops, and now and then a flurry of light snow whipped past the window. Late on the second day, he could restrain himself no longer. He threw tack hammer and needles aside, pulled on his heavy overcoat, and slipped the Navy Colt into his waistband.

His mother was at the kitchen table, a pile of woolen socks and a darning egg before her. She glared at him, her mouth hanging open.

"Where you goin' to?"

"I'm gonna have a look around," he said.

"If you ain't gonna take me out of here, you'd best stay right where you belong. Let them army people go about their business and you go about yourn."

"I'm gonna have a look around, that's all."

"Them army people got their own business to attend to."

"Well, maybe I got some business to attend to with 'em."

"You leave me here by myself, with all these soldiers around?"

"They ain't gonna bother you. If anything starts, just get in the root cellar."

"Root cellar? You taggin' off I don't know where, and you tell me get in the root cellar?"

"You'll be fine."

Spider Epp left his mother as he usually did, with her grumbling behind him. He got the horse saddled, thinking how much better all the Union army stock looked than this old gelding that had saddle sores and hipbones thrusting out against his scruffy hide like plowshares. He pulled the horse from the shed and went to the saddle, feeling the heavy grunt as his weight settled.

He rode west, across the wooded hollow cut by the water from Winton Springs, and on toward Wire Road. He passed the tentage and wagons of a quartermaster outfit where stacks of boxes and burlap bags mounded up like small hills. Stenciled across the bags were the words, *Potatoes, Desiccated.* He had no idea what that meant, nor would he have had even if he'd been able to read it.

Behind a long line of wagons were two soldiers, their pants down, squatting over a narrow ditch, one foot on either side. It was the first straddle trench Spider had ever seen, and it astounded him because he had never considered how an army takes care of such things. The two soldiers, facing one another and talking as they smoked pipes, paid him no attention, and Spider Epp shook his head. Right outside, he thought, and calm as church.

Riding on, he could hear the sounds of the army settling in for the night up and down the valley. Horses were everywhere. He couldn't have imagined there were so many horses in the world. The brassy sound of mules braying came to him, and the dull thud of axes on hardwood and bugles blowing the supper call. They sounded like echoes, from one bivouac to the next. The noise generated by so many men and animals made him shake his head again. If there's a rebel in ten miles of here, he thought, he'd sure hear this noisy bunch.

He skirted an artillery unit, expecting to be challenged. There was a battery mess tent and cooks bending over steel pots, the men lined up in a long queue with their soup cans. He licked his lips as the odor of cooking beans and pork came to him. Behind the mess tent were the guns, still in traveling position, trails attached to limbers and the brutal snouts slanted toward the ground.

He passed another wagon park, where a sentry made no move to stop him, and began to wonder why none of these blue-clads were interested in who he was and where he was going. He had no way of knowing that, on the whole, this was a recently recruited army, blooded only at Wilson's Creek and other skirmishes, mostly ignorant of how an army secures itself. Or perhaps overconfident and not caring.

Yet, from his dress, he might have been a member of some rebel regiment. But he was not challenged, except by a line of picketed mules who bellowed and bared their teeth as he rode by. Somewhere he could hear soldiers singing a new war song, "The Union Volunteer."

> *"Ye loyal Union volunteers, your country claims your aid.*
> *Says Uncle Abe a foe appears, are we to be afraid?"*

It was turning dark as Spider Epp reined into a path that led directly to Wire Road. An infantry regiment was encamped here. He could see their rifle stacks, each one looking like the bare poles of a Plains Indian tepee. And before the rifles, neat rows of two-man dog tents. If a man could count their stacks, he thought, he'd know how many infantry they got. Four men to the stack. At the end of each tent row was a company guidon, the swallow-tailed pennant with stars and stripes, replica of the national colors.

The troops here were in small groups of eight to ten men each, cooking their supper. Most of it appeared to be salt pork. These men wore long infantry coats with capes and havelock caps, like French kepis. Some still had the cloth hanging cover that dropped to the shoulder and around the ears and neck. But most of these had been torn off and put to use as coffee strainers.

Spider Epp rode directly in among them, drawing rein near one group squatting about a low fire. They were frying biscuits in pork fat, using the halves of canteens split in two as skillets. Over the fire was a chicken on a spit of ramrods, turned by a young man with a red beard. All of them were drinking coffee, steaming in metal soup cans.

"How'd do, boys?" Spider said.

A corporal among them, his rank marked by the inverted chevrons on his sleeve, rose and drew back the heavy overcoat to reveal the walnut butt of a revolver, in a holster with flap open.

"Where you boys from?" Spider asked.

"Illinois," the corporal said.

"Well, I'm damned! Us folks come down here from Illinois ten years ago. What part of Illinois?"

"All over the place. Some of us from Chicago," the red-bearded man said without looking up. Only the corporal showed any interest in Spider Epp's arrival. The rest stared intently at the browning chicken.

"I live right over yonder," Spider said, waving a hand back toward Leetown. His tongue flicked across his ragged front teeth, with the odor of the cooking strong on the evening air. "Say, boys, where could I find the head man of this shebang?"

For a long time the corporal stared at him, his hand near the butt of the pistol. Then he inclined his head.

"Old Curtis is over that way someplace and Osterhaus's headquarters is about half a mile."

Some of the men began to fish the biscuits from the pans, swearing as the hot grease burned their fingers. They ate these and chunks of salt pork, much of it looking raw. The corporal walked slowly over to stand near Spider's stirrup.

"What are you doin' out wanderin' around through the camps?"

"I live right over yonder," Spider repeated. "My people are free-soilers. I'm again' this slavery business."

The men around the fire stopped eating and looked at him then, and the red-bearded one laughed.

"By goddamn," the corporal said, and allowed the coat to fall back over the pistol. "Now what you reckon we got here, boys? A true rebel abolitionist."

"One of them nigger-lovers who wants to turn loose a bunch of darkies, come take our jobs," the red beard said.

"Hey there, Johnny, don't you know what we're down here for?" another soldier called. They were all watching Spider Epp, grinning.

"We're down here to stomp out this rebellion," the red-bearded one said. "We ain't here to free none of your niggers. You ought to find one of them New England regiments, you want to preach abolition."

"And there ain't no New England regiments in this army, Johnny," someone else said. They all laughed.

"We ain't fightin' no rebel army on thirteen dollars a month to set loose a bunch of darkies," a sour-faced older soldier said.

"You mean thirteen dollars a month when they decide to pay us anything." They all laughed again, and returned to their biscuits and pork.

The corporal, still standing at Spider Epp's stirrup, pointed toward the fire.

"You hungry, Johnny?" he asked.

"Yeah, you want something to eat, Johnny?" the red-bearded soldier said, slowly turning the spitted chicken with one hand, stuffing biscuit into his mouth with the other.

"Well, a mite of coffee would be good."

"Here, have some of this salt mule," Red Beard said, and

reaching into a pile of duffel came out with a slab of black meat the size of a clear-water catfish. He tossed it up and Spider Epp caught it. The thing, whatever it was, felt gritty and slick, like a stone that had been lying at the bottom of a stagnant pool. It was hard, and Spider knew if he bit into it he'd likely break his teeth. He slipped it into an overcoat pocket, where it lay like a five-pound shot.

"That's pickled beef," the corporal said. "The pride of the federal army."

"Yeah," the sour-faced one said. "They give us three days' rations before a fight, but they always have to throw in a mess of that goddamned slimy shit."

Spider Epp, who was not known in this valley for his clean mouth, had never heard such bitter and colorful swearing.

"We got them three days' ration this mornin'. We et all of it 'cept for that salt mule and some of these biscuits and sowbelly. You don't want that mule, feed it to your hogs. But soak it a week before you do."

Everyone laughed again, chewing their meat and swearing.

"I'd rather eat wood chips out of a whiskey-agin' barrel," someone said, and that brought more laughter.

"Three days' rations," the sour-faced one said. "That means the goddamned rebel army ain't far off."

"This chicken, now," the red beard said, grinning. "That's only for soldiers, you see. We cotched her back up the road because she didn't know the countersign."

"None of these Arkansas chickens knows the countersign. Nor the hogs, either, when we run acrost any."

"So they gets appropriated," the red beard said. "Like that pistol the corporal was about to draw on you, Johnny."

"Never mind the pistol," the corporal said, still watching Spider and grinning.

"They ain't supposed to be no infantry corporals with pistols in this goddamned army," the sour-face said.

"Never mind the pistol."

"You see, Johnny, we be an appropriatin' army," the red-bearded soldier said.

"You best get down for some coffee," the corporal said. "Then after a while, we'll get somebody to take you over to Old Dutch's headquarters. Else, you might get your arse shot full of balls, with dark comin' on."

"Old Dutch," the sour-faced man grumbled. "You don't have to spoil my supper mentionin' him. That son-of-a-bitch pumpernickel. He ain't nothin' but Saint Louis trash. Just trash."

"You let the cap'n hear you talk like that, you'll get gagged and bucked," the corporal said. "Come on down, Johnny. Have some coffee."

"Damned pumpernickel," Sour Face mumbled again. "I can't abide these goddamned foreign sonsabitches givin' orders around this army."

3   Colonel Peter Osterhaus's headquarters were a mile east of Leetown alongside Wire Road. There was a small frame building that had served the area for years as a general store, and around it were pitched the tents appropriate to a commander charged with direction of a division in Curtis's army. Mounted and infantry sentries were about the place, holding their capes close over their shoulders against the cold. Couriers rode in and out with that frantic haste common to the field headquarters of an army making itself ready for battle. Nearby was a cookwagon, where two black men in civilian clothing bustled about pots and pans suspended over three fires. There were flags before the largest of the tents, and beneath these the aides and officers of the staff milled about—talking, holding papers, smoking. A line of fine horses was tethered alongside.

Inside the tent where the colors stood, Colonel Osterhaus and certain of his subordinates bent over a field table, studying a map and making their comments, pointing with pencils or stubs of cigars. Some of them drank coffee from the tin cups provided in the mess kit of a divisional commander. In one corner was a smaller table, cluttered with plates and scraps of food left from the evening meal—bits of kipper and drying molasses, black as coal tar. Along the ridgepole sputtered two lanterns, giving off their smudge of light and smelling of kerosene.

Colonel Osterhaus was a native of Koblenz and had served in the Prussian army. He had come to Saint Louis as still a young man and enlisted in a Missouri infantry regiment when war came. He was soon raised to commissioned rank, and now commanded the First Division of Curtis's army.

Osterhaus apparently had never forgotten the lessons of hard times in a land without a strong central government, and for that reason was a dedicated, almost fanatic supporter of Mr. Lincoln's efforts to prove the Union indivisible. He was as German-looking as his name, with a high forehead and well-groomed brown hair, intense eyes under bushy brows, and a gigantic mustache that swept grandly over his mouth, clipped just short of sparse chin whiskers. He was thirty-nine years old.

The battle area, as Osterhaus expected it to develop, was in the shape of a triangle. The southern leg was Little Sugar Creek. Approximately at right angles to that, running north, was Wire Road, the other leg. Forming the hypotenuse was a road called the Bentonville Detour, which crossed Little Sugar Creek about three miles west of the Wire Road crossing. The Bentonville Detour angled northeast behind the Union positions, behind the hill of Pea Ridge, and came into Wire Road about two miles north of Elkhorn Tavern. This road was beyond the right flank of the prepared Union positions along the bluffs of the creek.

"We're felling trees along this road now, Colonel," the engineer captain said, pointing to the Bentonville Detour. "In case rebel cavalry patrols try to use it."

"Good, good," Osterhaus said, speaking with a slight German accent.

"Colonel," another officer said, "we need to position some troops near those tree-falls. An obstacle isn't of much value unless it's covered by fire."

Osterhaus's eyes lifted to the young officer. He tapped a pencil rapidly on the field desk, like a drumroll.

"Yes. I know. If we have to, we move troops there. Now, our battle position is here." He stabbed the pencil at Little Sugar Creek where Wire Road crossed.

"I was just thinking—"

Their discussion was interrupted by a provost sergeant pushing his head into the tent to explain that a civilian had been brought in asking to see someone in authority.

"Says he'd like to talk with the head man, sir," the sergeant said. "Should we take him over to General Curtis?"

"No. Don't bother the general. He wants something?"

"He says he's got information for the head man. About the country hereabouts and the people who live here."

Osterhaus frowned, tapping with his pencil. A lock of hair had fallen across his forehead. The staff waited, and for a time the only sounds were the rapping of the pencil on the field desk and the hissing of the lanterns.

"I can see him, Colonel," one of the officers said.

Osterhaus shook his head. "No. Bring him in here, Sergeant."

Spider Epp blinked in the lantern light as they pulled him into the tent, a soldier at each of his elbows. He stared quickly around at the blue uniforms and gleaming brass buttons. Osterhaus straightened and folded his arms, still frowning as he studied this man before him with the yellow eyes.

"Sir, I am Colonel Osterhaus. I take it you reside in this area?"

For a moment, Spider Epp's face was flat, his eyes blank. Then he smiled, showing his jagged teeth.

"Oh, yes sir, your honor. I resides in Leetown. I know this here country like the inside of my hat. And I know the people who live here."

"And how should we address you, sir?"

Again it took a few seconds for Spider to comprehend what he was being asked. His smile broadened and his eyes shifted back and forth across the tent, quickly, almost furtively.

"I'm Crawford Epp, your honor, and a cobbler by trade. Now, me and my people are good free-soilers, and I'd like to help you whup the rebels. Folks around here call me Spider."

"You come to enlist, then?"

"Well, no sir, your honor. I can't leave my sick old mother for any degree of time. But so long as your army's around these parts, I can show you anything you want to see, and I can tell you the people you ought to watch close."

Osterhaus's eyebrows went up, like arching feather dusters.

"People to watch? Do you mean there are spies here in employ of Confederate forces?"

"Well, no, I can't say about that. But there's a pride of folks hereabouts who are secesh rebels and wouldn't wish you no good."

"We found this on him, Colonel," one of the soldiers said, holding up the Navy Colt. Spider laughed nervously, shifting from one foot to another and twisting his slouch hat in his hands.

"Good many menfolks hereabouts carry iron, your honor. And a man's got to protect hisself from these secesh people."

"I see," Osterhaus said. He regarded Spider Epp with the same close attention he gave all details, a quality about him which many said would be better suited to a company commander than the leader of a division.

"I already have civilian scouts, Mister Epp."

"I'd wager none of 'em knows this country like I do."

"I have no funds to pay you for such service."

"Oh hell—beggin' your honor's pardon—I wouldn't want no pay. I'd just like to whup the rebels. Maybe now and again I could feed with some of your boys."

"That's small pay for any considerable work."

"Tell you the truth, your honor, I wouldn't want any of your salt mule. I seen some of that already."

Everyone in the tent laughed except Osterhaus, and because he continued to frown the laughter quickly subsided.

"Tell me, Mr. Epp, what do you know about this Confederate army we expect to fight?"

"Blamed little. Except I seen 'em go through here sometime ago, headin' south, and they didn't look no great shakes."

"Tell me, Mr. Epp, was you going from Fayetteville to Springfield, how would you travel?"

"I never been in Fayetteville, your honor. But that's south of here, and if I was south of here and wanted to go to Springfield, I'd travel by Wire Road all the way."

Osterhaus glanced around at his officers and a slight smile touched his lips beneath the huge mustache.

"Good! And you say you know the roads nearby?"

"The roads and the hog paths, too, your honor."

"Mr. Epp, you know that if a man comes to this army and claims to be a Union man and it turns out differently, the consequences can be serious."

"Your honor, I'm just a poor man and can't dress out like no buggy-whip salesman, but I am strong for the Union."

"Well, then," Osterhaus said, stroking his chin whiskers, looking down for the first time at the map. "Mr. Epp, please wait outside with these soldiers. And, you there, give Mr. Epp his pistol back."

Spider Epp bowed out of the tent, grinning and waving his hat. As soon as he was gone, all faces turned to the colonel.

"Well, gentlemen. What do you think?"

"I don't trust any of these people," one said.

"Nor me," said another. "But on the other hand, if this man knows the area, he might be of great use to us. So far as I am aware, none of our scouts with the army has ever lived here."

"We'd need one of our own men with him at all times," said the first.

"Yes, of course," Osterhaus said. He stared at the map, much of its patchwork of woods and fields inaccurately portrayed, as he knew from his own reconnaissance; a number of roads and byways he had ridden himself were not shown at all.

"Good," he said finally, and turned to the engineer officer. "Use him tonight, Captain. On the right flank of the army, where we are working to block roads. Take him there. See to it we have not missed anything. But get him out of the forward areas by dawn."

"Yes, sir. Where should I take him then?"

"Take him to Provost Marshal when you are finished with him."

"At the tavern?"

"Yes, yes," Osterhaus said sharply. "That's where Provost Marshal has his headquarters, is it not?"

"Yes, sir, it is."

"Tell Provost Marshal he can use this Epp person as a scout in rear areas. But always with one of our men, you see?"

He bent over the map once more, his fingers running the twisting length of Little Sugar Creek. As the engineer captain started from the tent, Osterhaus spoke again, almost too softly to hear.

"And, Captain. Tell Provost Marshal to get names of those people our Mr. Epp said would be a nuisance. Tell him to find out where they live."

"Yes, sir. Any instructions to the provost marshal about those people, your honor?"

Everyone laughed again, and the tiny smile touched the colonel's lips.

"No. Provost Marshal, he'll know what to do."

4 Calpurnia slipped from her bed and ran along the cold loft floor toward her brother's room. She could see him, sitting in his bed with a blanket across his shoulders, his face close to the small window that looked out over the garden patch north of the house. Along the edge of the woods, fires were burning, and the red glow silhouetted Roman's face as he turned toward her, his eyes startled.

"Scoot over," she whispered, pulling up one side of the blanket and moving under it. He jumped back, almost desperately.

"What in hell's name are you doing?" he asked, trying to wiggle back from her as she pressed under the blanket and close against him.

"You better watch your talk, else Mama will whale you. What are they doing out there?"

She looked through the small panes of glass that Martin Hasford had shipped in from Saint Louis the same year they had sided the house with cut lumber. Along the garden woodline there were three fires, and around them the dark forms of men rolled into blankets, and a few standing, their capes hanging out from their shoulders like old ladies' shawls.

"You're not supposed to be here," Roman whispered frantically. "We ain't little kids anymore!"

"Don't say ain't. You know better than that. Just hush and tell me what they've been doing."

"Your feet's cold, damn it. Get out of here."

She was sharply aware of his embarrassment, but she did not

draw away. She pulled the blanket tighter around her shoulders, forcing them close together. She reached down beneath the blanket and arranged her long nightgown around her feet, which were curled under her. She laughed.

"This is nice and warm. It looks cold outside."

There was a fine drizzle of rain dotting the windowpanes with glassy beads, and they could hear the wind in gusts cutting along the eaves. It was a sound familiar to them when there was any wind at all, the rough shakes on the roof creating the clefts and rents that gave off flute notes as the air passed through them.

"What are they doing?"

"What do you think they're doing, this time of night? They're sleeping."

"Some aren't. They're standing around."

"All right, some are standing around and some are sleeping," he whispered irritably.

Calpurnia could feel her brother relaxing, the tenseness going out of him like a sigh. Their faces were close to the glass. One of the figures at the fire walked off into the dark woods and after a moment returned, his shoulders humped against the rain.

"What's he doing?" she asked.

"Aw, for Lord's sake, Calpurnia, what do you think he was doing going off into the woods?"

"Well, at least he didn't come up here and use our privy," she said, and laughed.

"The way you talk sometimes, and you think Mama would whale me just for saying a few cusswords."

"Oh, Roman, you make me tired," she whispered sharply.

He shrugged. "Well, for hell's sake."

Except for the sound of rain and wind, the night was still. Some time ago the dogs—locked in the barn again—and the guinea hens had stopped bellowing, having become accustomed to the strange people around the farmyard. The soldiers had come at midafternoon, along with a young lieutenant on horseback. He had stood respectfully off the porch and asked Ora if he might use the spring, and she'd said water was God's own and welcome to anyone who needed it.

"Did you see that officer today, when he was talking to Mama?"

"I saw him," Roman said. "And I saw you looking at him, too, like you never saw a Yankee with a uniform on before."

"If he didn't have on the uniform, you'd never know he was a Yankee. He was a nice man, wasn't he?"

"He was just a Yankee officer, that's all."

Most of the day they had stayed close-in to the house, watching the watering parties going to and from the spring hollow with clusters of canteens. The soldiers avoided the yard at first, and then the old sow had begun to farrow. By then the small camp had been established in the garden patch, and some of the men from there came to watch. They stood around the pigpen near the barn, laughing and talking as the old sow's pigs came down. They were Germans, and Calpurnia had not understood anything they said, having lost what little of that language she had learned in her girlhood.

"We could speak German once," she whispered.

"No, we couldn't," Roman said. "Papa could speak it, but we never could."

"I wish he'd taught us."

"Well, he didn't."

"It sounds funny, hearing them talk and not knowing what they're saying."

"You hear some of those people over along White River talk, you can't understand a lot of that, either. Anyway, you likely got no business hearing what soldiers are saying," Roman said.

"Picture Grandpapa was a soldier, and so is Papa."

"Yeah, but these Yankees are from all those big cities and you never can tell what they might say."

"How do you know so much about Yankees from big cities?"

"Well, I do."

"I wonder if they'll steal the chickens?"

"They got their own grub," Roman said, sounding superior because, for once, he was on ground more familiar to him than to his sister. "They carry it all right along with them. That's the way armies work."

Calpurnia said nothing, but she wasn't so sure. She was almost certain that by evening there had been fewer chickens around the yard than usual. And with the guineas so quiet, she suspected they might have ended in a Union army cookpot.

"Have you ever tasted guinea?" she asked finally.

He looked at her, his eyes wide and shining in the light from the fires beyond the windows.

"You don't eat guineas!"

"Soldiers might."

She could feel him thinking about that one for a while and was sorry she'd mentioned it. She had learned from her mother that you don't burden your menfolk with your own imagination.

"They took all the fence railings along the road," Roman said.

"What were you doing down by the road? Mama told us to stay close after they came."

"I was just watching to see what was going on, late this afternoon. All the railings are gone. What do you think they're burning out there?"

"Why didn't you tell Mama about it?"

"She can't do anything about it."

"Maybe that nice officer will come back and pay for them."

"Oh, hell, Calpurnia. Armies just grind you down."

"They do what?"

"Never mind. You wouldn't understand if I explained it."

They watched silently for a while, neither of them sure what they were waiting to see. The sleeping soldiers made dark lumps on the ground, like giant mole eruptions across the surface of the garden. Now and again, one of the standing men would throw wood on the fire and the sparks would flare up.

"There goes another one of our railings on the fire," Roman said.

"They look cold, don't they?"

"Let 'em freeze."

Roman pulled violently against the blanket. "Listen, if you want to sit up all night and watch this, you go ahead, and I'll just go get in your bed."

"No, I'll go. I just wanted to look. My feet are warm again, see?" And she pushed a bare foot against his legs. He drew back and shoved her, and she laughed, sliding quickly from under the blanket. Even with her form hidden beneath the long gown, her movements had grace and sureness, like a willow whip. She ran silently along the loft to her own bed.

The Hasfords used flatirons for bed warmers, wrapped in flannel, and she pushed her feet against the heavy bundle deep under the covers, feeling its radiant heat. Against the window, the rain seemed to slacken. Calpurnia pulled the covers up under her chin, enjoying being there, warm and safe with bad weather outside. And she did not sleep at once. Unlike Roman, who could be asleep within seconds of resting his head on the pillow, she had always been slow to drop off, always running over in her mind the things of the day and imagining what might come next.

She had no idea what tomorrow might bring, but she felt secure. The young officer who came to their dooryard had been polite, touching his hat and saying ma'am when he spoke with Ora Hasford. His saber looked so big, almost as big as he was, and him a boy not much older than Roman. She wondered about his home and his family, for like her mother, home and family were to her the most important things in any person's life.

He likely has a wife and children somewhere up north, she thought. And here I am, waiting for the war to be finished and the young men back home, but by then I will be so old, nobody will want me.

Calpurnia had peeked through the window curtain as the young officer spoke with her mother. And while she watched, one of the soldiers had seen her there and smiled. And, she thought, winked. It was very serious business when a boy winked at a girl, and maybe this had been nothing more than a man winking at a girl in ribbons, like Uncle Tulip did when she was younger. But she knew this wasn't true. She was no little girl in ribbons. And a grown man winking at a woman was very, very serious business.

She thought a great deal about her womanhood, and these were personal and private thoughts, shared with no one. Her mother had never discussed such things with her. Except once. Calpurnia had been hoeing in the garden when the cramps came and, later, the bleeding. She had been badly frightened because she thought something had been torn inside with the hoeing. But her mother said it was just a thing all women had to do before they could have a family and that Calpurnia might as well get used to it because it came with the changing of the moon. It only stopped when one was old or with child.

Calpurnia had never expected explanations from her mother, or anybody else. She knew a great deal, living among livestock. The life cycles of horses, cows, pigs, and dogs were plain enough. She wasn't sure exactly how it happened between people, but supposed it took care of itself when the time came. If she needed instruction other than what she could observe in the barnyard, she was sure her mother would tell her. Besides, only the details were not clear. And those details were not discussed, even between a husband and his wife, she suspected. They just happened.

With a renewed fury, the wind whipped against her windows, and sleet began to peck the glass above her bed. She slipped deeper into the covers and thought she could hear distant thunder. With that low sound, she slept. But it was not thunder. It was artillery moving along Wire Road toward the south.

V

Major General Sam Curtis was having his breakfast, a bowl of oatmeal mush and a glass of buttermilk. His face was stern; some said the countenance of a good Presbyterian minister. Muttonchop whiskers framed his face, emphasizing the harsh turn of his wide mouth that seldom smiled. His eyes were deep-set and stony, and across his balding pate the few strands of remaining hair were plastered down like wet silk. He was a man of no frills and little sense of humor.

The wall tent that served as headquarters and bedroom was sparsely furnished—a cot, a small trunk, a field table that served as dry sink, another as desk and dining table, and a few stools. An oil stove in one corner gave off little heat.

Curtis could hear the wind tugging at the canvas. The rain and sleet had stopped, at least momentarily, but the mercury was sliding lower in the glass that hung from the front tent pole. His civilian scouts had told him that should the wind shift to the northeast, there would surely be snow.

While the general spooned the lumpy cereal into his mouth, the young captain sitting across from him sipped coffee, steaming in a tin mess cup. He was a small man with snapping eyes and the self-confident air of one who is aware of his own considerable capabilities. This was the army's commissary officer and his name was Philip H. Sheridan.

Curtis believed in doing one thing at a time. Until he had finished his meal, there would be no conversation. Sheridan respectfully kept his silence, too, although there was about him an attitude of suspended animation, as though he might be impatient with sitting quietly, even for a few moments. But if Sheridan was anxious for activity, Curtis was equally satisfied to enjoy a leisurely though spartan breakfast without concerning himself with the army's business. He was happy with his army, as happy as any commander ever is just before battle.

Among his subordinates there was considerable talent, some displayed in Missouri, some still waiting for opportunity. Foremost among these men were the two Germans, Osterhaus and Brigadier General Franz Sigel. Then, there was Colonel J. C. Davis, who had been a lieutenant at Fort Sumter when it was fired on. Colonel Eugene Carr had come from a frontier cavalry regiment and Colonel Grenville Dodge was a respected engineer-officer.

On this cold March morning, Curtis had no way of knowing how these officers would cooperate, or if they were up to the task of coordinating a major military operation. One thing he did know: the young captain sitting before him was largely responsible for bringing order out of chaos in the Army of Southwest Missouri.

When Sheridan had arrived, the army was incapable of supplying itself. There was little or no system for the purchase of subsistence from the local population, no method of processing the food for army use once it had been obtained. And the distribution of transport in the army was absurd, some divisions having over one hundred wagons, others none. All this Sheridan had corrected in an amazingly short time.

Sheridan's ability to manage accounts and wagonloads of salt pork had perhaps begun when he was a fourteen-year-old boy in Albany, where he took up clerking in a general store at the handsome salary of twenty-four dollars a year. His quick Irish temper had very nearly cost the Union his services when as a West Point cadet he had disagreed in some manner with a command given by a cadet sergeant and threatened the offender with a bayoneted rifle.

Now Sheridan sat before his chief, the bright eyes alert. He wore a well-clipped mustache and was beginning to go bald, although it had not yet become obvious. His fine thick hair was waved back across his head in a fashionable pompadour.

Curtis finished his mush with a clanking of the large army spoon in the empty cereal bowl. He wiped his lips with a handkerchief produced from the inside breast pocket of his uniform coat. After replacing it, he carefully fastened all the brass buttons and smoothed down the cloth over his stomach. He looked at Sheridan, blinking several times before he spoke.

"And now, Sheridan. You return to Springfield?"

"Yes, General. The mill operation there needs careful watching, and the collection of grains."

"And of meat?"

"The supply of meat to the army is of some concern to me, sir," Sheridan said. "There is no reason to suppose that we can subsist on the countryside in that respect. Which means all of our meat must be transported from Rolla or Saint Louis."

"And grain?"

"There is little wheat in southern Missouri. We are milling some white flour, but we depend mostly on corn. Resources in that regard are more than adequate."

"And wagons?"

"Each division has transport, and additional wagons I have pooled under my own supervision." There was the quality in his voice that suggested he would know at any moment the location of every wagon in the entire army. Curtis suspected that if any man was capable of such a thing, Sheridan was that man. Already, the nattily dressed Sheridan had the cocksure attitude that would mark his long career.

"You must make plans to move your base south of Springfield," Curtis said. He glanced irritably at the top of the tent as a gust of wind shook the ridgepole. "As we move south into Arkansas, I would like to have you near."

"Plans are already made, General," Sheridan said.

An orderly came into the tent with a blackened coffeepot. He poured a tin cup full for Curtis and offered it to Sheridan, who shook his head.

"You have bad weather for a ride to Springfield."

"I suspect it will snow soon," Sheridan said. "And we can hope that the ground freezes again. When the roads thaw, they are rivers of mud."

"Yes, well, I suppose we can be thankful—"

An officer aide thrust his head into the tent, holding back the flap. There was ice shining across his cap visor. He announced that the army's provost marshal needed a consultation, and Curtis waved his hand. Major Eli Weston pushed his way under the tent flap, bundled in overcoat and cape. He gave a short salute and Curtis acknowledged with a nod.

"Sir, I have a civilian, a Union man, he claims, who lives hereabouts. He's given me a list of people who might want to do us harm," Weston said. Sheridan smirked, but quickly hid his expression behind his coffee cup.

"Major, a good staff man does not come to me with problems, but with solutions," Curtis said, and the provost marshal flushed.

"Sir, I have no way of knowing what your policy is on such things, our never having been in a secesh state before."

"What kind of direction do you need, Major?"

"Should we take these people into custody?"

"What harm might they do this army, do you think?"

Weston glanced at Sheridan, who avoided his eyes.

"This informant says there are fanatics here, members of partisan gangs, people who might make mischief or even signal our positions to the rebel army."

"Captain, you operate in rear areas," Curtis said, turning his deep-set eyes on Sheridan. "Have you any reason to believe such things could happen?"

"I have no evidence of it, but we have only just begun to operate in Arkansas," Sheridan said. "However, if there is the slightest possibility of such a thing, I would recommend precautions be taken."

Curtis grunted and stroked the muttonchops on his cheeks. He shook his head.

"I hate to antagonize people who live in our rear areas. I hate to make enemies of people who by next week, next month, and for a long time to come, will probably be along our supply lines."

"My informant lives here," Weston said.

"Yes, I heard you say that, Major," Curtis snapped.

"He should know the intent of his neighbors."

The general drummed his fingers on the table, looking first at Sheridan and then the provost marshal. He shook his head again, frowning deeply.

"How many people are we talking about?"

"There are some thirty of them," Weston said.

"No, no, no. We aren't going to impound a whole platoon of civilians. Can this informant identify a few of the more radical ones?"

"Yes, sir, he already has. A few he feels strongly about. There is a family living near here, General, a woman and her two children—"

"No, no, no," Curtis interrupted. "I am not going to impound women and children! They should be moved out of the area."

"We should move them?"

"No, they should move themselves," Curtis said, unbuttoning his coat to take out the handkerchief to wipe his mouth again. "Although I suppose those who would leave have already gone."

"Some won't go, General. They insist on staying in their homes."

"Yes, yes, I know. It's a risk they take on themselves. Well, who else do you have that is a threat?"

"A few old men, sir. One in particular. An old Jew who is a rabble-rouser and firebrand and always causing trouble."

"An old Jew? What has being a Jew to do with it?"

"I'm only repeating, sir."

"Feeling runs high amongst these people," Sheridan said. "But I agree, General, that no consideration should be given to take women into custody. A few may wave rebel flags at the troops, but I doubt any will try shooting at us."

"Waving flags are the least of my concerns," Curtis said. "Of course, there is the problem of information concerning our movements being passed along to their armies."

"Once our troops are between them and their own people, there is no more likelihood of spying here than in any other place. And anyone caught at such a thing can be dealt with accordingly."

"But some of these rebel men in the area do concern me," Curtis said.

"General, I would recommend that you take advantage of any intelligence that might come to hand regarding these people," Sheridan said. "You cannot afford to endanger your army out of consideration for a few old men and half-grown boys who might do you harm. However, those taken into custody should be treated civilly, and made to understand that once the main body of our army has passed, they will be released. As you say, nothing is worse than having men in your rear area who feel themselves mistreated. Besides, we need them to plant their crops in a few weeks. The army may be needing those crops."

"Points well taken, Captain Sheridan," Curtis said. He turned back to the provost marshal. "All right. Use your own judgment, Major, but treat anyone you take with consideration and courtesy, and not like a bunch of convicts."

"Yes, sir. We can house them at the tavern, at my head-quarters."

"When I was there last night, the place seemed already congested to me."

"It is, sir, with the reserve trains and my own operation. But we can find room."

"And this Union man, this informant." He looked at Sheridan and his lips twisted down. "I hate informants. But what of him, Major?"

"Sir, Colonel Osterhaus suggested we use him with our own patrols in the rear areas. Because he knows all the roads in this place."

"Osterhaus suggested that, did he? Very well. Use your own judgment." Curtis rose abruptly. "And now, gentlemen, I go to visit the positions along Little Sugar Creek. Was that all, Major?"

"Yes, sir, and thank you, sir," Weston said, saluting and backing from the tent.

Sheridan was up, slipping into his greatcoat. His movements had a quick decisiveness. He flicked one hand to the bill of his cap.

"Good day, General. And good luck."

2 All the chickens and guinea hens were gone. And when Ora Hasford went through the coop, there was not a single egg. Most mornings she found at least a dozen. For a long time she stood in the coop, looking out through the open door across the wide yard where water fallen during the night had frozen in harsh little pools. She held an egg basket in one hand, milking pail in the other, and suddenly they had an oppressive weight. She could hear

the Union troops in the garden patch shouting and laughing, playing with the bluetick hounds. She had a fleeting moment of rage and despair, but clamping her jaw tight she willed that away and went out past the pigpen toward the barn.

The sow and her farrow were under the sty shed. She thought, One is too big to carry off. The other's too young to eat. She found the cow, the horses, and the mule waiting patiently in the barn for their morning feed. Using the pitchfork she pulled down hay from the loft and gave each animal a double handful of corn. While she milked, she tried to force her mind away from everything except the warm jets pumping into the pail with the strong pressure of her fingers.

When Ora came into the kitchen, Calpurnia was at the stove frying eggs from the last gathering. She glanced at the empty basket in her mother's hand and turned quickly back to her work without saying anything. At the rear of the stove, a pan of hominy warmed. There had been no coffee for a long time, not since six months after the war had started and the regular run of produce and grocery wagons from Springfield had ceased. But there was sassafras tea, and cold corn bread from the night before, and a small pot of honey from Tulip Crozier's hives.

"Is Roman up?" Ora asked.

"He's down at the road, watching the army."

"I don't want him wandering around those soldiers."

"He won't, Mama. He's just watching them."

Ora was not worried that anything might happen to her son. But she had seen the excitement in his eyes when the soldiers began to appear, even though they were Yankees. She knew the uniforms and horses and rifles made him want desperately to be a part of such things. It turned her cold to think of anything that might encourage him to go away.

Most especially, Roman had spoken of the Union soldiers' rifles. It seemed an obsession with him. And Ora knew why.

When Martin left, he had taken the family rifle with him, leaving only the old shotgun, and a stock of loose powder and shot in the little dugout shed alongside the back porch. Roman was fascinated with the guns that had paper cartridges. He wanted something he could load without using an old-fashioned powder horn.

Roman came in as Calpurnia placed the eggs on the table— somehow he was always appearing at the exact time a meal was ready. He was full of stories about what he'd seen. There wasn't a fence rail left in the valley, and even the telegraph poles along Wire Road had been pulled down for firewood. He talked with his mouth full until Ora scolded him. Neither of the women mentioned the chickens.

They were still at the table when the Union provost guard patrol rode up from the road and directly into the backyard.

There were three soldiers, one of them a sergeant. They carried Remington revolvers and curved sabers beneath their short cavalry tunics, and on each right sleeve was a black brassard, signifying their function as military policemen. With them was Tulip Crozier, his turkey vulture feather bobbing jauntily behind his hat as his horse moved about nervously. Another civilian named Ruter, who had three sons somewhere in the Confederate army, was there as well—an old man with a sparse beard, wearing a fur cap and a long, split-tailed coat. As Ora Hasford stepped onto her back porch, hands wrapped in her apron, Crozier lifted his hat and old man Ruter bobbed his head.

"Ma'am," the sergeant said, touching the bill of his cap with two fingers.

"So, Ora, a good morning to you," Crozier shouted, pressing his hat back onto his head.

"A good morning to you, Tulip. Mr. Ruter. Won't you men step down and have some breakfast?" She intentionally ignored the sergeant, not looking at him when she spoke.

"Why, Miz Hasford," Ruter said, grinning and showing teeth

worn down almost to the gums. "We done et. 'Sides, we can't step down. These here Yankees has arrested us."

"Nobody has been arrested," the sergeant said, his eyes now taking in the farmyard and outbuildings, casually and, Ora thought, without hostility.

The bluetick hounds ran up from the garden patch with a sudden barking, startling everyone. But at the horses, the dogs skidded to a stop and backed off, mouths open but silent and tails wagging. Behind them, a number of German soldiers appeared from their camp, but stopped well back from the house and stood watching, smoking pipes. The sergeant's eyes stayed on them for a long moment before he turned back to Ora.

"I hate to intrude on you folks," he said. His voice had the hard twang of a prairieland farmer, the words pronounced as though they were sharp-edged, to be flipped out before they could cut. "But I have instructions to take certain gentlemen into protective custody."

"Protective custody, and what do you think that means, Ora?" Crozier said, wallowing a large cud of tobacco in his cheek. "It means his army needs protection from us. From old men."

The sergeant turned in his saddle, his saber rattling in its case. There was a faint smile beneath his bushy mustache.

"Mr. Crozier, be still a minute while I talk with this lady. Don't cause trouble."

"Trouble, is it? You're the one causing trouble, you and your army."

The sergeant reached inside his tunic and produced a scrap of paper. His head was lowered, the bill of his cap hiding his eyes. He read deliberately, his lips moving, and after a moment he lifted his head again and looked at Ora, and his eyes went behind her to the door.

"Roman Hasford," he said. "I take it you're Roman Hasford."

"I'm him," Ora heard her son say behind her, and his voice was taut and high-pitched.

Ora Hasford's hands pulled free of the apron and went to her hips, and she stepped to the edge of the porch, open defiance in her face.

"That's my son. He's no man. He's just a boy."

"Ma'am, we've got men in this army younger than him."

"They are arresting old men and next children," Crozier yelled, spurting a long stream of amber juice toward the legs of the soldier's horse next to him. "So, I'm surprised you don't put the women and girls in chains, too."

Once more the sergeant turned, patiently, and sighed. The other two soldiers were grinning, and Ora saw with some consternation that they looked no older than Roman.

"Mr. Crozier, don't talk nonsense to this lady. You know better than that." He stuffed the paper back inside his tunic, looking then at Roman.

"And what if it is Roman Hasford?" Ora asked, still bristling, although she had begun to feel surrounded. The Germans were still at the edge of the yard, watching without expression, smoking their pipes, their collars turned high around their necks.

"We've got orders to detain him at the army provost marshal's headquarters until the army moves on, ma'am. It is just protective custody, not an arrest."

"My boy hasn't done anything to you people," Ora said, and her voice almost broke. "And you're not taking him anywhere."

"Well, ma'am, I'm afraid we've got no choice."

For a blind instant she thought of running into the house for the meat cleaver again. But she knew that was useless. All these uniforms and guns, all this polite speech overwhelmed her. The defiance began to seep out of her like milk from a cracked bowl, leaving her empty. Her chin quivered for just an instant and then she had it under control, but the sergeant looked quickly away and shook his head.

"He'll be well treated, ma'am, and well fed. We just want to have the menfolk around here who are in sympathy with the southern cause where we can watch them. Keep them out of trouble. Then afterward, he'll be released and no harm done. There's nothing to worry about, ma'am."

"Oh yes, you'll—" Crozier started and the sergeant spun around, his eyes glaring hotly.

"Shut up, old man," he bellowed. "Can't you see this is not a pleasant job for anybody?"

Crozier's mouth snapped shut, and on either side of him and Ruter, the two provost guard soldiers were no longer grinning.

"We've got our orders, that's all," the sergeant muttered.

Roman moved out beside his mother, and she knew he was there without turning to see him.

"It's all right, Mama," he said, his voice strained. "I'll go with them. I'll go with Uncle Tulip."

She knew then it was useless to argue any longer. Her hands dropped from her hips, and without looking at her son she spoke to him softly.

"Get your heavy coat, and a blanket," she said.

"I've already got on my coat, Mama."

"You won't need a blanket, boy," the sergeant said. "We'll give you all of that you need."

"Why do you have to take young boys?" Ora said, in one last effort.

"I'm just following my orders, lady."

"No need to fret, Ora," Crozier said, his voice not strident as it had been before. "So you think they're taking us in? Maybe we're taking them."

Old man Ruter laughed.

"You better be quiet, old man," one of the provost guards said.

"You can see, these men are not bound," the sergeant said. "And neither will your son be. Now come along, boy."

"Can he take his mule?" she said, trying to keep the anguish from her voice.

"Yes, he can."

"I'll be all right, Mama," Roman whispered. "I'll be with Uncle Tulip." She got the feeling he was looking forward to this as some strange adventure.

Roman moved off the porch, glaring up at the Yankee sergeant as he passed the man. He walked to the barn with a studied indifference, his back stiff and his heels kicking into the ground with each step. The German soldiers stood silently, watching him, and with a show of arrogance Roman waved to them. Ora thought, just a little boy, afraid and not going to show it. She had difficulty controlling her voice when she spoke.

"How long will you keep him?"

"Why, it won't be long, I suspect. As soon as the army moves on. A few days."

"When the army moves back to Missouri, we all pray," Crozier said quietly.

Roman came from the barn with the mule and went quickly to the saddle. He fell in beside Tulip Crozier, and the old man reached over and slapped his leg.

"So you never thought you'd be going to jail with your uncle Tulip, did you?"

"Good day, Mrs. Hasford," the sergeant said. "And your boy will be all right."

"Don't worry, Mama," Roman called, his eyes bright and his mouth set rigidly. Ora watched them as they turned about and disappeared around the corner of the house, the dogs following, yipping softly at the horses' hooves. Calpurnia stepped out and took her mother's arm.

"Come on inside, Mama. It's cold."

Then the sergeant, alone, was riding back into the dooryard. He drew rein and touched his cap once more.

"Ma'am. I'd like to advise you that you and that girl there should move away from here for a short time. Go visit neighbors or relatives."

"If I left here for a single night, your soldiers would steal the boards off my house," Ora said bitterly.

"Well, you might be safer someplace else."

"We stay here."

The sergeant scratched his mustache, his eyes moving from the woman to the girl, then quickly surveying the yard again, pausing on the row of Germans still watching, their pipes clinched between their teeth.

"I guess you'll be safe enough. If there's fighting, it'll be three, maybe four miles south of here. Along that little stream. But still, you here alone, with your man gone off from you. . . ."

He let it trail off, as though uncertain of anything else he might say. With a small shrug, he yanked his horse around and was gone.

"Mama, how do all these people know about us?" Calpurnia asked. "That awful old night rider and these Yankees?"

"I don't know," Ora said quickly, turning back to the door, not wanting to think about what was in her mind, trying to push it aside. "Let's get inside. We've got churning to do."

Then she paused and stared at the Germans standing at the edge of her yard. Her anger flashed up and she made a step toward them, throwing up her arms as though shooing chickens.

"Go back where you came from," she shouted. "Go back, you damned thieves. *Raus!*" The German soldiers instantly turned and moved quickly back toward the garden patch, looking over their shoulders furtively.

Watching them go, the fire left her. She was a little ashamed that she'd taken out her frustration on these poor Germans, who were only doing what they were told. But then she remembered the chickens, and seeing the soldiers as the only thing she had to attack, she turned again and shouted, her mouth turned down and fury in her eyes. Calpurnia had to take her arm and draw her back into the house.

3   Elkhorn Tavern was a two-story frame building with galleries that ran the length of the structure on both floors. An elk's skull, the antlers lifting upward like two unclasped hands, was nailed to the roof ridgepole midway between the high sandstone chimney at either end. There was an outside staircase that led to the guest rooms and the Baptist meeting hall on the second floor. The internees were taken there, to sit on the rough lumber pews or along the wall on the floor near the fireplace where oak logs were stubbornly refusing to burn. The room smelled of smoke and wood ash and hymnals.

"So. Roman," Crozier said, seeming to enjoy all of this, "your papa would have a foaming fit if he knew the Yankees had put you in a Baptist place."

With Roman Hasford, Crozier, and Ruter, there were about a dozen others, mostly old men from the valley who at one time or another had made plain either their loyalty to the South or their hostility toward the Union. Some, like Ruter, had sons or brothers in the Confederate army.

"Tulip, how you reckon these here Yankees knows so much about the folks in this valley?" one grumbled.

"How do they know? Somebody told them!"

"A damned Judas," Ruter said. "I'd like to let my dogs loose on whoever he is."

Bundles of blankets were thrown into the room, and the men arranged the benches three abreast and made beds of them. Roman moved from one to the next of the windows in the room. They looked out on three sides of the surrounding area.

Timber had been cut away from the tavern and its outbuildings years before, making a crescentlike clearing in the woods that opened to the south and the cornfields that extended to Leetown. Just a few yards to the west, Pea Ridge thrust up its limestone outcrops, showing dull gray among the leafless oak and hickory. The crest was heavily wooded, but along the south face of the bluffs there was only scrub growth that disappeared, too, where the land flattened out to cultivated fields.

In all the cleared areas around the tavern, and even well back into the trees, there was the casual yet continuous activity of an army support area, well behind the battlefield. Men and horses and wagons moved about in what seemed to Roman a studied aimlessness. A traveling forge had been set up near one end of the building, and from there the clang of metal on metal provided a constant bell-tone among other clamors. All about was the smell of horses and their droppings, of meat being cooked over open fires, of spilt gunpowder, of leather and wet canvas and axle grease.

Major Eli Weston, the provost marshal, came in to deliver a speech. Tulip Crozier insisted on calling him the unelected sheriff of Benton County. Weston said they were being held for their own protection against any overenthusiastic Union soldiers who might look on their political leanings as an excuse to do them bodily harm, and against local free-soilers who might have malicious intent. All of which Crozier labeled muleshit, and in words more than loud enough for Weston to hear. Weston left in disgust, posting two sentries on the upper gallery at the Baptist meeting hall door. They carried rifles with fixed bayonets.

They were left alone then, except when one of the sentries opened the door to inform them that from time to time they would be escorted in twos to an outside privy, of which the tavern boasted four, all three-holers. Later, food was brought in the china generally used to serve paying guests. Lark, oldest of the Cox slaves, carried it on top of a large wooden packing crate with *US* stenciled across it.

"Miz Polly and Miz Lucinda says dey ain't no Southern gentlemens gone eat Yankee grub long as dey in dis hotel," Lark said, laughing as he served out white flour biscuits, milk gravy, pork sausage, and boiled beans. "She done fix all dis from our bery own cellar."

Roman watched the black hands, fascinated with their delicate strength, ebony across the tops, the palms blue-white. After he had served them all, Lark pulled a small wooden box from beneath his shirt and laughed again.

"Now dis here, dis is Yankee grub. I jus' happen to fin' it ober in dat big ole tent where dey's got the stuff stacked up high as any man's head. De Yankees calls it kipper, but it smells mighty like fish to me."

While Crozier pried open the box, sending the strong odor of salt and herring through the room, Lark slipped a chunk of taffy wrapped in oil paper from his shirt and handed it to Roman.

"Miz Lucinda, she says you mot like dis, Mister Roman."

"So, Lark, you're a fine gentleman yourself," Crozier said, his brown eyes popping. "Why don't you give us a little song and a jig while we enjoy all this?"

"Aw, naw, sir, Miz Polly says dey ain't to be no singin' or jiggin' with the Yankees 'round. She says we don't wont no Yankees to think we's pleasured wif havin' 'em here. I ain't doin' no singin' and jiggin' for you tonight, Mister Tulip." He was shaking his head.

After he was gone, Tulip Crozier laughed.

"That old darkie sure likes to put on the dog when he's got tavern visitors, even ones like us."

"I can't understand half of what he says," Roman said.

"He can talk as good as you or me. Maybe a hell of a lot better, if he wanted to."

"Then I wish he would. All that bowing and grinning and such, and that talk. He acts like an old hound expecting to be switched."

"That's close to it, all right. He thinks that's the way a white man expects him to act, else he might get switched."

"The Coxes never whipped their slaves. Not that I've heard of."

"No, and Lark wants to make damn sure they won't. And besides, I'd guess he likes to playact in front of us, making us laugh a little. Only I'd expect he's laughing at us more than us at him."

Later, Lark returned with a bucket of drinking water and a dipper. It was icy cold. He had news, as well. The southern army had driven in the Union pickets around Bentonville and had begun to close on the main battle position along Little Sugar Creek.

"Dey talk 'bout shootin' an' killin' down there at Bentonville, and dey talkin' 'bout all dem southern gentlemens comin' on to Little Sugar," he said. "I don't care nothin' 'bout bein' 'round when dey start to shoot dem big cannon guns. Miz Polly says we all gone get in de cellar."

"You tell Miz Polly there won't be much happening around here," Crozier said. "You tell her and Miz Lucinda not to worry. We're so far away, we won't even hear the cannons when they shoot."

Lark scratched his head and grinned.

"I hopes dey ain't gone shoot 'round here. I done tole all of 'em I ain't got no use fer dem big cannon guns."

"Nobody else has, either."

"Dey take in to shootin' dem big cannon guns 'round here, ole Lark gone run off to the Indian Territory."

"You run off to the Territory, so one of them big Cherokee chiefs will cotch you and make you his nigger, too."

"I knows dat, Mister Tulip. I knows it," Lark said, bowing out of the room, grinning, still scratching his head.

Roman watched through one of the wavy glass windows as the weather grew worse. Cloud cover had been thick all day, and there had been a gray cast to the land. As evening drew closer, the clouds grew thicker, lowering toward the top of Pea Ridge, driven more slowly now by a wind that had shifted to the northeast and was dying. A few snowflakes began to fall, and then sleet, and then snow again, more heavily.

At Elkhorn Tavern, the fires blazed up. But south through the valley the fires were fewer and fewer, until at last, along Little Sugar Creek, there were none at all. There, the infantry pickets looked from their bluff positions across the creek, where the southern army had been marching up and going into position since before dark. The Confederate fires there grew in an ever widening arc across the front of the federal army. They blazed unusually high, to the disgust of watching Union troops who had been ordered to kindle no light of their own.

Along the front, where there were no tents, the men rolled themselves in their greatcoats and tried to sleep. A thin layer of cotton color began to pattern the earth and log parapets. The cannon barrels, muzzles toward the fords, were sheeted with ice and a covering of white. Some of the smaller tree branches began to snap in the darkness, giving off explosive little sounds that caused sentries to jump and look anxiously toward the creek, and beyond to the Confederate fires, blurred now in the falling snow.

By midnight, the wind had died completely. The snow was

coming in swift little flurries. It fell along Pea Ridge and across the old cornfields, and in the deserted streets of Leetown. And it fell along Little Sugar Creek, where the Union soldiers watched the fires of Van Dorn's army blazing still through the night. But Van Dorn's army was no longer there.

VI

The three men held their horses close together in the middle of the road, the snow slapping with moist little sighs against their hat brims. They were on the Bentonville Detour, well behind the Union army position and about three miles northwest of Elkhorn Tavern, whence they had come. Now they paused, and the tallest of them was trying to light a short cigar. In the flare that finally came from the sulfur match, Spider Epp looked at his face and thought once more that the man resembled a duck. The nose was long and flattened over upturned lips, and the blond mustache was the same color as his skin. His name was James Butler Hickok, a civilian scout for the federal army. The third man was an Illinois cavalryman, detailed to this dismal, deserted road for picket duty. All were in their twenties, but Hickok seemed older than the others.

"You will have a cold time here," Hickok said, puffing the cigar and slipping his hands out of sight in the folds of his buffalo-robe coat. Strapped around this massive garment was a heavy belt supporting two open holsters and a pair of percussion Colt pistols. "But you needn't worry too much about Johnny. We're so far behind the army, you may not even hear the cannons if the ball opens."

"Damned picket duty," the cavalryman grumbled. "Enough to make a man head out for home, and to hell with all of it."

Hickok's eyes glinted, reflecting the tip of his cigar. Spider Epp had noticed those eyes before, in the lamplight of Major Eli Weston's headquarters at Elkhorn Tavern. They were bleak and passionless, cold as chips from a blue china plate, set in a metal-hard face.

"No, sonny, you don't want to do that," Hickok said. "They might send somebody after you."

"So long as it's not you, Bill."

The cavalryman laughed but Hickok grunted, finding no mirth in the comment. He shifted in the saddle, his hands coming out again to settle the heavy revolvers more comfortably on his hips. He seemed to caress them with his fingers. There was about him the strong odor of old hides and cheap bay rum.

"You heard what the major wants," he said. "You ride this road about a mile west, then back again to here. And don't come fogging in with wild tales if you happen to see a rabbit."

"That's all we'll likely see out here."

Hickok pulled away from the other two and rode a few yards toward the west, staring into the snow. When the flurries did not come too thickly, the white ground gave off enough light to see some distance. For a long time he sat smoking, watching along the Bentonville Detour. Then he turned back to them, moving his horse with the pressure of his knees only, his hands buried in the buffalo coat.

"You do what the major says, and somebody will be out here to relieve you after daylight," he said. "That's only a couple hours."

Without another word, he left them, riding toward Wire Road. While they could still see him, he cut away toward the south and the tavern, pushing his mount into the ice-crusted timber. The cavalryman drew a deep breath.

"That man gives me the shivers," he said. "They say he's one mean son of a bitch." He turned back to Spider Epp. "Now, he'll go back to get some warm sleep and some good grub from all them victuals stacked up around Old Weston's place. And if they didn't need to put you out of harm's way, they might not even have me up all night like this, on some damned road where there ain't no worldly need for a picket."

Spider laughed. He thought, You son of a bitch, I'm as cold as you are. But he said nothing.

The cavalryman twisted in his saddle and shoved his carbine into the boot. He slapped his gloved hands together.

"Come on," he said. "Let's move a little, or we'll freeze to the ground. What'd you say your name was?"

"Epp. Spider Epp. I'm a free-soiler."

Riding side by side, they moved slowly, the sounds of their horses' hooves soft in the snow that covered the roadway.

"I never caught yore name," Spider said.

"I never throwed it. But it's Welsh."

"You been in this army long?"

"Less than a year, that being almost a year too much. Being in this army is mostly bad grub and sore tail, and goddamned little excitement."

They rode west along Bentonville Detour. Off to their left was high ground, visible only vaguely through openings in the snow curtain. Welsh waved one hand in that direction.

"What's that over there?"

"That's what we call Pea Ridge," Spider said. "Or sometimes we call it Big Mountain."

"It don't look all that big to me."

"Well, there's another hill south of it, smaller. And that one we call Little Mountain."

"I'll be damned."

They moved along for about ten minutes before Welsh drew rein. Spider's old gelding came to a quivering halt without bidding, staying close against the flank of the big cavalry mount.

"This ought to be far enough," Welsh said. "Now we turn and go back the other way. Damned foolishness."

Before he pulled his horse around, Welsh took something from a saddlebag and fumbled with the wrapping, throwing paper aside. He held out a handful of hardtack crackers and, after Spider took those, what appeared to be a potato pancake.

"What's that?"

"Fried desiccated vegetable," Welsh said with distaste. "It's a lot like muleshit, but it fills your belly anyway."

Spider bit into the cake and it was tough, like eating matted straw.

"Here, maybe this'll help wash it down," Welsh said, and he passed over a small bottle.

When he uncorked it, Spider could smell liquor. "Now, a little sip of whiskey's good on these kind of nights."

"It ain't whiskey. It's medical brandy. I liberated it from the hospital tent they got set up back at the tavern." They started back in the direction they had come. The fiery liquor burned all the way down Spider's gullet, warming his stomach. It felt good and tasted like rotten apples.

"Is this what you always do in the cavalry? Ride picket for the provost marshal?"

"Hell no. It's just a detail, like riding behind battle lines and catching stragglers. None of that's regular cavalry duty. More like punishment. These damned backside pickets, nothing ever happens. You just ride back and forth looking for something that ain't there."

"Looks like it'd be better than someplace you'd get shot at by the rebels."

Welsh looked at him, astonished.

"Damnation, Epp! That's why we're down here, to change shots with the rebels. What the hell you think we're here for?"

Spider didn't say anything. He didn't like this man, nor understand anything about him. Spider's idea of a good fight was to lay an ambush and do all the shooting before the other man had a chance to start. But here was a soldier complaining because he wasn't where the cannonballs would fly. He worked off another cud of the vegetable cake.

"I'd be obliged for another drink of that whiskey," he said.

"What do people do in this place?" Welsh said, handing Spider the bottle.

"Me, I'm a cobbler. Most folks hereabouts farm or cut timber."

"God-forsaken place. Hills and all this scrubby timber. I'll take the flatlands, and the open. You ever been in the south of Illinois?"

"God yes, my people are from there."

Welsh stared at him, unbelieving.

"Why in God's name did you come here, then?"

They paused often in their patrol, and Welsh produced more food from the saddlebag. Cold salt pork cooked crisp and hard crackers. Men and horses trailed breath vapor. Suddenly, Welsh reined in, his head turning from side to side.

"You hear something?" he asked.

"A few limbs breakin' under the ice," Spider said.

"No. Something else." Welsh listened, his head forward as though sniffing. "Well, maybe not."

They drank again from the bottle until it was empty. Welsh threw it into the timber alongside the road, knocking down ice that made a sound like glass striking the ground. The brandy had begun to warm Spider Epp's body. Only his toes were cold, and his nose.

They rode on, letting the horses set their own pace. The wind had died with approaching dawn, and the snow fell now only in scattered flurries. Finally, a dim light began to appear over the trees in the east.

At one point, the road made a slight bend toward the south. Here their vision was cut off from what was ahead by the trees crowded close to the detour. They were moving along this bend, heading west once more, when horsemen suddenly materialized before them, making no sound. Welsh gave a start and reached for his carbine, but then paused.

"Some of our boys," he said. "Cavalry patrol. What the hell are they doing way back here—"

His words were cut short by a sharp report, a flash of fire from the front of the oncoming group. Spider Epp felt the ripple of air as the bullet passed near his head. He yanked the old gelding around and drove hard for the trees. Another shot made a dull thud through the muffling snow, and then he was smashing into the wall of blackjack oak and persimmon saplings, the ice shattering like crystal and snowing down around him.

"Rebels! They're goddamned rebels," he heard Welsh screaming behind him.

Spider pushed on through the tangle of trees, headlong, slashing at the gelding's flanks with his heels. He could hear the pounding of horses and low shouts, but there were no more shots. Looking back once, he saw no pursuit. He crashed through the trees, making a terrible racket, lying low along the gelding's neck. The horse stumbled once and he pulled it up with a vicious yank on the reins. He broke from the thick timber and into a small clearing. The horse was grunting in protest, and in the far timber across the clearing Spider Epp pulled up. Behind him, he could see nothing.

There was a low mound of bald rock in one corner of the clearing, and although his heart was slamming against his chest, curiosity compelled him to take a look back toward the road. He tied the horse to a tree and ran to the rock, scrambling up on hands and knees, slipping often on the glaze-ice that coated it. Before reaching the top, he yanked off the slouch hat, then slowly lifted his head.

From this high perch, he could see a good portion of the Bentonville Detour as it bent back toward the west, now dim in the growing light. He was hardly in position when the Confederate patrol came into sight, going back the way they had come, prodding Welsh and his mount along with carbine muzzles. They made no conversation he could hear. Even their hoofbeats were silent.

"Jesus God," he muttered. "They done taken that boy a prisoner."

He started to slide back down the rock to spread the alarm, but stopped. The patrol had halted in the road, only a pistol shot away. They seemed to be conferring. Spider blew his breath into cupped hands to hide the vapor cloud, but he kept his eyes on the patrol. After a minute, all but two of the Confederates and Welsh turned back toward the east again and rode out of sight. Spider looked west along the detour. It was still only part light, a gray dawn, but he saw something coming along the road. More cavalry, he thought. I'd better get my arse out of here.

The dim shape took form, coming out of the snowy landscape like a fish groping through murky water. Spider lay on the icy rock, mouth gaped open. That ain't cavalry. That's infantry! He stared as they came closer, four abreast, rank on rank, their rifles at shoulder, a hedge of bayonets bobbing above their heads. He watched, uncomprehending, as an entire company passed. Then another. The increasing light revealed a solid column of them, as far down the road as he could see, walking silently.

Then he heard the rumble that he had come to recognize. Artillery! Between the infantry companies, batteries of guns. And more infantry, their flags up, each regimental banner showing dark in the dawn, the color of blackish red dried blood. From where the road disappeared into the snow haze, he watched them coming, the guns, the horses of more cavalry units, the officers on horseback, the foot troops crowned with their bared steel, moving silently along the Bentonville Detour toward Wire Road, where the two intersected a mile and a half north of Elkhorn Tavern.

"Oh dear old God," Spider whispered. He pushed back and slid down the rock, scrambled to the gelding, jamming on his hat. "Oh my dear old God!"

He leaped into the saddle and drove in his heels, and the gelding gasped. He plunged back into the timber to the south, going toward Pea Ridge. He would ride directly to Osterhaus, where the real Union fighting men were. Not to that damned provost marshal, but to the fighting men. And warn them that the rebels were directly across their rear with an entire army.

2   Broad daylight showed through the windows in the Baptist meeting room on the second floor of Elkhorn Tavern when Roman Hasford was wakened, Tulip Crozier bending over him. Even as he came out of sleep, Roman could hear horses running and wagon wheels grinding in the yard below, and the frantic shouts of men. A dog was barking hysterically, and somewhere nearby an artillery battery was wheeling into position, the thunder of limbers and caissons shaking the tavern windows. There was a bugle blaring, sounds gurgling out in no pattern or call, but only random, distraught notes. From the south along Wire Road, infantry drums beat the long roll, seeming to draw nearer even as Roman sat up on his hard bench and threw off the blankets to reach for his boots.

"So get awake, boy," Tulip Crozier shouted, his eyes bulging, his jaw working with quick little jerks on a cud of tobacco. The old beaver hat with the vulture feather was jammed down on his head, gray hair flying out underneath in all directions. "All hell's broke loose here. Get them boots on."

"What's the matter? What is it?"

"Who knows what's the matter? An army don't tell people anything about—"

At that instant, there was a tremendous explosion, the loudest, most ripping noise Roman had ever heard, cutting brutally across the clatter of other sounds. The walls seemed to jerk and glass in the window facing north came out in a spray of silver shards.

"Come on," the old man shouted. "We got to get off this high perch."

Roman struggled to get into his boots, with Crozier pulling him to the door by the coat collar. The two sentries had disappeared from the upstairs porch. As he ran out, Roman could see complete pandemonium in the yard below. Soldiers were dashing about the snowy grounds like chickens under a hawk. Some were trying to strike tents, throw boxed supplies into wagons, harness horses. Major Eli Weston was there, hatless, waving a pistol and screaming instructions. Directly in front of the tavern, and less than a hundred yards away, an artillery battery was going into position in the lane formed by the Huntsville Road that ran due east from Wire Road. The gunners swung the muzzles of the Napoleons to the north, where smoke had begun to rise from the woods in dense clouds.

An artillery shell plowed into the side yard, sending up a blast of earth and snow. Two horses sprawled to the ground, and with them their driver. Horses and men thrashed about, and in that instant Roman had no idea whether it was a man or one of the horses squealing horribly.

An infantry column was coming over the small crest of ground just south of the tavern, moving along Wire Road, running and shouting, their drummers beside them, beating out the rolls. Where are they going? Roman thought. Why are they coming in this direction? Then it came to him, in that wild moment of confusion and noise, that they were being shelled by southern guns—from where, he had no time to wonder. The yard was an uproar, being pounded now with solid shot, shell, and spherical case.

He ran for the stairs, following the bobbing buzzard feather in Tulip Crozier's hat. He tripped at the head of the stairs and fell headlong against Crozier's back, and they both tumbled and sprawled to the bottom. The other men who had been held in the Baptist meeting room came down behind, jumping over them and running out into the yard.

"Get up, damn it," Crozier bellowed, pushing Roman aside and then pulling him to his feet. "The cellar. Behind the tavern, there's an outside door."

As they ran around the building, the images that flashed before Roman's eyes were a kaleidoscope of violence and fury, destruction and panic. A large supply tent, half-down and left deserted, was already ripped with shards. Alongside one of the outbuildings was a blue-clad form, lying against the blood-splattered wall. There were other men scattered across the yard, some trying to get up, some motionless. Those are dead men, Roman thought. My God, those are dead men. Even worse were the horses, some of them hit and down, screaming, some charging riderless across the grounds, eyes rolled back. The walls of the tavern were being peppered now with small-arms fire.

The Union infantry drew abreast of the tavern and ran on past it, forming a line of battle north of the building, advancing to the fence line there and into the trees beyond. The battery along Huntsville Lane opened with a roar and was immediately enveloped in their own smoke. Artillerymen ran back and forth in the murky, sulfurous fumes, hauling up paper-cased charges from the limbers.

Major Weston was trying to form a line with his provost guard soldiers, facing the draw between the tavern and the rising high ground of Pea Ridge. Up there, Roman now realized, there were Confederates, and their rifle fire slashed down through the yard.

He ran wildly behind Tulip Crozier, stumbling. The outside cellar doors lifted steeply against the rear wall of the tavern. Lying squarely across it was a dead horse, and beneath the horse, a man with sergeant's chevrons showing on his arms. Roman saw it was the young man who had ridden into the Hasford farmyard with the provost patrol only the day before. Below his still-natty jacket was a jelly of smashed bone and flesh, and Roman felt the bile rising in his throat.

"Help me get this goddamned horse off here," Crozier yelled, the tobacco juice spraying from his mouth. The other internees had gone, Roman had no way of knowing where, and the two of them heaved on the half-ton deadweight of the horse. Roman tried not to look at the sergeant's face, now the color of old flour paste, the eyes open and dull.

From the north they could hear rifle fire in growing volume, and then the crash of a regiment firing in volley. Smoke began to rise more densely over the trees there, and they could hear men shouting.

Near them, his face pressed to the side of the building, was a Union soldier, shouting prayers.

"Oh dear God, forgive my transgressions, and save me from perdition."

A sergeant ran to him, pistol drawn, and kicked the man viciously in the ribs. The soldier fell back, his cap flying off, his glassy eyes staring, his face incredulous.

"Get up off your arse, you son of a bitch," the sergeant screamed. "Get over there in that goddamned line or I'll shoot you right here."

The soldier grabbed at his rifle, had to make a second try before his fingers would close around it, and then was up and stumbling toward Weston's little line. The sergeant ran alongside him, banging at his back with the pistol barrel. Weston's troops were firing, their carbines slanted toward the trees of Pea Ridge.

Artillery was coming in faster now, splattering the yard with earth geysered up, the shards whistling through the air like malevolent wasps. Roman's ears were ringing, his nose stinging from the thick and oily clouds of smoke. The shells had already blown much of the snow off the yard, leaving it a reddish brown hash of raw earth.

A number of horses and mules had been corralled in the pigsty, and now a shell exploded at one corner of the enclosure, releasing the fear-crazed animals across the yard. Hogs, horses, and mules bolted from the shattered pen—squealing, braying, charging out in all directions like a massive covey of quail gone mad. Roman saw his mule among them.

"There's my mule," he shouted, and started running to cut him off. Before he could reach the walleyed animal, the earth before him suddenly erupted, knocking him backward with a mouthful of hard dirt and heat and acrid fumes cutting into his nose. Another horse was screaming as Roman lifted his head, stunned, his hat knocked off and one boot as well. Then he saw it was not a horse crying out, but his own mule, down and kicking violently. But only for a moment. Then the long legs seemed to reach out and stiffen, and the mule was still, lying with a rear leg thrust awkwardly toward the sky.

Roman sat for a moment, spitting wet earth from his mouth, eyes watering from the smoke of the exploding shell. He stared, uncomprehending, at his one bare foot. He seemed suspended in all this havoc, sitting there, staring about him. He heard Weston shouting orders, saw some of the blue-clad provost troops running back away from the draw where they had been firing. A wagon careened past, the teams whipped into a frenzy by a coatless soldier on the box. Another wagon sat near the barns, one wheel shot off and leaning crookedly, like a stool with only two legs.

Roman crawled over to the dead mule, put his head against the still-warm flank, and began to cry, his nose running. At first he thought it was blood. There was a roll of small-arms fire from the woods just north of the tavern yard, the sound of infantry savagely engaged at close quarters. Roman heard the sound with only a blur of understanding. A heavy form fell across his body and he started in terror. He tried to roll from beneath the oppressive weight and then heard Tulip Crozier's words, shouted into his ear. He looked up and saw the old man, his eyes wide and showing the brown veins, the gaping mouth in the stained whiskers. Crozier was holding the boy tight to the ground behind the dead mule.

"The damned Yankees killed my mule," Roman screamed.

Tulip put his mouth close to Roman's ear. "It wasn't the Yankees, boy—it was our own artillery. Stay close down, behind this mule. Just stay close down to the ground."

Wagons were still being driven from the yard, drivers slashing at the panic-stricken teams with loose lines. A shell of spherical shot exploded, knocking down the lead horses of an ammunition wagon. The wheel team tried to clamber over the two animals thrashing before them, tangled in harness. The driver leaped down to cut them loose, swearing furiously.

Another Union infantry regiment was running past from the south, their faces streaming sweat. The clouds had begun to break up, and the sun shone like a pale orange disk above the eastern woods.

As suddenly as it had come, the artillery fire ceased. But there was the increasing snick and thud of bullets. Small arms made a constant roar from the woods, and then they began to see blue-clad soldiers coming back, some of them running, others stumbling and supported by comrades, red across their uniforms. Behind these were other infantrymen, falling back, firing and loading, aiming into the wall of smoke that crept out to obscure the line of trees.

Watching over the mule's flank, Roman saw the first southern infantry. They came in a solid wave through a break in the federal lines, walking steadily ahead, firing as they came, bayonets gleaming. Above the sounds of the firing their shout lifted, raised as on a single tongue, a high-pitched, spine-tingling trill that made the skin on Roman's neck move.

Along what was left of the snake-rail fence north of the tavern there were a number of vicious little fights, the contending forces going at one another hand-to-hand. The figures were like shadows, moving with jerking motions in the haze of smoke. The blue figures were emerging from the fog in greater and greater numbers, many without their weapons. At last, from the wall of smoke, a solid line of southern infantry appeared, mouths agape in that dreadful yell, faces smudged from biting off the ends of powder cartridges. They moved relentlessly toward the tavern, pressing the federals before them, and behind, a second line appeared, and then a third.

There at one corner of the tavern a tall man stood, with a drooping blond mustache, wearing a buffalo-robe greatcoat. In one hand he held the reins of a prancing bay horse. With the other he calmly, almost casually, drew from his belt a heavy revolver and took deliberate aim at the advancing line. He fired once, then again, and yet again. Then, reholstering the pistol, he turned to the horse, mounted, and rode around the corner of the building, never ducking as the answering shots splattered around him.

After a last frantic volley, the battery along Huntsville Road was limbering up and dashing off. But bursting from the woods along the lane, rebel riflemen surrounded one of the guns before it could be pulled away. There was federal infantry there, too, just come up Wire Road. For a moment a desperate struggle surged, all of it swallowed in the pervasive smoke. Then the blue-clad men fell back and the Confederates lifted a cheer around the captured gun.

Southern soldiers were spilling down off the near end of Pea Ridge, screaming their defiance, driving back Weston's pitifully small defense. The tattered men in butternut and shoddy were into the yard from two directions, pouring across it, only a few now dropping from the fire of the federals falling back. Along the small rise of ground south of the tavern, mounted Union officers were re-forming lines, and fresh troops were joining them from the south.

"Put your hands out in plain sight," Crozier shouted. He pushed his hands, palms forward, over the body of the mule, so the onrushing infantry could see he was unarmed. "Else our own boys may shoot us as Yankees."

The two of them lay there, hands extended, their wide-eyed faces up because neither of them could bring himself not to look. They watched one barefooted southerner stop and peer down at a fallen blue-clad. The soldier bent and removed the shoes from the federal soldier, then sat down in the midst of his running comrades and pulled the shoes onto his feet.

There was a scattering of dead and wounded all across the yard, and where the old fence had stood they lay thick, one on top of another. Over almost each of these, a southern infantryman bent, taking wallet, shoes, ammunition, watch—anything that wasn't bloody, and many things that were.

A tall soldier ran across the yard, stopped short, and began to urinate, his breath heaving. He saw Roman and Tulip Crozier, their empty hands extended. He grinned, his teeth shining in the black smudge of powder around his mouth.

"Goddang, ain't this one helluva shoot?" he said, then finished with his business and rushed on, trying to reload on the run, scattering cartridges on the ground like fat paper sausages.

Another, running close by, suddenly stumbled and went to ground like a rag doll, his expression never changing. And yet another was caught in midstride, head snapped back and hat flying off in a spray of brains. A federal soldier crawled across the yard, retching blood and gagging, a great jagged hole torn in the back of his jacket.

The soldiers began to pillage the wagons left behind, breaking out cases of food, stuffing raw pork into their mouths. A cluster of them were around the springhouse with canteens, near where Weston had tried to make his stand. One soldier ran to the rain barrel at the corner of the building and plunged his head and shoulders into the water, then, dripping and gasping, went on toward the federals, his rifle up.

Midway down the slope of the yard, Roman saw a Confederate officer, lying spread-eagle. Above his yellow collar there was no head, only a wide blackish stain on the patch of snow where he had fallen.

Impressions came to Roman like those in a dream—unreal, unthinkable. Bodies were lying in clusters along the northern edge of the grounds and scattered across the yard, as though the sweep of southern infantry had been a sickle, leaving behind shocks of matted cornstalks all wadded together in bloody stacks. He saw men trying to rise, some with legs twitching, others with pants blackened by their own urine. He watched a Union soldier on hands and knees, head hanging, bawling like a disemboweled cow. It left Roman shocked but strangely untouched, a casual observer of someone else's nightmare.

Far down the lane formed by the Huntsville Road, a line of federal cavalry appeared. But they were wary of the infantry weapons and stayed well back, apparently trying to determine the flank of this Confederate attack. After a moment, they disappeared back into the timber.

"Lookee them mule riders," one lanky southern rifleman shouted. "Like to see 'em ride in here."

"Hell's fire. We'd clean their plow."

"Them Yankees ain't dumb enough to send horse again' us. Whoever seen a dead cavalryman?" There was loud laughter.

Confederate batteries were coming south along Wire Road, the drivers whipping teams out of the woods, following the fence lines around the tavern, into position behind the infantry lines. The empty limbers bounced over uneven ground, giving off a hollow rumble. Crewmen leaped down to swing the guns into place, shouting for the caissons and more ammunition.

An officer on a magnificent sorrel rode through the yard, a saber in one hand, blood running from the fingers of the other. His dark eyes were shining above his well-trimmed mustache and beard as he shouted orders and encouragement.

"Get ready to take a charge, boys," he yelled. "They'll be coming back. Colonel, get your regiment back on line. Get those men up front."

His sleeves were heavy with golden sworls, and on his collar was the wreath and stars of a Confederate general.

They began to take position, checking their rifles, swilling down water from canteens. They rammed in fresh charges, pressed percussion caps to nipples—some kneeling, some standing and looking toward the rise of ground only a hundred yards away.

"You best piss now, boys. You may not have another chance," someone shouted, and there was a ripple of laughter down the lines and many men began unbuttoning their trousers. Roman could see the blurred figures of federal infantrymen, moving up and forming into line along the little ridge. They were so close that no skirmishers were sent forward.

Amazingly, a Confederate soldier suddenly dashed back from

the line and around the tavern building. He dropped his rifle and yanked down his pants and squatted, then, still squatting there, took up the rifle again and began to load it. Some of the men in the line he had left were laughing.

"You can't stop the flux—you can't even slow it down." And they all laughed louder.

"It occurs to me," Tulip Crozier said, "that we're on the wrong side of this mule."

The two of them scrambled over the big gray body and lay on the other side, between the legs, still watching, looking now past the tavern toward the south.

"Here they come," an officer shouted. The blue line came through the smoke that had eddied out of the yard and drifted to the south. The line took shape slowly in the haze, showing ranks aligned, rifles lowered, and battle flags up. They began to shout, not the high trill of the southern men, but a deep-throated hurrah, in cadence with their marching.

"They ain't much account for yellin', air they," a soldier shouted. All along the line, the southern rifles were coming up.

"Hold fire, there, hold fire. We'll volley those goddamned bastards."

"If you can't see 'em through the smoke, aim just above the dead horses," an officer commanded. "Steady now. Steady now."

The federal line came, along both sides of Wire Road, back toward the tavern. Behind them drums were playing.

"Now," the Confederate officer shouted.

The fire ripped out from the southern line in a single vociferous crash, the smoke abruptly obscuring everything. A second volley came, and then the rapid fire of individuals shooting as fast as each could load. The federal line shuddered, torn apart, but came on still. More of them dropped, and then the drums were silent and the few remaining turned and moved back to the rise where they had started and threw themselves on the ground. The rebel yell went up again as the firing died in the yard. From the woods to the east the din continued for some time, then it, too, was finished, and there was cheering. Both lines sagged to the ground, panting.

Roman began to hear the cries of the wounded, many moaning now in agony as the pain returned to nerves at first shocked into insensibility with the strike of bullets. One, leaning against the rain barrel, was still trying to scream out the triumphant shout, his voice almost gone, his eyes glassy, but trying to yell as he attempted to reload his rifle with a bloody hand that no longer had fingers.

The general rode along the lines, and now many of them cheered him and called his name. Van Dorn. He was bleeding still from the hand and from another wound in the side.

"Up now, boys, and drive them," he shouted. "Up, up and drive them."

More Confederate infantry was coming from the north, passing through the yard with impassive faces unmindful of the ones gone before and fallen. They moved out into extended lines of battle and passed on beyond the men who had just repulsed the federal charge. Approaching the low rise where the federals lay, they began to fire, creating their own smoke cloud, into which they disappeared. For a while the battle flags were visible above the gray pall, then those, too, moved forward and out of sight. There was the roar of an answering volley from the federal side.

And now Union artillery from somewhere in the valley began to register on the tavern. The screeching shells and solid shot came in, gouging up more of the scarred ground.

3   Van Dorn, unable to remain in his ambulance cot while his troops fought, had mounted his sorrel and led them personally in this surprise attack from the rear. He was exultant, the thrill of

combat and of success flushing his dark face. Yet, as his infantry-men stormed across the grounds of Elkhorn Tavern, there was the crease of worry on his forehead.

He had heard nothing from the other wing of his army. For this was a plan for attack in two places—at Elkhorn Tavern along Wire Road, and a slashing down along the western slopes of Pea Ridge to strike the federals around Leetown. McCulloch was there somewhere now, for the smoke and low grumble of his fight were evident far down the valley. But Van Dorn had received no report from him. Nor from his ammunition trains, either, left the night before with an entire division to stand along the south bank of Little Sugar Creek until first light.

But surely this growing success at Elkhorn Tavern augured well for the whole front. Van Dorn determined not to take coun-sel of his fears. As the fighting surged within a few hundred yards of the tavern, he established a headquarters there, where already his medical corps had set up a field hospital. He allowed his wounds to be dressed; there were by now three. He moved among the wounded, trying to cheer them. He greeted Mrs. Polly Cox, who with her son and daughter-in-law had come up from the in-side door of the cellar to help. And he shook the hand of a tall man with white beard who was assisting the surgeons, too. His name was Tulip Crozier and he had served in the Mexican War. For a moment, the two stood together recalling stories of that conflict.

More good news came to him while he stood beneath the yellow hospital flag on the tavern porch. Enough of the small rise of ground to the south of the tavern had been secured to allow placement of guns that could command much of the broad valley beyond. And standing there, he could hear between the nearby bursts of firing the growing roar of a battle being fought some-where to the southwest, near Leetown, and he could see more smoke rising there as well.

He looked at the high ground of Pea Ridge, where his infantry regiments were taking position, and beyond, toward where McCulloch must be engaged. He could not keep the frown from his face, for still he had no report of that action, nor was there any message from his ammunition trains. Already some of his infantry units were out of ammunition, and all the batteries were running dangerously low. The sun was beginning to emerge from the clouds, warming the day as it advanced, but it did little to comfort him.

4   Just to the north of Leetown, alongside an old cornfield, the Thirty-sixth Illinois Infantry Regiment waited at the edge of a fringe of woods. Before them were open fields, some stretching out for more than a mile to the dense timber that stood along the western flank of Pea Ridge, and at a closer range and to the right, the knob of Little Mountain. These were the troops of Osterhaus, who had faced about with the first warnings at dawn that rebels were in their rear. Now they watched the battle of Leetown developing before them, far enough away to make them feel detached from it, as though they were watching some vast Punch and Judy show at the county fair.

With them crouched Spider Epp, at his side the saddle and bridle he had stripped from the old gelding, played out with the furious ride down from the Bentonville Detour and probably dead by now. He had at last found the general's headquarters in all the mad scramble of men and guns and horses, but not soon enough to give his vital message. Other scouts had already warned the federals that Van Dorn had enveloped them.

Spider Epp had stood, watching in astonishment the activity around him, watching an entire army turn itself around. He had stood with saddle and bridle in hand, the old horse wheezing beside him, head-down. A column of infantry had passed and he hardly noticed until someone among its ranks shouted, "Hey there, free-soiler." It was the red-bearded soldier of two nights before, and he saw as well the sour-faced man and the corporal who had offered him coffee, and taken him to Osterhaus's headquarters. "Come on, Johnny. They've started the ball!"

He had fallen in beside them, trotting to keep up, the saddle swung across his shoulder. They hurled insults at him, laughing, but he knew they accepted him and it made him feel good, made him feel a part of this army, his army. It made him feel brave. No concern at having been taken in the rear by the enemy showed on their faces. It gave him confidence, made him proud of these men from Illinois, men from his own native state. Even after he had panted out the story of the columns of rebel infantry he had seen going toward Elkhorn Tavern, they were serious for only a moment, and then were joking about it again, except for the sour-faced soldier, who said it was going to be a dreadful day.

They had hardly been stationed in the line of trees facing the fields when the grumble of artillery came to them from the north, and closer, other batteries began to bark viciously. They watched the cavalry of both sides exchanging shots and screening flanks. Then the advancing line of Confederate infantry appeared, coming down from the Bentonville Detour, their skirmishers out in front. Smoke rolled across the landscape in lazy billows, and each individual cannon produced its own cotton ball of haze with every shot. And they could hear the rattle of musketry from far up the valley, coming with a sharp violence between the bursts of fire in their own area.

"They're having one helluva fight someplace," the sour-faced man said.

"Sounds like they're tying into one another around that tavern we passed the other day," the corporal said.

"I'd wager them's the rebels I seen this mornin'," Spider Epp said.

"I hope Old Curtis and his pumpernickel generals gets something turned around to stop 'em, else the sons of bitches are gone be in our laps before night."

Across the field to their front, miniature figures moved amid the smoke, hidden for long moments, then reappearing. They could make out massed formations of rebel regiments and brigades, the lines advancing with an undulating movement, like waves on a sandbar after a catboat passes. There was no wind, and the smoke drifted upward slowly. To their right was federal infantry, falling back now, and between the smudgy billows they could see a battery suddenly caught without support. Cavalry appeared near the guns, the cries of the charging horsemen coming across the field in sharp, staccato patterns unlike anything they had ever heard. Even at this distance they could see the garish color of sashes and turbans and decorated coats. The artillerymen tried desperately to turn their guns to this new threat, but they were too late.

An officer was watching with field glasses and he swore.

"My God," he said. "Those are red Indians."

An angry murmur went along the line as the Indian troops overwhelmed the federal gunners, striking them down with clubbed rifles. There were a few rifle shots.

"They're armed with flintlocks," the officer said incredulously. "It's unbelievable. Red Indians and flintlocks!"

"Those dirty, slimy secesh trash," the sour-faced soldier spat. "Using red Indian heathens again' white men."

"They've gone crazy," the red-bearded man said. "They're climbin' all over the cannons."

"What's happening, Lieutenant?"

"I can't tell," the officer said, glasses to his eyes. "They seem to be milling around. Dancing? My God, I don't know."

"They're scalpin' our boys. I'll wager they are," someone shouted.

"I don't know," the officer said. "They're just running around the guns. I can't tell."

"Goddamned miserable rebel trash. Heathen red Indians in a white man's fight!"

"There's an officer, trying to make them move on," the lieutenant said. "They're paying no attention. They're waving their arms, and sitting on the guns."

"Look! There!" someone yelled, pointing. Federal batteries were moving into position, with infantry. The men watched, cheering as the battery horses galloped up, swinging around in a half-circle to bring the gun muzzles toward the milling Indians. Trails were dropped and limbers run back, and then there was the spouting smoke, and after that the low thump of the muzzle blasts seeming to bend the cornstalks like a gentle breeze. Shells began to explode around the captured guns, and another cheer went up along the line as the Indians scattered, running their horses back into the timber.

"Run, you sons of bitches!" the red-bearded soldier shouted, waving his hat. "They got little taste for artillery. They don't like them shells, no, sir."

But now Confederate infantry was coming across the far fields from their left, advancing toward the woods where the Thirty-sixth Illinois crouched. They came in good formation, driving everything before them. There was a scattering of Union foot troops there, and some were quickly captured.

"We'll be kissin' those bastards before long."

Behind them, other federals were moving in, forming lines. They could hear the soldiers shouting back and forth in German.

"I hope them boys can fight better than they can talk."

More artillery, supported by horse and foot, were aligning themselves along the fence lines running down from Little Mountain. The noise and smoke increased as the fighting drew near. More units were marching up to the battlefront as commanders brought their troops from the positions along Little Sugar Creek.

The ice had begun to melt on the trees around them. Chunks fell to the snow below with sodden thumps, and cold water dripped down on them. They damned the weather. The sun was out now, the clouds dissipating, but under the trees they were cold. Across the fields the snow was disappearing fast and the soil was turning soft. Smoke clung to the ground everywhere, and most of the federal right was obscured by it, but they knew there was heavy fighting there now from the racket of rifle fire. Once, a rebel yell came to them, dimly heard yet clear, making some of them shiver.

"Why do they do that goddamned yelling?" someone asked.

"Same reason we do it, son," an old soldier said. "To make the blood run hot."

"That ain't no soldier yell, no proper yell at all. It's like a pack of hounds bayin' the moon."

"Yes, sir, and them hounds got big teeth."

Nervous laughter ran along the line, and hands were gripping rifles tighter now, lips gone whiter. Spider Epp's heart seemed to beat louder with each step the Confederate formations took toward him.

But they waited, the day slipping past quickly in the roar of guns. Time seemed suspended, yet rushed on unnoticed. The woods smelled of wet wood and sulfur from the powder smoke. From along the woodline, an early lark swept up and past them, yellow flashing across its breast.

"Goddamned bird ain't got a lick of sense," the red-bearded soldier said. "What the hell's he doin' here?"

"Some winter here," Spider said, and he hardly recognized his own voice, coming from his tight throat.

They saw Osterhaus once, riding a gray, going along his infantry lines in the woods behind them. Other officers moved constantly among them, checking percussion caps, muttering words of encouragement. Then the order came along the line to fix bayonets. The clatter of metal on metal as the long, vicious spikes were attached to rifle muzzles made Spider Epp shudder. He knew they were about to go forward, and he edged back into the woods.

A little over one hundred yards out into the field was a rail fence. It was made of sturdy oak saplings strongly wired together, which explained why it had not been carried off for firewood. The rebel infantry was nearing the far side of that fence when the order came to advance.

"There's the colors," someone said. Spider Epp could see four soldiers, all noncommissioned officers, moving out from the regimental front and into the open field. They carried the national standard and the regiment's own banner.

"By God, boys, when them old flags come out, we're about to see the elephant."

"You'll be one of them color-bearers one day, Corporal, you stay free of trouble."

"I decline your kind invitation, sir," the corporal said. "Colors draw fire like a flue."

A line of federal skirmishers ran from the trees, their bodies low. The popping rifle fire from the Confederate formation grew more intense, but it took no effect because the range was still too great. The skirmishers made the fence, crouching down there and leveling rifles across the top rail.

"Now, men," an officer shouted, almost directly behind Spider Epp, "move double quick to that fence. Keep it dressed—keep those lines dressed. Now!"

"Come on, Johnny," the red-bearded man yelled, laughing. Spider thought, Why in hell does he keep laughing? Then he realized this man was actually exhilarated by the coming fight.

Spider was swept along with them, unwilling but somehow

compelled. They ran across the rough ground, mud collecting on their shoes. Midway to the fence, Spider remembered his saddle and bridle, left back in the woodline. He paused only a step, then ran on to catch up to the red-bearded man. I'll pick it up later, he thought. If I ever get my arse out of this foolishness.

The regiment came to the fence and took cover, arranging themselves in firing positions. Before them, the rebel formation came on. Part of it dipped out of sight in a low depression, and after that, the advancing line was suddenly very close. They were not shouting, but coming on grimly toward the federal position.

"Pre-sent," an officer screamed, and the rifles came up, leveled across the top fence railing, the massive hammers rolled back. "FIRE!"

Spider Epp jumped with the shock of the volley. Smoke billowed out, and he could see men falling, others coming on. Those still standing were shooting back, and Spider heard the harsh hornet snap of bullets passing near his face. He could hear them thumping into the hard oak wood before him, and there were other sounds as missiles struck softer stuff. Near him he heard a gasp of expelled air and watched the corporal who had given him coffee flop back and jerk on the ground, his face a mash of blood. Another young soldier slid down, clasping his neck, the thick red color showing between his fingers.

"God, Mama, they've killed me," he choked.

Spider pressed his face against the railings, far down from the top, his hands clawing into the ground, shivering, cold sweat running into his eyes. Through a crack, he watched the Confederate line melting away under the intense fire.

Suddenly a Confederate officer rode out of the cloud of smoke, his darkly bearded face contorted as he shouted. He wore a white hat and a black velvet jacket, and he ran his horse directly at the fence.

The red-bearded soldier was frantically ramming in another load, pressing cap to nipple. And then the long Springfield came up to his shoulder and bucked violently as he pressed the trigger.

The officer in the black coat shuddered and slid across the flank of the horse, his hat flying off and rolling along the old furrows. One foot caught momentarily in the stirrup, then came loose as the horse turned and bolted back into the rebel line. A shout went up along the federal position.

"I got me a goddamned officer," the red-bearded one screamed.

Spider Epp watched in amazement as the Illinois soldier dropped his rifle and leaped over the fence. He ran toward the fallen man, then bent quickly and went through the pockets, yanking back the black velvet coat. For an instant it seemed he would run after the hat that lay some distance away, but he thought better of it and ran back to the fence, crouched low. Something in his hand shone yellow in the sunlight.

He was back across the fence then, panting as he grinned at Spider. He opened his hand, showing a large gold watch and chain. The company officer ran over and looked down for a moment, shaking his head.

"You know you're not supposed to do that." But he said no more, and turned away. The red-bearded soldier snapped the watch open.

"God, look at that," he said. "It's even got an inscription."

"Get back to your firing position and start working that rifle," the officer shouted, looking back at him. The red-bearded man laughed, slipped the watch into his coat pocket, and grabbed up the Springfield again.

The rebel charge was broken. Remnants of the line fell back toward the woods far in the distance. It was a long way to go. Artillery sought out each group and peppered them with spherical shot. The Thirty-sixth Illinois continued to fire, taking careful aim as their targets drew farther away.

They began to sweat under the sun. The black powder was gritty on their mouths and hands, and stinging in their eyes. Spider Epp peeked through cracks in the fence and saw the Confederate formations fading away. Far to the left were horsemen, but he had no notion of which cavalry it might be. There was no longer any sign on the field of Indian troops.

Spider's eye returned again and again to the end of the golden watch chain dangling from the red-bearded man's pocket. Once, he reached out and touched it for an instant, and the soldier paid no mind, intent on his work. Spider looked back across the field to where his saddle lay in the edge of the woods. Beyond was Leetown.

This war has cost me a horse, he thought. It's only right I take some pay in return.

The red-bearded soldier was biting off the end of a paper cartridge, then tamping it home with the rammer. He had to force it now that the rifle bore was caked with black powder. He placed a cap on the nipple and lifted his body to sight over the fence. With the shock of the recoiling rifle, his body jerked, and with two delicate fingers Spider Epp lifted the watch from the soldier's pocket and turned quickly back toward the woodline in their rear.

Running, he expected a shot in the back, or at least a shout of rage. He ran as fast as he could, stumbling through the muddy furrows, the skin along his back squirming with the expectation of a bullet. But nothing came, no shot or shout. Panting, he was into the woods. He took up the saddle and bridle and rushed on. He kept going beyond Leetown, skirting the scatter of buildings where Union hospitals were operating. He went into the deep timber east of the town, where Winton Springs had cut deep little hollows, thickly timbered.

He stopped at last, sinking down against a large hickory and whipping off his slouch hat. His shirt felt gummy and wet, stuck to his skin, but he hardly noticed. He slipped the watch from his pocket and stared at it. The metal was slick and rich, and heavy in his hand. He held it to his ear and it was ticking loudly, steadily. A broad smile crossed his face, exposing his uneven teeth. He snapped the watch open, and although he could not read it, the engraving was impressive.

BENJAMIN MCCULLOCH, UNITED STATES MARSHAL,
BY APPOINTMENT OF PRESIDENT JAMES BUCHANAN, 1857.

VII

The federal army was almost completely faced about to meet the threat from the north by late afternoon of the first day. The firing near Leetown and Little Mountain sputtered to a halt, and soon all the southern forces there had withdrawn back to the Bentonville Detour and started to move along it toward the fight at Elkhorn Tavern. But there, too, the firing had become desultory and scattered, each side seeming to lie exhausted, waiting for night and rest.

All day, Ora Hasford watched from her windows as blue-clad soldiers marched through the yard and into the trees north of the house. The German soldiers had gone. Cavalry troops galloped before the front of the house, through the garden patch, and into the woods beyond. Federal artillery that had rumbled south for two days was coming back, taking positions all across the valley with muzzles pointing north.

And all day, too, random Confederate artillery shells burst in the trees along Wire Road and in the timber behind the house. Ora could see the scarred white wood where bark had been blasted off, and from many trees the limbs were shattered, hanging down like drooping feathers.

The hounds shivered on the back porch. After each shell exploded, even though far out in the valley, they whined and pressed against the wall. They had heard gunfire before, but never of such magnitude and always with Martin or Roman nearby with the shotgun. Ora started to pen them in the barn but changed her mind, although their whimpering set her nerves on edge.

She watched the smoke rising from the eastern end of Pea Ridge and heard the sounds of firing there. She was vaguely aware that another fight was in progress at Leetown throughout much of the day. But though that one was closer and much louder, she paid it little mind because she knew Roman was somewhere near the tavern. A hard knot of apprehension almost choked her each time she thought of him. She fought the bitterness at being left alone by her husband. In a sudden fit of anger, she took down the watercolor of Picture Grandpapa in his Prussian uniform and placed it facedown on the library table. But loyalty to her husband and his wishes helped her control her temper. She tried to conceal her concern from Calpurnia, but the girl was quick to sense her mother's mood, this one not too well hidden. Ora paced the floors, her hands clutched in her apron.

Once, a spent bullet whined across the yard and struck the house like a gigantic hailstone. We'd best get in the cellar, she thought, but changed her mind again. If the house caught fire, they would be trapped, the only entrance to the cellar being in the kitchen. She brought a quilt from her bed and made a pallet along the inside kitchen wall and ordered Calpurnia to sit there and occupy herself with sewing quilt pieces together.

Each time an artillery shell struck in the woods near the house, they both jumped, were stock-still for a moment, and then went on as though nothing had happened.

"I've stuck myself three times with this needle," Calpurnia said.

"All right. Just bear with it. Just think of what's happening to some of those men out there, and your own little hurts won't matter."

Partly as a precaution and partly to occupy time, Ora removed her plates and platters from the china closet in the parlor and arranged them on the floor under the table. Once, she went

out for water. She did not go to the spring hollow, because that
was too far away, but drew up a bucket from the well beside the
barn. Martin and Tulip Crozier had dug that well years ago,
mostly to water the stock, and she could recall them sweating over
the work, pausing now and again to take a sip from the jug of
whiskey Martin always kept in the cellar. It had concerned her a
little because she had never seen her husband drink that much
before. The well came in with clear, cold water, although not so
cold as that from the springhouse.

She put on a kettle for sassafras tea, but neither of them had
any stomach for it. With the sun out the day was warming, but
she continued to stoke the cookstove, throwing in the thin-cut
staves of oak and hickory. The day dragged on endlessly. The gunfire sounded in low grumblings and then rose to such a pitch that
the house shook.

"I've got to go outside," Calpurnia said, rising from the pallet.

"What are you talking about?"

"I've got to go to the privy, Mama."

"Use the chamber pot under my bed," Ora said.

"Oh, Mama, for goodness' sake—"

"Do what I tell you," Ora said sharply. "Take it in the parlor
if you're afraid I'll look at you. And stay away from the windows."

The firing in the north began to die out. God's will be done,
Ora thought. Whatever has happened, has happened, and all that's
left to do is wait. She kept watching the slope below the house,
half expecting, half hoping Roman and the mule would appear.

Instead, toward evening, a long column of Union cavalry
came up from the road, guidons snapping above them. They
passed alongside the house, through the dooryard, and on by the
pigpen and the barn, finally out of sight in the timber beyond.
They made an infernal racket of chains and sabers rattling, hooves
thudding and leather squeaking. The troopers were silent as they

rode by, faces drawn and expressionless. The horses were lathered as though they had been ridden hard. Ora and Calpurnia watched them, wordlessly, and then the girl went back to the pallet and the quilt pieces.

The passage of so many animals near her pen made the old sow nervous and she began to squeal and run back and forth in the small enclosure, scattering her pigs before her. They set up a whining noise, high-pitched and grating on the ear.

"Damned pigs," Ora muttered. "They'll drive us out of our minds with all that ruckus."

"What's the matter with them?"

"The horses got the old lady upset, I guess."

Light was still in the sky when Ora said, "We'd best fix some supper."

"I'm not very hungry. And I'm getting tired of these old quilt pieces."

"You'll be happy to have your own quilts someday," Ora said, going to the stove. She put on a pan of water and dumped in dried apples. She was making corn bread when the shell exploded against the barn with a shattering detonation.

Ora dropped the corn bread on the floor, the mixture splashing over her shoes. Calpurnia covered her ears with her hands and screamed. Their heads rang with a strange sound, going on and on, high-pitched and harsh. Then Ora knew it wasn't shell noise, but the pigs. There was in it an hysterical note she had heard once before in her life.

"Come on, hurry," she shouted, and ran for the door.

The shell had ripped away the siding from the barn just above the pigsty. In a panic, the old sow had begun to eat her pigs, possibly because a shard had bloodied one of them, or perhaps the unfamiliar din throughout the day had finally driven her mad. But after the first bite of her massive teeth into one of the farrow, the taste of blood sent her into a frenzy of killing lust. She was shredding her pigs as fast as she could reach them.

Ora ran for the barn, the hounds off the porch and yammering around her, then dashing for the pigpen, running along the fence, trying to get in. She was back with the pitchfork in an instant. The dogs were clawing and jumping against the sty, and Calpurnia was at the fence, staring in horror. The pigs were squealing with terror, blindly scrambling about, trying to avoid their mother's jaws.

"Open the gate and stand back," Ora yelled.

Trancelike, Calpurnia yanked the gate open and Ora stepped in, the dogs tumbling around her feet. Two of them ran directly at the sow, and the pig threw one back with a toss of her head, the dog howling with a slash of red showing along his ribs. The other hound attacked the sow's flanks. But the third dog was after one of the surviving pigs, trying to kill it. Ora stabbed at him with the fork, and with the tines under his belly threw him away. The dog snarled and snapped at her, teeth clicking.

"Get the pigs, get the pigs," she shouted.

The sow turned toward Ora, eyes red-rimmed, bloody chunks of meat hanging from her mouth. She snorted and came at Ora with a low squeal. Ora leveled the fork like a bayonet and lunged for the pig's face, all the anxious fury of the day in her movements. The sow rammed into the tines, shuddered and backed away, the two dogs still at her. She shook them off and came again, and Ora caught her in the nose with the fork. It was difficult footing with raw meat and intestines and blood all over the pen.

Calpurnia was inside the sty, grabbing for the two remaining pigs. The voracious hound made a lunge for her and she kicked him in the belly and he backed off, coughing. She caught up one pig by the hind leg and dropped him into the front of her skirt, held up before her to make a sack. She cornered the other pig, still walleyed and screaming, and dropped him in as well. Holding the squirming bundle against her belly, she ran out of the pen.

"I've got 'em, Mama. I've got 'em!"

The two hounds were hanging on to the sow now, one with jaws clamped on a rear leg, the other pulling back on the twisting tail—all four feet planted, he was dragged across the pen as the sow made yet another charge. Ora met the sow with the fork, and the handle bent. But this time as the pig scrambled backward away from the tines, she got around Ora and raced through the open gate, Calpurnia screaming and running for the porch. The sow turned toward the woods and ran on, the two dogs at her back, snapping at her rear hooves. But the third dog was still in the pen, gobbling up great mouthfuls of meat from the scattered remnants of pig, his teeth crunching on the tiny bones.

"Damn you," Ora screeched, and drove the fork at the dog. He turned to her and bared his teeth, growling. Ora threw the fork to the ground and ran to the house. Roman's shotgun was leaning in one corner. She took it and found the box of caps on the rafter niche above it, then ran back to the yard, her face dark and working violently.

"Mama! Mama, what are you doing?" Calpurnia screamed. She was still on the porch, holding the pigs in her dress.

Ora capped the shotgun as she ran. The dog was still dashing about the sty, scooping up pieces of pig, swallowing them whole. He looked up at her as Ora ran to the fence, and she shot him in the face. The dog howled and leaped straight up, legs stiff. He ran from the pen unsteadily, toward the springhouse hollow, and Ora shot him with the second barrel from the rear. He skittered along, running only on his front feet for a few yards, then was down and quivering.

All the day's pent-up anger was gone, and Ora was exhausted. Holding the still-smoking shotgun, she looked at the dog. With a shudder she turned back to the house where Calpurnia stood on the porch, ashen-faced and wide-eyed.

"I won't have a dog around that'll turn on you," Ora said. Her face was drawn, her jaw tight-set, and Calpurnia followed her inside without a word.

Now, thankfully, there were things to be done, to occupy the mind. They put the pigs in the half-empty woodbox behind the stove, and when Calpurnia asked what they would eat—not yet weaned and their mother run off likely all the way to the White River bottoms—Ora sharply said they would eat whatever they were given. Calpurnia had the feeling that the pigs would dare not refuse anything Ora offered them, on forfeit of their lives. She had never seen her mother's wrath explode so openly and violently, and it frightened her a little.

"Now clean up this batter mess and make some more while I reload the shotgun."

Later, while her daughter prepared the evening meal, Ora went down into the cellar and groped in the darkness until she found the jug of whiskey. There was a heavy dust on it and she wiped that off and pulled the cork. Holding the jug across her elbow as she had seen her husband do, she took a long swallow. It scalded her throat and she gasped. The cellar had a musty odor of old potatoes and cobwebs, and now the oily smell of white whiskey as she stood in the dark with the uncorked jug in her hands. After long enough for the fire to leave her tongue, Ora took another drink. Then she corked the jug and went up to feed the stock, to milk the cows, and to bury the dog.

2   Spider Epp stole a federal horse. There was no difficulty about it. With night coming on, the timbered hollows around Winton Springs were full of them—riderless cavalry horses or

officers' mounts. He selected a fine bay stallion that had no trace of blood on his coat. The horse was skittery and Spider had to follow him a long way through the wooded draw, coaxing in a low voice until finally he had his hands on the trailing reins. He stripped off the army gear and replaced it with his own bridle and high-horned saddle. He worried for a moment about the large *US* branded on the stallion's left flank, but overcame that with a smear of mud across the incriminating mark.

Twice during all of this he almost stepped on wounded Union soldiers who had somehow struggled back to the springs and were lying along the banks, drinking. There were stragglers here, too. They made him uneasy, shifting along under the trees in the growing darkness, faceless forms like shadows. Now that he was a man of means, with a gold watch and a fine horse, he was disposed to suspect each dim figure of designs on his holdings. Even the ones badly wounded and able only to crawl.

He felt for the Navy Colt in his waistband to reassure himself. His fingers explored each cylinder nipple to make sure a cap was in place. But none of the skulkers came near him, and he walked his new horse out of the hollow unmolested. He passed out of the timber and on toward Leetown. In the west was a strip of light still, but the ground had become dark. Around him he could hear the Union army medical corpsmen looking for wounded.

There were more lights among the buildings of Leetown than he had ever seen before. Much of the place had been taken over by the surgeons, with yellow hospital flags up before many of the homes and small businesses. Carrying parties moved along the streets with litters, and there was a general movement between the town and the surrounding area. As he drew near, Spider Epp could hear the crying and groaning of the wounded. It failed to touch him in any way. He was concerned only with getting the stallion into his stock shed.

The search parties had lighted lanterns and torches now. The pinpoints of light moving among the trees looked like fireflies in summer, and in fact the night had a feeling of spring about it. It was warming, and there was no wind under cloudless skies where the stars shone sharp and clear. All of it gave Spider Epp a sense of deep satisfaction, just to be alive after what he'd seen this day—a quiet exuberance that blood still flowed in his veins undisturbed. And now a new season was coming, the season of mockingbirds and cicadas and tree frogs and rising sap in the trees . . . and in Spider Epp's loins. He thought for a moment about Calpurnia Hasford.

The army had not taken over the cobbler shop, and he found his mother sitting in the low lamplight of the kitchen. She began to whine at him for having left her for so long, with all the noise and smoke and strange people moving through the town in their blue uniforms. He tried to explain that these were their own people, but she hardly listened, droning on as she sat with bony fingers clasped in her lap. He was a useless son, she said, going off for excitement and fun, leaving his poor old mother alone and defenseless.

There was a pot of baked chicken at the back of the stove, largely picked over but with some meat left on the bones. He scooped up a handful of it from the congealed grease and went out to the shop, where he stood eating, looking through the window at the activity in the street. His mother's voice went on behind him, low and monotonous. He ignored it.

There was a row of strange bundles lying in the street beneath his window, stretching as far as he could see in either direction. At first he supposed them to be supplies of some sort, but as his eyes grew accustomed to the darkness once more, he realized they were bodies. They were neatly aligned, like a company's dog tents, with blankets pulled over them. The federal litter parties were collecting not only their wounded, but their dead as well.

———

3   The federal line had been withdrawn from the southern positions won just south of Elkhorn Tavern. Units on both sides coming from the Leetown fight were being moved into place along either flank, until finally the lines were extended from Pea Ridge on the west to well beyond Wire Road on the east, a distance of more than two miles. Had one been able to look down from above on the evening of March 7, 1862, they would have observed that the dispositions suggested a pair of lenses. On the north the Confederate lines were concave, and on the south the federal were convex; they faced each other at an interval of about a half-mile from flank to flank.

Van Dorn's men lay exhausted, sleeping on the cold ground wherever they happened to be placed. There had been no distribution of rations, for they had carried everything available on their backs, and the supply wagons were still somewhere to the south. Many suspected that by now the Union army lay directly between them and their food and ammunition, for they could not expect the federals to leave Bentonville Detour open a second time. The wagons had been slow in moving, and now it was too late.

Southern soldiers built fires in many places along the front. Orders passed down the lines to extinguish them, but many burned well into the night, like beacons marking the defensive positions for enemy gunners. Down Wire Road and across the fields to the front of the Confederates, there was only darkness.

Officers listened intently as the sounds came to them across the windless night. There to the south, only a half mile away, the federals were massing their army, arranging themselves for tomorrow's assault. They could hear artillery moving into position, and sometimes the shouts of command among the infantry regiments. There were federal skirmishers between the lines, and throughout the night the pop of a single rifle broke across the stillness whenever some Yankee soldier saw a moving shadow. It was like the nervous tic in the face of a man drawn tense with the knowledge of what would come with daylight.

No one who thought seriously about it could doubt what Van Dorn would do. He was squarely across the federal line of supply; he would stand on the defensive and make them come to him. Yet, the disquieting thought recurred that the only ammunition they had for tomorrow's fight was what they already possessed. A redistribution was taking place among the batteries—units that had not been so heavily engaged during the day giving up some of their supply to those that had been.

The situation was almost as dismal for the infantry. But their spirits were still high. In the flush of temporary victory, they exclaimed up and down the line that they would meet anything the Yankees had to offer with the points of their bayonets—although not one among them had ever seen an enemy killed with that weapon.

Van Dorn perhaps did not realize that he outnumbered Curtis in both men and guns. Had he known, he would still have been troubled. For unless the ammunition trains arrived, victory on the morrow would have to be won quickly or it would not come at all. And this Yankee army had shown itself to be stubborn and hard-hitting. What made matters even worse, two of his best generals and many other able officers had been killed in the abortive attack at Leetown.

Van Dorn did not show his concern outwardly. He moved among his troops and the wounded, offering congratulations on the job done this day and encouragement for what was still to be done.

Burial details had been busy since nightfall, collecting southern and federal dead alike, hauling them north along Wire Road in captured Union wagons. Their instructions: Bury as many as you can before first light, then return quickly to your units for the expected encounter. It was the soldiers' most abhorrent duty.

Elkhorn Tavern was a blaze of light. It was now a southern hospital, with a collection of regimental and army surgeons working in a number of the rooms. Beneath one window a growing pile of amputated limbs—arms, legs, hands, feet—was carefully guarded by one of the Cox slaves to keep the dogs and pigs away until all of it could be buried. Opiates had soon run out, and all operations were being done without anesthetic. Where the wound allowed it, generous doses of whiskey from the Cox cellar were administered, but even with that was considerable screaming.

Under normal conditions, many cases would have been removed to field hospitals to the rear. But here, the Confederate rear was behind the federal lines. And so the tavern became not only a field infirmary but a hospital as well. Tulip Crozier, Polly Cox, and her son, Joseph, helped as they could, and before the night was old their fronts were covered with red.

Roman Hasford and Lucinda Cox sat on a cedar chest in the outside kitchen. This was a small building detached from the main tavern and used as a cookhouse when the number of guests in the inn taxed the resources of the family kitchen. It was far enough from the work being done in the tavern to make the moans of the wounded almost inaudible, except for occasional sudden cries of agony. But that had been going on for so long, they were hardly aware of it, and what they did hear they made a studied effort to ignore.

Old man Ruter was sleeping on the floor across the room, against the woodbox. They could see his stumpy teeth between parted lips. He had returned after running away in the first bursts of Confederate cannon fire. He had been leading Tulip Crozier's horse and his own, found wandering in the timber. The animals had been terrified at the noise and the old man had claimed the devil's own time catching them.

"I didn't find your mule, Roman," he'd said.

"No. The mule's dead in the yard."

"I declare. You'd never suppose there'd be so much livestock killed when they fit one of these battles. It's a shame."

"They make big targets," Roman had said, trying to sound hard and ruthless, stating a common fact.

Now the girl and Roman sat together, he trying to avoid looking at her swollen belly. She wore a high-waisted dress designed to hide her pregnancy, but it seemed only to emphasize it. It embarrassed Roman to look at her, or even think about her condition.

"Old man Ruter can sure snore, can't he?" she said. Roman shrugged. When he had first looked into the parlor and seen what was happening on the dining table under the surgeons' knives, he had thought he'd never eat again. But soon the odor of Mrs. Cox's famous white bean soup had revived a hunger denied all day, and he ravenously ate two bowls with cold corn bread and a chunk of raw onion. Now, the shock of the day's events wearing off, all he wanted was sleep.

"What's Calpurnia been doing?" Lucinda asked.

"Aw, just helping Mama around the house, I guess. Like she always does." What the hell does she think Cal's been doing? Why doesn't Joseph come and take her away from me and hide her someplace?

"She's such a pretty girl. Prettiest girl along Wire Road."

"I guess so," Roman said, leaning back against the wall and closing his eyes, hoping Lucinda would shut up.

"I hope I have a little girl," she said, and giggled. "Joseph wants a boy. I guess it don't matter. But I'd like to have a little girl and I could dress her up in ribbons and lots of lace and everything."

Roman squirmed, saying nothing. There was some satisfaction in what Lucinda said about his sister, but not enough to make any of this worthwhile. Talk of Lucinda's approaching confinement he found extremely distasteful. He was enough like his father to resent this casual reference to birthing, and all that implied. Even discussions of livestock in a similar condition had always been rather guarded in the Hasford household.

"Did you hear those horses screaming today?" Lucinda said, going off on another tack. "It was just awful. I never heard anything like it."

Maybe if I act like I'm asleep, she'll go away, or at least be quiet, Roman thought. He tried to breathe more heavily.

"Sometimes, during butchering time, when the hammer doesn't hit just right, a pig will squeal. But it doesn't sound near as bad as horses. Horses sound like people screaming."

And that's another thing, he thought. People who kill hogs with a hammer are crazy. His own father and Tulip Crozier always shot them, one ball just behind the ear, and there was no fuss or bother with squealing.

When he thought of his father shooting hogs, he thought of the rifle Martin Hasford had taken with him to the army. I ought to be out in the woods, looking for a gun. I'll wager there's plenty, just lying around, dropped by soldiers.

"I don't know what we're going to do with all those dead horses scattered around the yard," Lucinda was saying. "Mama Cox didn't want me to see, but I looked out the window and saw them when we came up from the cellar. They're all over the place."

A group of officers clumped into the kitchen with muddy boots and dished out mess tins full of the bean soup. They touched their hats to Lucinda, and she smiled and blushed. Roman kept his eyes closed, hearing the clink of their saber chains. They trooped out to the front gallery to eat.

"Some of those army people have such nice uniforms," she said. "But some are just ragged and dirty-looking."

Oh God, Roman thought.

"Have you ever trapped a possum?" she asked, her face close

to his ear. He shook his head impatiently and crossed his arms on his chest. "Joseph traps them all the time. He caught one last week. Have you ever ate possum?"

"No," Roman said explosively. "They're not fit to eat. Mama cooked one once and the stink ran us all out of the house. She threw it out and even the hounds wouldn't eat it."

"Good gracious, Roman, we don't eat them, either," she said, giggling. "Joseph skins them and cuts them up and puts pieces in trees to attract hawks so he can shoot them."

"Well, then, do you eat the hawks?"

"Of course not, that's silly. Joseph kills all the hawks he can, 'cause they kill chickens."

Everything she says rubs me wrong, he thought. You don't kill wild things without you plan to eat them, or 'less you catch them in the act of going after your livestock. Except maybe copperheads. Or crows.

"Mostly," he said with resignation, "hawks kill field mice and ground squirrels. They scare chickens, but they don't kill many."

"They do, too! And eagles will carry off kid goats and shoats, too."

Oh horseshit, he thought. This talk of killing and hanging raw meat in trees had begun to make him a little sick.

"Joseph ought to go out early in the morning, because there's plenty of meat hanging in trees north of the house. Where soldiers were blown to smithers by those cannons."

Lucinda gasped and drew back from him.

"I wasn't talking about anything like that. . . ."

"And besides, I like hawks," he said. He felt her leap up and move off, and his satisfaction was so complete he chuckled. Girls are such fools, he thought. Being around one with a loose mouth and a big belly was almost unendurable. Yet, there was something exciting about having a girl close. He wished Calpurnia were here. Although he had protested that night she'd come to his bed to watch the Germans in the garden patch, it had given him a warm, choking feeling that was better than it was bad. Why aren't there more girls like Cal, and not so damned many silly ones talking about hanging possums in trees . . . to fetch hawks for killing? What a peck of foolishness!

Someone touched him on the shoulder, and he tried to squirm away, thinking it was the girl back again. Then Lark's voice came, the words softly spoken but startling him just the same.

"Mister Roman. You awake?"

The face was close over his, and he saw the large mouth and bloodshot eyes and sweat across the black forehead like beads of clear wax. It occurred to him that he had never been this close to a colored man's face.

"Mister Roman, you and me, we're gone go," Lark said. There was nothing about him now to suggest the shuffling, joking darkie Roman and the other internees had seen in the Baptist meeting hall. The speech was clear and direct, and he looked squarely into Roman's eyes without flinching or lowering his head.

"Time to go where?"

"Mister Tulip says you ought to get on back home. He says he don't know what might be goin' on over there, what with it bein' so close to the Yankees' flank."

"Close to the Yankee flank?" Roman sat up, his fatigue forgotten.

"Don't get all upset now. Mister Tulip says it'd just be best iffen you was in your own place, 'stead of here."

"How does he know about the Yankee lines?"

"I been doin' a mite of scoutin'. I been out along Huntsville Lane, seein' what I could. Them sojurs is off down in that direction towards yore mama's place. Now Mister Tulip says you ought to go along Huntsville Lane for a couple miles, then you could cut back through the woods and get home all right. Mister Tulip says this place gone be hot tomorrow, wif the Yankees comin' back and lots of shootin'.'"

On the floor beside him was a rolled blanket and something the size of a grape basket wrapped in cheesecloth. Lark grinned.

"This here's a chicken got hisself stricken by a Minié ball this afternoon. Miz Polly says you take it along home to yore mama. He's some busted up, but he'll still eat good."

They went out through the back door and into the lighted yard. But within a few steps, they were in darkness, and Roman could see nothing at first. Lark guided him across Wire Road and into the Huntsville Lane. They walked east, and soon the stars were visible and the woods edging down on either side of the road. Off to their right, they could hear horses and the voices of men. Mounted troops came along the road a number of times, and Roman and Lark would move off into the shadows to let them pass. No one stopped them, and soon they were well away from the tavern. After about half a mile there were no longer any sounds of the army.

Roman guessed they had walked more than two miles when Lark touched his arm. They stood facing each other in the dark. Roman could see the shine of the black man's eyes, and of his teeth when he spoke.

"Now, you go on from here, Mister Roman."

Lark handed Roman the blanket and the wrapped chicken and put his hand on the boy's shoulder.

"You go right on south from here, then cut back east after 'bout a mile or so. Maybe two miles. Then you be in yore own backyard."

"I know the way."

"Now, Mister Roman, you be careful. You get tired, you

stop and wrap this blanket around yoreself and rest. And don't get lost. We don't want nuthin' happenin' to you. Get home to yore mama."

Roman set off into the woods, holding the rolled blanket before his face to ward off low branches. After a few steps he stopped and looked back. Lark had disappeared into the blackness. Toward Pea Ridge he heard the faint thump of a skirmisher's rifle. In the east, along White River, a dog was barking in some farmyard with monotonous regularity, the sound faint and sorrowful.

He shivered and plunged on into the timber, bearing due south. From time to time he looked back over his shoulder to check his course by the Big Dipper and the North Star.

4   Ora Hasford stood on her back porch, a shawl around her shoulders. Her arm ached and she massaged it gently with her right hand. The sounds from the troops a short distance north of the house were mostly still now. She had heard them late into the night, moving into position and cutting trees, scraping in the ground with bayonets, making shelters from southern fire. She knew this battle was only partly finished, and that with morning it would erupt again, some of it only a few yards away.

There was a narrow strip of timber north of the garden patch, and then the land opened up into a large meadow called Ruddick's Field. She knew from the sounds that the Yankee soldiers were in the line of woods just short of that field. She suspected the southerners were on the far side. And before dark, a reserve infantry regiment had moved into the trees between the house and Wire Road. She felt choked with blue-coated soldiers, and was unable to sleep although it was well past midnight.

Behind her in the kitchen, Calpurnia was asleep on the pallet, well back from any window. Having seen what had happened to the barn, Ora supposed the walls of the house would offer little protection in the morning if artillery shells came this way. But the building was much stronger than she imagined, with oak logs laid well beneath the lumber siding.

We should have left here yesterday, or whenever it was that soldier came for Roman, she thought. But he said the fighting would be south of here, and it hasn't been south of here at all. Who knows where it might be tomorrow? Besides, the cow moves so slow, getting her out on the roads might tempt some of these hungry Yankees to see her as skinned, quartered, and roasted over one of their fires. Too late for that, now. Too late for a lot of things. If we'd gone to Texas with the rest, long ago, maybe it would be better. But then she realized that had that happened, she might never have married Martin Hasford, and such a thing was incomprehensible.

She heard a dog barking far off to the east. She wondered for a moment if it might be one of the blueticks. They had not returned after chasing the sow off into the woods, and she doubted they ever would. Do Yankees eat dog, too? she wondered. She listened intently to the dog's voice, but was unable to tell if it might be one of her own. She knew that Martin and Tulip Crozier, and sometimes even Roman, could recognize individual dogs in a racing pack when they were fox hunting, but she had never developed that knack.

When she thought of Tulip Crozier, she frowned. Sending Roman off with him had seemed good at first, but the more she thought about it, the less she liked it. The old man with his loud bullheadedness might get Roman into all kinds of trouble with the Yankees. Who could tell what he would say? Just to show his disrespect for the blue army.

And where was Martin? In his last letter, he had written that he was in some place called Russelville, to the south. She had no idea where that was, nor for that matter, where this Confederate army had marched from to the valley of Little Sugar Creek. Perhaps at this moment, he was out there along the wooded slopes of Little Mountain where she had seen the lanterns of the Union men searching for their fallen. But she put that quickly out of her mind. She felt sure in her heart that if her husband was with these southern forces so near at hand, he would somehow have let her know. But except for those two letters there had been no word since the day he'd walked off in the fall, after butchering, never looking back as he went down the slope to Wire Road and along it to the south, the rifle across his shoulder.

Damn these Hasfords, she thought. Damn them and their marching off to fight somebody else's war!

At least Martin had not taken one of the horses. They would be needed for spring planting soon. What is the first day of spring? I've forgotten because it never mattered before. We'll need to plant the garden as soon as we can, and get in some corn and maybe barley in the fields below. Because grub in this valley is going to be scarce after the armies leave. And who knows when one of those night-rider bunches will be back, gobbling up everything in sight the way the hound had done in the pigpen this afternoon, eating it whole before anyone could get it away from him. Well, she thought, he hadn't had time to digest much of it.

She thought of the girl lying inside. Calpurnia. The name was dear to her. Maybe we should have arranged to find a good husband for her before all this took place, before all this war business. Then she'd be off away from here, and safe. But we protected her like some kind of precious stone, or like the twenty-dollar gold piece Martin and Oscar tossed that day to decide who would be husband on this farm. That coin is buried now behind the fireplace, and only Martin and I know where.

A precious stone, she thought. A jewel. Why does she have to grow to the hardships of womanhood? She was meant to be a little girl, full of life but innocent and beautiful and natural as the swarms of purple flowers that came in the woods after the April rains. Ora ached with her own impotence, her inability to make time stand still, to have stopped it forever when the children were fragile and dependent. Well, not so fragile, maybe. They have always been pretty tough, and she thought on that with some pride.

Somewhere near Leetown, a bugle sounded, rousing cavalry troopers to some early-morning duty. The notes came faint but clear across the silence, and Ora thought of the line from the second chapter of Joel. "Trumpet in Zion."

As the last note died, she stiffened. Had there been something moving in the trees behind the barn? She listened, and heard nothing. But after a moment, it was there again. Someone was coming along the slope from east of the farm. She could hear the footsteps. She started inside, but something kept her on the porch. Something she did not think about, much less understand. She moved to the edge of the porch and peered into the darkness before the late moonrise.

A figure came around the corner of the barn. She shifted her eyes to the side, not looking directly at it. It was a man, a tall, slender man, coming closer, carrying something under each arm, wearing a small brim hat. He was into the yard and only a few feet from her before she let herself be sure.

"Roman," she whispered, and ran out to meet him.

He stopped then, and she threw her arms around him and held him close for a minute and neither of them spoke. She felt the tears well into her eyes as the boy stood stiffly, allowing himself to be hugged tight. Ora stepped back, wiping her face.

"Mama," he said softly. "They killed the mule."

"Don't worry about that now. You're home."

"You haven't come to any harm?"

"No. I'm fine. Now."

"And Cal?"

"Sleeping. And fine, too. Come on in before you get cold."

"I'm not cold, Mama," he said. "I brought you a chicken."

"Come on. Come on inside."

They walked toward the house and she held his arm tightly, as though afraid he might somehow disappear back into the night.

VIII

Old Sam Curtis sat his dapple-gray gelding and watched a bloodred sun rise over the eastern woods. There was no breath of wind, and the smoke of yesterday's fight hung like gray fog in the timbered draws. Stretched across the fields and woodlands before him was the army, guns in position and four infantry divisions ready for the assault. The lines lay in disciplined ranks, the blue uniforms looking almost black in this early light. To the far left was Pea Ridge, the crest held by the Confederates, rising like a hog's back above the gun-smoke haze beneath. His right flank was anchored in the woods near Ruddick's Field, and there he could see the outlines of a farmhouse and barn through the trees.

The sun lifted slowly into a cloudless sky, warming a land that but for the scarred trees looked calm and peaceful, a land waiting to burst forth into the green of springtime. In this first flush of the new season, birds that had wintered here were out and sending their calls across the valley. Curtis could hear the slurred whistle of a meadowlark, the call of jays in the timber along Wire Road, and somewhere the rapid thump of a woodpecker pounding at the bark of an oak snag. All other sound seemed suspended, the thousands of men lying on their weapons, silent and waiting.

The general was confident. His artillery had been resupplied overnight with ammunition from trains he had drawn close into the battle area before the rebels cut his line of supply. Now there was more than enough for the day's battle, and he had no intention of allowing it to go further than this day. Only one of his divisions had been badly mauled at Elkhorn Tavern. The others were relatively unscathed. His staff reported to him that the men were in fine fettle, ready and itching to make a fight of it.

The officers around him watched his face, tense to his every move. He sat quietly, now and again taking a handkerchief from his coat and wiping his mouth. To some, he seemed reluctant to disrupt the pastoral tranquillity. He gazed up at the blue sky and around him on all sides, where fields were waiting for the plow, the snow gone from them. The trees in this warm sunlight had already shed their ash color of winter and were brown and tan. One would almost expect to see buds appearing along the lacy limbs.

"Not an altogether unpleasant country," Curtis remarked.

"No, sir," an officer nearby replied. "But the weather is a mite unpredictable."

From along the low rise of ground just south of the tavern, there was a lazy blossom of smoke and flame, and in a few seconds the sound of the cannon shot reached them. Curtis pulled a watch from his pocket, snapped it open, and glanced at the time. It was seven o'clock. He turned slowly to a waiting officer.

"General Sigel, you may open on them, sir."

Within moments, the federal front was outlined with flame and smoke as batteries that had massed the night before began their volleys, the crash of sound rolling back across the country-side like thunder close after the lightning flash. The earth trembled with it, and soon there was the echo of descending shells bursting on southern positions, where earth and trees were seen spouting up like black fountains. The stink of burnt powder drifted across the fields.

Gunners worked feverishly. After each shot, the barrels were swabbed and a new shell positioned with the ramrod; a man with leather thumbstall to protect his hand from heat held a thumb over the firing vent. Trails were positioned, barrels aligned with targets, a sharp pick was thrust into the vent to puncture the paper cartridge, a primer pressed in place, and the lanyard attached. As the crew jumped aside, the lanyard was pulled and the gun roared and leaped backward in a cloud of smoke. And the whole process was begun again.

The southern lines seemed stunned at first, but slowly their own guns began to reply. They were most effective on the Union right, near Ruddick's Field, where the smoke of their firing drifted like a rain cloud over the trees, obscuring the sun. But even there, after a short time, their cannonade began to slacken.

Curtis gave the signal for infantry formations to move.

The blue lines surged forward, but were met in many places with devastating rifle fire. The steep outcrops of limestone on the Union left were more hindrance than the defending Indian regiments of Albert Pike, and soon the federals were in control of the crest. Near Elkhorn Tavern, rebel positions were penetrated, flags and prisoners taken, before the Union infantry was driven back. Near Ruddick's Field, there was the sharp clatter and crash of infantry in close contact through the woods.

Watching the lines of foot soldiers advance, their bayonets gleaming in the sun, Curtis sat unperturbed as southern case shot began to explode near his field headquarters. The bombardment lasted only a few moments and was silenced by the overwhelming weight of federal shell. The general turned to an aide and smiled grimly.

"We are going to drive those people from the field," he said.

The colors of each regiment moved in through the smoke, floating above the blue lines that heaved against the metal coming out to meet them. As color-bearers went down, the standards dipped momentarily, then were taken up by others. There was the swelling chorus of steadily repeated hurrahs across the front—deep-throated, the notes unanswered from the rebel lines except with fire.

Federal batteries continued to pour their shot into the smoking ruins of the southern position, but even so the advancing infantry met determined resistance. Soon it was apparent that rebel riflemen, like their artillery, were running out of ammunition. Yet, as each blue regiment struggled forward, they left behind the huddled, bloody markers of their passage.

2   They heard the battle start to the northwest, at the center of the lines near Elkhorn Tavern. It rolled toward them with surprising speed, like breaking waves on a hostile shore, closer and louder until the foundations of the house shook and the fragile glass in the windows quivered like paper held taut in a high wind. When the batteries near Wire Road opened, only a few rods away, their harsh barking was almost lost in the constant smash of noise.

Soon there was the ring of musketry from Ruddick's Field, giving a sharp high pitch to the overwhelming roar. They were only vaguely aware of men shouting and running through the yard, of horses galloping past the porch. They huddled on the pallet in the kitchen, a heavy comforter pulled over them, and waited for the storm to pass.

The two suckling pigs, saved from their mother on the first day of battle, were in the cellar. At first their whining squeals raked against the ears like fingernails run along a rusty stovepipe. But soon the noise seemed to mesmerize them into walleyed silence.

Bullets whacked against the north side of the house, and they could hear glass breaking. One slug came through the back door, splintering it, and rang against the front of the cookstove.

Another hit the ax in the chopping block just outside the kitchen door and ricocheted off into the trees with a dismal whine.

For a while through the din, they could hear the cow bawling, and then she was still. The horses were setting up a racket, too. Ora thought perhaps all the stock should be brought right into the kitchen, where the walls were thicker. But the splat of Minié balls in the yard dissuaded her from that, and she could only hope the two mares would not kick their way out of the stalls and leave the small protection the barn offered.

Damn all this, she thought. Martin gone off to find the war someplace and now it comes into his own backyard. She heard a tree falling somewhere, and a buzzing bullet strike the fireplace chimney with a solid crack. There was a rain barrel at one corner of the house to catch water for washing clothes in dry times, when the spring and well had to be conserved for drinking. Twice she heard bullets strike it with a hollow thump. Damn the Yankees for coming into this country, she thought. And each time a new sound came to her, she damned something else, silently and furiously, the muscles along her jaw working into knots.

For the second time in two days, Roman was under Confederate fire, and once again he felt the frantic impotence of soldiers on every battlefield realizing that all metal is hostile, no matter its origin. He began to think himself a veteran, like one of those southern infantrymen he'd seen charging across the grounds at Elkhorn Tavern. The noise set his head spinning, and he felt the strange elation of danger, uncommon and incomprehensible to all but a few.

Calpurnia sat beside her brother, her hands over her ears. But she did not scream, as she had done yesterday when the shell struck the barn. She could sense her mother's anger, a strength that somehow transferred to her and made her ignore the possibility of disaster. So much had happened so suddenly over the past few days that her senses had been stunned; she no longer reacted to any of this, except to wait patiently, watching her mother. From those moments at the hogpen, Calpurnia knew she would never again look on her mother without feeling her indomitable will.

The Confederate artillery on the far side of Ruddick's Field began to bombard the Union lines that ran near the house. Shells exploding close to them rent the air—a ripping sound that vibrated painfully against the ears. There were only a few of these, but the last of the southern shells struck very near, and the house vibrated like piano wire.

Ora smelled smoke. Not the acid fumes of black powder, but woodsmoke. She scrambled up.

"Get the buckets! The house is burning!"

It made no difference that rifle bullets were still pecking at the house, nor that it was dangerous to leave the floor and kitchen wall. The house came first, and Ora wasn't sure she could do it alone. They all ran into the parlor, where bright shards littered the floor. In the center glass panel of the china closet was a large hole, a spiderweb of cracks radiating from it. They ran to the loft, Calpurnia and Roman each with a sloshing water bucket from the kitchen washstand, Ora still clutching the comforter to her.

A hole had been blown in the roof directly over Roman's bed, shattering two rafters and filling the room with shingle splinters. Through the smoke, they could see a splattering of fire across the loft floor and the smoldering edges of the wound in the roof. But these were oak shakes, hard as iron, and they did not burn easily.

"One bucket there," Ora panted, and Roman doused the fire on the floor with a long sweep of the bucket, drowning the sparks. Ora dipped the comforter into the other bucket and began to sponge out the smoking shakes. But she could not reach the ones toward the ridgepole.

"Get a chair over here, quick," she said, and Calpurnia drew over a chair, directly beneath the tear in the roof. Roman went up with the comforter from his mother's hands and continued the work. "Can you see outside?" Ora asked. "Can you see if the roof is afire?"

Roman thrust his head through the hole and swabbed down the shingles, as far as he could reach. His mother and Calpurnia held his legs as he worked. Clouds of thick smoke drifted lazily across the rooftop from the woods along Ruddick's Field. Once more, Roman felt its sting in his nose. Suddenly the image of the officer at Elkhorn Tavern, lying decapitated, flashed through his mind, and he ducked his head.

"All right, let me down. I got it all. These shakes won't burn."

"Back to the kitchen," Ora said. She looked around the loft once more as the children ran for the ladder. It was still smoky, but there were no flames. Through the window over Roman's bed, she could see a dead horse in the garden patch, bridle and saddle already stripped off. Beyond that, in the woods, there was the vague outline of blue-clad troops, facing Ruddick's Field.

Calpurnia and Roman watched her as she came back into the kitchen. She saw no fear on their faces, and pride swelled up in her. They stared at her with wide eyes, waiting to do whatever she said needed doing. Bullets were still whacking at the walls, but she walked calmly to the stove, where the cast-iron kettle sat steaming. Just as it always was, and the sight of that familiar old pot gave her the confidence to think: no matter what happens, we'll always be here and the same.

She made sassafras tea, poured three cups, and dumped a tablespoonful of sugar into each, although her sugar was almost gone. She gave each of the children a cup, and sat down beside them with her own. They sipped it obediently, saying nothing, watching her over the steaming brew. Just like a rest in a normal day's work, she thought.

Slowly, then, the sounds of battle moved back into the valley, as though the shell burst against the roof had been one final, defiant thrust at them. Their ears were still ringing, and when she spoke her words sounded distant and strange to her.

"You did fine."

"Mama," Calpurnia said. "If it wasn't for the noise and the mess, it would be exciting, wouldn't it?"

Ora stared at her daughter for a moment, incredulously. Then she laughed, they all laughed, and there was a little hysteria in it. But they found it hard to stop, and it was satisfying.

3   Tulip Crozier helped load the wounded. There were only a few ambulances, and most of the bloody cargo had to be stacked into springless wagons captured from the federals during yesterday's assault. The Cox family was there, too, lifting up the sagging forms to surgeons' assistants in the wagon beds, all ignoring the occasional shells that exploded still on the tavern grounds and the whining solid shot that passed above and into the woods beyond.

The more seriously wounded were left where they lay, in the rooms of the tavern and outbuildings, to be abandoned because there was only space enough for those with the best chance of survival. There was the hope that when the federals came, their doctors would care for these men in their final hours, and then bury them.

The grounds were a shambles of discarded equipment and dead horses. The glass was gone from the tavern's windows and all the buildings looked clawed and chewed by shell and bullet. Directly before the gallery was a twisted limber, one wheel off, the seat cover hanging open to reveal empty ammunition bins. Rifles were strewn about like splintered toothpicks, and there were enough cartridge pouches, cap boxes, belts, and knapsacks to equip a company. A cannon barrel, blown off its stock, lay in the ditch alongside Wire Road, black muzzle pointed crazily toward the sky. Scraps of merion and flannel cartridge bags lay like patches of gray snow. There were shattered trees and fallen limbs, and the ground everywhere was tortured and gouged. About the place there hung an oppressive odor of charcoal and saltpeter.

The battle continued to rage only a few hundred yards to the south, the Union artillery thundering. But as the morning wore on, the answering fire from southern guns decreased and finally stopped completely in most places across the front.

The ammunition trains had actually approached to within a few miles of the battle area, having taken a long, time-consuming route around the federals' left flank. But Van Dorn had somehow lost his decisiveness under pressure of Union artillery fire. He had sent a courier to turn back the wagons—to avoid their capture, he said. With them went the last hope of victory for the Confederates. Now, the problem was to escape.

It was well before noon when the order went down for units to begin their withdrawal. Each company and battery were to accommodate their own wounded, there no longer being a medical facility to handle them in the rear. Soon there would be no rear at all, for reports indicated that blue cavalry was already well around the western flank of the Elkhorn Tavern position.

As the hospital train moved laboriously from the yard, the surgeons came from the tavern, carrying their bags of crusted scalpels and saws. They were haggard and red-eyed from the night's work and from too much whiskey taken to keep them going. One of them turned to Tulip Crozier and shook his hand before climbing into an ambulance.

"Sir, a surgeon's lot is not an easy one. To decide which ones you try to save and which ones you must move aside," he said wearily. He waved a hand in the direction of the tavern. "I'm sorry there are no opiates left to make it easier for them."

"We'll do what we can for them, Major."

"Be careful with the water. No water for those shot in the bowels."

With a heavy sigh he turned and mounted the ambulance, and the driver whipped the team across the yard and onto the Huntsville Road, the ambulance becoming the last in a line of slowly moving vehicles. Southern infantry companies had begun to move back, and the men walked alongside the wagons. Some were dejected, marching heads-down, but others were defiant, cursing an unkind Providence. The federal guns continued to roar, some of them very close now.

Once the wounded were away, Polly Cox began preparations to take her family out as well, having had enough of noise and smoke, curses and mangled bodies. While Joseph hitched the tavern mules to a small hack, she stood in her dining room and looked at the bloodstained floor, the bullet-pocked panels, the nicks and scratches in what had been her finely polished furniture. Wounded men lay along one wall, watching her with vacant eyes. She moved quickly out through the family kitchen, pausing only long enough to take a rose-painted china soup tureen from a warming oven where it had somehow escaped harm.

The slaves were sitting in back of the hack, their legs dangling off, wide-eyed and flinching with each explosion that came near. Joseph held the reins tight against the prancing mules while Tulip Crozier helped the bulging Lucinda onto the box beside him.

"If you see Calpurnia Hasford, tell her I bid good-bye," the girl said.

"I'll see her soon," Tulip said, "and tell her, and what a brave girl you've been. A very brave girl. You have yourself and Joseph a fine baby."

Polly Cox hurried across the yard to the hack and handed up the soup tureen for her daughter-in-law to hold.

"She ain't got much lap for holdin' things, Ma," Joseph said.

"I'll take it in a minute." Polly turned to Tulip and he took off his hat. "There's a little white flour left, and maybe some salt meat. You take it over to Ora."

"I'll do that, Polly, and she'll be much obliged."

"And, Tulip, there's a small trap under the woodbox in the outside kitchen. Mr. Cox keeps his private stock of whiskey in there. You and Ezra Ruter are welcome to it."

The old man was coming down across the yard to say goodbye, his hat in his hand, and he was a little drunk, but he heard the last of what she said.

"We'll drink your good health," Ruter said, grinning. "And all your kin."

"Drink it however you want. Just don't let the Yankees get it." She looked across her littered and wounded yard. Lark was standing far back, against the tavern wall.

"You've still got one boy left to load up. If this hack will hold one more," Tulip said. His hair was matted and dirty and his eyes were bloodshot, but when he put the beaver back on his head, the buzzard feather bounced jauntily.

"No, I've told Lark he can stay here if he pleases," Polly Cox said. "To watch the place, he says. But I expect there won't be much left when we get back. If we ever get back. Tulip, help me up. I'm bone weary."

Sitting beside Lucinda, she looked again at the grounds, then down at her hands. Dried blood was caked around the nails, outlining each in black.

"My land, here I am goin' visitin', and haven't even washed myself."

"Hang on," Joseph said, and whipped the mules. "Go on, there!" They wheeled around in the yard, onto Wire Road, going north. All the slaves waved as they went away, and Tulip turned back to the tavern.

"Come on, Ruter, let's get that whiskey."

Lark's face was forlorn as he watched the little hack, heavily burdened, disappearing into the trees where they had first seen the advancing southern infantry the day before.

"So Miss Polly has let you stay on?" Tulip Crozier said to him.

"She axed me did I want to go or stay, and I says I ain't got no business in Missouri or Kansas and I ain't acquainted with no folks there."

"Don't you know that in Missouri or Kansas you'd likely be a free man?"

"I don't know nuthin' 'bout no Missouri or Kansas. I been a southland nigger all my life and I aims to stay a southland nigger."

"Well, then, southland nigger, now that you're sole proprietor of this inn, why don't you go to the outside kitchen and get that whiskey Miss Polly was kind enough to leave us?"

A broad grin passed slowly across the black face and he nodded.

"Yes, sir. Yes, sir, we still runnin' a nice tavern here, and soon's the Yankees leave, we'll have jiggin' and singin' again."

"Lark, your days of jigging and singing are past, and you don't even know it. Get the whiskey and bring it inside. I'll take another look at them boys left behind."

Troops had begun to move across the yard, those who had tried to hold Pea Ridge and were now joining the retreat to the east. A regiment of Indian cavalry passed, their colorful clothing in sharp contrast to the drab and tattered uniforms of the other soldiers. The last of the artillery that had been stationed on the right quick-marched behind the tavern and onto the Huntsville Road, empty limbers bouncing as their wheels slithered into the deepening ruts of the lane where the ground, softened by the sun, was wet and spongy. The entire Confederate line was peeling back from right to left, like a page turned in a book.

Men in butternut inched back over the low ridge to the south, some shooting a last shot toward the federals before coming under cover of the ridge to form ranks and move off. Cavalry appeared, to screen the final withdrawal. Everyone moved in good order, without panic, toward the road that pointed in the direction of White River. Van Dorn and his staff sat their horses in the edge of the east woods, watching.

A group of southern infantry trudged along, up from the springhouse and behind the tavern. They proudly carried the captured standard of a Union regiment, taken at Leetown. Going past them on a lathered horse, a young officer shouted, his face red under a bloody bandage: "Case those colors, goddamn it! Or some of our people are liable to open fire on you."

From an artillery battery, the order was given, "Fix prolonges!" The guns were attached to limbers by long chains and dragged back, the crews running alongside and loading as they went. When each gun was charged, the teams were pulled to a halt and the piece was fired in the direction of the advancing federals, some of their blue ranks visible through the trees where Van Dorn sat waiting.

A detachment of southern cavalry rushed across the front, firing and dodging back into the woods. The last of the infantry, skirmishers, began to run into the Huntsville Road. The bellow of Union soldiers advancing could be heard clearly now, but they were coming on cautiously as the retreating guns peppered them with the few rounds of canister remaining in the limbers.

Tulip Crozier and old man Ruter had moved onto the gallery to watch, each with a jug of Cox whiskey. Before them, the Confederate army was quickly fading away into the east. Van Dorn and his staff rode over, and the general touched his hat.

"Gentlemen. We are grateful for your assistance here."

"So, a man helps when he can, General. Can I offer a little drink before you go?" He held up his jug, and old man Ruter snickered.

"No, I am grateful, but no. If you gentlemen would like to go with the army, I am sure we can find transport for you."

"I think not, General."

"Another day, then, and perhaps we will be back."

"We'll be here to greet you, sir. Good-bye."

Van Dorn lifted his hat, then he and his staff wheeled their horses around and galloped off into the eastern lane. Tulip admired it all, for he knew the most difficult task any army could undertake was to break contact with an enemy and get away unscathed. It appeared Van Dorn was doing exactly that, but there had been the stamp of defeat on his handsome face. The light had gone from his dark eyes and disappointment plain as the written page was there in the bitterly turned-down corners of his mouth.

"So, Ruter, we'd best get our arse into the cellar, else the Yankees may mistake us for one of the shooters," Tulip said, and they turned back into the tavern.

The federals came on slowly, expecting more deadly fire as they appeared over the rise of ground south of the tavern. They ran forward and threw themselves down, looking along their front with rifles ready. The artillery had finally subsided. For the first time since early morning there was a resounding silence almost as painful to the ears as the noise had been. The first mounted officer topped the rise, paused, his eyes casting about quickly. He urged the men on, and they came running, cheering now. Nothing came to meet them, and they leaped and waved their rifles. The sun shone down on their grimy faces, each open mouth coated with the powder from paper cartridges ripped open with their teeth.

The realization that resistance had finally collapsed brought the blue-clads across the sloping ground in a reckless charge, the excitement and joy at having been spared showing in their faces. They waved hats and rifles and battle colors. What had been well-cadenced shouts of regiments became the yips and bellows of individuals who were finally set loose across a recently contested ground, free now to surge down and around the structure that had become the symbol of this fight. It would never make an epic story, like those great struggles in the east—Chancellorsville, Gettysburg, Shiloh, Cold Harbor. But for these men, coming across the eastern spur of Pea Ridge, it would last forever in memory because they had survived it.

As the triumphant troops moved around the tavern, into it, beyond it, a mounted colonel drew rein before the neatly white-washed building now pocked with signs of violence. His eyes lifted to the ridgepole of the roof, and with a wave of his hand he stopped a soldier running past.

"You there," he shouted. "Climb up and pull down those antlers and bring them to me."

And thus the spreading horn that had given this place its name became a trophy of war.

4   General Sam Curtis sat his horse at the side of Wire Road, watching the day come to a close. The dense smell of burnt gunpowder drifted across the fields, and the haze it created turned the setting sun into a great umber disk, already sinking behind the far western horizon. Around him was his mounted staff, many of them animated, the excitement of the day making their voices sharp. Curtis was silent, his eyes searching through the growing gloom for couriers from the area north of Elkhorn Tavern, where reports had it earlier that the Confederates were retreating, toward Missouri!

There was good reason to be cheerful now—with the turning of the army and the stunning performance of the artillery, everything had carried through efficiently to bring victory from a field that had seemed at first to offer only disastrous defeat. But the general's face remained stoic, almost sour, as he listened to the mutter of far-off rifle fire, now diminishing and finally ceasing.

If the rebels were indeed retreating north, he would have

little choice but to follow. For though he knew they were beaten here, he could not allow even remnants of an enemy army operating in his rear areas. If only the first reports were incorrect, and Van Dorn had gone another way, then he could turn his army once more and proceed deeper into this rebel state, subdue and occupy it.

At last the awaited rider came. He ran his lathered horse down Wire Road and crossed the ditch with a bound and a grunt and pulled up before Curtis, raising his hand to his hat.

"Colonel Dodge's compliments, sir," he said. "He informs you that the resistance along Wire Road north of here has been nothing more than a covering force, and there is no evidence now of rebel forces going off in that direction."

"In what direction, then?" Curtis snapped.

"To the east, General. Into that wild mountain country."

Curtis frowned, stroking his side-whiskers. He slipped his handkerchief from the front of his coat and wiped his nose furiously. His staff sat silently now, waiting. Finally he turned to them.

"Do you hear, gentlemen? Dodge says the rebels are not retreating to Missouri after all. I was suspicious of that when we first heard it."

"Might they not swing north when they are clear of us, General?" one asked.

"Without ammunition? I hardly think so." Curtis turned back to the courier, his saddle creaking as his weight shifted. "Sir, Colonel Dodge is sure of this?"

"Colonel Dodge believes their whole army has gone off to the east. Toward some place called Huntsville. We have cavalry in contact now with their rear guard."

"Good." For a moment he sat in deep thought, his fingers playing with the frayed hair along his cheeks. Again, he turned to the staff. "Very well, gentlemen. Pass instructions to divisions. We will hold in place and reissue ammunition and rations and tomorrow prepare to move to the south once more. What's left of the rebel army will undoubtedly turn in that direction, too."

"We're not going to pursue them, General?" one of the officers asked.

"We will keep cavalry detachments on their tail temporarily. But I don't want any of our horse lost over there, wandering around in those hills. You must remember, gentlemen, our mission is to move deeper into this rebel state and secure what principal urban areas there are. We move south!"

The staff began to rein away, all except one of the general's personal aides.

"I want to see Sigel and Osterhaus and Dodge here, as soon as you can bring them," Curtis called. Then he looked back at the courier, who still stood before him on the blowing horse. "Don't you have a unit to which you should return? I don't want Dodge's men scattered all along Wire Road, chasing rebels that aren't there."

"Yes, sir, I'm on my way now. But, General. Colonel Dodge asked that I pass congratulation to you. Missouri is saved for the Union."

Curtis grunted, and wiped his nose again.

"Yes, I suppose so," he said. "Saved for the Union."

With all the sounds of his own army around him, Curtis looked off into the blackening east. He thought of Van Dorn, there somewhere, his units badly used, his ammunition gone, his horses spent, and no rations for the men. From all his reports of that day, Curtis had assumed that the Confederates had no trains with their combat elements. He thought of the wounded, carried away in springless wagons, groaning through the night, and with nothing to eat until . . . until when? Until they had moved back to the south—and, Curtis suspected, far to the south, perhaps at least to the Arkansas River. For there was no place north of that where an army could be provisioned, except in the vicinity of Fayetteville, and Curtis intended to be there himself, long before Van Dorn.

He slowly reined around to his aide, a young man with a gigantic cud of tobacco bulging his cheek.

"Well, Charles, what do you think of this army now?" And for the first time that day, his face softened.

"General, we have whupped them clear and simple," the aide said, and sent a long stream of tobacco juice off into the darkness.

"Yes. But not without cost," Curtis said. He looked to the east again, where stars were making a thin dust of cold light. "I wonder what Van Dorn is thinking now?"

He seemed to shake away his reverie and turned to the aide once more.

"Charles, be sure the divisions have parties out to collect the wounded. I suspect we will find many of them in these woods. And the dead. We cannot leave the dead."

"No, sir," Charles said. "We won't forget the dead."

5   The single rider detached himself from the flowing stream of Van Dorn's army as it wound down into the White River Valley along the Huntsville Road. It was dark, and as he moved away from the thickets beside the road, then into the tall timber beyond, he could hear behind him the scrape of steel-rimmed wheels being braked along the rocky surface where it turned sharply downward. He continued to move, allowing his small pinto pony to pick its way through the trees.

Though not a large man, he was large enough to make the pony appear overburdened. He wore a knee-length jacket with beadwork across the breast, and on his head was a scarlet turban with two cuckoo tail-feathers curling down the back like white spotted shoehorns. His face was broad, with high cheekbones, and his nose was long and straight over a wide mouth. His name was Spavinaw Tom. He was a member of the Cherokee brigade, and he was deserting.

He drew rein in a stand of hickory and listened. Now, after only a moment of riding away from the army's line of retreat, he could hear nothing from the long columns. Still farther into the deep woods, Spavinaw Tom dismounted and felt the pitch of ground under his feet, sloping toward the river somewhere in the dark timber below. White River it was, the place where he was born. His father had told him the story many times, of how the Cherokees had come from the east—his own family from the hills of Tennessee—and marched cross-country to this place, where cold weather caught them well short of the Indian Territory.

There had been many signs of game then, but the trees were bare and the bed of fallen oak leaves made stalking difficult. Or perhaps the scent of coming bad weather kept the deer and turkey secluded in tangles and briars, quiet and watching. The people had found little to shoot. They ate the fish taken from the streams and the salt pork the army gave them, and some died from want of food and exposure.

His mother had delivered him in a willow thicket along a sandbar where the people caught snapping turtles and roasted them, eating the sweet white meat out of the shells that were like deep platters. His father had named him Going Turtle because of that, but he'd never appreciated the value of the name. Later, after he entered into commerce with whites, running a cotton press and selling them timber, he took the name Tom, which was a name the whites could understand. That was after he'd attended the boys' academy at Tahlequah, and learned English.

The family farm was on Spavinaw Creek, and when anyone

asked him who he was, he'd say Tom from Spavinaw Creek. It soon became Spavinaw Tom for good, and the old child's name was forgotten.

Now he was back in the land where he was born, the land his father had told him looked much like the old country in the mountains of Tennessee. He took a deep breath, trying to smell the water, but the river was still too far away. It didn't matter. As soon as the Confederate army—and after that the Yankee patrols—cleared out of this wild country, he would live here for a while, hunting and fishing and reliving the times of his fathers in Tennessee, recapturing some of the old freedom. Not that he was unhappy with the hills and woods of the Cherokee Nation. But if he went directly back there, General Pike's men might arrest him for leaving the army after having enlisted with the promise to fight for this new country, this Confederate States of America.

He turned back to the pony and took from the saddle an old flintlock rifle, the kind of weapon the Confederacy had given its Indian troops to fight the bluecoats. It was worthless, and he had never been able to make it shoot. He threw it into the brush and reached back to the saddle once more and pulled forth the second gun. This was a short Yager rifle he had taken from a dead Yankee soldier near the hill called Little Mountain, before the artillery had fired at them. He ran his fingers along the smooth surface, feeling the snakelike contours of the wood and metal. It was a .54-caliber, and when he had picked it up from the battle-field, he had read the inscription on the side plate: *Harpers Ferry, 1858*. And with it, he had found paper cartridges and buckshot and caps, and he knew it would be good for taking deer and turkey, perhaps even geese that might be going north now and stopping in their flight to rest on White River.

Spavinaw Tom unsaddled the pony and, long-tying him to a tree, wrapped himself in the saddle blanket to sleep. The ground was cold, but most of the wet was gone from it. Through the bare lace of tree branches overhead he could see the stars. They shone as brightly and in the same positions he recalled from his own hills near Tahlequah. He was satisfied. He had seen many men die, but he was alive. Now, the war was no longer his affair. When old General Pike with the long hair on his face had come among the people to recruit troops, he had joined because many of his brothers joined. But he'd had no passion for it.

There were many things about the white man he could not understand. They had a strange medicine, if any at all. The elders of the tribe sometimes spoke bitterly of them, but for Spavinaw Tom the only bitterness was from the memory of others, and such a thing never carried the bad taste in one's mouth left by personal experience.

He had grown up among white men, learned their trades, and spent their money on good things. He could speak the white man's language as well as he could speak his own. He had even acted as their intrepreter at Fort Gibson and at the Tahlequah agency.

But still, there was an uneasiness in his belly when he stayed around them too long. Even those white men who had become his friends and the business associates of his father. Perhaps it was because of what his father had said about them. That the white man would eventually swallow the Cherokee, like a snake with extended jaws crawling slowly around a quail's egg.

Spavinaw Tom sat up to unwrap the turban, and his hair fell straight to his shoulders, thick and black like fine silk thread. He felt for the golden earrings in each ear, and satisfied they were still there he pulled the blanket across his shoulders and lay down.

He was wakened once in the night by the sounds of rifle fire, somewhere along the road he had left, and he thought perhaps a blue patrol had caught up to the rear guard of the retreating army. But it did not concern him because it was no longer his affair, and he was quickly asleep again.

PART TWO

IX

There were three days of sunshine. The earth turned warm and soft and the birds began to announce spring as they always did, a little early but confident it was not far off. Turkey vultures made lazy circles in a cloudless sky, their black wings arched at the splayed tips in a motionless dihedral. They were everywhere along Wire Road, spiraling down to the dead horses the federal army had left behind. The crows came, too, feeding on the horses and making a great racket. The smell of wet cornstalks and unplowed ground came on the westerly breeze, along with the overpowering musty-sweet scent of carrion.

The litter of an army caught in desperate struggle was everywhere. Wagon wheels, cannon barrels, bits and pieces of clothing and personal equipment. And in some of the stands of oak where artillery fire had fallen heaviest, the graying fragments of human flesh hung like Spanish moss. Here, the redwings flocked and disputed over the leavings, like clouds of bluebottle flies swarming to the odor of decay.

The valley was like a room suddenly emptied of its people. The quiet that settled over the hills and woods was the natural state of things, yet with the noise and violence abruptly cut off there was something ominous in it. When Ora Hasford looked across the landscape, she found herself watching for a solitary band of approaching horsemen, though with no conscious thought of returning jayhawkers.

There was a constant haze in the west, like pale blue gauze drawn across the horizon, and Ora knew more bad weather was on the way. A great deal needed doing while the sun lasted, and after Ora outlined each task they went about it, an organized family unit working like a disciplined machine—just as they did during haying time, or butchering, or harvesting and cutting apples to be dried on the smokehouse roof.

Roman hitched the team, and using a length of log chain dragged the dead horse from the garden patch, down the slope before the house, across Wire Road, and well out into the field beyond. He looped the chain about the dead horse's neck, and as he whipped the team along, walking to the side with the reins in his hands, he was afraid he might pull the head completely off. It was a heavy, sweating job, for horses and Roman both.

The milk cow had taken a stray bullet that had splintered through the flimsy barn wall and gone into her flank. She died that first day, after the battle. Ora hoisted the carcass head-down on the extension of the barn's summer beam where Martin Hasford had attached a heavy pulley for lifting hay into the loft or raising hogs for bleeding and gutting. Ora had never butchered a beef, but she had watched it done. She opened the cow's throat in a wide slash just behind the ears, and while the blackish blood splattered around her feet she slipped the knife into the thin belly hide beside the udder and sliced all the way to the rib cage, pulling out with reddened hands those entrails that didn't spill out with the cut.

When a beef was butchered, the meat was usually distributed among neighbors and eaten fresh. There was no way to preserve the meat except in winter during a hard freeze. Salt was used almost exclusively on pork. And although there was considerable commercial canning in metal containers, the time of home canning in glass jars had not come to these hills. This cow she would cook, all of it for her own family, and store in the root cellar. A little she would strip-cut and dry. But she knew most of it would go to waste. As she worked, Ora tried not to think about the loss of her family's milk supply.

Using butcher knife and hatchet, which she honed now and again with the grinding wheel on the back porch, she cut a number of large roasts from the chuck and the round. There was little meat along the back, and she hacked out the ribs and sliced them individually for roasting. She saved only a little of the liver and the heart for making stew. Before she was finished, she was bloody as a battlefield surgeon.

After disposing of the dead horse, Roman cut shake shingles with a broad ax, piling them alongside the chopping block where he had stacked a number of beams and strips of lumber taken from the barn for repairing the roof on the house. They would peg in the broken rafters and slats, and Calpurnia was whittling pegs from persimmon wood, using one of Roman's pocketknives and blistering her hands. The front of her dress was plastered with corn mush from the last feeding of the suckling pigs. Shoving spoonfuls of gruel down the protesting throats had left more on her than got into the pigs' bellies.

Roman worked without a shirt in the sun, and his underwear soon showed damp under the arms and across the back. But it felt good to be using his long, hardening muscles, and his strokes with the ax were quick and sure. Each strike with the blade sent the solid sound of steel on oak across the yard. It was a sound so unlike the ones they had heard over the past few days that it had some reassuring quality.

"Roman, get Bess hitched and take all this leavings down to the field before it starts smelling," Ora said. He stared at the pile of entrails and the cow's head and the stripped carcass, still hanging by the hind legs, the chopped-off ribs protruding like the pink stalks of broken rhubarb.

"How am I gonna get that mess down to the field?"

Ora was carrying a bundle of dripping meat into the kitchen. She snapped at him, "Make a drag with two of those fence posts in the barn and some of your papa's old burlap. Do I have to tell you everything?"

Roman went about it sullenly, muttering to himself. He made what amounted to a Plains Indian travois and dumped what his mother had left onto it. I hate feeling slick guts, he thought. This is worse than cleaning out the privy. Twice on the way down to Wire Road and the field beyond, the cow's head rolled off the drag and he had to pull in Bess and lift the thing back on. At least, Calpurnia was not laughing at him. She had grown quieter in the past days, her eyes somehow darker. Already Roman could see new freckles appearing across her nose and cheeks.

"You better get a sunbonnet on or you'll end up looking like a peach orchard mushroom," he said.

Later, with Ora cooking in the kitchen and the smell of roasting beef coming to them strongly, Roman and Calpurnia went up on the roof and started boring holes in the old rafters with a hand auger to seat the pegs and jury-rig the splints taken from the barn. The shakes along the ridgepole were nailed down, but the rest had to be wedged in because there were so few shingle tacks. Roman had watched and helped his father work with wood in every way, and he went about the task quickly, without thinking.

Calpurnia was wearing a bonnet now. The long hood shaded her face, and beneath that her hair curled down across her damp temples. Looking at her, Roman thought he had never seen anything so grand. Then suddenly she slipped off her dress to work in chemise and long bloomers. Roman was astonished,

"What in hell's name are you doing?"

"I can't climb around here with that dress catching on everything," she said, and there was no teasing in her voice. "Hand me some more of those shakes."

Below on Wire Road, they could hear wagons and horses passing. They paused to watch, sitting on the roof, drawing their knees up under their chins and holding their arms around their ankles.

"We'll likely be seeing a lot of that," Roman said. "With the Yankee army south of here."

"What is it?"

"Some supply wagons, I'd reckon, and a few cavalry. When I was at the tavern I heard the Yankees talking about their supplies being at Springfield." He looked at his sister, and exasperation came into his voice. "What if some of those Yankee soldiers saw you squatting up here half-naked?"

"They can't see me for the trees."

"We can see them, so they can see us, if they just looked."

"They're too busy to think about it."

"Soldiers never get too busy to stop thinking about pretty girls."

She turned her face to him under the bonnet hood and some of the old mischief came into her eyes.

"You think I'm pretty, Roman?"

"For hell's name," he exploded. "Let's get back to work. They're gone now, anyway."

Ora draped strips of beef on a clothesline strung between house and barn. But the foxes came on that first night, and leaped up to pull it down, and by morning not a scrap of meat remained. The cooled roasts she put in the cellar, where she knew the mice would get at them. The white flour Tulip Crozier had brought to her from the tavern she saved, except for a small batch to start a crock of sourdough. They ate each meal of roast beef and corn bread, stuffing themselves, trying to get as much down as they could before it spoiled.

The glass was cleaned off the parlor floor, and oilcloth was tacked over the broken windows that had been shattered by rifle fire along the north wall. Replacing her china in the bullet-marked cabinet, Ora thought of armies and plagues of locust. She thought of the trials of Job, and of the Teachings, of turning the other cheek. She found it odd that now, with Martin gone, her thinking came more and more to the Scriptures. It made her feel closer to him. He had always been the one who read his Bible every day, the one who quoted from it and sometimes even hinted that he would have been fulfilled only as a minister in the church. And always that damned contradiction popping up: his admiration for the Romans, the very ones who had executed Christ, however reluctantly after His own people had denied Him.

The final and, therefore, the most hateful indignity she found on the second day. Many of the hill people harvested their potatoes and stored them in cellars. But the Hasfords put them in field dugouts. Along the edge of the garden patch, they would dig small holes, line them with straw, dump in a few dozen potatoes, cover them with straw and clay, and mound the whole thing with loose earth. These little bunkers kept potatoes all winter. When the Yankees had come, there'd been two such mounds remaining. Now she discovered each one despoiled, the potatoes gone.

She stood in the garden patch, the warm windless day making the sweat run across her face, and she cursed them. She cursed them for having come, and she cursed them for having gone as well, leaving this valley to whatever breed and brand of men might appear to savage it again. She went back to the house and down into the cellar and found the jug in its dark corner and drank twice before slapping the cork back home.

"I'm about give out," she said aloud, and that annoyed her, too, because she had never talked aloud to herself.

They spoke little to one another in those three days. They were in bed each night while there was still light in the western sky. Once, Ora started a harangue against Tulip Crozier, who had come by the farm from Elkhorn Tavern with old man Ruter, both of them drunk. But she cut it off, as though ashamed of attacking a friend when they had many more serious concerns, and abruptly changed the subject.

"Cal, tomorrow while Roman finishes the roof, take a grub hoe and go along the old potato rows in the garden and see if we missed any last fall."

Throughout this time Roman said nothing about what he'd seen at the tavern, nor did they ask him. Each time he thought about it, there was some black, terrifying aspect to it that seemed to lie just beyond any words he might use to describe it, ready to drown him in darkness if he said too much. Yet there was also a savage fascination and excitement that disturbed him a great deal.

At the end of the third day of sunshine, Roman was tapping in the last of the shake shingles with a leather mallet when the rain began. It was a slow, drenching downpour, coming out of a gray and windless sky. That night with their beef, Ora cooked a batch of sourdough biscuits and a little white gravy made with flour, water, and meat drippings. Stacked in the warming oven were the cow's ribs, like a rick of firewood, roasted brown and crisp, and she rationed one each to them.

Night came on quickly, and with it the chill that accompanies March rain. But it would not freeze. They had seen the last of ice and snow until November. Roman grumbled and moved his bed from beneath the leaks in his new roof. He thought about the two armies, out there now and moving away in the rain, one far to the east, the other south.

Ora and Calpurnia washed the dishes and fed the suckling pigs and put them back in their box in the cellar. Soon they would be large enough to go in the sty and eat table scraps and corn. Ora wondered what kind of table scraps they might have then and how long the shelled corn would last. After Calpurnia went up to the kitchen, Ora took another sip from Martin's white whiskey.

They were drying pans and putting them in the safe when they heard someone calling to the house from the dark woods behind the barn.

2   Spavinaw Tom saw the lights go out inside the house and half expected gunfire. He was sure someone had come onto the back porch, but the night was so black he could hardly see the outline of the barn close by, and beyond that everything was veiled by rain. He called again.

"Hello the house!"

He straddled the pony's croup, holding a blanket over his head and shoulders. Before him on the saddle lay a man, facedown. Spavinaw Tom edged the pony away from the barn and into the yard.

"Hello the house," he called. "I got a hurt man here."

No sound came back except the fall of water, like ice pellets shot against the wet ground.

"I got a hurt man here!"

"What do you want?" Spavinaw Tom thought it was a woman's voice, but he couldn't be sure.

"Somebody needs to take this hurt man out of the rain." There was another long silence, and he could feel cold water running down his back. The man lying across the saddle was wearing only long underwear, and beneath his hand Spavinaw Tom could feel the soaked flannel. "Somebody needs to take care of this hurt man."

"Who are you?" Now he knew it was a woman. He hesitated, not knowing the sentiments of these people, and with no men here, with only a woman to call back to him in the night, he knew they would be very nervous. Or maybe, he thought, she is there alone, which would be even worse.

"I was a soldier in this battle here," he shouted above the

rain. "But I'm not a soldier now. I found this hurt man in the woods. He needs to get in out of the wet."

A lighted lantern appeared, making a fuzzy ball of light in the downpour. He could see three figures. One held a gun, but he kneed the pony forward, toward them. They remained under the porch roof until he was close, and then the woman and a tall girl ran out to the horse. Spavinaw Tom slipped down and helped them pull the man off the saddle and onto the porch. The other one, a man, stood well back, his eyes sharp and intent like a dog watching a rabbit being skinned. He held up the lantern; the weapon he held in the other hand was a shotgun.

"All right, let's get him inside," the woman said. Spavinaw Tom could feel her eyes going over him, combing him from top to bottom, looking at the turban and the feathers and the beaded jacket. They pulled the deadweight of the man across the porch and into the kitchen, where it was warm and smelling of cooked meat. The man with the lantern followed, watching closely, paying no attention to the soggy form they dragged across the floor, his eyes strictly on the Indian. I hope I haven't made a big mistake, Spavinaw Tom thought. This is a very young man with that shot-gun, and his eyes are very blue and hostile.

They laid the man on his back before the cookstove, his bare toes pointing up. They were the color of putty. His face was drawn and covered with a sparse blond beard, and his eyes were only partly open, showing the marble shine of fever. He was trying to talk, his lips making formless sounds. The woman lighted a lamp, and Spavinaw Tom backed off and stood against one wall near the door. He watched the tall young man, who returned his look evenly, still holding the lantern and the shotgun.

"Who is he?" the woman asked.

"I don't know him. I found him in the woods."

They were all watching Spavinaw Tom, and he did not allow himself to look directly at the girl because it sometimes caused trouble to look at a white girl. But he knew she had blue eyes, too—wide now as she stood behind her mother. They were all tense, like a strung bow, ignoring the mumbling man on the floor. Spavinaw Tom stood very quietly, for he did not want to be lying there like the other one in the flannel underwear. The man on the floor thrashed feebly, moaning, still trying to speak.

"All right," the woman said finally. "You can go out to the barn and stable your horse and fix a bed in one of the stalls. I'll send grub in a minute."

He felt some relief then. These people were perhaps like his own, and others who lived in Indian country, who always fed a man even if they were unsure of his intentions.

"I thank you," Spavinaw Tom said and moved to the door, keeping his back along the wall and watching the young man with the shotgun. As he slipped outside, he heard the young man slide home a wooden bolt, and he heard the girl say something about the Yankee officer who had come "to ask for water."

Spavinaw Tom led his pony across the yard to the barn, finding the door in the darkness. Inside, there was the strong odor of hay and he could smell horses and hear them snorting at his intrusion. One nickered softly, but that was all, and he guessed there were only mares here and no feisty stallions. His own gelding stood silently at the door, ground-hitched, the reins trailing down loose. He moved slowly, groping in the dark.

He felt his way along the walls and the stall partitions. His fingers moved across the warm rump of a horse and found the studs along the wall, and the upright oak beams. There was an empty stall next to the door. He pulled the pony into it and stripped off bridle and saddle. With handfuls of straw from the floor, he wiped down the pony. Then he mounded straw against the wall for a bed and squatted there to unwrap his turban. He was soaked through, but it was cold, so he left the jacket and pants on and sat squatting there in the darkness.

When the young man came, he carried an oilcloth bundle and a lantern, but he no longer held the shotgun. He moved into the barn with hesitating steps, the lantern high, his eyes on the squatting Indian, his face suspicious and taut. The young man placed the bundle before Spavinaw Tom and backed away to stand with his back to the door. Wet, straight hair lay plastered across his forehead. Spavinaw Tom opened the bundle and there were roasted beef ribs and corn bread.

The Indian lifted a rib, a foot long, and holding it in two hands began to rip off the crusted meat with his teeth.

"I thank you for this food," he said, chewing. He moved his mouth along the bone, taking off the meat as though he were playing a harmonica. His earrings gleamed in the lantern light and his long hair was swept back across his shoulders to show his broad face and black eyes.

"My name's Roman Hasford," the young man said. "This is our place."

"I thank you for the food, Roman Hasford," the Indian said. "My name is Spavinaw."

"My papa came here and settled this place when he was a boy."

Now he's making his claim to the land, Spavinaw Tom thought. "Then your family has been here longer than mine," he said.

"Are you Cherokee?"

"Yes."

Roman Hasford saw the Yager short rifle leaning against the barn wall, and the suspicion began to leave his face. He lifted up the lantern and hung it on a nail and moved closer to Spavinaw Tom, squatting before him, his eyes bright as he looked at the weapon.

"That looks like a fine rifle," he said.

"Yes." Spavinaw Tom wanted to ask where the other men of

the house were, because that might tell him how hostile this farm was for him. But he felt the tension going out of the young man and he waited, eating the ribs. It tasted good, but the corn bread was dry in his throat. "Is there water for the horse?"

Roman Hasford ran out into the rain and was back after only a moment with a bucket of icy water. Spavinaw ate the last of the corn bread and lifted the bucket to his face and drank. Then he took it into the stall and let the pony drink.

"I can pitch down some hay," Roman Hasford said. He took a fork and pulled hay from the loft, then went back into the dark barn and returned with a double handful of corn. "We haven't got much corn left, but he can have a little."

"He don't eat much corn anyway," Spavinaw Tom said. "He's a prairie horse. I got him from a Delaware, who traded him from a Comanche."

They squatted again in the straw, Roman Hasford closer to him now, watching him eat the last of the ribs, and looking at the rifle.

"Where'd you find that fella you brought in?"

"In the woods."

"He's a Yankee officer. He came to the house before they had that battle, asking for water for his men." Spavinaw Tom stopped chewing for a moment and stared into Roman's eyes. "He's out of his head now. Mama says he's delirious. I guess you couldn't tell he was a Yankee, dressed like he is."

Suddenly they both laughed. Now Spavinaw Tom felt he knew which side this family favored.

"No. But you can't leave even a hurt dog in the woods," he said.

Spavinaw Tom could see the other two horses in the lantern-shine, looking over the stall partitions, their large eyes shining. He began to feel better, but he was still wet and cold. He picked up the bare ribs he had cleaned of meat and began cracking them with his teeth, sucking out the marrow.

"You were a soldier with Van Dorn?" Roman Hasford asked. The Indian looked at him, his teeth shining as he cracked the bones.

"Yes. But I'm not anymore."

"You were with that bunch from the Nations, I'd wager. That Indian brigade."

"Yes. A Cherokee regiment of cavalry. My people came through this country a long time ago," and he added quickly, "after your papa was already on this place."

"Papa told me about you people coming through here. He told me and my sister Calpurnia all about what he saw. He said you were bad put upon by the government."

"Yes." The bones cracked loudly between his teeth.

"Are you going home now?"

"Maybe. After a while. You know White River?"

"Sure. Me and my papa have hunted a lot of deer there, before the war. It's not far from here."

"I know," Spavinaw Tom said. "I saw it a few days ago. I was born in that valley."

"On White River? Why, in hell's name, you ought to feel right at home, then."

"I don't remember it. My father told me about it. There's not much game there."

"Sure there is," Roman Hasford said. "But this is a bad time, just before spring and rain coming on. They're hard to find. They don't move around much in bad weather. But there's lots of game over there."

"Maybe. Maybe I'll hunt some, then go home."

Abruptly Roman Hasford took up the oilcloth and ran from the barn, leaving the Indian squatting there cracking the last of the bones. After a few minutes he was back, two blankets wrapped in the oilcloth to keep them dry.

"You'll need these," he said, dropping them on the straw. "That's sure a nice rifle you got. We haven't had a rifle on the place since Papa took ours off to the war."

"Which army did he go with?" Spavinaw Tom thought he knew by now, but he wanted to make sure.

"Confederate."

"Was he in this battle here?"

"No, we don't think so. We didn't see him anyway. That's sure a nice rifle."

Spavinaw Tom reached back and took the rifle and tossed it to Roman Hasford, who caught it and admired the heft and balance of it. There was no cap on the nipple, but that didn't matter now because Spavinaw Tom trusted the boy. He could sense that Roman Hasford was a boy quick to make up his mind. And all signs of hostility had gone now that they were away from the women. Spavinaw Tom could see in the lantern light that Roman was much younger than he'd thought at first. Maybe that's because he has stopped looking at me like he wanted to shoot me. Maybe that makes a man look less old, when he's not ready to shoot.

"Where'd you find that Yankee officer?" Roman asked, his thumb caressing the large hammer on the gun.

The Indian waved his hand vaguely. He was finished eating now and wiped his hands on his damp jacket below the beads.

"In the woods. A ways from here. He has an old wound. Maybe he got it in the battle. Maybe later. He didn't take care of it and it made him sick. Some stragglers must have taken his clothes after he fell off his horse, in the woods."

"I didn't see any wound."

"In the hand," Spavinaw Tom said, raising his left arm. "Not a bad wound, but he didn't take care of it."

"There's still a lot of Yankee soldiers around. I guess they won the battle."

"Yes, maybe so."

"There's still a few at the tavern, but mostly just passing up and down the road. You'll have to watch out for them."

"Yes. I'll have to watch out for Confederates, too, now that I've quit their army. Maybe they wouldn't like that." They looked at one another and laughed. As his wide mouth moved up at the corners, Spavinaw Tom's eyes looked lighter than before, not so black and expressionless.

"Well, you can hide here. We haven't got much to eat, but you're welcome to it."

Roman Hasford reluctantly passed the rifle back to the Indian, his hands lingering on it. Spavinaw Tom placed it carefully against the wall.

"Have you got cartridges for it?" Roman asked.

"A few."

They heard footsteps coming across the wet yard, and Spavinaw Tom's hand moved back to the rifle.

"It's likely just Mama," Roman said.

The woman came into the barn quickly, a shawl over her head. Her eyes went to Spavinaw Tom's face, her lips hard and tight, her eyes bright. Spavinaw Tom stood up and nodded his head in greeting.

"I thank you for the food," he said.

"You're welcome to what we've got."

"He's a Cherokee," Roman said. "He was with the Indian brigade that fought in the battle."

"I'm called Spavinaw Tom. My people live near Going Snake in the Cherokee Nation. My sister went to Miss Sylvia Sawyer's female seminary in Fayetteville. A lot of our young girls go there." He felt as though this woman had him on trial and he wanted to get the part about his sister going to a white school into the evidence.

"Mama, he was born over along White River. During the Removal."

"All right," she said, her eyes on the Indian's face, searching his features. "You're welcome to sleep in the barn tonight. But I don't want you near the house. No disrespect, but I don't know you."

"I thank you," Spavinaw Tom said.

"You'll have to give me your matches or flints or whatever you make fires with. I don't want you smoking and setting my barn afire."

"My matches are used up and my tobacco is wet," he said. "I won't make any fire."

She looked at the Yager rifle, and for a moment he thought she would ask for that, too. But she said no more and turned to the boy. Her voice changed when she spoke to him—some of the edge went off her words, as though she were instructing someone half Roman's age. Spavinaw Tom could feel the boy's irritation, and he recalled his own growth to manhood and how during that time he felt somehow belittled whenever his elders spoke to him like a child.

"Roman, saddle Bess. You've got to go someplace for me."

"Now?" he asked incredulously.

"Yes, right now." She glanced at Spavinaw Tom and paused a moment before making up her mind to say more. "I want you to ride over to the tavern and see if there's an army doctor there who can come help that man we've got in the kitchen. He's bad, and I don't know what to do for him."

"A Yankee doctor? Mama, we can't bring a bunch of Yankees over here with Mister Spavinaw. He fought against those people."

"We don't aim to bring any Yankees to the barn," she said. "We can tell them we found the man ourselves."

"Why don't we just hitch the wagon and carry him over there, and dump him with his own folks?"

"We're not dumping him off on anybody. He's been out in the weather too long already."

"But there's likely no doctor there anyway. Just supply troops and—"

The Indian saw her jaw set and her lips go thin, and he knew this woman was not accustomed to having her children argue with her decisions.

She cut off the boy. "Saddle Bess and scoot. And if there's no doctor at the tavern, then go to Tulip Crozier and bring him. But the tavern's closer so try that first, you hear? Now get along."

Roman started back into the darkness of the barn, and her voice followed him, more gently now.

"And get your papa's wide hat and slicker on. I don't want two sick people on my hands."

After the woman had gone, Roman leading the saddled mare, Spavinaw Tom undressed and hung his wet clothes across a rafter support. He wrapped himself in the two blankets, leaving the lantern burning. He thought about the woman and the set of her jaw, and judged her to be capable of defending herself. Unlike some white women he had seen, there was little of powder puff and lace about this woman. She reminded him of women among his own people and judged himself fortunate that he had seen the light of this farm instead of some other.

After a while, thinking about what the woman had said about fire, he got up and blew out the lantern and wrapped himself in the blankets again in the dark.

I swore an oath, he thought. With old General Pike. And I wonder if maybe I broke that oath when I helped a Yankee officer? Of course, he had not known it was a Yankee, with the blue uniform stripped off. He recalled seeing other soldiers in Van Dorn's army helping Yankee wounded, and he knew it worked the other way as well. It wasn't like the old fights with Osages, when an enemy was an enemy no matter what his condition. These whites fight like wolves, tearing each other apart with those big guns, and then they stop and treat one another like brothers, like old friends, he thought. They are hard to understand, these whites.

But he liked that woman, with her mouth set hard and her eyes bold and not looking down. He liked the boy, too. And the girl, from what he'd seen, was a pretty one. As some white girls were, he had found. Even the blue-eyed ones.

3   The windows of Elkhorn Tavern shone through the darkness in patches of phosphorescent light, looking like foxfire in the falling rain. The dark lift of Pea Ridge was a forbidding shape in the west, its wooded outline showing as lightning played across the horizon of the Indian Territory. Thunder grumbled there, too, with the flaring glow fading and growing and fading again, the dying embers of a blue-flame fire.

Two fiddles were sounding a scratchy tune from the tavern's downstairs dining room and feet stomped the floor. One of the tavern dogs howled with the music from the shelter of some outhouse shed. There were the voices of women raised in shrill banter and laughter.

Roman pulled Bess in and sat well out in the yard, suspicious of this place and not wanting to go in closer. The rain was seeping through the felt of his father's hat and making cold traces down his face. Then, remembering his mother's urgency, he edged the horse forward until he could see figures dancing across the light of the windows. The music was suddenly finished and he could hear shouting and a heavy thump, as though someone had fallen on the floor. Then the fiddles started up again.

In the rear of the main building there was a dim light, and he knew it was the window of the outback kitchen. He reined Bess in that direction, and she moved carefully. Roman gave the horse her head and she picked her way, avoiding a shattered tree stump in the darkness. With the pressure of his knees, he guided her toward the backyard.

Drawing close to the kitchen window, Roman looked inside and saw Lark sitting on a wooden box before the big cookstove. The lids had been removed and the fire sent flickering red light across the dark face. He was playing a Jew's harp, his eyes vacant and reflecting the flames, his long fingers gently strumming the sounding bar. Along the walls were stacks of boxes and burlap bags, but there was none of the furniture in the room that Roman remembered from the night he sat there with Lucinda Cox. Roman slipped from the saddle and went to the door. He hesitated a moment with his hand up to knock, but changing his mind he lifted the latch and stepped inside.

Lark's face turned to him slowly and his eyes widened in surprise, but he did not smile. Roman pushed the door shut behind him and stood against it, dripping water on the floor.

"What on earth you doin' out a night like this, Mister Roman?" He still held the Jew's harp up near his face, as though about ready to play again. Roman whipped off his hat, spraying water across the room. "Is somethin' the matter?"

"We need a doctor over at our place," Roman said. He wasn't sure how much to tell, not knowing what had happened here since the battle, not knowing the black man's loyalties now. But he had to come at it head-on and waste no time. "Is there a Yankee doctor here?"

"Ain't no doctor here," Lark said, shaking his head violently. "Ain't nuthin' here but a bunch of them soldiers. You got folks sick?"

"It's a man. We found him wounded in the woods. Mama needs a doctor for him, or he may die."

"They carried them wounded and dead men out of the woods around here for two days, Mister Roman, and cart 'em off someplace. I ain't never thought to see so many dead men."

"Then you're sure there's no doctor? It's important."

"Ain't no doctor now. They all went off with the army, and dem Yankees say they goin' all the way to Fayetteville," Lark said, still shaking his head. "Now, they's jus' them soldiers. They always unloaded stuff from wagons and stackin' it all over. An' they brang in a load of red whiskey and two trash women from Springfield, they say to do the cookin' and cleanin', that's what they say. But ain't no doctor. Miz Polly done lef'."

"I know that. Tulip Crozier told us when he came by the place after the fight here."

"You hafta go plumb to Bentonville for a doctor, Mister Roman, an' they may not be ary one there neither, with all this shootin' and Yankees runnin' up and down."

"Well, I'll ride to Tulip Crozier's, then, and get him to help us. What's in all these boxes and sacks?"

"Them things full of Yankee army grub," Lark said. Roman moved over and looked intently at the stacked boxes. Some of the smaller ones were stenciled *Pork, Salted.*

"I guess I'll just take one of these along," he said. Lark began to grin, rising and coming to the boy, stuffing the Jew's harp in a pants pocket.

"If you was to have a wagon, you could take a load," Lark said. "Them soldiers is drunk and rowdy and you could take a whole load was you to have a wagon."

"I'm riding Bess, and I need to get along. Mama's waiting for me and it's a long way to Tulip Crozier's."

Roman moved to the door, a box of the salt pork under one arm. Lark followed closely, still grinning. He touched Roman's arm with one tentative hand.

"Mister Roman, why don't you take me along. I'd like to go along with you."

"It's wet outside. Why'd you want to leave a nice warm kitchen?"

Lark rolled his head back and lifted his arms in exasperation. "God Almighty, Mister Roman, this ain't no place for me anymore. I tole Miz Polly I'd watch this place, but them Yankees tell me I can go off anywheres I want 'cause I'm free now. They say they don't want some ole nigger underfoot and eatin' up their grub. An' they done burn all Miz Polly's furniture in the stoves."

"Well, I don't know."

"Mister Roman, I ain't gone be no bother. This place ain't no good for me now. They ain't gone be no tavern business with them soldiers here, and I ain't got nuthin' to do but stay away from them Yankees. They want me to chop their wood, say they feed me if I do, but I say I ain't choppin' no wood for people that come in here and burn all Miz Polly's furniture and kill her livestock with all that shootin' they done."

"You've chopped plenty of wood before."

Lark stared at him, frowning. Roman could see the spark of anger growing in his eyes.

"That ain't the same thing, Mister Roman. You let me come with you."

"What in hell's name would I do with you?"

"Nothin', you don't have to do nothin'. I'll stay with Mister Tulip. That good ole man let me stay with him. I can help him run that mill and milk his goats till Miz Polly come back."

"Well, maybe. Have you got any stock left, any riding stock?" He said it reluctantly. He wasn't sure how Tulip Crozier would react, but somehow he couldn't say no to this man who had slipped him away on that first night before the Yankees came and recaptured the place.

"Miz Polly taken the last two mules wasn't shot and killed when they done all that shootin'."

"All right," Roman said. "We can ride double. Unless you want to steal a Yankee horse."

"No, I don't want to do that," Lark said, his eyes rolled back.

Roman guessed the rolling eyes were a thing he had always been expected to do before, and now he did it out of habit even though the Yankees had told him about being free. "No, I don't want to do that. They tole me when I lef', if I take anything belong to their army, they'd string me to a tree."

"All right, get a hat and coat and Bess'll take us both. But I'm leaving you at Tulip Crozier's when we get there. My mama would scald me if I brought home another hungry mouth."

"Mister Roman, I aims to stay with Mister Tulip and help him run that mill and milk his goats."

"He may not have any goats left to milk," Roman said. But he felt good about the companionship on the long ride across the valley to Little Sugar Creek.

X

On the ride to the Hasfords', Tulip Crozier fell off his horse three times. They came the long way, taking Little Sugar Creek trail to Wire Road and along that to the farm. The old man refused to go the shorter route over the mountain and through the woods because he said in his condition he might run into a tree in the dark and brain himself. It was still raining, it was cold, and it took a long time.

Crozier would lurch in the saddle, swear a mighty oath, and pitch forward into the mud with a loud splat, his beaver hat rolling off into the darkness. He would thrash about in the muck, cursing, finally sitting upright with the rain running through his beard until Roman got down, found the hat, and helped him back onto the old chestnut he was riding. He smelled vilely of corn whiskey and wet leather.

"Me and old man Ruter finished off the last of the Elkhorn Tavern private stock," he bellowed at one point. "So! And a goodly part of my own supply. And I sent him home to his woman this evening before you came and brought that free nigger to eat me out of meal and meat. She likely has been over there on that rock farm of theirs thinking all along the Yankees carried him off or else he got himself shot and was roasting in hell. Which appears to be a more pleasant climate than what we got here. We been drunk for four days, you know that, Roman?"

The boy rode slumped in the rain, saying nothing, soaked through and shivering. He kicked Bess along and pulled at the reins of Tulip Crozier's chestnut. It was all a little disgusting to him, never having seen a man as drunk as this old man was now. But it was funny, too. At least it was funny until he thought about what his mother was going to say when they trooped into her clean kitchen, Crozier dripping and caked with mud and filth like a hog that had been wallowing in slops.

As they rode along, the old man alternately lectured him on the wickedness of whiskey and sang ribald songs from his soldier days during the Mexican War.

"So, by God, boy, do you see me here," Crozier bellowed, beating his chest with one clinched fist. "Never fall on evil ways like I have, with whiskey and bad womenfolk. And you'd better stop sneaking those chews of your papa's tobacco that I've smelled on your breath every time you come to the mill. You ever hear a tune called 'The Leather-winged Bat'?"

Without waiting for reply, he launched into the song, shouting it out into the night, his voice a discordant bray. He almost fell again, but Roman grabbed his arm.

> " 'Hello,' said the baboon, sitting on the bench,
> 'Once I had me a lively wench.
> But she got too saucy and from me fled,
> And now, you see, my arse is red.' "

"You best not sing that song where Mama can hear it," Roman said.

Crozier sang the same verse again, and a few more in like vein about various members of the animal kingdom. Then abruptly he stopped, sniffing, his head back and the rain falling onto his closed eyes.

"Smell them dead horses! Nothing makes a worse stink than a dead horse, unless it's four dead men. Maybe five. I can tell you tales about the time I served with old Zack Taylor across the Texas border. . . ."

His voice droned down to a low mumble, as though he were talking in his sleep, and Roman could make nothing of what he was saying. It was just as well. Roman wanted no war stories now. The images of Elkhorn Tavern when the southern infantry came charging from the woods were still too starkly vivid in his mind. Crozier's stories had always fascinated him, stories of the Mexicans and guns and cheering and flags waving. But there had never been mention of men torn apart, of the screams and moans, of the young soldiers crawling like cut grubworms puking out their blood and crying like babies before they died. There had never been any of the reality of war that Roman had seen now. He was glad the old man this night relived his memories incoherently.

It was well past midnight when they turned off the road and up through the trees toward the house. Crozier was reluctant to go in alone. He waited on the back porch, hanging on to one of the roof supports while Roman stabled the horses. The barn was dark, and as soon as he stepped inside, pulling the two horses behind him, Roman thought he heard the metallic click of a gun's hammer being drawn back.

"It's me, Mister Spavinaw," he said quickly. "It's Roman Hasford."

He waited a moment, but from his corner the Cherokee said nothing. Roman pulled the horses into stalls and stripped off the saddles. Roman knew the inside of the barn as he did his own fingers, and he found burlap bags in the darkness and rubbed down both horses. But he did it quickly, thinking, If I let Uncle Tulip stand too long, he's likely to fall off the edge of the porch and drown in the yard.

Ora Hasford confronted them from the center of her kitchen, hands on hips and mouth drawn tight, as though she might have suspected Tulip Crozier's condition before they came through the door. Crozier slipped off his mud-splattered coat, his eyes wavering in the lamplight and avoiding her icy stare. Then he shrugged, dropping the coat on the floor.

"So, Ora," he said thickly. "I didn't know you'd be needing me."

Roman hung the slicker and the wide-brim hat on rear wall pegs, waiting for his mother's fury to break. But she said nothing to the old man, though her fierce glare continued to stab his face.

"I brought some sowbelly from the tavern," Roman said. "But the Yankee doctors have all gone."

"I reckoned as much, the time it took you," she said, still watching Crozier. "I'm surprised you got him here at all."

"Now, Ora—" Crozier started, but she cut him off.

"Roman, get up to the loft and out of those wet clothes and into bed. Right now!"

The tone of her voice left no room for argument, and besides, he was bone tired. Leaving the room, he glanced at the federal officer in his mother's big bed, covers drawn around his neck. He looked dead, his cheeks sunken and his high forehead beneath a shock of blond hair shining like old wax. He stirred restlessly, eyes bright and unseeing, mumbling.

In the loft, Calpurnia called to Roman from her bed. He paused in her doorway, his eyes adjusting to the darkness. She was sitting up, blankets drawn around her shoulders.

"I've been waiting for you to get back. Where have you been, anyway?"

"Had to get Uncle Tulip. He's drunk as a goose."

"Where's that Indian?"

"In the barn. Mama told him he could sleep there."

"I know she did. I wish she'd run him off. He scares me. I never saw anybody with eyes like that."

"He's not going to bother you. Did you find out who that Yankee is downstairs?"

"No. He tries to talk. Something about horses and soldiers. You can't make sense of it."

"He looks dead to me," Roman said.

"He's the one who came here for water. Remember?"

"I remember you mooning over how grand he looked in his uniform."

"He looks different now. He's skinny as a kid goat. We got him cleaned up and dry and put one of papa's nightshirts on him. He's helpless as a rag doll."

For a moment Roman tried to understand what he'd just heard.

"You and Mama took his clothes off?"

"Well, he didn't have much to take off. Just longhandles. Did you expect us to put him in Mama's bed all wet and dirty?"

"In hell's name, you helped get him undressed and dried him off?"

"Oh, Roman, for land's sake, what's the matter with you? He's sick. And besides, I've seen you naked enough times."

"When I was little, maybe," he said, growing more angry as he thought about it. "But seeing a baby and a grown man naked are two different things."

"You make me tired, Roman," she said, lying back and pulling the covers up to her chin. "You act like I don't know anything. Besides, Mama did most of it. Now why don't you take your sore tail and go to bed?"

Roman started to say something more, then clamped his jaw shut just as his mother did when she was completely exasperated. He turned and moved back along the loft to his own room, stomping his feet. Another leak had developed in the roof patch and he had to shove his bed from beneath it, mumbling some of the oaths he'd heard Tulip Crozier use. He hoped his sister heard them.

This war business turns everything inside out, he thought. You'd think the armies would just go at one another, and when one got whipped that would be the end of it and everything would be like it was before. But here I am, nearly frozen after riding halfway across the county to get a drunk old man to come fix some Yankee stranger that Calpurnia talks about undressing like it was the kind of thing she does every day, and then scolding me for being mad about it.

It was all crazy. Dead horses and blown-up trees and some wild Indian sleeping in the barn and cocking a rifle when he tried to go in and stable the horses. And now, with the armies gone, who knew when those night riders might come back?

Roman woke in the night from a dream of dancing at Elkhorn Tavern. All the dancers had been wearing nothing but shoes. The shapes were indistinct and he tried to recall what the women looked like, feeling aroused. But he turned to his side and drew deeper into the covers, forcing his mind away from it because he knew such things were a sin and, if allowed to run free, could bring shame on the family. And besides, he knew that self-abuse could cause him to go insane. After a short agony of time, he slept, feeling empty and unfulfilled.

But before he was asleep, lying there listening to the rain on the shakes above him, slackening and finally stopping, he thought about the song Tulip Crozier had been singing along Wire Road. He wondered if there were such things as baboons with red arses.

2   The kitchen was warm and smelled of cooking food, and Tulip Crozier felt his stomach churn at this sudden heat after the chilling ride from Little Sugar Creek. His curiosity concerning the young man in the bed was almost overwhelming. But even in his state, he knew his stock with Ora Hasford was at dangerously low ebb. He was also afraid if he moved he would fall on his face. He held the beaver hat in both hands, staring at the

bobbing turkey-vulture feather with that vacant, glassy-eyed intensity of drunks trying to concentrate on something to avoid throwing up.

"So. You see this old buzzard feather? The wild Indians of the Plains use buzzard feathers on their arrows. Do you know why? Because blood don't affect the vane and make it soft. And neither does water."

"Keep your voice down," she said. Her words were not spoken loudly, but the old man felt them like cold raindrops running down his neck. She sat at the bed, drawing back the covers and gently pulling forth the federal officer's left arm. The hand was bandaged and she began to unwind the stained cloth. "And this is no time to be worried with your stories about wild Indians."

"Not worried about wild Indians? Roman said a wild Indian brought this wounded Yankee to you and you've let him sleep in the barn," Crozier said, dropping the hat on the kitchen table and staggering closer to the bed.

"He didn't seem so wild to me," she said. "Now, come look at this hand."

"Well, I'm a mite unsteady, Ora."

"You're worse than that. You ought to be ashamed, getting yourself in a condition. Don't fall on him," she said sharply.

"I told you, Ora. I didn't know you'd be needing me. How was I supposed to know, how indeed? Your boy comes in the night banging on my wall, and bringing that damned nigger with him besides."

"Bringing who?"

"Lark. That old tavern nigger. He wanted to get away from the Yankee soldiers at the tavern, so your boy just up and brought him to me."

"All right, look at the hand," she said, holding up the limp arm. "And stop calling Lark what you call him"

"What I call him? I call him what he is, a nigger—"

She broke in, suddenly savage. "Shut your mouth! Lark sent my Roman home and maybe saved him and now he's just a scared old man. In this house you call his name or you call him a colored man. You teach my children enough bad habits without throwing that one in, too."

Crozier's mouth gaped open, his eyes started from their sockets. He'd never heard such fury in a woman's voice, never been so lashed by women's words. And certainly not from this woman, who mostly joined conversations of the menfolk only when invited, deferring to their opinions and decisions as a good woman was supposed to do. He swallowed audibly and stumbled to the bed, going to his knees beside the wounded man.

"So, Ora, I didn't know you'd be needing me," he repeated for the third time.

"I wish to God I didn't, the way you are now. But you're all I've got. Now look at the damned hand!"

Her words shocked him, and she was aware of it and glad. She knew he was of the school of men who supposed decent women didn't even know such words, much less say them.

"Look at the color."

A large-caliber bullet had entered the back of the hand near the wrist, leaving a bluish puncture and swelling along the lower arm. Ora turned the hand over, and Crozier could see the palm had been shattered, shards of pale white bone protruding from a jagged, gaping tear. Red streaks extended along the wrist, and the flesh around the wound looked like fish scales or an ear that had been frostbitten. The fingers were putty-colored and had begun to turn purple-black, and they were puffy as new-stuffed sausage.

"Can you still smell?" she snapped. She lifted the hand to his face and he bent to it, sniffing elaborately. He wrinkled his nose.

"Smells like tainted pork."

"And he's got a fever, too. A lot of fever."

She waited impatiently, but he said nothing, swaying back and forth on his knees and looking owlish.

"Well? Is it blood poisoning of some kind?"

Tulip Crozier bent to the hand once more, sniffed it, his whiskers almost touching the wound. He sighed heavily. The young man in the bed whispered and turned his head from side to side, eyes glassy. Then, with a sudden clarity that was startling, he looked at them and spoke.

"The term *tort* comes from the Latin *tortum*, meaning 'to twist,' but the meaning in law is 'a wrongful act or injury done willfully or with negligence.'"

"What's that he's saying?" Crozier asked.

"He's out of his head with fever. I haven't been able to make any of it out. Don't pay any attention."

The young man's eyes were turned away once more, glazed and unseeing, and his lips moved without any sound coming.

"Well? Is it blood poisoning?" she asked impatiently.

"Blood poisoning? So, something like that. I think it's gangrene."

Ora slowly moved the arm back to the bed and let it rest there above the covers. She looked at the wound, remembering that Martin's mother had died of blood poisoning in her hand, from a wound almost indiscernible.

"How bad is it?" she asked.

"It's bad enough to kill him in a few days." He paused and blinked a number of times and shook his head violently, as if to clear it. "Unless it comes off. I've watched surgeons take off hands hurt less. And even before the wound was allowed to rot. Why wasn't this taken care of when he was shot? Why didn't the Yankee doctors take care of it? There hasn't been much blood getting into those fingers for a spell."

"I don't know how it happened or where or anything else

about it. That Indian just said he found him in the woods. He didn't say where, even if he knew. He doesn't know this country and he didn't say much. This boy hasn't said anything. But what's the difference? He's here now."

"And his army passed him by. That's a cruel thing."

Ora looked at the pale face on her pillow, the lips open and the breath coming only faintly between them. Some of the men this very officer had commanded were likely responsible for her lost chickens and potatoes and fence posts, and certainly because of his like, her roof had been blown nearly off, her dogs and pigs were gone, and the lives of her children had been placed in jeopardy. But she could not help thinking of Roman or Martin in the same situation, helpless and dying and at the mercy of chance. She had determined from the first that if she had the power to make it so, this young man would live.

"I thought maybe it was that bad." Now her voice had lost its harshness, gone almost pensive. She looked at Crozier, her eyes clear but the heat gone from them. "So you'll have to do it."

Crozier gave a start and swayed back from her.

"Do what?"

"Take it off," she said. "Or else he'll die. That's what you said."

"God Almighty, woman, let him die. He'll likely die anyway, no matter what we do."

"We have to try. And you'll do it." She was speaking softly, watching his face. "If you won't, I'll do it myself."

"God Almighty, I knew that's what you were going to say. I knew it."

"You've helped do such things. In the army."

"I never said that."

"You have, too. You were one of those medical soldiers who helped the doctors."

"Well, I've helped do it. All right. But God Almighty, Ora."

"And Roman said you helped at the tavern, too. You can still remember that, can't you?"

"Of course I can. I remember all of it," Crozier said, rubbing his already unkempt-looking hair with both hands.

"Then you can do it."

"I'm mighty shaky, Ora."

"You can do it. I've got a good stew on the stove. I even managed to get some of it down this boy a while ago. Now I want you to eat a good bit of it and, while you're doing that, tell me what we'll need."

"God Almighty!"

She knew he accepted it, no matter how reluctantly, and her mood toward him changed to one of near-tenderness as she helped him to his feet and over to the table. She dished out a large bowl of stew. He ate with considerable noise, and she could see him grimace with each mouthful, forcing it down. But it was good stew, made from beef heart and roast with a few potatoes Calpurnia had salvaged from last summer's garden. As he ate, he began to instruct her, his voice growing more stable as he appeared to assume responsibility for what was about to happen and the hot food settled in his stomach.

At first he argued with himself about how best to stop the bleeding. He finally convinced himself, speaking aloud, that cauterizing would be too much of a shock without any sort of opiate to kill the pain. He would use ligatures, fashioned from the silk thread he had sent to Ora some time ago. She produced her largest butcher knife and a bone saw, but he said an ax would be quicker, and she pulled a shawl over her shoulders and lit a lantern.

"This is good stew," he said, wiping the juice from his whiskers with the still-damp sleeve of his coat. "Once a body gets used to it."

"It's made from my milk cow." He started to respond but she was already out the door. Soon he heard the grindstone on the back porch cutting against the hard steel of an ax blade.

It was growing light in the east behind Plum Thicket Ridge before they were ready. Everything was arranged at bedside. The woodlot chopping block had been brought in, a two-foot length of hickory log that stood about the same height as the bed. Waiting were the double-bitted ax, its metal head shining from the wheel, the butcher knife, just in case, that she had sharpened at the table with a milkstone as Tulip Crozier finished his meal with scalding-hot sassafras tea. There were clean rags for bandages, a length of leather strap and a round sandstone the size of a goose egg for a tourniquet, the silk thread, a ball of twine, tweezers from Ora's sewing basket, needle-nosed pliers from Martin's toolbox, a can of coal oil, a jar of pork lard, and an empty water bucket sitting on the floor beside the chopping block. And if Crozier's ligatures failed, there were two iron pokers heating to a red glow in the kitchen stove, standing up from an open lid like the handles of umbrellas.

Ora was glad to see the old man looked a little less drunk. Not sober, but less drunk. His eyes seemed not to waver so badly. As she arranged their gear, he stared at the floor.

"So, Ora, I'm sorry about tracking in all this mud and water."

"There'll be more than mud and water after a bit, and if you feel bad about it, I've got a good mop."

As gently as they could, they pulled the federal officer to the edge of the bed. His left arm was extended and they rested it on the block, palm up. He made no sound, but his eyes were still open. He tried to resist weakly, but they held the arm in place.

"I hope he don't get wild," Crozier said. "Sometimes they get wild as an acorn boar when they've got that much fever. Or else go into convulsions."

Crozier thought about something else then, and Ora regarded him with some suspicion for a moment before going down into the root cellar and bringing up Martin's jug of whiskey.

"Afterward, we need to give him a little," Crozier said.

They worked on the arm at the shoulder, feeling for the axillary artery on the underside, between the muscles and next to the bone. Ora seated the round stone against it, cushioned with cloth to avoid any more bruising than necessary. She cinched the stone in place with the leather harness strap, but they could not draw it tight enough. They ripped a tea towel and twisted it like a rope, then tied it and slipped a butcher's steel between the ends. Using the towel to hold the stone in place, they turned down the steel like a screw until there was no longer anything but a faint pulse at the wrist.

"We need it tight against that one artery," Crozier said. "There's only one big one this far up the arm, but it branches down about the elbow and when we cut we'll find two." He was working with a feverish intensity, his eyes bright.

"If we get it any tighter, we'll squeeze his arm off," she said.

They tied the steel to the biceps with a length of twine string, to keep it from unwinding the tourniquet when they released it. They worked close to one another, and she could smell his foul breath, but she tried to ignore it. They made the final adjustments of the young man's body, both on the bed on their knees.

"So, Ora! I've always wanted to be in bed with you, but not under this set of circumstances." He giggled.

"You're a drunken old fool, Tulip Crozier, and if you ever come here in your cups again, I'll set the dogs on you."

"I thought your dogs ran off." And he giggled again.

"Then I'll take the shotgun to you." She almost laughed, because she was tired and because all of this had taken on a dreamlike quality. And because here was this bleary-eyed old man talking like a young snort, after something he knew, and she knew, he would never try to claim, even if he had the capability. "Let's get along with it."

The old man rose unsteadily and took up the double-bitted ax. It was heavy, and he seemed to have trouble fixing his hands on the haft. He bent to the arm, staring at it a moment, licked his finger, and traced a line midway between the wrist and the elbow.

"Hold it tight, now," he said. He raised the ax, let it down, and raised it again halfway. He was shaking, and his eyes were bleary. He tried to set his feet more firmly, and swayed, almost falling. He shook his head. "I don't think I can do it, Ora. I'm afraid I'll miss the damned thing. Maybe I'd best use the knife and saw."

"No," she said, rising and pulling the ax from his hands. "You said it has to be quick, so you could get at the blood vessels in a hurry. Can you do that part of it? Now be sure, damn it!"

Crozier blinked a moment, still unsteady on his feet.

"Yes. I can do that. It's just my strength, Ora. I've had a few days of whiskey. . . ."

"You don't need to tell me that, God knows. Get down there and hold his arm."

Crozier sank to the floor beside the bed. He held the arm tight against the block while she lifted the ax, measuring its weight and balance that she already knew well.

"Where do I hit it?"

Once more, he wetted a finger and drew a shining line of spittle across the arm. He raised his head and their eyes met for an instant.

"Hit it hard, Ora. It'll be tough as an oak sapling."

She spread her feet, squaring her body to the arm, holding the ax handle at its end with both white-knuckled hands. Her jaw set, and leaning back slightly, she brought the ax up behind her left shoulder and quickly swung it down with all her strength, the big double-bitted blade just clearing the ceiling. It made the sound of a wagon wheel going over a chicken's neck, and there was the dull thud of the blade biting through flesh and bone and driving three inches deep into the wood beneath. The cleanly severed hand seemed to leap back from the blade in a spout of red, hang for an instant, then drop into the waiting bucket.

The young officer tried to rise up, his eyes staring wildly now, a low cry coming from deep in his throat. Crozier held him until Ora dropped the ax and came to help, and then the old man was at the stump with tweezers and the silk thread.

"By God, it's not bleeding as bad as I'd thought it would," he gasped. The young man lay quiet now, unconscious, his eyes closed and his breath coming harshly, like a snore.

"Can you do it?"

"I can do it!"

He found the radial artery at once, where it passed down the arm toward where the thumb had been, and he tied it off. The ulnar was harder to pull from the surrounding flesh, and before he was finished with the ligature blood was running deep red off his hands.

They released the tourniquet only a little, and there was still considerable bleeding. Reluctantly, Crozier went to the stove for the pokers. He cauterized the stump away from the silk ligatures, allowing the glowing iron to touch only for a second, long enough to sear but not so long that the hot metal burned into the flesh. Ora struggled to hold the officer down, and his wailing was a terribly low cry in the house. The room was suddenly filled with the odor of bacon dropped into live coals.

"Now the lard," Crozier said. He took it from her and smeared the burns with the thick grease.

They released the tourniquet again, very slowly, and the ligatures held. It was finished then. They bandaged the stump with the coal-oil-soaked rags, which Ora then wrapped in oilcloth before placing the arm across one of her doubled pillows, elevating the stump well above the young man's chest. Crozier brought the jug, and Ora pressed a few drops between the young man's lips with her fingertips. He was moaning softly, his eyes open and glazed.

"So, keep him warm now," Crozier said. He was shaking visibly, as though with a deep chill. He turned unsteadily and moved to his overcoat, still rumpled on the floor where he had dropped it. "Keep him warm and get food down him, as much as you can, and a little whiskey now and again."

"Where are you going?" she asked sharply.

"So, I'm going home. I won't burden you any longer with my wickedness."

"You're not going anywhere," she said. "Take this hand out and bury it in the woods. Shovels are on the porch. And then get back in here and sleep, and when you're rested, I'll fix your breakfast."

He did as he was told, not looking back at her. His eyes had filled and she could see tears running down into his whiskers. He took a long drink from the jug, and without a word took up the bucket. After he was gone, Ora daubed more of the clear liquor between the young man's lips. He was breathing harshly and his eyelids fluttered and finally closed.

She went to the stove, thinking, God's will be done. We've done our part. She stabbed at the fire with one of the pokers Crozier had used, replaced the lid, and slid a flatiron onto it. She would heat the iron, wrap it in flannel, and put it at the young officer's feet.

When Crozier returned he looked haggard, his eyes sunken and red. He had washed the bucket at the well and now it was filled. He sat it on the stove beside the flatiron.

"I drew up fresh water," he said. "We'll need it to scrub that floor."

"I'll scrub the floor. You take that block out of here."

He took up the hickory chunk and moved toward the door, pausing. The block was splattered with crimson.

"I'll wash it off," he said.

Now that it was all over, Ora was exhausted, her legs weak and her arm aching painfully. But she did not sit down. She was afraid she'd fall asleep at the table. She poured two inches of the white whiskey into a teacup and took it in one swallow, without a shudder.

The light of the new sun came through the rear windows with blinding brilliance. But it was only for a short time, and then more clouds pushed in from the west and it started to rain again.

3   Tulip Crozier sat up in his bunk bed, fully clothed and a little damp still from his ride home in the rain. This was a small room, cluttered beyond belief, looking as though nothing had ever been dusted, set in place, arranged, or assigned any function except to lie where it happened to fall. There was a table stacked with dirty dishes, a small cookstove with a jumble of food-marked pots and pans, a few shelves along two walls, and one window with four panes, one broken and patched over with burlap sacking. There were two chairs, one without a back, and on it Lark perched, watching the old man lift himself up from the covers and throw them off with a grunt of dismay.

"So, you're still here. I thought maybe you'd gone."

"Yas sir, Mister Tulip, I'm here sure as rain," Lark said, grinning. He watched fascinated as Crozier licked his lips elaborately.

"Still here. I thought maybe you were never here at all, but just something I dreamed. Corn-whiskey dream."

"Yas, sir, I'm still here," Lark said.

Crozier, sitting in the bed with his arms back to support him, stared about the room owlishly.

"This place needs swamping out."

"Yas, sir, it sure does."

"Where were you when I came in? I didn't see you any-where."

"In the millhouse, wropped in some of them old sacks. I seed you come, but you looked wore out, and so I jus' stay in the mill-house and let you sleep awhile. Then I comes in and makes a fire."

"By God, that was the longest ride I ever took," Crozier said, swinging his feet out to the floor and scratching his belly. He began to look for his coat. "She wanted me to stay on and sleep there, and feed me. But I think I wore out my welcome at the Hasfords'. They're a hard-judging breed, Mister Lark. You don't ever want to get crossways with that family. 'Specially with the mama. I felt like hell, once I started to sober up. So I came on home."

"It was past sunup."

"I know when it was," Crozier said, finding his coat and struggling to get his arms into the tangled sleeves. There was only a small fire in the cookstove and the room was cold. He rose un-steadily, Lark watching wide-eyed, as though expecting him to fall back into bed. "What's for grub? I'm hungry as a wolf."

"I ain't fixed nuthin', Mister Tulip. I didn't know what you wanted."

Crozier walked to the stove, weaving a little, one hand to his head. He groaned and lifted the lid from a cast-iron pot, revealing a whitish-gray substance. He bent and smelled it and gasped.

"Old turnip soup," he said. "Rank as a goat's tail."

He slid the pot over the fire, clattering the other pans on the stove, knocking a lid off onto the floor, which he ignored. He went to the window and glared out at the rain, scowling.

"Speaking of goat's tail, somebody's got to milk the goats. I don't remember if me and old Ruter did that the last few days."

He turned bloodshot eyes to the black man and blinked. "You know how to milk a goat?"

"Yas, sir, Mister Tulip, I can do that. But I ain't seed no goats around here."

"Up on the hill, behind the hives," Crozier said, waving his arm impatiently. "There ought to be a bucket here someplace."

He went back to the bed and sat down heavily, glaring around at the disheveled room.

"We got to get this mess cleaned up."

"I can do that, Mister Tulip."

Crozier rubbed his face with his hands, opening his mouth like a lion yawning, stretching his jaw muscles.

"So, by God, I don't think I've been that drunk since they signed the treaty of Guadalupe Hidalgo back in 'forty-eight. Watching men shoot each other down develops a fierce thirst. 'Specially good men. What day is this?"

"I ain't kep' track, Mister Tulip."

For a long time Crozier sat staring into the black man's face, and Lark continued to grin at him.

"How old are you, Lark?"

"I ain't kep' track of that, either, Mister Tulip."

"So, haven't kept track? Well, it doesn't matter. You get older whether you keep track or not. You're almost as old as I am, I'd wager on it."

"I guess maybe I am, Mister Tulip."

"You don't look it, though. That's the difference. All right. Now tell me again what you said last night when that boy brought you in here."

"I come to hep' you with your place, Mister Tulip. Ain't nuthin' lef' at the tavern I want anything to do with."

"What about Polly Cox? What if she comes back and needs you?"

"Then I go where I's supposed to be, at the tavern. But she

ain't gone come back with them Yankees there. She may never come back. Nobody knows where Mister Cox is at. Maybe they won't none of 'em ever come back. So I'll hep you on your place."

"Help me with the place, is it? Now, how can you do that?"

"I make the bes' cracklin' corn bread in the county, Mister Tulip."

"You can't make cracklin' corn bread without hogs. Where you going to find a hog in this valley?"

"I can make hominy bread, too, and I can run a sorghum mill."

"Can you run a sawmill?"

"No, sir, I ain't ever done that."

"You'll likely cut off a hand before I can teach you—" He stopped and turned his eyes to the window for a moment, his face twisting as he recalled the scene in the Hasford kitchen. He rose and found the beaver hat, mud-splattered and soggy. He passed his fingers along the vane of the buzzard feather, as he always did each time before placing the old hat on his head. "Lark, you know why the Plains Indians use buzzard feathers in their arrows?"

"I don't know nuthin' 'bout them folks. Mister Cox say some of them folks is pure heathens."

"So. Well, I'll tell you about it someday. Get your coat and fetch that bucket over there and push the turnip soup off the fire, and we'll go out and find the goddamned goats. Is that jug empty?"

"Yas, sir, it was empty when I come las' night."

"Then we can assume it still is. I wonder if old Ruter's got any."

4   Roman hurried out to the barn as soon as he was up, but Spavinaw Tom was gone. In the back lot, Roman could see the pony's tracks in the mud, going toward Plum Thicket Ridge, in

the direction of White River. He found the two blankets neatly folded on the back porch.

He stood for a while under the eaves, watching the rain, wondering why the Indian had gone. He somehow felt disappointment, a sense of loss. Later, his beef stew breakfast lying heavily in his belly, he halfheartedly cut more shakes on the back porch, and then went up on the roof in the rain to try and find the leaks.

He thought about the young man lying close to death below him in the kitchen. He had begun to understand some of the things that were happening and the things that could happen. In a war, he thought, it is hard for a body to mind his own business. If the jayhawkers come, they will likely pay us a visit, knowing we are southern people. And now that we're tending to that man, the bushwhackers may come too, wanting to know why we are nursing a Yankee. He would not think beyond that. He would not think what night riders would do once they paid their visit. But somehow, he knew they would come.

5 There was no pain in his arm, only a throbbing, searing torture through his chest, pounding with each beat of his heart. Lights and shadows moved across his vision, even when his eyes were closed. And more clearly then than when he opened them and tried unsuccessfully to see. The great, cloudlike masses closed around him, swallowing him, creating a soundless wind that threatened to toss him from the bed like a dried leaf, although in fact he lay motionless. Across the blackness of the rolling shapes, a bright light appeared now and again, moving slowly from side to side, passing before him as though some invisible specter were walking through his mind with a lighted lamp.

Even in his tortured brain he could recognize the massive movement of formless darkness, for he had seen it before, when a child and with scarlet fever upon him, and his mother coming into the bedroom throughout the night with her small bed lamp, to bend over him. Now he could see her face, pained and thin, and her cool hand on his forehead. Then, the vision would disappear, and once more the tidal wave of crushing weight would roll across his mind.

When he had suffered scarlet fever, he had screamed in his delirium, had tried to claw his way out of the bed and away from the consuming shapes. But now, he lay quietly, quivering as the sensations passed through his fevered body. As each attack passed, he lapsed into dreams, sharply defined and somehow terrifying.

He could see his father, carrying his mother about the house, she in the long lace-covered gown she almost always wore, often too weak to walk from rocking chair to dining table. He could see her wan smile, and the total acceptance of her affliction, acceptance of the unknown, for no doctor had been able to diagnose the sickness that left her weak after only the slightest effort. And he dreamed of the later days, too, when he himself had carried her about the house, frail and delicate and light as a peacock feather.

But his dreams were only quick and jumbled impressions, and then were gone. Now he could hear in the darkness—the voices around him, a low murmur of varying tone, like the distant movement of water along a rocky shore, the sounds beating into his brain softly. During the daylight hours there was some vague glow, bluish and weblike, across one corner of his awareness, even though his eyes were closed. And at night, when he tried to see with his eyes open, there was the harsh orange blur of light from lamp or fire. But he was unable to focus on any of it, not even the shapes that moved just above him.

The violent seizures of delirium came at less frequent intervals, and he dreamed more, peacefully and sometimes breaking into a cold sweat as his body fought off the fever temporarily. He saw in his head the stacks of produce on the Saint Louis docks, where he had earned money as a boy on Saturday afternoons. Then the streets of the city at dusk, the lights coming on in shop windows as he hurried along to be home with his father, just returned from the lead mines south of the city.

His dreams had no order to them, no continuity. And although they were not as frightful as the nameless shapes, there was violence there. The horsemen in Union blue surging about him, and the snap of bullets in the trees from unseen enemies. The first red stain of metal on the breast of a companion, the shouting and the smoke of artillery fire rolling across brown fields. He could hear the drumrolls and a band, and see a line of young girls, waving handkerchiefs, and then a horse, beheaded by a solid shot, writhing mightily as he tried to disentangle his feet from the stirrups.

Faces appeared, floating in smoke, and he recognized his two friends from school days, wearing the insignia of sergeants, one of them bellowing and showing gold teeth. And the defiant glare of a captured rebel, looking like some hairy beast of the forest, snarling and held between two horses, the troopers in blue taunting him.

And a woman's sweet mouth, sipping cider from a crystal cup, and once again his mother's face above the tiny coffin of a baby girl, his sister, taken by that same scarlet fever after two months of life. He saw his father's tears, and the open hole in the ground, and he heard the sounds of spades in the loose dirt as his father pulled him away toward the waiting buggy.

The afternoon sun, coming through the window beside his bed and shining across his face, began to feel warm. He dreamed of another sunlit window, and the row of large books, leather-bound and massive, and his father, older then, with gray sparse hair and his false teeth clicking, explaining the majesty of the law and how it operated in civilized nations.

And he felt himself rising slowly, to conscious sensation,

with the pain now localized along his arm and shoulder. It was like surface diving in the river below the docks, once again as a boy, plunging down into the cold water, then up again, head held back and eyes open, seeing the clear light of the water's surface coming swiftly to meet him as he rose from the blue depths.

For two days cold cloths had been applied to his head and food forced between his lips, along with a little of the whiskey. And then at last his fever broke completely, and he was bathed in sweat that had to be mopped constantly from his brow. His eyes opened fully then, and clearly, and the first thing he was conscious of seeing in this house was the face of Calpurnia Hasford, bending over him.

XI

A week after the young man in Ora Hasford's bed regained consciousness, one of the bluetick hounds came home. It was a late-March day that smelled of spring, with the sky cloudless and the oaks and hickories standing bare, waiting for the burst of new foliage. Already a few sparrows had arrived to camp in the barn, and twice they had seen Carolina chickadees, with their tiny white-and-black faces, masked like a Comanche painted for war.

Ora was in the backyard boiling clothes in a cast-iron pot over an open fire when she saw the dog coming down through the woods behind the barn. He was mostly hide and bone, and the joints of his slowly wagging tail showed like great peas in a tight skin pod.

In the garden patch, Roman pulled in Bess, wrapped the reins around the plow handles, and came over, clucking to the dog in a low voice. The hound stood with his tail whipping, head down, and allowed Roman to pat his flanks a few times. And then he walked over to the porch and lay down beside the grinding wheel, head on paws, watching with doleful eyes, as though he had never been gone.

It was a time to be remembered, because on that day, too, the young federal officer began to talk. For the entire week, he had said little except "Thank you, ma'am," when they fed him or combed his hair. Calpurnia in particular had wanted to ask him who he was, where he came from, how he came to be there. But

Ora refused to allow it, her respect for the man's privacy stronger than her own curiosity.

The stump had begun to heal well, to Ora's considerable amazement. Color had come back into the young man's face, and he had become more and more aware of what was happening around him. He seemed to accept his maiming without emotion, except for once when Ora came in from the parlor quietly and found him crying. They had strung a clothesline hung with quilts across the kitchen, creating a makeshift bedroom. Usually the quilts were drawn back so he could watch the family move about the kitchen and hear their conversation.

Calpurnia did most of the nursing, although there were a few things Ora managed herself. She bathed him and helped him out of bed and onto the chamber pot when the situation required, and on each such occasion she sent her daughter out of the house on some errand. His increasing embarrassment when he needed the pot seemed a good sign of returning health.

And as the days passed, his eyes became more alert and seemed constantly to follow Calpurnia as she moved about the kitchen helping her mother prepare the frugal meals. Mostly, they were eating corn bread and fried squirrel or rabbit.

"Don't waste shot on quail," Ora had told Roman. "It takes too many of them to make a meal, and there's no fat in them for gravy." She was still hoarding the sack of white flour that had come from Elkhorn Tavern, using only a small handful each night.

It was going on toward sundown that day, Calpurnia at bedside spooning corn bread and gravy-squirrel stew into the young man's mouth, when he looked at her for a long moment and smiled. It was a weak smile, barely showing the straight but slightly yellow teeth beneath the cornsilk mustache Ora had left when she shaved him with one of Martin's old razors.

"Calpurnia's a nice name," he said. At the table, Ora and

Roman stopped eating, startled, and looked toward the bed. The girl's face reddened only a little, and she returned his gaze directly.

"What's yours?" she asked.

"Allan Eben Pay," he said. "I live in Saint Louis."

Once he had begun, they could not stop him. Ora came to the bed and felt his forehead to be sure he wasn't feverish again. He seemed intent on spilling out everything about himself at once, leaving nothing for a later time, as though anxious to have them know whom they had lying in their bed and eating their food. Even when Ora remonstrated with him about exerting himself, he went on. Roman stayed well back in the room, treating this Allan Eben Pay as he might someone with a catching disease.

Pay's voice came haltingly at first, it having been a long time since he had spoken at any length. He constantly wet his lips with the tip of his tongue. Beneath the mustache, his wide mouth and rather full lips moved elaborately, Calpurnia thought, the enunciation exact and the words coming sharply, so unusual in this country where most of the people rolled their vowels in a long slur.

Had Pay known precisely the order of Ora Hasford's priorities, he could not have better impressed her, for he told first of his family. They were Welsh, and in America only a generation before he was born. His father had worked the lead mines, but studied at night, and never having had any formal training, passed the bar in Missouri. Saint Louis had been a booming city of commerce before the war, with money to be made. And when it came Allan's time, he had been sent to college in Illinois.

But his own emergence before the Missouri bar had been short-lived. A year after his name had been burned into the shingle that already bore his father's, the war had come. When Sterling Price took the state militia out against the Union, he had been swept up in the passion of the moment and entered his name on the rolls of a federal cavalry regiment. He was commissioned at once, being a young man of means and education, although of no experience whatsoever in the tactics of horse soldiers.

He had fought at Wilson's Creek with some distinction, and then at Pea Ridge, as the federals were now calling it. On the days of battle, here in this valley, he had done the duty of cavalry, screening the eastern flank of Curtis's army. He was surprised and pleased to learn that it was this very house to which he had come asking for water for his troops.

"Now I recall," he said, looking at Calpurnia's face. "I had wondered how it was that you seemed so familiar. You watched us through the window. And you were kind to us that day, too," his eyes turning to Ora. "Now I remember."

But his recollection of what had happened after the battle was hazy. He had been wounded in the hand, and seeing the nature of it and knowing how many of the field surgeons cut quickly, he had avoided the medical corps, hoping the wound would cure itself.

At this point he stared at the bandgaged stump still elevated on one of Ora's pillows. His face twisted, and they thought he might cry again. But he smiled instead, and shrugged his slender shoulders under the blankets that covered him to the chin.

"But it was something I could not avoid, it seems."

"You'd have died if we hadn't taken it. You'd been better to have let the doctors see it early because it got gangrene," Ora said quietly. "Now, you've talked enough. You shouldn't excite yourself."

But he went on anyway. Two days after a rebel rearguard patrol had fired the shot that found his hand, he had lost his senses during a night skirmish and fallen from his horse. His own men had gone on and left him, pressed by rebel cavalry and not knowing where to find him in the dark. That was all he could recall until he opened his eyes and saw Calpurnia bending over him, wiping his brow.

"Somebody took all your clothes," Ora said.

He lay for a while, his eyes moving back and forth between the women, his brow wrinkled as he tried to remember. Now, in the lowering light from the windows, his gray eyes were darker. He finally shook his head slowly.

"I can't seem to recall. I would imagine it was someone who had straggled from the battlefield. I am afraid that such things are not uncommon among armies. And I assume they took my pocketbook as well?"

"Everything," Ora said.

He sighed and a wistful smile touched his lips.

"There was good currency there. I had just been paid, a few days before the battle. The first time since I enrolled in the regiment. All my identification gone as well. So you have cared for me this while without knowing who I am."

"Only now, when you've told us," Calpurnia said. "I've been wondering who you were and giving you all sorts of names."

Across the room, Roman scowled.

"I hope my real one, now you know it, is not such a great disappointment," Allan Pay said.

Now Ora would not be denied. She pulled the covers up tight under his face and shooed her daughter back from the bed. Pay looked through the open window, listening to the calls of birds.

"What is that I hear? There. Hear it?"

"Yes, that's a cuckoo," Ora said. "He'll be making that racket well into the night, and then the mockingbirds will start. I'll close the window."

"I had no idea there were cuckoos here," he said. "It's a pleasant and soothing sound."

Suddenly he looked at her and there was anguish in his eyes. "My family. I need to let them know I'm not lost."

"There's not much mail now between here and Missouri," Ora said. "But we'll manage it somehow. Don't worry. Try to rest."

"I thank you. For everything you've done. But I do not know your name. Only the others calling you Mama."

"I'm Ora Hasford. This is my husband's farm." She paused, then continued, watching his face. "He's off in the army. In the southern army."

Their eyes met for an instant, and some understanding passed between them, an agreement that here in this room the war did not matter.

"I had assumed as much," he said softly. "I am therefore doubly grateful."

Later, splitting wood in the backyard, Roman said to her that he thought it best he ride over to Elkhorn Tavern.

"You'll do no such thing."

"If he's well enough off to do all that talking, then his own people ought to come get him and take care of him."

"In the first place, I don't want you around that tavern," she said. "Maud Ruter rode by here the other day and said those soldiers over there are nothing but rowdies. And besides, there's no one there to take care of him. No doctor, you found that out yourself."

"There's no doctor here, either," Roman said.

"The man was brought to our door, and we'll take care of him. For the time being, anyway. He seems a nice young man, and from a good family."

"Well, he's just a Yankee as far as I'm concerned," Roman muttered.

"If you don't stop leaning on that ax, it's going to take root. Now split a few more for me, and hush about the tavern. We'll bide our time."

Muttering sullenly, Roman turned back to the still-stained chopping block. He began to swing the ax with a vicious snort, cleanly splitting oak chunks into cookstove staves with each stroke.

"If the bushwhackers come riding in here, you know what they'll do to him, don't you?"

It pained her that Roman spoke so harshly. She knew he was unsettled over the Yankee officer lying in their house, but she wasn't sure exactly why.

"Though I have faith to move mountains and do not have charity, I am nothing," she said.

Roman paused, the ax half-raised.

"What?"

"Nothing. We're finished talking about it," she said, bending down to take up an armload of split staves. "We'll just wait and see. Nobody's going to move that wounded boy just yet."

But she would find herself arguing that point with the Yankee army sooner than she could have imagined.

2 Commerce along Wire Road had come to a virtual stop. No stagecoaches ran, no Springfield wagonloads of flour and cured meat and rice came down from Missouri to be marketed in the small stores throughout the valley. The stores themselves were largely deserted now, as was most of Leetown, the people having departed as the armies came together. And not yet returned—if they ever would.

Food had become scarce everywhere. Soldiers had taken most of what there was, without benefit of requisition, usually at night and without knowing or caring that the rightful owners would go hungry as a result. Like soldiers in all times and all places, the men in both armies looked on livestock and poultry as fair game. What most of them would have considered common thievery in usual times became under the circumstances of war highly praised enterprise. And always there was the excuse, no matter true or not, that their own commissary department provided rations fit only for slopping hogs. As they passed on, they left behind a land scourged as if by locusts, in a valley which had barely had enough for its own people to start with.

Money was scarce as food. And those who had it could find no place to spend it, for there was little to sell. Everyone kept what was his, uncertainty of tomorrow making hoarders of them all.

News of what was happening passed more slowly, with less traffic on the roads; those people remaining in the valley stayed close to their farms. But news did pass nonetheless, carried by the few who braved any unknown danger simply to "visit," as they called it. Thus it came to Ora Hasford that old lady Epp had died. She had been one of the few still in Leetown, and they all said she had gone because she had grown tired of living. Of course, it was expected that the family would attend the funeral.

It was a small gathering, in the cemetery near the fields where the battle of Leetown had been fought. A Methodist minister came over from Bentonville to read some Scripture and lay the shriveled old body to rest in its wretched oak coffin. There was Tulip Crozier and Lark, the Ruters, the Hasfords, and perhaps a dozen more. They stood in two groups, widely separated across the open grave, those with sympathies for the south on one side, free-soilers on the other. They held no converse with one another and seldom exchanged glances, silently acknowledging what the war had done to former friendships.

"She had no friends, poor thing," Ora whispered.

"Her menfolk soured her," Maud Ruter said. "They ain't nobody I know was as ornery as her husband, less'n maybe it's that boy of hern."

Ora Hasford was surprised to see that Spider Epp was crying as the preacher said his piece. The wolf-eyed young man stood beside the grave, turning his hat in his hands, the wind blowing his straight hair down across his face. Tears wetted his cheeks and his nose was running. He wiped at it with a sleeve.

They began to lower the coffin into the hole with long ropes, and Tulip Crozier went over to help. Spider Epp clapped his slouch tight onto his head and glared at the old man.

"Get away from here, you Jew trash," he said, his jagged teeth showing as his lips peeled back in a snarl.

Crozier's face went livid. He stood uncertainly for a moment before turning away. Everyone had heard it, and there was an almost inaudible sigh among them as they began to drift back to their horses and wagons. Ora watched Spider Epp bending over his mother's grave. There was a bulge in his coat, and she knew he had a pistol there. Something about his long face, dark in the shadows of the wide-brimmed hat, made a cold knot grow in her stomach. Then she knew! This was the man who had come to her house that night with the jayhawkers, the man she had helplessly watched carry off two of her chickens. And she realized in that moment the thing she had secretly suspected. Someone in this valley was capable of turning against his neighbors and leading marauders to their dooryards. And that someone was Spider Epp.

Maud Ruter was saying something to her, but she hardly heard.

"They say you folks got a wounded man at your place," the old lady said with some hesitation, not wanting to be accused of prying.

"Yes, he's a nice young man," Ora said absently.

"They say he's a Yankee," Maud said. The sun shone on the white stubble across her chin.

"He's just a young man, and he was bad hurt," Ora said, a little impatiently. "He had no one else to take care of him."

"Ora, you're too kind for your own good. Well, you folks come see us."

They rode home in the wagon. Calpurnia sat in back, cross-legged in the wagon bed, and said she wished she hadn't come at all. It was depressing, and besides, they shouldn't be leaving Mr. Pay alone in the house. Roman, reins in hand, grumbled something under his breath and scowled.

"He's able to move around enough to take care of himself for a little while," Ora said.

But then she said no more, the shock and anger with the thought of Spider Epp making her face stony. She could recall times past when Martin had hired the boy Epp to help with timber cutting, before the elder Epp had died. His strange eyes had always fascinated her in some terrible way, yet he seemed a good worker, a good boy. When they drove in from the woods with a load of cut oak, he would come to the back porch for a cool drink of water, and there tease Calpurnia about her freckles, and she only a very young girl then.

Worse than Judas, she thought, to bring harmful men to the homes of people who had been his neighbors. But she said nothing of her discovery to the children. There was enough else to fret them.

3   Day was fading from the shoe shop, but Spider Epp did not light a lamp. He looked around at the hanging leather strips and the cutting table and the lasts and bins of needles and awls. He spat on the floor and walked slowly back into the kitchen, then into the lean-to bedroom where his mother had slept, and where once he had, too, on a floor pallet, before his father died and he'd moved onto the bunk in the shop.

He sat on the edge of his mother's bed, a lumpy cotton mattress on a crookedly grotesque iron bedstead, painted over long since with coats of white paint that were chipped and scarred. The single flannel sheet and the old quilt, the pieces coming apart in frays and looking dirty, were rumpled, and he could almost see the form of her frail body where he had found it.

He could not remember ever having seen his mother and father going to this bed together. From the time he was too young to think about such things, in Illinois on that dismal little farm on the edge of a dusty cornfield town, they had slept apart. Now, he wondered if perhaps his father had always found his mother a little repulsive, and marveled that he himself had ever been conceived.

She was ugly, all right, he thought. And the old man treated her like he did the horses they'd owned. Like a brute good only for work with the least amount of fodder possible, and with a whipping thrown in now and again just to let everyone know who was boss. The old man was good at whipping, all right. That son of a bitch!

Somewhere, his father heard about those big southern plantations, with all the slave labor working them, and the master sitting in the shade with a glass of cool whiskey. He always figured himself as good as any such so-called gentlemen, and when he found such things beyond his reach he came to hate them and their system. Not because he had any compunction about slavery, but because he felt left out of the better things, like lazing around with that whiskey while somebody else did the work. He had come to believe that there was nothing in the South but the big farms, the rich ones. It came as a rude shock, once he'd decided to emigrate there, to find out that everybody in the South wasn't rich, and he never forgave the South for his disillusionment. And he passed that down to his son, too, all the bitterness of disappointment.

The old man left off farming, taking to the cobbler's trade, before they came to the Ozarks. What work was done in the puny field behind the house was done by Spider's mother, and then by him as soon as he was big enough to handle a hoe. Spider didn't mind. He hated even the thought of school, and when his father put him to the field, like a mule, he was happy for it. Then came the time for learning this marvelous trade, the trade that would make them money enough to buy one of those big southern farms. Rich enough to own a milk cow as good as anybody's, and have beefsteak or fried chicken on the table on special Sundays.

But coming to Benton County, Arkansas, had cost them everything they had, and they never quite made it back. By then the boy was in his early teens, and he'd come to know well the leather strap across his back when the old man was displeased. He took his beatings like his mother always had, with the unblinking, soundlessness of a yard dog, flinching only a little at the heavier blows, even on the two occasions that had brought blood, and thinking all the while, You son of a bitch, why don't you up and die?

In this new country, Spider's father made no effort to school him. The valley boys came to know him. He was a bully with those he could bully, cowering before those he couldn't. They never took him to the woods to hunt, nor asked him to help them make traps for crawdads in Little Sugar Creek. They called him Spider, and taunted him for crawling out from under a rock, saying he was an outlander and his father was mean and his mother ugly. And sometimes, when he was caught shoving and kicking some smaller boy, the big brothers would appear and beat hell out of him. Then when he got home, his long, pinched nose streaming blood, his father would belt him again for getting himself into a fix of trouble.

That son of a bitch, Spider thought. He pulled the Navy Colt from his waistband and caressed it, liking the smooth surfaces. At least I got this out of him, even if it took his dying to do it. I could have used it to kill those cats.

Spider laughed abruptly in the quiet room, remembering. He'd contracted with people to get rid of cats they didn't want. He used the old man's single-barrel shotgun and his technique was simple enough. He would capture the offending cat, stuff it in a burlap bag, go into the woods behind Little Mountain, and throw the sack on the ground. When the cat clawed its way out, hair up and wild-eyed, he'd let go with the shotgun.

He charged people a penny a cat. When his old man found out about it, there was another thrashing, one of those that brought blood. Because the profit he made didn't even pay for the powder and cap, much less the shot.

He fingered the long octagonal barrel of the pistol, thinking of Tulip Crozier back then. Crozier had heard about the cat-killing and had come storming into the shoe shop one morning threatening all kinds of mayhem if it kept up. Old man Epp had just bowed and scraped, never attempting to defend his son by explaining that it wasn't Spider's fault if people wanted to get rid of their excess cats. He'd just stood there like a nigger, taking it all from that Jew bastard.

After Crozier left, Spider expected another beating, but all he got was a tongue-scalding. Old man Epp raved about the indecency of doing things that would bring a dirty Jew into their house with threats, and from that moment Spider hated Crozier as much as he did his own father.

If there was one thing his father ever taught him besides the leatherwork and hating southerners in general, it was that a Jew was a blight on the earth. If the old man had no respect for any of his fellows, he had even less for a Jew. He never explained why he felt this way. It had just sprouted in him somewhere along the line, and he planted it in his son, and Spider had the same thing growing inside himself across the years.

Spider never tried to reason it out. He took things as they came in a hard world, his mind incapable of sorting it all out. It was just there, like owls hating crows and women despising snakes.

Spider laughed again, thinking of the time he had taken payment from a customer who'd picked up his boots from the shop after they'd been repaired. Old man Epp had been along the creek, trying to catch sun perch. When he came back, he saw the boots were gone and wanted to know about the money they should have brought. Spider was as big as his father by that time, so he just smirked and shrugged his shoulders.

"You're worse than some goddamned Jew, stealing your own father's livelihood," he shouted, and Spider hit him in the mouth with his doubled, bony fist. There was a sudden thrill of satisfaction, seeing the startled fear in the old man's eyes. So Spider hit him again, and there was blood across the old man's face.

"Don't never call me no Jew!"

By God, Spider thought, he never tried to whup me anymore. But the old man got more vicious mean with Spider's mother after that. He did little, spiteful things. Once, the old lady had a table set with a jar of wood violets in the center, and the old man glared at them a moment and then flung them against the wall.

"Iffen you can't eat it, don't set it before me on my table," he'd said, and Spider thought it was funny at the time. Now he wondered why he hadn't hit the old man again, right there at the supper table.

He looked at the rumpled bed, where his mother had lain all these years, awake in the night, thinking of ways to bedevil her menfolk, to pester them like a stinging gnat as some small revenge for the dismal life she'd led. Spider was not at all sure of his feelings for her. He'd never thought too much about it. She had always been just that ugly old woman, paying him little mind except when she was nagging. He wondered why he had cried when they put her in the ground. She was no longer any earthly use to anybody, even to him, and he was embarrassed that the tears had come.

Well, to hell with it all, he thought, I surer than shit ain't gonna be no shoe cobbler all my life. Rising, he went back to the kitchen. One of the ladies at the funeral had given him a small pot of boiled turnips with a little bacon fat, and he ate that cold, thinking about the armies and wishing they would come back and fight again on this same ground.

I wonder what it was that made the old man ask a promise I stay here with her, take care of her till she was gone? Then he laughed bitterly. That son of a bitch. Likely he done it just for a last slap at me, makin' me take all her spit and prattle, and him gigglin' in hell thinkin' about me still having to put up with her. Well, what he never knowed was, I'd have stayed on anyway, promise or not. I don't know why, but I would.

When he was finished, he wiped his mouth on his sleeve and made a last walk through the rooms, gathering his few articles of clothing. He pulled them into a tight bundle, spat again across the darkening kitchen, and went out to the shed to saddle the army stallion.

4 The two pigs were back in the sty. There was little enough to feed them, except the acorns Calpurnia gathered in the woods each day for that purpose. They were scrawny and red-eyed, more squeal than meat, Ora said. Yet the temptation to roast them was great.

Great, too, was the temptation to cook the few seed potatoes that lay on their dark shelf in the root cellar, waiting to be halved and planted as soon as Roman had the ground ready. They lay in the darkness, sprouts already pushing through the shriveled skins, and they were much on Ora's mind each evening when there was little to cook except the constant corn bread and whatever small game Roman had brought in.

If the season would only hurry. There were other seed waiting, the corn locked in a wagon box in the barn loft, selected last fall by Martin before he marched away. There would be radishes and onions and cucumbers and watermelons, but all had to wait their season. Ora thought that spring had never been so long coming.

When her desperation had almost gone beyond endurance, they found half a venison hanging one morning from the rafters of the back porch. It was cleanly dressed and ready for butchering, and in one flank was a large, ragged hole.

"Spavinaw!" Roman said when he saw the wound and thought of the Indian's Yager rifle. "He's still hunting the White River country."

"You see? It always comes back to you when you're decent to people," Ora said, but Roman frowned, thinking of Allan Eben Pay still getting most of the attention from everybody as he lay in the kitchen bedroom or moved cautiously about the house with his stump in a tight sling against his chest.

The weather was warming fast and they had to eat the deer meat quickly. For four days they gorged themselves on venison steak, then Ora made a giant stew in her wash kettle with what was left. It went sour before they were finished with it, and they fed it to the pigs.

And two days after that, Lark appeared in the dooryard leading one of Tulip Crozier's nanny goats. He seemed reluctant to come near, but finally did when Ora called that the sassafras tea was hot. Lark sat on the edge of the porch, loudly sipping the tea and grinning at the goat tied to a porch roof support. The goat pulled back on the tie rope and set up a great racket, her marble eyes glaring about.

"This here is a goat that's half-wild, Miz Hasford," Lark said. "But she gives a little milk. Ain't no good for butter. But Mister Tulip say it's all right for a cool drink now and again. You set it in the springhouse, and it'll make good sop." Which was his way of saying gravy.

"She looks to me like she might butt," Calpurnia said from the doorway.

"Yes, ma'am, she do, a little. You tie her to a tree to milk her. And you can let her graze in the woods, but you best tie her on a chain lead, 'cause she'll eat through a rope and run off."

"You tell Tulip Crozier we're beholden," Ora said. "And tell him our young officer is going to be well before long."

Lark looked up at her and shuddered.

"He tole me you all cut off that man's han'. I seen enough of that at the tavern to las' me my lifetime."

"He'll be fine. You tell Tulip Crozier."

"Yes, ma'am, I will. Mister Tulip, he'd have brang the goat, only he say his welcome done wore out here."

"Well, I knew something was chewing on him. He hardly spoke to us at the funeral. You tell him his welcome is never wore out here. So long as he's sober."

"Oh, he's a sober man, now, Miz Hasford. He done drank up all his whiskey."

Roman came over from the garden, his shirt plastered with sweat and his boots gummy with fresh-turned earth. Lark grinned at him and bobbed his head.

"You's almos' as wet as you was las' time I seed you."

"It's mule work," Roman said. He sat on the edge of the porch and wiped his face with his hat.

"Mister Roman, you know ole man Taliferro, live up on that farm outside Mudtown?"

"Sure. We sold some timber to him one winter. A while back."

"Well, sir, the other night they was four men with pillow-cases on dey heads come in his house and hole his feet to the fire to make him tell where his money was hid at."

"I don't want to hear such things," Ora said sharply. "And thank God, we haven't any money for such people to be after."

"No, ma'am," Lark said, turning his face up to her, his eyes wide. "Mister Taliferro didn't neither."

5 He could feel the itch between the fingers of his left hand that was no longer there. He had heard old veterans talk about such things, but never until now quite believed it. It was not painful, but irritating. He gingerly felt the stump with the fingers of his right hand, probing against the thick bandage that Ora Hasford changed every day, but it only brought a sharp pain and no relief from the itching. The best way to control this, he thought, is to pretend it isn't there.

Since morning, he had wanted to be outside. It was a bright day, with clouds lying like explosions of cotton in great patches across the blue sky. The westerly breeze coming through the open windows brought the scent of newly sprouted things. He felt an urgency to be out of the confines of this room, to move with earth beneath his feet and where his vision would not be limited to the rectangles of the windows.

He thought, I have seen men at Wilson's Creek with amputated hands, walking back toward field hospitals within a few days of the knife. I don't know how many days, but surely no more than I have spent in this room.

Not that he disliked this room. He had become accustomed to its smells and its sounds and the people moving through it, sometimes in a dim haze as he lay dozing, but at other times sharp and clear, their voices sounding the soft slurs of hill folk.

As the late afternoon wore on, Ora went to the garden with Roman. Calpurnia was in the woods behind the barn. He had no idea what she might be doing there, being as yet only vaguely aware of what went on around this farm, but he did seem constantly to be wondering what the girl did when she was out of this room, out of his sight.

I have never seen a people who live so much in their kitchen, he thought. It is the center of their existence. In his own home, he had seldom seen his mother in the kitchen; with her frail constitution, there had always been the necessity of hiring a cook. And so they lived in their parlor and on the verandas in summer, in hanging swings and cushioned rockers. But largely, his mother lived in her bedroom.

He walked a little unsteadily across the room and stood in the open back doorway, leaning against the frame. He was dizzy, although just standing there and looking into the wide yard seemed to clear his head. But the movement made the stump throb with a deep pain that ran up to his shoulder.

Then he saw Calpurnia coming through the woods toward the barn, pulling the goat along on a ten-foot chain lead. Now and again the nanny would lower her head and make a short charge at the girl's back, but every time Calpurnia seemed to sense her there and turned to switch at the goat's face with a willow stick. Allan Pay laughed, watching the goat making her fake charges and stopping just short of the stick.

He could see the lines of Calpurnia's legs under the gingham skirt as she moved with long strides. The front-buttoned dress was tight around her small waist, and even though it was fuller across the chest, he could see the uplifting outline of her developed breasts. Her hair was pulled back into a braid, as she always wore it when she was doing chores. To keep it out of her face, he supposed. For whatever reason, it exposed her long neck, and he thought perhaps that was the most beautiful thing about her. That long neck.

No, not that, he thought. The eyes. What eyes she has, looking directly at you and suddenly appearing to have the wisdom of old age, but clear and bright, too, and penetrating. Yet only a girl.

No, not a girl, either, he thought. She's no girl, but a woman, and all of it. Even with those childish freckles. And *childish* was a word out of all context for Calpurnia. She had that quality to confuse him, to make his mind leap from one contradiction to the next. But thinking about her made the low throbbing pain in his arm less bothersome, and it seemed to dispatch the itching between the vanished fingers completely.

Perhaps it is the spring coming on, he thought.

Allan Pay stepped off the porch, unsure of his strength. His legs were wobbly, but he walked slowly to the barn, where Calpurnia was snubbing the goat close to an oak sapling. She went into the barn and quickly reappeared with stool and pail. She placed the stool close against the goat's flank and the pail beneath the two teats that thrust downward like horns.

She saw him then, and her eyes widened. She was standing half bent above the stool, holding her skirt in a wad between her legs, as though about to mount a saddled horse. He smiled at her, coming closer, and she straightened and put her hands on her hips, looking at that moment very much like her mother.

"What are you doing out here?" she asked.

"A little fresh air might be beneficial," he said, still smiling.

"Your teeth aren't very clean. You've got to start scrubbing them with salt and a willow stick. That's what we all do." And as though to show him the results he might expect, she smiled, too, showing her own strong, gleaming teeth.

"I suppose I could manage that," he said, clamping his lips shut.

"Papa says two sets of teeth are all you get. If they fall out before you're well on the way, then all you can eat is soup and honeycomb." She laughed, and he knew she was teasing him, though not about the willow stick and salt. "Did you ever milk a goat?"

"No. I've never milked anything."

"Then come on, and I'll show you how."

She pulled the stool back from the goat, to allow for his longer reach, and, with her hand under his good arm, helped him onto it. Her fingers were long and gripped his arm firmly, and he thought perhaps their touch alone helped dispel the ache in his arm.

"This goat doesn't smell too good," he said, and laughed.

"A goat's a goat," she said. "I like cows better, but for now, the goat's all we've got. Now, here's how you do it. Just take hold up close to the bag, with your thumb and one finger, and squeeze down, and then close your fingers all down on it at the end."

She took one of the teats and pulled down gently, her hand closing as she stroked it, and a jet of bright milk rang into the pail. She did it a number of times, the milk quickly spreading across the bottom of the pail.

"See? That's all there is to it. Go ahead."

The goat had settled against the oak sapling, waiting patiently for her milk to be taken. Allan Pay took a tentative grip and pulled, and Calpurnia laughed. The goat kicked and bleated again, her glassy eyes rolling.

"Not too hard. You're not supposed to pull it off. Just squeeze down, like this."

She showed him again, reaching past him, and the milk came down effortlessly. She moved back and Pay reached under the goat's belly. He was acutely aware of her closeness, and he could feel her breathing on his neck as she bent behind him. His second effort was no more successful than the first. At least the damned goat is standing still, he thought.

"It feels like a banana," he said.

"I don't know what a banana feels like. I've seen pictures of them, but I've never tasted one."

"They're firm and creamy and very good with milk and sugar, sliced in a bowl."

"I guess you've got lots of bananas in Saint Louis."

"They come upriver from New Orleans on boats. Or they did before the war. Clusters of them on stalks, mostly green, so they have to ripen on the river docks."

"You're still yanking on it. Be gentle with her. Where do bananas grow?" she asked.

"In Central and South America, I suppose. I've never made a study of bananas." He laughed once more, becoming accustomed to the feel of the goat and of Calpurnia's nearness. "I think the goat knows she's got a novice at this."

"Let me show you." She reached past him and her hand closed over his. "Just hold your hand loose and let me do it."

Calpurnia moved her hand on his, pressing his fingers against the soft teat, and a dribble of milk came and he laughed again, somehow feeling it an important accomplishment. He turned his face to her and she was very close, her eyes on the goat and their hands together beneath the goat's belly, and when she realized he had turned she pulled back, a faint dust of pink on her cheeks.

"Go on, you can do it by yourself, now."

He made a number of futile efforts before the milk began to come down, even then without the hard force he had seen under Calpurnia's hand.

"This would take me all day, to get that pail full," he said. A wave of light-headedness came over him and he bent his head to the goat's side.

"What's the matter?" she asked, and he was aware of the concern in her voice. "Are you all right?"

"Just a little dizzy."

"Come on," she said, and her strong hand was under his arm again, lifting him from the stool. "You're going back in the house, and no arguments."

He allowed himself to be led across the yard, glad of her support because he wasn't sure he could do it himself. There was a little difficulty making the step up onto the porch, but she half lifted him, and soon he was back in Ora Hasford's bed, panting a little, his arm throbbing.

"I guess milking a goat takes more strength than I thought."

"You be still, now," Calpurnia said. "I'll do the milking. But later you can try again if you want to."

When Ora came in, she made a great fuss that he'd been in the barn lot, but there seemed a note of pride in her voice as well. Roman was there, too, his hair and face still dripping from a dousing in the washbasin on the back porch. He listened to his mother's scolding, cutting his eyes now and again to Allan Pay's pale face. When Ora had finished, she drew a light comforter over Pay's legs and went to the safe to take down pans for cooking. Roman walked over to the bedside, beads of water running down his face.

"You try to milk that goat?"

"Not very well, I'm afraid."

"Well, a goat is easier to milk than a cow."

"I wouldn't be surprised."

"Cal's the best milker in the family. It takes a certain touch," Roman said, a little petulantly, and turned and walked away.

She's more than that, Pay thought. She's cool as winter ice, that girl, but with a heat from somewhere inside that would scorch you if it came out. Not a bad kind of burning, either. Better maybe than any brandy, better than any bananas with milk and sugar. Or if she wanted to, it could scald you and leave a scar that would last to the grave.

6 The Union army in the person of Captain Philip Sheridan arrived at the Hasford farm one morning when Roman was plowing one of the far cornfields across Wire Road and Calpurnia was on Plum Thicket Ridge collecting white-oak acorns for the pigs. Sheridan was in a dour mood. Since the battle of Pea Ridge, he had been in bad odor with General Curtis over the matter of mules and horses.

As the army's chief quartermaster officer, Sheridan had refused to pay for livestock brought to him by various groups of unsavory men, having decided that these animals were stolen. He had taken to the practice of confiscating them as captured enemy property, branding them with a *US* and sending the ruffians on their way without a cent. There had been considerable grumbling about this, particularly from his own assistant quartermaster officer.

This same man had complained to General Curtis about other aspects of the supply situation. Sheridan wasn't sure the exact nature of the complaints, but he knew they had come increasingly to the commanding general's ear. This assistant quartermaster was a scoundrel, Sheridan believed, looking for the opportunity to better himself by turning the war into a profitable business enterprise. There were such opportunities for the unscrupulous, and Sheridan loathed the thought of it.

This assistant quartermaster was supposedly a banker from Iowa, no proper soldier at all, and till now unsuccessful in any civilian venture. To Sheridan he was no better than the men who made up the bands of thieves and cutthroats operating along the borders of Kansas and the Indian Territory, preying on helpless citizens in the expectation their plunder would be cheerfully purchased by the United States government.

But sometimes rogues will out, even in the army, he thought. And now he was facing a court-martial because he had refused a Curtis order to pay for those stolen horses and mules. He often thought that a good brigade of cavalry should be dispatched to this place for the sole purpose of rooting out and hanging partisans, those soiled and hairy men who plagued the countryside and created the very conditions that made corruption in any army such a great temptation.

Now if a band of them could find a willing quartermaster, they could, for a small fee to him, create a ready market for stolen loot, and make a profitable game for all concerned. Such is the nature of those gone money mad, he thought, even be it money bought with the suffering of the innocent. They should all be hanged, as we hanged those Yakima braves for their outrages on Columbia River back in 1856.

He would ask the departmental commander to relieve him of his duties soon, so that he might get into proper field service. His efficiency in establishing the army's commissary service was partly due to an urgent restlessness at being relegated to rear-area duty. He wanted action, the command of men in battle, and he was sure Old Halleck would be sympathetic to his request regardless of the stories being circulated about disobedience of orders and other such foolishness.

But first, he had to deal with this federal officer, wounded and being cared for by a family identified long since as having southern leanings. Hiding a man in one's home is difficult, even in a wilderness community, he thought, and perhaps *hiding* is not the proper word. These people, whoever they were, had apparently made no effort to conceal the fact from their neighbors. As Sheridan had it, word had passed along the valley from an old man who ran a mill and had been involved somehow. Finally and inevitably, the information came to a man of Union sympathies. What was his name? Eads? No, the name was Epp, and although Sheridan had never seen him, the provost guards had indicated that he was a font of intelligence. Like Curtis, Sheridan hated informants, but their value could not be ignored. Still, the whole business was distasteful to him.

He found Ora Hasford, whose name he already knew through the agents, on the front porch with an old-fashioned stone mortar and pestle, grinding shelled corn. Sheridan could not recall ever having seen anyone make cornmeal by hand. She watched him ride up through the oaks with a calm face, her hand working the pestle. Behind her, in a rocking chair, was the young man whose identity Sheridan did not yet know, his left arm secured tight to his chest with a white cotton sling. As Sheridan approached, the young man started to rise, but the woman spoke to him and he remained seated in the rocking chair.

"My name is Philip Sheridan, ma'am, captain and chief quartermaster officer for the Army of Southwest Missouri," Sheridan said, doffing his hat. She continued to work the corn, looking him squarely in the eye.

"My name is Ora Hasford, and this is my farm. What is it you want?"

Looking at Pay, his hat in his hand, Sheridan said, "I believe I have come to inquire about this gentleman."

"This is Allan Eben Pay. He's part of your army. Or at least, he was once," she said.

"Captain," Pay said, nodding.

"What was your unit, sir?"

"I am a lieutenant of the Seventh Missouri volunteer cavalry."

"Information came to me that you were wounded and being held here."

"Sir, I would hardly say that I am being held. I am being cared for here," Pay said, and Sheridan noted some resentment in the young man's voice.

"A poor choice of words. May I inquire of your wound?"

Ora Hasford rose and turned toward the open front door.

"Light down, and I'll have some tea in a minute," she said.

"Thank you, ma'am," Sheridan said and quickly dismounted.

He tied the horse to a porch post and sat on the top step. "I see you have lost a hand, as I had heard. You should have come to the army field hospital."

"I had little choice in the matter, sir," Pay said. "But I doubt I could have had treatment any better, no matter where I had been taken."

"Then you were carried in to this place?"

"Yes, sir. My wound was taken on the last day of the battle, in a pursuit action, and became infected later. I was lost in the darkness. Lost from my troopers. Someone else found me and brought me here. I am really unsure of the details, because I am afraid infection came quickly and much of that time is hazy to me."

"This may seem a brutal question, Lieutenant, but are you convinced that there was a need to take the hand?"

"I have every confidence," Pay said, his face flushing with anger. "These people did what was necessary to save my life. There was another man here, a civilian, who had experience, I am told, in the medical department during the Mexican War, and has since acted as somewhat of a doctor in these hills."

Ora Hasford reappeared with a tray and cups of steaming tea, and Sheridan rose to take one, bowing slightly. Sipping the tea, he found it without sugar and rather bitter to his taste. Nonetheless, he continued to drink, and when the woman seated herself, so did he.

"I saw as I rode up that there are many marks of battle on your house and outbuildings," he said to her. "Where were you, Mrs. Hasford, when the battle was fought?"

"In this house," she said, a little defiantly, he thought. "Where I belong, with my children."

"You have children?"

"A boy and a girl. He is off plowing in one of our valley fields and she is out back collecting acorns to feed our pigs because your army left us little else to feed them. Only two little suckling pigs. That's all your battle left us in livestock."

"A battlefield is a dangerous place, Mrs. Hasford."

"This is not a battlefield, as far as I'm concerned. It is my home."

"I can appreciate your feelings."

"And in the midst of it, your soldiers came and carried my boy off because he was a danger to your army. Only a boy. And you took him to a place where the battle was fought, and very nearly got him killed."

"Those were not my soldiers, Mrs. Hasford. They were provost guards, and it was only their duty."

"They were wearing blue uniforms, whether your soldiers or someone else's."

Sheridan decided to change the subject, asking about the details of Allan Pay's wound. He listened attentively to the story of the ordeal, and continued to be uneasy with the idea that Pay had refused medical attention when he was first wounded. Such a thing went against form. Yet he had to admire the young man's determination to remain with his troops despite such a wound. Sheridan was aware that many soldiers ignored wounds, even serious ones, and went on with their duties through some sense of honor, or else because they were afraid of the surgeon's tent. In Pay's case, he suspected the former. He found the woman's part as surgeon with an ax almost unbelievable, yet there was the stump to give it credence.

"I would suggest that it is now time for you to move to an army hospital, in Springfield," Sheridan said.

"No!" the woman said. "He isn't ready yet for a ride over these bad roads."

He was startled at the vehement response. "I had supposed from looking at him that he was doing rather well," Sheridan said.

Turning to Pay, he continued. "Don't you feel well enough for travel, Lieutenant? I could send an ambulance."

"A wagon would be worse than horseback," Ora Hasford said quickly, before Pay could reply.

"I am still weak," Pay said. "For the time being, I think this is the best place for me."

"What is at stake, sir, is the best interest of the army."

Pay laughed. "Captain Sheridan, I suspect that our cavalry units are not that desperate for officers with only one hand."

"There are a number of men serving with greater disabilities."

"Perhaps among your regulars," Pay said. "But I am a volunteer and I was only just passable with two arms."

"There are other positions than the cavalry," Sheridan said.

"Perhaps later, Captain. But I doubt there is any great urgency anywhere for a man such as I am now. Besides, even in hospital, I would require some convalescence. I prefer to take mine here, so long as Mrs. Hasford will allow me to stay."

"Very well. I will so report to your superiors."

Having satisfied himself that Pay was perhaps as well off here as anywhere else, Sheridan allowed himself a few moments of idle conversation. Neither of the other two could fully appreciate this, not realizing that idle moments were rare with Phil Sheridan. He spoke of the many birds in this section, and of the profusion of oak species. Ora Hasford said that within a few weeks the hills would be blanketed with jack-in-the-pulpit, deer's-tongue, wild verbena, and violets. And soon the wild strawberries would be coming ripe. She said that he should try a cup of them, although they were devilish hard to pick. Her words were not completely warm, but neither were they discourteous.

"How long have you lived here, Mrs. Hasford?"

"All my life," she said. "Our families came from Georgia, and before that from Germany. A long time ago. We have always been farmers."

"My parents came from County Cavan, in Ireland. My father and mother were second cousins," Sheridan said.

Ora Hasford's face showed some subtle change—Sheridan wasn't sure exactly how, but she seemed to be almost smiling.

"My husband and I are second cousins, too."

At last he rose, and extended his hand. She took it.

"I have been pleased with your hospitality, Mrs. Hasford," he said. As had been the case throughout much of their conversation, she returned his look directly.

"I have nothing to fear from a man in uniform," she said. "Now that everything I had has already been stolen."

Sheridan's face turned slightly pink, but although there was no show of friendship from this woman, neither was there hostility. He took her words as a statement of fact and said his good-bye graciously, doffing his hat again and bowing.

As he mounted, he was aware that Pay had followed—over the protest of the woman, he was sure. Sheridan looked down into the gaunt face, and the young man appeared to hesitate a moment before speaking quietly, so the woman could not hear.

"Captain Sheridan, these people have done everything they can for me. But I am concerned about my mother and father. I am concerned that they likely think I was lost in the battle."

"You may rest assured on that, Lieutenant. I will send a note to your father as soon as I return to Springfield."

"I thank you for that, Captain."

"I will tell them that you were wounded but that you are doing well. However, you should write them yourself and explain the nature of your wound. It needs telling before you arrive at their doorstep. And better you tell it than I."

"Yes," Pay said. He hesitated again, as though unsure of how to express himself. Then he went on haltingly. "Captain Sheridan, these good people here are very nearly destitute."

"I am sorry to hear that," Sheridan said.

"Their milk cow was killed, their hog run off by all the racket of battle, their potatoes stolen by our soldiers, I'm afraid."

"I had heard that many of these people are in dire circumstance."

"In your position, sir, might it not be possible to provide some small amount of foodstuffs?"

"The army cannot feed the entire state of Arkansas, Lieutenant."

"I implore you to consider this case, sir. Any small thing, any gesture might help heal the wounds we've inflicted on these people."

"These people were the ones who desired to dissolve the Union, sir. There are those who feel they are getting only what they deserve."

"Captain, this woman and her children hardly understand the concept of Union. Their lives have been here, in the wilderness."

"Having been in the army such a short time," Sheridan said, "you apparently do not understand that material and rations purchased by the United States government must be accounted for, item by item. I cannot ration unauthorized civilians, even those who are providing hospital for one of our soldiers. This is not a case of the army making requisition on a civil community. It has been done by their own choice and free will, and now by your own."

"I ask you to reconsider, Captain Sheridan," Pay said. Sheridan reined his mount around and gave a short salute.

"I am afraid such a thing would be impossible."

But two days later, a pair of mounted soldiers arrived and deposited on the front porch ten pounds of salt pork, a fifty-pound sack of white flour, another of dried navy beans, five pounds of sugar, and two dozen lemons. Before Ora Hasford arrived from the backyard, the soldiers had ridden off, down the slope to Wire Road, and she found Allan Eben Pay alone, standing over the plunder with a wide grin. She stared a moment, only slowly realizing what had happened, and then with a shout of delight threw her arms around him and kissed his cheek.

XII

The beginning of dawn was fading the eastern sky pale gray, so the tops of the trees showed along the slope behind the farmyard. Roman was on the back porch, recharging the shotgun for hunting. It was an easy operation. He always loaded the gun with a felt wad on top of the shot, which came out quickly when he used the worm attachment on the ramrod, and then the shot would roll out as he tipped down the barrel. Normally he kept the gun charged with number-four shot, a good all-around load, but for hunting he used eights in one barrel for squirrel and rabbit and buckshot in the other on the chance of seeing deer or turkey.

Finished, he swung the powder horn over one shoulder. In one pocket he had shot, in the other caps. He was ready to move off into the timber when he heard a soft shuffling sound behind him. Allan Pay was standing in the kitchen doorway, clumsily pulling on one of Martin Hasford's old woods jackets.

"Are you going out to hunt?" he asked softly.

"I thought I might," Roman said defensively, a slight irritation in his voice, which Pay ignored.

"I'd admire going with you."

"Well," Roman said reluctantly, looking at the loose sleeve of his father's jacket where it hung below the stump of Pay's left arm. "If you think you can keep up. The way they treat you around here, I thought you might still be peaked."

"I feel good. I think I can keep up, if you'd have me along. If I can't, I'll sit and rest and then come back into the house."

Pay was smiling, and against his better judgment Roman could not refuse him.

"Come on, then," he said brusquely, and set off toward the woods, intentionally walking faster than he usually did. The dog started to follow, but Roman sent him back to the porch with a word. They were well into the timber before Pay spoke.

"Why don't you hunt with the dog?"

"Because that's a coon dog," Roman snapped impatiently. "I don't want him ruined chasing squirrels and rabbits. I always still-hunt squirrel and walk-hunt rabbits."

"Walk-hunt?"

"Yes, you just walk along one of these roads around here early in the morning or at evening, and they come out to play in the dust in front of you. I guess you've heard of still-hunting." His voice was sarcastic, but Pay seemed not to notice that, either.

"Yes, I know what still-hunting is. You find a place and wait. I've never done either kind. I've never hunted at all. I've fished a good deal, but never hunted."

"Well, a coon dog or foxhound don't make a very good squirrel dog, anyway. What you need for a squirrel dog is some brown mongrel yard-breed. But then he'll keep you awake nights, barking at everything and running around treeing squirrels when you're not even hunting him. Coon dogs you want to sound for coons only, and foxhounds for fox, and nothing else."

"Do you eat raccoons?" Pay asked, and Roman slowed enough to look back at him, marveling at such ignorance.

"Hell's name! You don't eat coons, nor fox either. You take 'em for hides. When you take 'em at all. Mostly you just run fox to hear the dogs sounding him. Coons you sometimes take, but just for the hide."

Roman began to feel a great sense of superiority. This dumb Yankee doesn't know anything about the woods, he thought. No wonder he had to be dragged in half-naked by some Cherokee Indian.

"And coons aren't all that easy to take. If a coon can get to water, deep water, it takes one fine dog to pull him out. Best dog we ever had was drowned trying to pull a big he-coon off a log in the middle of a hole of water in White River once. Papa got so when a coon went into water, he'd not let his dogs go in after him, if he could get there in time to stop 'em."

"I never knew a raccoon was that capable of taking care of himself."

"They are. They're a nice little critter, except when dogs take in after them, and then they're hellish mean. Now, stop making so much noise. We'll run the squirrels clear to White River with all this talk."

Roman had slowed by now, searching the trees ahead. He moved back along a bench, where hickories and walnut trees vied with the oaks for growing room, found an old log he had used many times before, and sat down on it, head and gun muzzle up. He was pleased to note that Allan Pay was breathing heavily, and that there was high color in his cheeks.

They waited, listening to the woods awakening, the birds beginning to move through the trees, and off to the east a late-hunting fox yipping to warn her cubs that she was coming back to den. It was Roman's favorite time in the woods, when everything smelled fresh and every detail and outline was clearly defined in various shades of gray, slowly going lighter and taking on color as the sun rose. They waited only a short time before Roman shot the first squirrel from a tall, half-dead hickory, reloaded, and waited for the echoes of the shot to die and movement to start again in the trees. The second he shot without changing position, less than ten minutes after the first, and out of the same hickory.

The squirrels had fallen ten yards apart, and Roman went

directly to them and carried them along the bench to a small, clearwater spring, Allan Pay moving behind and making a great deal of noise in the leaves and underbrush. Roman skinned them quickly, slicing a small cut through the skin along the back, then slipping in his fingers, pulling the hide off toward both ends all the way to neck, tail, and lower joint of the four legs. He cut off the head and tail and feet with the large blade of his pocketknife, gutted them, and tossed the entrails into the brush. The whole thing took less than a minute.

"That old gun shoots a good pattern," he said proudly, picking shot from the small, red bodies with the point of the knife blade. He was feeling a little better about having this Yankee watch him work the woods. It was a thing he had confidence in because he'd been doing it a long time. "She'll shoot a pattern not much bigger than your fist at fifty paces. That's all right for birds, if you lead 'em far enough and just let 'em fly into the pattern. But with squirrels, you end up with a lot of lead in your meat."

"Can you kill deer with that thing, too?"

"Sure, for close shots. In brush country, and most of the hunting around here is in that kind of country," Roman said, warming to his subject. "It's not much good for long shots, say over fifty paces, but inside that, buckshot works all right. But I like a rifle for deer."

"I don't see how you clean them so fast," Pay said, and Roman looked closely to see if he was serious, not making light of anything.

"It's easy. A deer takes a little longer." And he laughed.

Overhead, there was a scrambling of gray bodies, and looking up they saw two squirrels frolic among the branches, out to enjoy the new sun after only a short time of impatient waiting, too young yet to know the danger of woods where there had been gunfire. Roman had not reloaded the gun. He and Pay squatted by the spring, watching the squirrels play.

"You're not going to shoot them," Pay asked.

"Two's enough. You don't want to overhunt your woods. You want to leave a few for tomorrow."

"I'd thought from what I'd seen that there are plenty of them for tomorrow."

"There's plenty for tomorrow because I don't try to kill them all today," Roman said derisively.

They started back, more slowly now, and Roman picking the best pathway through the timber and brush.

"Did you like being in the army?" Roman asked.

"Not very much."

"I wanted to join the army once," Roman said, as though it had been ages ago, and him not yet a man. Allan Pay smiled, but he was walking behind and Roman did not see it.

"Are you still so inclined?"

"I don't guess so. I've seen enough of armies to last me my life," Roman said expansively. "If a body could see armies first, before he joined up with them, he might not ever join up at all."

"Some men enjoy it," Pay said. "It takes a particular kind of man, but some do."

"Well, Papa had to join up. I don't guess there was a single way to keep him from it, once he'd set his mind. When Papa sets his mind, he goes ahead and does it, whatever. We've had two letters from him."

"Yes. Calpurnia told me about it."

With mention of his sister's name, Roman's jaw clamped tight, and that was the end of the conversation.

2 Seventy miles northwest of the Hasford farm, in a sycamore grove along the banks of the Neosho River in upper Cherokee Nation, Colonel Clarence Caudell was holding his band in readiness for their next foray into northern Arkansas or southern Missouri,

depending on his whim. It was a filthy, ragged crew, fully bearded and with hair hanging to their shoulders under wide-brimmed hats caked with sweat and dust. They moved about the encampment slowly, eyes wary and heads thrust forward as though sniffing the breeze that blew in from the high grass flats along the river. Their long coats, frayed at the bottom, almost brushed the ground as they walked. They looked like a pack of beasts that had just emerged from long hibernation. Their eyes were red rimmed from too much wood smoke, their skins leathered and wrinkled from too much wind and sun.

Despite their appearance, they had gold coins in their pockets and silver plate in their packs, taken from various farms and settlements scattered over a three-hundred-mile radius. Their horses were sleek and strong, and their weapons Colt or Remington percussion revolvers. There were even a few Spencer carbines, the brass cartridge repeater patented in 1860.

Squatting before the fire, one of the men slowly turned a spitted calf over the coals. The aroma of the cooking meat drifted through the grove, making the others smack their lips.

On a campstool facing the fire, legs spread on either side of his massive belly, was Colonel Clarence Caudell himself. Of all the men in this band, he alone showed any sign of grooming. His blue cavalry hat was well-brushed and the gold band and acorns on it gleamed. His cape showed only a few stains of mud and grease, and the pistol belts about his middle shone with leather polish.

He was, in fact, a fastidious man in everything except his table habits. Even now his men throughout the grove quietly joked among themselves about it, saying the old man would likely eat half that calf himself. But at least they knew the cooking would not take long, because the colonel did not enjoy waiting for his meals, and sometimes, therefore, they all ate their meat half-raw.

And they joked, too, about his bib, though not loud enough

for him to hear. To avoid splattering his clothing with hard-to-remove grease, he carried a bedsheet in his saddlebags and draped it about himself when he ate. By now the sheet was a smudged, dirty gray, but it continued to serve its purpose.

Those same saddlebags were on the ground beside him now, and he took from them a small Bible. He read a few chapters, as was his custom before eating, or at any other time the spirit moved him. Sometimes he gathered his men about him and read aloud, concentrating on the heathen-in-the-land passages, or the fall of Jericho in the Book of Joshua, or the destruction of Dagon in First Samuel. He inclined toward stories of nonbelievers being smitten, and he never touched on the charity of the New Testament. Judges was his favorite book.

Once, he had been a lay minister in some church none of them had ever heard of, but it was most certainly of the hell-and-brimstone variety. He had taken his wartime mission from the testaments, with the inspiration of old John Brown always before him. Not a single one of his followers shared in his sense of mission, though they enjoyed the spoils from it.

Nor did any of them complain about the little sermons he sometimes preached, especially before a raid, because they had seen his wrath rise up like thunderheads, his eyes going glassy with rage. They had, in fact, seen him hang two men in his own band for contradicting him on some minor point of tactics or doctrine. And so they listened in silence to his roaring exhortations, because they did not want to feel about their necks the bite of the baling wire he always carried in long coils.

He was zealous in his aims, to the point of self-destruction. Had he known what was going to happen, he would gladly have joined old John Brown at Osawatomie and later at Harpers Ferry and even later still on the gallows at Charles Town, Virginia. He considered that day in December of 1859 when they executed the fiery abolitionist to be the darkest in man's long history. There were times, in his daydreaming, when he expected John Brown to be resurrected from the grave.

But even though he professed—and believed in—his mission, his holy crusade, he was not beneath taking a profit from it. He called it reaping from the collection plate of the Lord God of Hosts, passed amongst the heathens. And when there were particularly rich takings, his spirit rose to such a dizzy height he felt compelled to help it stay there by the use of strong drink. Therefore, when on campaign, his men were accustomed to seeing him tight as a tick, as they said, and sometimes dead drunk.

Caudell was reading his Bible and combing his great black beard with his fingers when two of his men brought Spider Epp into the camp. One of them led the army stallion stolen at Winton Springs, and the other held the Navy Colt.

"We found this one comin' upriver, Colonel?" one of the shaggy men said. "Says he's been out lookin' fer us. Says he's rid with us before, over in Arkansas. I don't recollect ever seein' him."

The Colonel's hard black eyes examined Spider only for an instant, then turned back to the Bible. He continued to comb his whiskers with his fingers.

"Your memory is somewhat less than admirable, Henry," Caudell said.

"You remember me, don't you, Colonel?" Spider Epp said, grinning and showing his deranged teeth. "I was with you a while back, in Benton County, right before they had that big battle there. I showed you boys the best way out of that valley, remember?"

"I recall, sir. There is no need to refresh my memory. My mind is a map, a map of all past campaigns, and our allies in them." He stared at the calf, dripping and hissing on the spit. "What are you doing here?"

"Well, Colonel, I decided to join up with you," Spider said. "I closed up my shop, and left."

"You told me you'd wait there for me," Caudell said. "You

told me you'd play agent for me and watch the secessionist rascals, and play guide to my regiment if we returned."

"Oh, I can still do that all right. I can still guide you. But that valley was gettin' a mite hostile."

"Hostile, sir? To you? Where is the federal army? We had supposed after the battle the federal army would be occupying that country."

"Well, a few are still there. But not many. Mostly, they all moved off to the south."

Caudell looked at Spider again, and there was a growing interest showing in his bright eyes.

"The army's mostly out of there? What does *mostly* mean, sir?"

"Colonel, about all's left is this bunch at the tavern you visited." And Spider laughed. "You know where that's at. Maybe six men. They just stack supplies and load wagons is all. Then there's a train now and again that goes along Wire Road from Missouri, but they always go on south. They don't stop nor nothin'."

"And cavalry? Is there no cavalry patroling that section?"

"Not much. All the fightin' troops has gone off far south. They say they'll go all the way to Fort Smith, and even south of there."

"And infantry? We have little fear of infantry, provided we stay well clear of them. But infantry, Mr. Epp, is a deadly and devastating thing to horsemen, if the horsemen are caught unawares."

"There ain't no infantry anywhere in the valley. They've all gone to the south."

Caudell's fingers moved up from the beard and caressed his fat, sensuous lips. He began to smile.

"No cavalry. No infantry. Splendid. We've been wondering since we saw it last what had happened in that pleasant valley. It appeared to me from our short stay there that horses and mules could be found in plenty, for requisition." His smile broadened.

"We always requisition in the name of the cause, you know. Mr. Epp, do I recall your name correctly?"

"That's it, Colonel."

"Good. Henry, bring me a bottle from my gear. Mr. Epp has come a long way and shown great enterprise in finding us. Now, about those horses and mules."

"There's still livestock there. Not so many as before maybe, because lots of people has moved out. But there's still stock there, all right. Though all of it don't belong to rebels."

"Of course, Mr. Epp. But you see, when we are out requisitioning for the cause, we have little time to determine loyalties, do we?" Caudell laughed, rubbing his stomach with both hands. On one finger was a massive ruby ring set in gold. "Soon, we expect to have a ready market for all the livestock we might obtain. A ready market with the great army of the republic. Excellent prices. Isn't it a convenient situation? The supply in Arkansas and the market close by in Missouri, at the army quartermaster depots.

"Ah, here's the bottle, Mr. Epp. A brandy with some distinction. We requisitioned it from a white man near a place called Going Snake. A man who trades in whiskey with the Indians. Now, everyone knows it is against the law to trade with whiskey to the Indians, and we advised this man of that fact, but unfortunately he took issue with us and had to be dispatched."

Caudell handed the bottle to Spider, still smiling.

"Consider yourself enrolled in our glorious regiment," he said. "Henry, give him back his pistol. And by the way, Mr. Epp, don't get caught by any of our friends in blue uniforms while you're riding that horse you came here on. I can see his brand from here."

"I don't aim to get caught by nobody," Spider Epp said, and he lifted the bottle to his mouth.

"And, Henry, take Mr. Epp's fine horse over and rub him down."

Spider Epp's eyes watered from the fiery liquor and he wiped at them with his coat sleeve. He looked around, through this sycamore grove. He could hear the waters of the Neosho running slowly between its banks. Somewhere beyond the trees, two catbirds were making their mewing call. The smoke wafted through the trees, moving gently before the breeze. The roasting meat smelled good, and he could hear its juices popping in the fire. Men stood all about him, or squatted in their long coats, among the trees and along the horse-picket line. They watched him with flat, expressionless eyes, like caged cats, a deadliness about them. Spider Epp grinned. He felt completely at home.

XIII

They sat on the front porch in the evenings, Calpurnia and Allan Pay, watching the spring come on with an explosion of greens and yellows and deep blues, all the trees suddenly bursting at each twig with new foliage, and the smell of fresh-plowed, newly planted fields coming on the breeze. Above them scissor-tailed barn swallows swept through the growing dusk, making their quiet *wit-wit* calls as the day's last light faded brilliantly from the western sky. There was a growing chorus of tree frogs and early jarflies, and then the mockingbird continuing its program of imitations from the churn-house hollow well into the night.

Ora Hasford watched, and left them to themselves, usually occupying herself at such times with some chore in the rear of the house. She could not fully analyze her feelings toward this young man, but she knew that he was well bred, well educated, and a gentleman. She found herself comparing him to eligible young men who would return someday to this valley after the war was over, and each of them she found wanting. They were an illiterate group by and large, hard-handed and rough-talking, with little to give a woman except the prospect of a short life of bone-grinding subsistence farming. And some of them would never return at all.

But most persistent in her mind was the thought that the valley could at any time become a dangerous place for a girl such as her daughter. Perhaps nonetheless so for herself and Roman—still, whenever she wondered who might ride down Wire Road on any given day, she thought mostly of Calpurnia. And she finally realized that she wanted very badly to have the girl away from here.

He's a Methodist, too, she thought, which makes up a little for his being a Yankee. He had not once spoken an oath or sworn a single word. Surely he had been sent for some purpose, had not come to their hands by chance alone. She had never been comfortable with the idea of preordination, as Martin often was, but if the good Lord has put him here, she thought, there is no reason one cannot do what one can to further His design. And so, during the quiet of the day, when the two of them were together, Ora left them to themselves.

On the day before Martin's letter came, there were clouds in the western sky. Calpurnia sat on the edge of the porch, her feet drawn under her full gingham dress, holding her knees beneath her chin with both arms. Leaning against a roof support at her side was Pay, wearing Martin Hasford's clothes and shoes, all slightly large for him. They watched the changing colors as the sun set, painting the clouds purple and red and gray.

"I had never thought there could be a place so peaceful," he said.

"It's not so peaceful, with all those bugs and birds making such a racket."

"Those are peaceful sounds. They are even quiet sounds."

"You haven't spent much time on a farm, in the country, have you?"

"I am a city boy, Calpurnia. Where the noise is often harsh and unending, and where there is little spaciousness. The people all crowded together. But there are nice things about the city, too."

"Papa took us all to Springfield once," Calpurnia said. "But that isn't much of a city, I guess."

"When I was a boy, my father worked in the lead mines south of the city. He knew a great deal about mining. His brothers and his father had been in the pits all their lives, in Wales. He was a supervisor, and came home often. We would walk along the riverfront together. We'd watch the steamboats at night, going along the Mississippi with their lights, looking like little beehives floating above the water."

"Have you been on a steamboat?"

"Yes. Sometimes, after he began to practice the law, my father would take us down to Saint Genevieve and we'd set trotlines for blue catfish in the Kashaskia River."

"All of it seems so far away."

"You'd love the little shops. Where you could buy lovely dresses and shawls, and lace and ribbons. You should have lace and ribbons, Calpurnia."

"And a big sunbonnet to keep me from freckling," she said, and laughed because her freckles no longer embarrassed her.

"All pretty girls should have a few freckles," he said, and they both laughed.

"I suppose there are lots of pretty girls in Saint Louis."

"There are a good many. When my regiment was presented their colors, pretty girls came in flocks, wearing large flowered hats and carrying little parasols. And afterward, before we paraded off with the band playing and everyone waving handkerchiefs, our boys ran among them and stole kisses."

"Right in front of everybody?"

"Of course. Pretty girls expect to be kissed by brave soldiers marching off," he said, teasing her.

"It's a funny way to be kissing," she said. "With strangers. Kisses are supposed to be more important than that." It was very daring, talking about kissing, and she knew the color had risen in her cheeks. But it gave her a tingle of excitement.

"Has it ever been important to you?" he said, still teasing.

"We don't do much kissing around here," she said. "Except

sometimes with kin. One of the Ruter boys kissed me once, behind a wagon when we were having a singing convention and dinner on the ground at the church."

"Did you like it?"

"I boxed his ears for him."

Pay laughed, and bent quickly to her as she looked at him, and his lips brushed hers for only a second. He drew away, seeing the darkness come into her eyes like a faint shadow.

"Don't box my ears, Calpurnia. I meant it with respect," he said, no longer teasing her.

"That's the way you do it, then. Just a peck?"

"I didn't mean it for just a peck." He fumbled in a pocket and brought out the old pipe Ora had found for him, and a small sack of tobacco. Ora had cut up some of the drying leaves in the barn that were usually twisted for chewing. Calpurnia started to take the pipe, to fill it, but he drew it back.

"Let me try myself. I don't like feeling completely helpless."

He held the pipe between his knees and pressed tobacco down into the bowl with his right hand. She watched his fingers, long and slender and moving with supple strength.

"Do you play the fiddle or anything like that?" And as soon as the words were out, she realized what she'd said. "Oh, I'm sorry, Allan."

"No need for that," he said, and smiled at her. "I have never been a carpenter or a freight driver or a musician. And a lawyer can work as well with one hand as with two."

Even though he protested on every occasion possible that he was good as ever, she could feel his torment. Often she had seen the arm move in the sling, as though he were trying to use the left hand, starting to reach with it before realizing that the hand was no longer there. Calpurnia had developed a deep attachment for this young man, and all along she had assumed it was pity, and pity only. It was beginning to trouble her now that perhaps more was involved, as though any feeling other than compassion was somehow disloyalty to her own kind.

From far across Wire Road they could hear the sharp, distinctive whistle of a bobwhite. Allan Pay smoked for a while, Calpurnia rocked back and forth with her arms locked around her knees, and both of them were silent. Knocking out the pipe at last, he began to speak of his work with his father. Although he did not mention it again directly, she knew he was trying to reassure her that he would suffer no real handicap as a lawyer. In fact, he said, a one-armed war veteran might be good for business. She had the feeling that he was trying to reassure himself as much as her. It made her uncomfortable, and she rose and moved down the steps to the bottom one and sat again, bent over and staring at the ground.

"Look here," she said. "Doodlebugs have made their little holes in the dirt."

He moved down beside her once more, and she pointed to a number of small, conical depressions in the sandy soil. She moved a finger slowly in a circle over one of them and repeated in a low monotone, "Doodle, doodle, doodle."

"What are you doing?"

"Trying to make one come up," she said. "Papa can make them come up. They're little bugs at the bottom of the hole, and when other bugs fall into their trap, they catch them."

She continued the droning sound, her finger just over one of the conical traps. He sat close beside her, their shoulders touching. After a moment there was a movement in the sand, and the tiny legs of a black insect appeared for a few seconds, and then, discovering the trap was empty, were buried again.

"I did it," she laughed. "I made a doodlebug come up."

"That's an ant lion," Allan said. "I've never seen such a thing done before. But that's what it is, an ant lion. He thinks the noise you make is an insect caught in his trap."

"You try, Allan. See if you can make one come up."

He began the ritual with his finger over one of the traps, his voice droning. But the ant lion would not come up, and she laughed again.

"What perfect little holes they make," she said, bending forward. She felt his hand on her hair and for a moment was perfectly still, and then his hand drew away. She straightened and looked at him. His lifted his hand to her face and touched her cheek and kissed her for a long moment.

"All right, there's a proper kiss," he said, drawing back his face and his hand. "But I'm afraid if your mother saw me do that, she might not like it very much."

"I don't care," she said, and moved her face to his and kissed him again, but very quickly, and then she was up and running into the house.

She paused in front of the china closet, her fingers tracing the sharp outline of the bullet hole in the glass. She waited for him to follow, but she heard nothing, and it infuriated her—either at him or at herself, she wasn't sure which. She ran up the loft stairs to her room.

Kissing is a very, very serious thing between people old enough to marry, she thought. Yet she had felt some urgency to kiss again. It had been unlike it was with the Ruter boy, or anybody else.

Calpurnia knew how the hill people thought and acted, she being one of them, and she knew that marriage generally happened when two people decided they would settle down and live out their lives together. When the time came, you married whoever was at hand. It wasn't a thing she had often worried about. And it wasn't a thing she connected necessarily with love, whatever that was.

After all, her own mother and father had likely never said "I love you" to each other until they had been married for ten years, and maybe not even then.

Of all the girls she knew, she could not remember any ever talking about love seriously. They talked of marriage, when the time came, of establishing their own household, of bearing and rearing their own children, of cooking and caring for their man, whoever he was. It didn't seem to matter. What mattered was a woman creating her own family, separate and apart from the one she had always known. That was the excitement of it, beginning a new home, and she the ruler of it even though subservient always to her husband. The man's duty was to feed her and keep a roof over her head and protect her from harm while she had the children. To everyone she knew in these hills, and to her, it always had been that way, and any love involved was almost incidental. Except in later years, when love might grow, and if it didn't, then hate instead.

But the family was kept together, no matter love or not. The family was begun in the first place, no matter love or not.

Love was when a new schoolmaster arrived, she thought, the girls watching with eyes like deers being stalked. A man with a coat that matched his trousers, and who talked with elegance and grace. To have him make an approving mark on your slate sent shivers up the backs of your legs, and sometimes, at first, you thought of him at night before you went to sleep. But soon all the giggling stopped and love passed and he was just another dowdy man in rumpled clothes with chalk dust on him.

Or maybe love was that first time a young lieutenant came to the door, and you peered through the window and thought perhaps his eyes had met yours for just an instant. But then he was gone, and inside a few days forgotten. Only now, this one had returned. And his eyes did not touch for only an instant, but seemed to caress, constantly.

She knew that Allan Pay was close to asking her to come with him to Saint Louis, to leave her family. And she thought that she might say, "But I don't know if I love you. A one-armed man. Maybe I'm only sorry for you."

And she knew he would say, "It doesn't matter what the reason, just come with me."

2 When Allan Pay had begun to regain his strength, Ora Hasford had moved to Roman's loft bed, thinking it the correct thing to do now that she was no longer needed as night nurse. Roman slept on the parlor daybed, where his mother had spent every night for two weeks after the amputation. He liked it because he could come and go in the night without waking anyone.

Now he could walk through the open front door whenever he had the call, and stand on the porch to send out a long, arching stream into the yard without his mother knowing it. She had always insisted he use the privy on such occasions, but he found the barefooted trip across the backyard tiresome, and besides, it was hellish hard to hit one of those holes in the dark; the next morning Calpurnia would complain about him spraying the whole seat.

But on this night he was thinking of more serious things than his mother's objections to wetting down the yard. Through the kitchen window just before dark, he had seen what happened on the porch. It had given him a brassy taste in the mouth, not unlike the experience he'd had when he saw his mule cut down by artillery fire at Elkhorn Tavern.

Just when he'd begun to accept this Yankee, even talk with him a little, he caught the bastard kissing Calpurnia. Not that Roman had made his presence known. He had watched, and then, the lump in his throat almost choking him, gone out the back, kicking at wood chips viciously as he crossed the yard. His mother had been at the well, drawing up water for the horses.

"What's the matter with you?" she had asked.

"Nothing." He had slammed into the barn, through it, and out the back, kicking at the horse apples.

Who does he think he is, coming into this family and acting like that? Kissing and touching her. And what galled him most was that it had been his sister who had done a large part of the kissing.

Now, in the darkness, he lay listening to Pay's steady breathing from the next room. By God, I'll go off and join the army and let everybody try and get along here with just that one-armed son of a bitch, he thought, working himself into a second rage, thinking all the things he could say to wound his sister and mother.

That's another thing. Mama seems to be blind as a bat about what's happening, turning her back when they touch hands, finding things to do off someplace when they start talking, letting Cal sit there by his bed and read all that poetry trash.

Roman rose and sat on the edge of the bed. The house was quiet, only the night sounds coming from outside. He stood up and walked into the kitchen. The quilts had not been drawn across the room, and he could see Pay's head outlined on the pillow from the light of a quartering moon coming through the window like a pale mist.

He knew exactly where the shotgun stood, and he went to its corner without a sound. This is not the time to get a splinter in my damned foot, he thought. He took up the gun and held it, breathing heavily, his heart pounding. He found the caps and slipped one on each nipple. He stood stock-still for a moment, the steel of the gun barrels cool under his fingers.

What in hell's name am I doing? he thought.

He went to the door, carrying the gun, and slipped outside noiselessly. He sat heavily on the edge of the porch and stared through the moonlit trees. The bluetick hound ambled up, yawning and stretching and wagging his tail.

"Get on, I don't want you," Roman muttered, and the dog turned away casually and ambled off, into the deep shadows at the end of the porch.

His anger had abruptly gone, leaving him with an empty feeling in his belly. He tried to fan it up again, but it was useless. He thought of Spavinaw Tom, back along White River. He thought of the steep, oak-covered slopes in that country, the limestone cliffs overhanging flowing water, the thickets of chokecherry and red birch. I just ought to light out and find him, and live in the woods like a red Indian.

Then he remembered the day with his father, there on White River, when a lovely six-point whitetail had suddenly appeared from a stand of willow twenty feet away, walking slowly toward the river. It was his first deer, and he lifted his father's rifle. But nothing happened. He tried to shoot, tried to press the trigger, but his body was suddenly bathed in sweat and he was paralyzed. The deer walked slowly out of sight, never seeing them, never knowing his mortal peril, the rifle still impotent in Roman's hands.

Buck fever, his father had said, and laughed about it.

If shooting your first deer is that hard, he thought, I wonder what it would be like to shoot a man. I wonder what awful thing he'd have to do to make it easy. Maybe nothing would ever make it easy. Maybe I'll never have to find out.

I could shoot a panther, he thought. I've only seen two, and had no shot at either, but I'll wager I could shoot a panther. A man, I don't know about.

He rose and went back into the kitchen, closing the door gently, and replaced the gun in its corner. As he started across the room to the parlor, he saw Allan Pay's head rise from the pillow. Roman could see the shine of moonlight in his eyes.

"Who is it?" Pay called. "Is that you, Roman?"

"Yeah, I had to get a drink of water," Roman said, gruffly, and went on to his bed.

3 Ezra Ruter brought the letter, and as soon as Ora saw the handwriting on the crumpled, dirty envelope, she began to tremble. It was all she could do to be civil. Old man Ruter's eldest boy had come home from the army, and he'd brought the letter. No, he wasn't with Martin Hasford. The letter had just been passed along through many hands until it finally came to his. It was not an unusual system of postal service in the South. No, his son was not out of the army. No, his son had not deserted, just slipped away for a short time to visit his folks and help with getting the crops in before he went back.

After an eternity, the old man rode off, saying he had a few more letters to deliver before dark set in. Ora ran into the kitchen and slipped the envelope open with a carving knife. She was glad she had this time to herself. The children and Allan Pay were in the woods somewhere behind the barn, gathering acorns, Roman with his shotgun in case he had a good shot at a squirrel.

Her hands shook so badly she had to lay the wrinkled pages flat on the table before she could read them. Her lips moved slightly as her eyes ran hurriedly across the words.

IN CAMP NEAR PETERSBURG, VIRGINIA:

My Dear Wife, I take pen in hand once more, far from home. I hope that a kind Providence has continued to look over you and the children. I am well, thanks to God, who looks to all things.

Since last I wrote, the company has traveled greatly.

We departed Russelville more than a month ago, traveling down the Arkansas River and I seemed to recall some of that country from when the family came upriver in '36, but it may have been my imagination.

My company and one other traveled to Montgomery and then to here before the Confederate government recognized that we were fighting men and organized us into what they call the Third Arkansas Infantry Regiment. We will be traveling north soon, and it looks as though we will be brigaded with some boys from North Carolina.

Army life is a long succession of drills and rifle practice, even though we have nothing yet to shoot with the rifles Captain Reedy bought for us. We pretend like small boys that we shoot, and watching grown men biting imaginary cartridges becomes a laughing matter until one of the officers come round to tell us how serious it is.

The food we get runs from bad to worse. Some days there are good victuals, but I have learned like all good soldiers that when you get it, you had best eat it before someone steals it or it goes rotten. After that, we starve for three days until the commissary department issues more. The meat is very bad. Most of it can be thrown against a tree and will stick there and quiver like axle grease. Sometimes the flour and meat is so full of bugs and worms it can walk by itself. The boys say you need to post a guard on such grub to prevent its marching off.

But with God's grace, I am in good spirits and wait with these other men for our first chance to strike at the invaders. Some of them are hot for a good fight, and I must say, the same mood has infected me.

Virginia will be turning green soon. There is much tobacco here, which they tell us is in short supply in the Yankee armies. People here are most kind to us and many times ladies have come out of farmhouses along the route of march and given us buttermilk and johnnycake, so long as it lasts. For such things, a man needs to be at the head of the column. If he is at the rear, he will get none.

There are many vices in this army. We have been near Petersburg these past days, and it is a Sodom and Gomorrah, leeching on the soldiers. There is much play at Bluff and other gambling games and hard spirits are consumed in great quantities, even by the youngest of us. Bad language is so common I have almost become accustomed to hearing it. With God's help, I will manage to avoid all such things.

The worst part of being here is that I am lonesome for the family. War is a young man's business, when he has no wife and children at home to worry over. I often think of being there now, in the fields or at the kitchen table eating some of your sweet buscuits and listening to the children whispering in the loft before they sleep. Since I have been here, I have learned to cherish each of you more than even before.

I am writing this on an old stump, by firelight, and the camp is sleeping all around me. I must stop now, and sleep, because gossip has it that early tomorrow we will start for the Rappahannock. Have no worries for me. This is a time for men to do what they must, and trust in God.

Your husband, Martin.

She read it a second time, and then, clutching it to her bosom as though it were a newborn infant, she went to the back porch, sat down, and leaning her head against one of the roof supports, wept. Soon, she heard the children coming back through the woods toward the barn, Calpurnia laughing. She quickly wiped her eyes with the hem of her apron and went back into the kitchen and hid the letter in the safe. She would keep it to herself tonight and perhaps tomorrow, too, and then let Roman and Calpurnia read it. But for a short time, at least, she wanted it to be hers alone.

XIV

One night in the second week of April, a party of men rode into the yard of a man named Claiborne who lived with his eldest daughter, on a farm about ten miles north of Elkhorn Tavern. The men entered the house where the girl was preparing the evening meal and assaulted the old man with pistol butts, demanding his money. They wore soiled pillow slips over their heads with eye slits cut in them. The girl threw scalding water on one of them and wounded another in the arm with a hatchet. They retreated into the night but returned later to ride around the house, firing pistols through the windows before going off to the west, taking with them one mule, two chickens, and a shoat.

A week later, a man named Cole was riding along the Missouri to Bentonville Road after dark when he was waylaid by a group of armed men on horseback. His money was taken, his clothes stripped from him, and his horse stolen. As his attackers rode away, he ran after them, cursing, and two of the group turned back and shot him dead in the road. His naked body was found the next day by a local farmwife.

Three horses were stolen from a farm in the western section of the county, two more from their stalls behind a small roadside general store near the Missouri line. No one knew how many horses and mules had been taken since the battle of Pea Ridge, because after the occupation by federal troops the county government had ceased to function.

The forays came suddenly, furiously, and with impartiality. A man known for his Union leanings who lived along Little Sugar

Creek was called to his door one evening and shot as he stood on his front porch. In his barn were two horses and a colt that were left untouched. Two nights after he was buried, the horses and the colt were stolen by three night riders who left a hayrick burning when they rode off.

The Epp store in Leetown, empty now, was mysteriously burned to the ground on an early morning in May.

Ezra Ruter's son, home without leave to help get in crops, was weeding the new-sprouted corn in one of his father's fields. It was midafternoon. Hoeing near a line of scrub timber that marked the course of a small stream, he thought he saw movement in a stand of sassafras. As he stood looking toward the trees, a fusillade came at him. He could see leaves blowing back from the muzzle blasts before he was struck three times by heavy-caliber bullets. He managed to walk the mile to his parents' farmyard, where he collapsed and died as his mother ran screaming from the house.

Twice during that month, Roman Hasford stood on his front porch and watched the light of buildings burning in the night, far across the valley.

Roman thought of Tulip Crozier, because he knew the old man had two horses in his stalls. And he thought about Bess and the other mare. Normally they would be grazing in spring pasture, but now they were being kept close to the barn, grazing only in early mornings in one of the small woodland meadows near Plum Thicket Ridge. Roman took them there each day, on short leads, and he never allowed them to move into country where there was no timber for concealment. He and his mother never mentioned it aloud to one another, but each knew as well as if words were spoken that it would be better to keep livestock out of sight. Ora had never revealed to him her discovery of Spider Epp.

On two occasions during that period, Roman had found fresh tracks in the woods behind the barn. It had been a shod horse, but he knew it belonged to Spavinaw Tom because the tracks were small, a pony's tracks. And each of these times, they found hanging from the back-porch rafters fresh-killed game, once another half of venison, and the other a small tom turkey.

The rains of spring came and the new fresh vegetables began to come in and the days grew hot, and there was more food to put on the table. And each night, after he supposed the others were asleep, Roman stood on the front porch, watching for the fires. Ora was often awake at the window upstairs, watching as well. No matter what they saw or imagined of what was happening in the darkness, they said nothing. But when they looked at one another each morning, an understanding passed between them. This was a dangerous time.

2   White River headed in the rough high country of the Arkansas Ozarks, flowed between its primeval limestone bluffs north into Missouri for a short space before turning back south again, and then ran down into the Mississippi Delta a hundred miles away. In its upper reaches, where Spavinaw Tom was reshaping his mind to the terrain of his birth, known until then only through the stories of his tribal fathers, it was a clear cold-water stream of magnificent beauty. There, only a few miles from Wire Road, the river flowed during the spring beneath the outcrops and overhanging foliage—actually a hardwood jungle—like a slowly winding snake in a deep, lush carpet, the green almost as solid and unyielding as the rocks in which the trees along the steep hillsides took their purchase.

Spavinaw Tom roamed along the riverbanks, waiting for some hidden meaning to come, expecting some mystery to unravel, revealing to his conscious thought the unknown quality of kinship he felt for this land—some rocky cliff or twisting pool where sky and overhanging trees were mirrored, that would awaken in him some remembrance of his own world's beginning. But nothing came.

He made a shelter high above a bend in the river, at the top of a stony bluff that dropped straight down a hundred feet to the water. He had never left his farm without fishline and hooks in his jacket, nor had he gone to war without these things, and now he set trotlines each night and cooked the sweet blue catfish over an open fire, fastened to a split hickory log stood upright beside the flames.

There was game here, too, but to save cartridges he trapped rabbit and squirrel and even a few quail in upland meadows where woods fires had burned off the timber and left only scrub and stubble. Now and then he saw a turkey or deer, and these he stalked with the Yager. But he lived, except for the rifle, like a stone-age man, keeping his fire, once started, going always under a bank of ash, hidden from rain and wind by a sharp overhang of the white-streaked limestone bluff.

He kept clear of the few roads that ran through that country, and when he moved he stayed in heavy timber, as though hiding his presence even from the hawks and eagles overhead. He found the tracks of wolves, and twice saw wild hogs, whose ancestors had escaped from pens perhaps as much as four generations before. And the prairie pony flourished on natural graze, like a deer.

Along the edges of the river, and high in the rocks above, he found flint arrowheads. They meant nothing to him, and he doubted any of these had been left by his own people as they passed through. Rather, from some ancient folk, even far back beyond the Osage, forgotten now and leaving no trace in the mountains except these delicate little water-chipped flints, the fluted edges still sharp as honed metal. He pondered the variety of men called Indian by the whites, but men to him—an Indian, too—as foreign as South Sea headhunters.

He rode often to peer along the valley of Little Sugar Creek. He came to know it from a distance, and the people who lived there. He watched the white-bearded man and the black moving among the mill buildings and hives, and he saw many times the white girl at the farm where he had brought the wounded man, and her brother as well, and later the wounded man himself, walking in the woods behind the house. Always he watched from a distance, and none of them ever knew he was there, his black eyes on them.

On one of these occasions, when he was close in to the Hasford farm, the bluetick hound came out to challenge him. Spavinaw Tom went down from the pony quickly and talked the dog in close, and then scratched his ears and gave him a chunk of rabbit meat from his saddle pack, and then simply sat, allowing the dog to have full measure of his scent. Before he rode off, Spavinaw Tom took the dog's muzzle in his hand and blew his breath into the dog's nose, talking softly all the while in Cherokee, and after that the dog never barked at him again in his wanderings near the Hasford farm.

Once, during a moonlit night, he rode around Elkhorn Tavern, close enough to hear the soldiers laughing and dancing. He rode along Pea Ridge, and tried to look across the land below and recall what had happened on the day of the big guns and all the killing. But none of it was clear to him, and before dawn he was well back into the rough White River country, where he felt at home. And beginning to dread more and more the eventual return to his own country, the cotton presses and the sorghum mills and the stone and lumber houses—all the trappings of the white man's world that the Cherokees had now, for a generation, taken as their own.

3 "We don't enjoy things like we used to," Ora Hasford said. She sat on the edge of the back porch, her sunbonnet hang-

ing from its chin strap at the back of her head. Moisture at her temples made little ringlet curls in her hair, and a few strands showed gray. Allan Pay sat near her, his head bent, tracing designs in the dust between his feet with the fingers of his hand.

Roman was carrying buckets of water from the barn well to the garden patch because it had been some days since rain, and the vegetables on the high side of the slope were becoming parched. Each time he worked the well pulley, the wheel squeaked. Calpurnia was in the garden, too, pulling potato bugs off the plants.

Far along the wooded ridge behind the barn, two jays were scolding one another. The great leaves of the white oaks hung rigid in the windless air, and among them the pale green leaves of the locusts made only a delicate movement, as though breathing.

"On some afternoons, we'd all sit here after supper, and Martin would cut willow whistles for the children and we'd eat wild strawberries. Those were good times."

Her eyes moved slowly along the scarred outlines of the barn, marking each bullet pock and the jagged tear in the siding over the pigpen. From inside the sty, the acorn-fed pigs, bony and grunting, peered through the slats with their tiny red-rimmed eyes, watching Roman in his endless trips back and forth across the yard. Each time, a bucket in both hands, he sloshed a little water out, splattering his bare feet.

Ora was barefooted, too. She could feel the hot dust of the yard between her toes. Hanging limp from her hand was a bunch of green onions, just pulled, the reddish earth clinging to roots that looked like an old man's whiskers.

"The children played a counting game," Ora said. "With birds. We'd be sitting here and Cal would take one side of the barn and Roman the other, and they'd see how many birds they could count on their side, and Martin would keep time with his watch. Once, it was in the fall, and they were playing that game, and a whole flock of little yellow birds with black faces flew into the garden patch, and that was Cal's side. There must have been a hundred of them. Martin called them canaries."

"They were likely warblers," he said. "If it had been spring, it was likely goldfinches. They go in flocks when they migrate. I remember seeing them in the city."

"Maybe it was spring. But it was a good game. Cal was the one who made it up. She was always making up games they could play, and then she'd always win and make Roman mad. But he didn't stay mad long."

The bluetick hound came up from the garden, looking despondent and listless. He came into the shade, his tail making a tentative wag, and stood before Allan Pay to be scratched. Pay pulled back his ears and found a number of ticks and he pinched them off. From back in the trees, where she was chained to a tree, the nanny goat bleated.

"It's time I go," Pay said abruptly. She did not look at him, but nodded. She had been expecting it.

"A few more days," she said. "That will be time enough. Where will you go?"

"Springfield. To the army depot there, and let the sawbones look at the arm before they muster me out."

They had long since pulled the ligatures from the wound, an agonizing few moments neither would forget. But it had drained well, with no infection, and the skin was healing over the stump now. It was still sensitive, however, and they kept it well bandaged and in a sling so it wouldn't bump into anything when Pay tried to use the hand that was not there.

Calpurnia was coming up from the garden, and Ora saw Allan Pay's eyes go to her quickly and then turn away. His expression was almost as dismal as the hound's, looking up walleyed. The girl went to the well, drew up water, and washed her hands, dashing some on her bare feet.

"There is a great deal I need to say to you," Pay said softly.

"Not now," Ora said, rising and shaking the onions so that the dirt clinging to the old-man's-whisker roots showered onto the ground like tiny pellets of hail. "Tomorrow, I'm going to Tulip Crozier's. We're out of salt for the table and for the stock, too, and he's likely the only one in the valley who's got any. You can come with me. We'll talk then. And besides, you need to see the man who helped with the hand, before you leave."

They had all come to refer to it as "the hand."

"Yes. I want to. I'd been hoping he would come by sometime. I can't even remember his face."

Ora laughed. "It's a face you won't forget. But he's a strange old man, and very proud. When he was here last time, I think I hurt his feelings. Or maybe he hurt his own."

"I'll be glad to see him. But we need to talk, Mrs. Hasford."

"Not now," Ora said. "We'll talk tomorrow."

She turned and went across the porch silently on bare feet, and as Calpurnia came up and passed him to follow her inside, the girl's hand touched Allan Pay's shoulder for a brief moment.

She wears that bonnet right into the shade, Ora thought. Roman was turning brown as a berry, but Cal was taking care to wear the sunbonnet and her face was still creamy white, with only a few of the brown freckle blemishes that usually by this time of year covered her nose and cheeks. A good sign, Ora thought. A very good sign.

What will I do without her? Recurring in her mind these past weeks had been that question, and with it the memory of her daughter's life. Born here, in this house, reared and taught and nurtured. Ora could recall all the parts of it, almost all the separate days. Those first months of Calpurnia's being, lying at Ora's breast, the large eyes staring up with the intensity that only a baby's eyes can have, seeing her world opening up before her. The first smile on the finely arched, tiny lips—a slobbery, toothless, glorious smile.

And that giving way to the toddling months, the fumbling explorations, yet with a fine inquisitiveness, small hands reaching into everything. And that giving way to early speech, and the seriousness of her first communication, always frowning with the effort as the words bubbled out incoherently. And the supple grace of her movements, growing more confident each day, and her coming to know the power of a smile or a tear, learning to assert herself.

The little mother to Roman, then, scolding and placating and petting and soothing—and agitating, too, with a teasing, sparkling eye even at seven. After that, the awkward period—had she ever been awkward?—the legs and arms growing out like willow shoots, too fast for the flesh to fill the bone. The blossoming of young girlhood, when her body began to take shape and every boy who looked at her was suspected by Martin of wicked intent.

And at last, her womanhood, when she was no longer just child to Ora, but friend as well. Yet even now, Ora could see that crooked little first smile as though it had happened yesterday.

Her heart ached at the thought of Calpurnia leaving this farm. But she could put that from her mind, as she did the pain in her arm and shoulder. If I had to, I would even force her to leave, Ora thought. Because even with all the bad about it, there is more to it that is good.

She would be in a place where she'd have others outside the family to talk with, some even as bright as herself. New faces and new voices. She would be out of harm's way. She could live out her life undisturbed.

Nor was Ora oblivious of Roman's attachment to his own sister. He hovered about her like a hummingbird at the hollyhock stalk. It would be good to have her gone for his sake, to where she could rear her own family away from her brother's jealous eye.

There was such a thing as too much family, she thought.

Martin had always been anxious to isolate himself with his brood, and she had known there was always disappointment in him because the rest of the clan had gone off to Texas. It left no Hasford second cousins for his own children to marry. But she'd seen some of these hill families that had become so inbred they had a strange cast to their eyes, with some of their children still baby-slobbering at ten. And she had seen vacant-faced mothers nursing a child until it was old enough to stand beside her chair. Yes, there is such a thing as too much family, she thought.

But such thinking did little to ease the pain of losing Calpurnia. She did not cry about it yet, but the tears were there, inside.

4 The dogwood and redbud blossoms were gone, and Pea Ridge was an uplifting wave of jade-colored foliage, the long bare winter branches heavy now with fat new leaves. The valley below lay in shimmering haze, the woodlands and fields making a patchwork-quilt pattern of browns and greens. There were not so many cultivated fields this year, and the plots lying fallow were already being reclaimed by a dense undergrowth of weeds and brush. The land stretched away toward Little Sugar Creek, and the ridgelines beyond seemed to move gently like the waters of a pale lake against the shores of the sky.

Spider Epp sat the big army stallion well back in a hickory grove along the crest of the ridge, near a limestone outcrop that overlooked Elkhorn Tavern. His wolf eyes watched the comings and goings of the few blue-clad soldiers there, and the long face under his slouch hat moved as he mentally calculated their number. Soon, now, he would ride back west, drop down into the wooded draws, and angle toward the Missouri line, where the others waited.

He was indistinguishable by now from the men with whom he rode. His beard, coming out spotty, was fully three inches long at the edge of his jaw. His shirt was ripped across the back, revealing dirty red flannel underwear, and the knees of his trousers were threadbare. One of his boot soles had come loose at the toe, and when he looked at it he grinned, thinking of the shoe shop that he knew by now had been turned to ash by some secesh rebel. Somewhere, he had acquired a pair of cattleman's spurs, and although the rowels were rusty he liked the sound they made when he walked, like little bells at his heels. With the ragged beard and the clothes hanging in tatters around his lank arms and thighs, he gave the impression of an ill-tempered billy goat with a slight case of the mange.

Like so many men in this war, the only thing about him that looked well kept was his weapon. The Navy Colt thrust out from his waistband at the belly, the brass backstrap gleaming between the polished walnut grips.

Spider Epp searched the valley with the field glasses Colonel Caudell had given him, for just that purpose. He saw clearly the trace of Wire Road as it ran straight south from the tavern, then bent back into timber short of Little Sugar Creek. Along the low slope beyond the road stood the Hasford farm, although it was hidden now in dense oak foliage. But he knew exactly where it was, and his eyes, magnified by the glasses, lingered there a long time. He licked his lips and caressed the butt of the pistol, feeling the barrel move against his groin.

Spider Epp's thoughts sometimes failed in getting anywhere. They started, but they never finished. His thinking would come in formless lumps, often connected, often not. His conclusions, if they could be called that, were usually vague, with smoky edges hard to define. He was a fox, unable to concentrate on one bunch of grapes because the next bunch always looked juicier.

He was capable of singleness of purpose, else he would never have stolen that watch and horse, nor gone to search out Colonel

Caudell's light irregular cavalry. But making up his mind was often painful, especially now that he didn't have to worry about decisions, because the Colonel made all of them for him. Such a thing had never happened before, not with his father, and certainly not with his mother. With Colonel Caudell he felt a new freedom, wherein he could allow his thinking to wander grandly without worrying about deciding anything.

So on this day his eyes raced back and forth along the familiar valley, creating some quick and inviting image for only an instant before leaping to the next.

He sat throughout much of the afternoon, watching. He searched each woodlot and field.

Army's all but gone, he thought. No cavalry patrols, no supply trains on the road. He suspected Colonel Caudell had been right: they had shifted their base to Fayetteville, relying less and less on their Missouri depots. Plenty of mills around Fayetteville, he'd heard. And now there was likely some winter wheat coming in, some from as far away as the Indian Territory, maybe. And before long, the corn.

There was a sudden, furious movement in the leafy limbs above him, and he looked up to see two gray squirrels, one dashing madly after the other as they leaped through the trees. Spider grinned, his crooked teeth showing. Old boar squirrel after that young one to bite off his balls, he thought. Them old boars want it all for their own self.

He turned the glasses down the valley, toward the line of Little Sugar Creek. Back along that hollow was the old Jew, the secesh trash Jew whose time it was to be scalded out, he thought. More money than anyone else in this country, likely hiding his coin in burlap bags under his mill, and all manner of livestock. Well, he thought, it's about time you was scalded out, you damned old secesh trash Jew.

Then one last time before riding back to the others, he studied the trees that surrounded the Hasford farm, and he grinned again, his tongue flicking across his lips like a pink snake's-head.

5   Along the steep slope behind Tulip Crozier's buildings was a line of whitewashed beehives. They stood like fat gravestones in the weeds of the hillside where a burn had long since scoured out the timber and left a small meadow. The hives were like most in that country, some three or four boxes without tops or bottoms, called supers, stacked one on the other, a lid at the top that came off to give access to the frames inside, and vents at the bottom of each super to give the bees entrance.

Tulip Crozier moved among the hives, with a flat lady's hat on his head, hung with a thick brown veil, and a bee smoker in his hand. Lark was standing a few paces down the slope, looking like a grieving widow with a veil of his own draped over his round head.

"So, you have to check bees each spring," Crozier was shouting. "Bees can starve, you know. Before the blooms are well out, they'll starve if the winter supply of honey has run short, and then you have to give 'em sugar water."

"I ain't partial to no bee," Lark said, his voice muffled under the veil. He watched the sluggish fat insects crawling from the vents and across the hives, some of them on Crozier's hands and on the veil that hung over his face, well down past his beard.

"No, but you like the honey."

"Yas, sir, I likes honey. But I don't like them stings."

"They won't sting you unless you step on one. Besides, that thick hide of yours would break off their stingers."

Crozier opened one of the hives and lifted out the frames, one at a time, looking at the combs. He was not a scientific beekeeper. He did little to create new broodnests and nothing to kill off excess drones. His hives gave the impression of well-tended bees, but other than giving them sugar water during those springs when they needed it, he left them alone. Sometimes a swarm would take off from a hive and go into the woods, where some queen created a new colony. And sometimes wild bees invaded his hives. He didn't care, and as a result the quality of his honey was mixed. He didn't care about that, either.

"So, you see that," he said, holding up a frame, showing the white glaze of wax over each cell in the comb. "Honey. They've come out good. That comes from not taking too much away from them last fall. Some people are greedy and take too much honey for themselves, and their bees starve. Come on up here and see what I'm doing."

"Mister Tulip, I ain't fixin' to come too close to none of them bees."

"Not come close, you say? You ought to be ashamed," Crozier shouted, brushing a few of the insects off his hands and moving to the next hive. "Best beekeeper I ever saw was a darkie. A slave, down in Texas, on a farm there. He kept about thirty hives. They said his honey was the best anywhere along the Guadalupe. When his bees swarmed, they'd sometimes hang on to his chin like whiskers, and he'd just swipe 'em off like shaving soap."

Lark moved farther back at such a prospect, down the slope and away from the hives. Crozier muttered to himself, or to the bees, going from one hive to the next, lifting off the supers one by one, inspecting the frames. Finally satisfied, he came down the slope, pulling off hat and veil.

"Damned hot under that thing," he said. "So, the truth is, Lark, I should have done this a few weeks ago. By now there's plenty of flowers for 'em. But I wasn't a mind to do it, so I didn't."

He puffed a cloud of blue-gray vapor from the bee smoker

into Lark's face, and the black man moved back, coughing. Crozier chortled and squeezed the smoker again.

"Before long, now, some of those queens will come out of their hives and go off someplace else to make a new broodnest. That's when the drones swarm. Then one of the new little queens in the hive the old lady left will start her own batch of eggs. Bees are funny. The old lady leaves and the new girl takes over the household."

Lark seemed uninterested. He peeled the veil off his head, looking back up the slope once more to ensure that no bees were following.

"I seed a man onct. Got a bee sting and his foot swell up like he was bit by a cottonmouth snake."

"Cottonmouth snake? Why, hell, there aren't any cottonmouths around here. This is copperhead and rattler country."

"Over White River they's cottonmouths. But most I seed was in Mississippi when the folks'd fish in the sloughs back from the river. And that's where I seed the bee-stung man."

"That man likely smelled bad to the bee. Me, they like the way I smell, so they don't sting me. They're like a dog. If you haven't got any confidence, you smell bad. Then they're likely to bite. That's been my experience, with dogs and bees."

Along the valley on the far side of the creek, the leaves were turning up, looking like frogs' bellies. Crozier wiped his face with the bee veil and shook his head,

"Looks like a storm before long," he said. "Feels like it, too. Muggy spring day and leaves turning up, that means a storm, did you know that, Lark?"

"Yas, sir, tha's what they say. You gone go over to the Hasfords' and visit like you say you was? Miz Hasford say tell you welcome anytime, when I took that nanny goat over there."

"I know that. You've told me a thousand times. So, maybe in a day or two, after the weather breaks. And speaking of goats, in the morning early I want you to go back along the ridge and see if you can find that old nanny of ours that got loose yesterday. I think I heard her bell last night. She ought to be close by."

"Mister Tulip, that goat so old, you can't even milk her no more."

"No, but you can sure as hell make stew out of her. Tomorrow, you go find her. I don't want to lose that goat."

"Mister Tulip, I don't like wanderin' aroun' an' leavin' you alone with all these things happenin' in the valley an' all them men ridin' 'round."

Tulip Crozier glared at him, his eyes bulging and showing the brown veins. With his eyes shining and his white hair and beard blowing back in the breeze, Lark supposed, he might look like one of those old men that Polly Cox was always reading about in her Bible, who went around blowing up sandstorms and making buildings fall down just by looking at them.

"There's not going to be any of that around here," Crozier said. "Don't you know those sneaky bastards only hunt out old women and children?"

"Mister Ezra Ruter's boy warn't no old women and children," Lark said stubbornly.

"So, don't sass me! Anybody comes nosing around here will get what for. Now, hush about it and get over there and feed the horses. I think I'll give the old pistol a good cleaning."

XV

Wire Road was shaded in the early morning, but they drove along it without enjoying the freshness of the new day, thinking of the serious business that had to be discussed. Ora Hasford leaned forward on the wagon seat, elbows on knees, loosely holding the reins in her two hands. She was wearing one of Martin's old felt hats, the brim pulled down all around, her hair done up in a bun under the crown. Beside her, Allan Pay rocked with the movement of the wheels over the shallow ruts, clutching his left elbow with his right hand.

"Does it hurt you to ride?"

"No. I am only apprehensive that it might, I suppose."

Meadowlarks were calling from the fields they passed, and twice rabbits bounded out to run frantically in front of the horses for a few yards before dashing headlong into the brush alongside the road. On a high, shattered oak snag, a redtail sat, his cruel beak curved like a scimitar as he watched for some field mouse strayed too far from the burrow.

They were almost halfway to Little Sugar Creek before she broke the silence again. Her voice was low, but there was a sharp edge to it that made him start visibly.

"All right, Mr. Pay. You said you needed to talk. There won't be a much better time."

She could see confusion across his face, hearing himself addressed in a formal way after having been called by his first name so often in recent days. She had done it deliberately, putting him on the defensive. He will have to make his case without help, she thought. I owe Martin that much.

He hesitated, unsure of his ground, and she had a moment of sympathy for him. But she thought, I am mother and father both now, and I don't want to leave anything done partway.

"Mrs. Hasford, you are aware that I am not in my own world here. Your ways of doing things are in some respects foreign to me. Or at least unknown," he said uneasily, not looking at her.

"They are the only ways we know. We don't try to hide them."

"I don't mean that you do. I mean that I am concerned with saying and doing the right thing in your eyes."

"There's no need to be uncomfortable with yourself," she said. Her insides felt lumpy, like a potato sack half-full. It occurred to her only in that moment that maybe she had allowed too much time alone between this man and her daughter, and she added, "Unless you've done something to be ashamed of."

"No. No, I don't mean that, either. I have never had such a wonderful few weeks in my whole life. And I am forever beholden to you for what you've done."

"Mr. Pay." She said it again deliberately. "You know and I know that this little talk you wanted doesn't have anything to do with your being in debt to me."

"Yes. I know." He was silent again, for a long time, and they came down to Little Sugar Creek ford. Ora pulled in the team at midstream to give them their drink. The water was shallow, flowing over the rounded limestones with a muted music. Finally, he spoke again.

"She has become very precious to me, Mrs. Hasford," he said, and there was no need to explain whom he meant.

"She is precious to me as well," Ora said. I must make myself sound like I was trading for mules with some Missouri traveler, she thought. I must not make it soft. I must test his mettle. She wasn't sure exactly what that term meant, but she had heard Martin use it many times.

"Among my people, there is a period of courtship," Pay said. "A man asks permission to call on a young lady. With intentions honorable, and well chaperoned."

"It's not much different among our people," she said.

The silence came between them once more, and they sat watching the water. The eastern sun was well up now, and its light came through the leaves of the trees along the creek, casting bright patches of rippling, crystal brilliance across the surface of the stream. The horses finished drinking and stood heads-up, but Ora let them stand.

"The days seem to have gone so swiftly," he said at last. "And now I must leave and there is so much to ask in so short a time."

"Then now is when you'd best say it." Despite her resolve to keep this on a coldly impersonal basis, she had to give him at least that much encouragement. Else, she was afraid he'd never say the words she wanted to hear.

"I know I should be speaking to her father," he said. "But that is obviously impossible and I have no intention of waiting out the war."

Now, he's about to say it, she thought, but she said, "You can speak with me in his place."

She saw his right hand, gripping tightly the stump that still hung before his chest in the sling. She tried to avoid watching the anguish in his face.

"It is difficult for a man to state his cause when he is only part a man."

That almost broke her, but she set her jaw against any softness toward him.

"The only man who is not whole is one who feels sorry for himself."

She felt him tense, and looking at his face she saw the burn of quick anger in his eyes.

"I am not speaking now of myself and how I judge such things. I am speaking of your daughter and of you," he said, looking directly into her eyes with a controlled fury. "I watch each of you here in this place and see the kinds of work you do, and a one-armed man is mostly useless for any of it. I simply want you to understand that I am no farmer, nor stock tender, nor woodcutter, and I have never thought to be. I expect to continue in what I had started before this war came, and I will do it as well as if nothing had happened to me, perhaps better."

He paused and looked away from her then, his jaw muscles working. He stared along the stream for a time before he spoke again, but she waited, feeling somehow very glad that he had lashed out.

"And I apologize for saying a thing that you would so badly misunderstand," he said.

"Sometimes it isn't easy for us to understand you. But then, you may have some trouble with our talk, too."

"That's precisely my point, Mrs. Hasford. We come from different worlds, even though we are separated by only a few hundred miles."

"But it's important you don't feel sorry for yourself."

"I don't. There was a time when that was likely not the case. But I don't worry about it anymore. Not in that way. It is not me that I am concerned about here. It is you and your daughter and Roman. I want you to know what I am."

The words came with less force, but were spoken directly, each pronounced clearly and slowly, as though he were afraid she might miss their import.

"Well, we may be backwoods people, but we know there are other things besides farming and stock tending and woodcutting, as you put it."

"All I am concerned about here is that you realize this is not my kind of life. It is not my family's kind of life. We are city people, and we think we have a good life. It doesn't take away from what you and your people are, it is just different."

He fished the pipe from his coat pocket and, holding it between his knees, loaded it with the rough-cut tobacco. After he fired it, he puffed awhile, and she said nothing.

"Mrs. Hasford, having said what I already have, I ask now if Calpurnia is spoken for."

She sighed, because now it was out. And she wasn't sure she knew how to manage it, especially now that he had shown a flash of temper. Almost like Roman sometimes, she thought, except that Allan Pay does not stomp around and shout, but lashes with hard words carefully selected.

"How would you support a wife?" she asked.

"I had supposed you'd know that an attorney, particularly one in a large city and going into an established firm, is not poverty-stricken." Although he spoke coolly now, there was no sound of sarcasm in his voice. "Before I joined the lists for this war, I was already making well in excess of five hundred dollars a year, and only just started."

He puffed his pipe, clicking the stem against his teeth and watching the bright ripples of water where the rising sun cut its light through the lacework of leaves.

"I am graduated from a good college in Illinois, where I intend sending any sons I may be lucky enough to have. I am twenty-six years old and believe myself well matured and with some sense beyond that of my profession. I am not addicted to strong drink, although I have developed a taste for good brandy from my father's cabinet. I do not use profane or abusive language, nor do I enjoy going about the town with young blades. If this all sounds self-serving, perhaps it is. But it is also true."

He turned his face to her once more, and his eyes were calm, his features composed. A not altogether unseemly-looking man, she thought, although not so handsome as my Martin.

When he spoke again, there was a small smile about to break across one corner of his mouth. "And I am kind to cripples, old veterans, children, and stray dogs."

He is taking control of this, she thought, and spoke more abruptly than she had intended.

"Where will you live?"

"My parents live in a well-accoutred house on the west of Saint Louis—"

"No, I don't mean your people. I mean you," she cut in. "I'm not interested in what your family has. I am interested in what you can give her. Not ten years from now, either, but right now. I don't want her living among strangers."

"Surely, we are not strangers."

"No, but your people are. If she married right here in this valley, I would want her to live in her own house. A woman is no proper wife unless she lives in her own house."

"I can assure you, I will have my own house. Until now, there has been no need for it."

Ora flicked the horses with the lines and they moved across the ford and up the far bank, pulling the wagon into the trail that wound through the narrow valley toward Wolf Cove.

"Then you're asking to marry her?" I hope I'm doing this right, Martin, she thought.

"That's what I'm doing, Mrs. Hasford, with all respect."

"Have you asked her?"

"No. But I believe there is an understanding between us."

She started to ask again if there had ever been anything more between them, but decided against it. She knew the answer anyway, so why try to embarrass him?

"And you would take her away soon?"

"As soon as possible."

"And if I said I would not consent?"

"I would ask her to go with me anyway," he said. He puffed the pipe, looking at her from the corners of his eyes, but she showed no reaction. She was, in fact, glad he had said it. "However, she is so strongly attached to you and to Roman, I don't think she would go unless she had your well-wishes."

"If she wants to go," Ora said, "she will have our well-wishes."

The wagon rocked along the grassy ruts of the road that was more path than road. Allan Pay knocked out his pipe on the sideboard and slowly replaced it in his pocket.

"I know what she means to you," he said. "And I can appreciate your reluctance at seeing her go. But she needs to get out of this valley and it does me great honor that you consider me worthy of her."

They looked at each other, and suddenly she extended her hand, like a man, and he took it, and for a moment their fingers were gripped together.

"This valley has been her home for as long as she has lived," Ora said. "But I agree that she needs out of it now, and quickly. And I am happy with the bargain. I think you are a good man."

He looked away for a moment, his jaw tightening again, but she saw he was not struggling with anger but with some other emotion. Finally, when he spoke, it was quietly but with some urgency.

"I'll go tomorrow," he said. "I'll walk to Springfield and telegraph my father. Or perhaps there is a line working as far south as Cassville."

"That's close by," she said. "But you can't walk, even that far. You're not strong enough yet. You'll take one of the mares."

"I'll be back as soon as I can. Perhaps in two weeks. I'll take quarters somewhere here in the valley, and pay proper court to her."

She looked at him and laughed, but there was no humor in it.

"Where do you think you could find a place to stay in this valley now? The tavern isn't open. The Yankees are there."

He laughed, too. "You must remember, Mrs. Hasford, I *am* a Yankee."

"I'm trying to forget it." And they laughed together. Then he turned serious again and shook his head, frowning.

"That's another thing I appreciate. That I'm from the city might be bad enough, but a northern city besides. Yet you have graciously agreed to my marrying your daughter."

"There's not much to be gracious about. I'm only thinking of what's best for Calpurnia. Besides, you're not all that different, in the important ways."

"Then I'll impose on your hospitality when I return."

"Yes. There's been enough of courting. If she doesn't know now, she never will. And I suspect she knows well enough."

"I could bring all of you to Saint Louis. My mother and father would be unhappy to miss the wedding."

"Any of your family is welcome."

He shook his head.

"No, I doubt they will come. My mother has never been a very healthy woman. She's of a delicate nature, and Father won't leave her for any length of time. Perhaps later, after the war is over, they can come and see this country, and you can bring Roman to visit us in Saint Louis. It is a little unusual, perhaps, but these are not usual times."

"We'll send for that Methodist minister in Bentonville. I guess he's still there. We'll invite the neighbors."

"It is a very happy moment for me, Mrs. Hasford. Knowing there is a chance she will go with me."

"She'll go," Ora Hasford said. She was frowning, looking at the road ahead.

Here it had narrowed to little more than a path winding beneath the overhanging trees, following the course of Little

Sugar Creek's south bank. The ground was in shadow most of the time, still moist and soft. There were tracks in the grassy mound between the ruts, tracks of many horses. Their shoes had cut deep divots into the sod. And there were fresh droppings.

"What is it, Mrs. Hasford?"

"I don't know. A lot of horses have come along here, and not too long ago."

"It's likely a cavalry patrol."

"Maybe. But why would they be going to Tulip Crozier's?"

2   Around the hives there was the low hum of the bees working, bringing in the nectar and pollen from the new wildflowers that covered the hillsides in pale blue and violet clusters under the oaks and among the rock outcrops. Down the slope, where the buildings stood, there was a bright silence, the sun drenching the cleared spaces between the hickories.

Elderberry bushes, like great green fountains, stood sentinel along the back of the pigpens, their white blossoms bunched in rosettes big as a man's hat. The sties were empty, as was the horse paddock, its gate standing open. The top rail of the corral was bare in the sun, the peeled pole like a naked bone where saddles and bridles and blankets and hackamores were usually hung.

The windows of the buildings stared out blackly into the bright clearing. One was broken, a dirty once-white curtain fluttering out from it, a flag of surrender. And across the clearing, alongside the stream, the mill stood like a vast gray chunk of stone, with sparrows fluttering and darting under the eaves. The mill wheel was turning slowly, still shaded by the tall sycamores that stood in gray-and-white-dappled ranks along the bank of Little Sugar Creek where it made the oxbow bend that had been incorrectly called a cove for as long as any man could remember.

The unengaged wheel made a dry, wooden moaning, turning

on its oaken shaft. Lifted paddles dripped back to the surface of the stream with the sound of tiny summer rain. Water moved sluggishly over the limestone rocks of the millpond dam, hardly distinguishable from the rush of water between the steep banks below.

Emptiness and silence hung over Wolf Cove like a dense haze, suspended and impenetrable. Even with the soft breeze that came along the hollow from the west. Even with the sounds of the stream and the wheel and the chirping sparrows, and the scolding of two bright jays that whipped in and out of the dooryard before Tulip Crozier's store, where the door hung crookedly on its hinges and where a spilled sack of cornmeal made a yellow splash on the doorstep.

There was a clutter of debris across the mill yard between the smaller structures and the mill itself—bottles and empty burlap bags and corks and a strip of old harness, left on the barren earth where the grass had long since been trod down by years of passing feet. A few paces from Tulip Crozier's door lay the old horse pistol, its hammer down on an exploded percussion cap. And close by that, a stain of umber, blotted now by the soil into a dry scab. A boot lay on its side before the sliding doors of the mill room, half-open into the dark interior, and against the wall, a crumpled black beaver hat, the buzzard feather still standing stiffly from the brim.

3 Lark lay belly-down in a new growth of dogwood just short of the heavy oak timber on the south slope of the hollow. His tongue tasted like metal, as hard and hot as the sunlight slanting down through the dogwoods. Tied to a sapling behind him stood the wayward goat, old and tired and not bleating, having been found a little after dawn far along this ridge that extended toward White River Valley. But he was not thinking of the goat. He had completely forgotten that she was there. Below him were the white beehives, and beyond that the buildings of Wolf Cove. He could see the dark doorway of the mill, and he could see the speck made by Tulip Crozier's hat lying there against the wall in the sun.

He had been lying in this position for some time, the shade spotty and the sun making him sweat. It glistened across his dark face, and now and again he wiped at it, and fanned away the early-morning gnats that swarmed around his head.

To any casual observer, Lark seemed always to be occupied with such things as fanning gnats away from his head. But inside his brain there were many strange and marvelous shapes and forms that he sorted constantly, putting each in its place, irritated when one of them tried to take some other position. He kept them all polished and aligned, and from time to time he inserted something new and then spent days deciding where it fit into the arrangement. This was how he had survived, all his life, for his ordering of the shapes and forms constantly indicated to him that simplicity, even stupidity, was the thing that had to show through, regardless of what might be inside.

Lark had always been a good slave. He had done his work well, generally without complaint; he had been courteous and had slept with only a few slave women who were willing, causing no row among the other men. Each of his successive masters had believed that they alone had created Lark, had cut him from their own piece of cloth. But they had all been wrong. Lark acted as a proper slave should act because of the constant arrangement and polishing of the shapes and forms. He had allowed the white man to think whatever pleased the white man. It was a matter of survival, with a few creature comforts thrown in besides.

But as he lay among the dogwoods, all the shapes and forms were in turmoil. Since he had been told that he was free, and since Tulip Crozier had begun to treat him as though he were white, everything needed rearranging. He was unsure about what he should show outwardly now. I don't have to be no dumb nigger no more, Mister Tulip says, he would think. But I ain't gone be one of them uppity niggers like I seen sometimes in Mississippi, gone to readin' and writin' lessons with the white man on the quiet, helpin' with accounts then or speakin' that French in New Orleans and ridin' in carriages with stiff collars on, and actin' like they was white colonels. I gotta be somewheres in between. Somewheres between grinnin' and scrapin'.

And now there was this new thing, that blotted all the others from his thinking. The thing that had happened in this valley, and was still happening. As he lay there in the mottled splash of sunlight, he wondered how long it would take to walk back to Mississippi, where he might find things easier to handle, although unjust. But at this moment he was no more concerned with justice than with the goat. His concern was staying alive, and from what he had seen in this valley since the end of winter he was convinced that staying alive here was very difficult indeed.

He had almost made up his mind to go back down to Wolf Cove, an act needing a great deal of courage. On this clear spring morning, with the leaves full out and the water behind the mill making its soft music, there was a brightness and beauty in the valley of Wolf Cove. But to Lark, the place had become a scalding pot. He tried to think of what he would do down there. He tried to arrange the shapes and forms in his head, so he would know how to act. Then he saw the wagon pull into the edge of Tulip Crozier's clearing from the direction of Wire Road.

Someone with a large hat was driving the team, but he knew it was a woman from her gingham dress and the white half-apron hanging from her waist. She stood up, holding the reins taut, and Lark could see the horses fiddle-footing nervously. Sitting in the seat beside the woman was a man, bare-headed, who seemed to be hugging himself.

"God Almighty, who's come?" he muttered aloud.

He watched the woman shake the lines, still standing with one foot on the dash. The horses moved on into the dooryard and the rattle of the wagon boards came to Lark softly on the breeze. He could hear the woman calling.

"Tulip Crozier. Hello, Tulip, are you here?"

There was no answer, only the faded curtain waving from the broken window. Lark watched them drive to Crozier's store, and he watched the jays flash away and into the sycamores, still scolding raucously.

The man jumped down from the wagon, and Lark could see now that his left arm was bound close to his body in a sling. That's the man they cut off his han', he thought. The man bent and picked up the pistol. Even at this distance, Lark knew it was the pistol because he had seen it drop from Tulip Crozier's hand. The man smelled the muzzle and cocked it and carried it back to the wagon and handed it up to the woman. She smelled it, too, then wrapped the reins around the brake handle and stepped down to the front wheel and onto the ground.

Now Lark was sure who this was, because he had seen this same woman coming off her wagon in just that fashion many times at Elkhorn Tavern when she'd come to visit Polly Cox.

"Gawddamn, it's Miz Hasford," he grunted, and rose and started running down the mountainside toward them, shouting her name. Behind him, the goat lifted her head but still made no sound. Lark leaped the brush in high bounds, his heart pounding as it had once before this morning. He fell near the elderberry bushes, but scrambled up and went on again, calling her name.

They waited for him before the broken door of Tulip Crozier's store, looking grim. He saw as he ran into the yard the man's bandaged stump where a hand should have been, and he saw Ora Hasford's face, her lips set in a hard line under the shadow of the wide-brimmed hat. Lark fell against the store's wall, panting, leaning there with the sweat running off his black face. Ora Hasford moved quickly over to stand before him.

"What is it? What's happened here? Why's all this stuff scattered around? Where's Tulip Crozier?"

"They come, Miz Hasford," Lark gasped. "Some of them nightridin' men on horseback, and they taken Mister Tulip's stock and they taken his stuff out'n the store."

His eyes went to the slinged stump of the young man, and he seemed to draw away, but Ora Hasford grabbed his suspenders with both her hands and pulled him close, her face glaring into his.

"All right now, settle yourself and tell me slowly. Where's Tulip Crozier?"

"I was afeared, Miz Hasford. I never had no gun nor nothin'. I was afeared, but I seen 'em come in here and I was hid in them trees up yonder." He pointed toward the far line of trees on the hill behind the hives. "I was up there lookin' for a goat run off. I was jus' comin' back, and that's when I seen 'em. They come in the houses and they—"

"Where is he?" Ora Hasford cut in, shaking him by the suspenders like a misbehaving child.

"Jus' a while ago, Miz Hasford. Mister Tulip run out'n the store and shot one of 'em, and then them others put that shot man back up on his horse. One of 'em had a pillowcase over his head, with holes cut to see through, and they was wavin' guns, and one of 'em, the one with the pillowcase, he knock Mister Tulip on the groun', and then Mister Tulip pull that ole gun out'n his boot and shot this big fat man with a fancy hat, and the fat man fell offen his horse."

"How long ago, damn it?" she shouted, yanking on his suspenders.

"Jus' a while ago, Miz Hasford. They drag Mister Tulip over

yonder, into the mill," and he pointed to the open door across the yard.

She released him so suddenly, he almost fell. They were running toward the mill, and Lark pushed himself away from the wall of the store and ran after them.

"They drag Mister Tulip right in there, Miz Hasford, then rode out of here with Mister Tulip's horses and his pig."

Then they were inside. The main grinding room was dim after the bright sunlight of the yard. Lark could feel its coolness and smell the musty sweet odor of grain. The other two were across the wide room, looking behind the gears and the stones and the hopper. Lark moved deeper into the room, backing away toward one wall, and his shoulder bumped against something that swayed back away from him and then bumped him again. He turned and at the level of his eyes were two feet, one without a boot, gently swinging back and forth before his face.

"Oh my Lord Gawd, Miz Hasford," Lark cried, jumping back. She and the man turned, and he saw their eyes go wide in horror and heard the man swear and Ora Hasford's breath catch in her throat.

Tulip Crozier was hanging from one of the massive rafters, his hands bound behind his back with baling wire. Another strand of wire was twisted around the beam and suspended him by the neck. It made a soft glimmer of metallic light in the gloom of the mill, the long slender thread coming down from the oaken rafter and then buried in the swollen flesh of his neck. His eyes were bulging, as though he were ready to shout one of his terrible oaths, but his mouth was choked with a tongue gone black, protruding between his lips.

"Dear God," Ora gasped. She pushed against Lark, trying to move him back from the ghastly swinging body. Her eyes were up, on Tulip Crozier's bloated face, and her teeth ground together. She pushed Lark back through the door, her face looking sick, leaving Allan Pay, still staring, transfixed. And in the sunlight, with a sudden fury, she turned on Lark and held his suspenders once more, drawing him close to her and those furious eyes.

"I couldn't hep it, Miz Hasford. They was so many of 'em and they had guns and I couldn't do nothin'—"

"Stop babbling, you black fool," she screamed. "I know you couldn't help it. Where are they? Which way did they go?"

"They come out'n here where they done that to Mister Tulip—"

"Where did they go, damn it? Tell me where they went!"

"Off yonder," Lark said, and he pointed across the stream to the high slope north of the valley.

For an instant she stared across the stream. He could hear her breathing hard, and he saw the muscles along her jaw work.

"Dear God, the farm's that way. And she's there alone, with Roman out making fence." She said it to herself, but loud enough for Lark to hear. Lark opened his mouth to speak, but she was running toward the wagon.

"Mister, she's goin'," Lark shouted, and Pay appeared in the mill doorway, looking ashen-faced.

Ora Hasford held up her apron as she ran, her short legs stretching the long gingham dress. She scrambled up over the wheel and into the bed behind the seat, wrenching the lines from the brake handle. She screamed at the horses and slashed them with the lines and they grunted and leaped in surprise, eyes walling back as they bunched their rear legs and jerked forward in the harness.

Lark dashed frantically to leap over the tailgate, going headlong into the wagon. Ora was turning the team, whipping them hard, and the wheels cut deep into the hard earth, the wagon careening wildly.

"Help me up," Pay shouted, running along behind the wagon. Lark reached out and, taking the man's shoulders, pulled him up over the tailgate and into the wagon. He heard Pay grunt with pain as he fell into the wagon bed. Lark crouched at the tailgate, holding on with both hands. Ora Hasford was lashing the team out of the clearing, bellowing at them, cursing them as Lark had never heard a white woman curse, standing in the wagon bed with legs spread wide, the man's hat blown off. She slashed at the mares, driving them hard into the pathway toward Wire Road.

XVI

Calpurnia went slowly toward Plum Thicket Ridge, stopping often to watch a pair of pileated woodpeckers that seemed to follow her, high in the hickories, rapping each tree tentatively before flapping on to the next, their great outstretched wings showing black and white stripes and the red crest flashing like pennants in the sun. Across the carpet of the slope were the delicate wood violets, blooming among the moss-covered outcrops, and she thought she must pick a bunch for her mother on the way back. They grew in fluffy bunches, the tiny blossoms looking as though someone had needlepointed them across the faded gray moss. There were spots of lambency on the ferns, where sunlight penetrated the foliage, the brilliance appearing to come up from the earth like a shimmering issue of clear spring water.

She moved with her usual easy grace, swinging a wicker basket in one hand for acorns or wild strawberries or anything else she might find, and a stout hickory stick in the other. The stick was for snakes, although the only ones she feared were those she could not see. She had grown up in this country among them, the copperheads and rattlers, and they were only another part of the wild timber, although due considerable respect.

Once—when only six years old—she had been walking with her mother along one of these woodland paths when she stopped short and pointed to a five-foot rattlesnake just ahead. Her mother had leaped past her with that amazing speed she could call up on demand, throwing rocks, killing the rattler without ever going within striking distance of it. Calpurnia had often tried to remember seeing her mother pick up the rocks from the ground that day, but she never could. The flinty missiles had simply appeared in her mother's hands. And then she had thrown them with fierce velocity and accuracy, overhand—as Martin would have done, or later Roman.

The windfall of last year's leaves lay in small pillows under the oaks, reminding her of cast-off cuttings from some woodland quilting party, brittle and crisp and making a soft rustling sound as her feet passed through them. Now and again she stepped over tiny rivulets, where running water seeped from the hillside with a faint fairybell sound, and she half expected, as always when walking here, to see the footprints of the fairies themselves that some of the hill people said lived under the green sworling deer's-tongue and in the dusty underside of rotting logs.

The woodpeckers followed behind her, seeming to take her pathway as a guide to some juicy grub buried beneath the decaying bark of a hickory or walnut snag. Gray squirrels whisked through the branches, some of them stopping, their great liquid eyes peering at her with that sharp inquisitiveness of their kind before making a chattering bark, then disappearing in a quaking flurry of leaves.

She was happy to be here, alone. It had been a long time since she had walked among these familiar oaks, going to her favorite place where she could sit beneath the wild plums and watch the timber moths and bumblebees and the playing squirrels safe from Roman's gun.

There was a book in her gathering basket, but she knew she would likely do no reading this day because there was too much else to think about, too many of the old sights long remembered but at this time of year bursting forth with a rebirth that always startled her, even though she had seen it each spring from the beginning of her life. She knew she might never have the joy of being here again.

Ora Hasford's request that Allan Pay accompany her to Wolf Cove had been too adamant for Calpurnia or anybody else to overlook or misunderstand, even though her mother had disguised it as a suggestion only. Calpurnia knew the time had come for her mother and this young man from Saint Louis to have their talk together, about her and her future, and she knew Roman was aware of it, too. She had watched her brother walk out of the house this morning, sullenly, taking the broad ax and wedges and hammer he would use to split rails for fences, working in a jack-oak grove far across the valley. He said nothing, but he would go as far away from the farm on this day as he could go, to show his disapproval. She felt compassion for him, but only a little. She was too excited, quietly excited, to worry with her brother's moods. Because the time had come. She knew what Allan Pay would ask, and she knew what her mother would answer. There was much of her mother in her, the same intuition. Nothing had yet been said between the two, but she knew as surely as her mother knew. She would go with this man wherever and whenever he might go.

For a time, she wondered if she would have been so willing to go had her mother been opposed. She doubted it, but thought of it only fleetingly because she had never dwelt on improbabilities. She knew her mother well, and she knew herself, almost as though they were one. So there was no uncertainty. She knew.

Then she was out of the green gloom of the timber and into the open glade where the plum trees had just finished their budding. Behind her she could hear the woodpeckers still, rapping against dead bark snags. She looked carefully along the stony bench for snakes, found her usual place, and settled down against a large gum tree. She could smell the plum leaves and the pungent odor of wild onions.

There was a quiet turmoil in the woods, sounds she knew well and loved. The insects and squirrels, and perhaps a movement in the dead leaves of the deep timber where there might be a deer or even a turkey, watching her. The sounds seemed to intensify as she sat there, rising to a crescendo as the day warmed around her.

But suddenly the pileated woodpeckers flew off frantically, away to the east, and the scrambling gray squirrels disappeared like blown smoke, and even the buzz of wood flies ceased. She thought she heard the bluetick hound bark once, far down the slope, but she gave it hardly a thought. There were too many other things to occupy her mind, and she sat with the sunlight slanting under the brim of her bonnet, smiling, thinking of large boats like lighted beehives in the night, moving down a great, dark river.

2   They came in a straggling column, over the ridge from the south and into the churn-house hollow and up again to the yard. The bluetick hound saw them while they were still deep in timber and let off one warning bark before retreating. He ran to the garden patch, looking back over his shoulder, and finally took his stand among the potato plants, with tail erect but making no sound other than a low growl in his throat. The horses pounded into the hard beaten space between house and barn, sending up a fine dust.

There was no semblance of order in their movement. They came with leather squealing and bit chains clanking, shouting and whipping their horses on because they were in a hurry and not accustomed to riding in daylight. And because they were anxious to be away from here after what the man named Henry had directed them to do at Wolf Cove mill. Many of them still carried the image of the old man with the white beard hanging from his own rafter by baling wire, and perhaps that scene suggested what could happen to any one of them should they be caught by a cavalry patrol or some partisan band from the other side.

At their head rode Colonel Clarence Caudell, swaying in the saddle just as he had that first night he came into this farmyard. But he was not drunk now. His great belly was reddened with blood from the .50-caliber pistol ball that had ranged upward through the right side of his chest to lodge against his shoulder blade. With each movement of the horse beneath him, he could feel metal grinding against the bone. Beside him rode Henry, one hand extended to steady his commander in the saddle. Henry—the dirtiest, hairiest, most disreputable-looking man of a dirty, hairy, disreputable lot, and most faithful, too.

Henry guided the colonel's horse directly to the house as the others dismounted in an unorganized scramble to run into all the buildings. He leaped down and tried to help his colonel to the ground, but the massive weight resisted him.

"Come hep me with the colonel," he called, and two of the others ran over and the three of them dragged Caudell down and onto the porch.

"By God, boys, it's a deep one," Caudell gasped, and there was a froth of red at each corner of his mouth.

"Let's take a closer look, Colonel," Henry said, unbuttoning the greatcoat and ripping away the bloody shirt. There was a puckered, bluish hole just beneath the ribs, almost swollen shut now, bleeding only a little.

Caudell groaned, and his fingers, where the golden ring seemed swallowed by the bulging fat, groped for the wound. Henry pushed the hand aside. In those last frantic moments at Wolf Cove, he had done little other than have the colonel hoisted onto his mount, and now he examined Caudell closely, feeling along the back where he found no exit wound.

"Goddamn ball's still in him," he muttered, as two other men came up to bend over, peering at the wound with bloodshot eyes.

"Whiskey, Henry. In my bags. Get the whiskey," Caudell said, and his voice was weak and hardly heard at all.

"Colonel, we better not give you no whiskey jus' now," Henry said. "I ain't sure where that ball went."

"He don't look gut-shot to me," one of the others said dispassionately. "He looks more like he was lung-shot."

"You can't ever tell what them old punkin balls will do. We ain't givin' him no whiskey, ner nothin' else to drink," Henry snapped. He slipped off Caudell's hat and bunched it under his head, making a pillow. "We got to get to a doctor, Colonel. With a doctor, you'll be jus' fine, jus' fine."

"Lord God of hosts will bless our arms," Caudell croaked, a note of hysteria creeping into his voice. His eyes were turning glassy and the blood had begun to collect in small foamy driblets at his mouth and to run down into the great beard.

"Rest easy, Colonel. For jus' a minute while the boys see what we can find here," Henry said. "You there, draw up some water from that well over yonder. I'm gonna clean this hole."

"It ain't gonna do no good," the man said, but he went across to the well and drew a bucket of water. Others were coming from the barn now, one carrying a saddle.

"Ain't no horses here, Henry," he shouted.

"That goddamned Epp, where's he at? He told us they had horses here," Henry said, daubing at the colonel's red-smeared side with a dirty handkerchief. "And don't mess with that saddle—it ain't nothin' but deadweight."

"By God, I'll take her my own self," the man said.

"Then take 'er and be damned."

"Well," the other said, staring down at the saddle, then shrugging and throwing it aside. "To hell with it."

Henry bent over the colonel's face, and he could feel the breath coming harshly and loud from the parted lips. "How you feel, Colonel?"

"What's that? What's that about saddles?"

Another of the shaggy men came up behind Henry, bending, too, and staring at the swollen wound as Henry washed it with cold water from the well.

"Ain't nothin' in the smokehouse, Henry," he said.

"That goddamned Epp. Where's he at?"

"That crazy bastard? With that pillowcase over his head all the time?"

"He's afeared same of these people around here will recognize him."

"He'd be a damned fool to ever come back to this part of the country again, anyway."

"Well, he can burn in hell's fire. We gotta get the colonel to a sawbones."

The man turned away, shrugging, and said to another, "That old fat man ain't never gonna see no more sunrises."

"He don't look to me like he's gonna see sunset today, even."

Inside the house, they kicked furniture about in a fury at finding so little, broke a sugar bowl and dumped sassaffras tea roots from a tin tub. They were looking for money. One of them slashed open the kitchen bed mattress with a knife, but found only feathers.

"They bury it someplace," one growled. "They always bury it where you can't find it." He picked up a small silver pickle dish, stared without comprehension at the German mark of weight on the bottom, and slipped it into his pocket.

They were down in the root cellar, too, groping for potatoes that were not there, finding only a few fresh vegetables taken from the garden the evening before, stuffing these into shirtfronts. One dusted off a handful of green onions and ate them, roots and all.

In the smokehouse, one man was on his knees, scraping up the salt that had dripped to the floor over many years of curing meat; he put the stained crusts into a loot bag. Another was in the pigsty, grabbing each of the pigs in turn and striking them across the head behind the ears with a pistol butt before tying them and lashing them to his saddle.

"They's some dry beans, is about all," one said from the kitchen doorway.

"Leave 'em," Henry said. "Too damned much trouble to fix. Colonel Caudell, can you hear me?" He bent close over the colonel, shouting in his face. The eyes there, in their blankets of putty-colored flesh, tried to focus on him.

"Henry, is that you? Is that you, Henry? It's beginning to hurt very much."

"Colonel, we need to get you to a doctor, real fast," Henry said. "Now, it ain't far to Cassville, so we'll jus' put you back on your horse and ride up there and you'll be jus' fine."

More of the others had gathered now, looking at Caudell with expressionless eyes.

"Where you reckon everybody's at around here?" one asked.

"Damned iffen I know. But they ain't here anyways, you seen that."

"Maybe they pulled stakes."

"Hell, they's a fire banked in the stove. They jus' off some-wheres."

"I don't like this here valley. I'll be glad to get back to the Territory."

"Lord God of hosts," Caudell suddenly cried, stiffening.

"Come on, boys," Henry said. "Let's get him back in the saddle."

"We could make a drag litter," one said.

"We ain't got no time for drag litters. He'll ride. You can ride, can't you, Colonel?"

"Lord God, Lord God, I'm bad shot, boys," the colonel said, his eyes out of focus and the blood running from his mouth. Henry swiped at it with the stained handkerchief.

"Come on, boys, let's get him to Cassville."

"Goddamn, Henry, we ain't got no business in Cassville."

"We ain't never done nothin' to nobody in Cassville. Besides, maybe we can find one of them army sawbones where we been dealin' horses."

"That's a helluva long ways from Cassville."

"Colonel, we gonna ride now. We're gonna take you to a doctor in Missouri."

But Caudell was past hearing, his eyes already going vacant and staring. He was trying to speak, his lips moving, trying to give commands. Henry shook his head.

"Well, come on, boys, let's give her a try. Help me now. It ain't easy liftin' him. Hold that horse steady."

They lifted the deadweight into the saddle, the colonel groaning, his lips moving soundlessly. Some of them backed away then, wiping the blood from their hands onto their trousers. Where he had been lying on the rough boards of the porch was a small red stain.

"He's gonna bleed like a stuck hog, ridin' like this," one said.

"I can't help that. We got to get him to Cassville."

"Hell, he'll never make the border, much less Cassville," the same man muttered, but not loud enough for Henry to hear.

"Hold him there till I get up," Henry said, and he mounted, moving his horse in close to the colonel's. "Where's that damned Epp at?"

"I seen him ride off through the woods yonder."

"That son of a bitch!"

"Hell, Henry, we can find Missouri without no help from him."

"All right, let's get on out of here. If some of these people catch that slab-sided bastard and make hog slop out of him, it won't trouble me. I ain't waitin' for him. One of you boys ride close on the colonel's gee side."

They mounted hurriedly and followed Henry and the colonel through the garden patch. The bluetick hound was still there, growling but backing off again as they came on. The horses roiled up dust from the dry dooryard, and even more of a dense cloud going through the garden, trampling down the potato plants.

One man remained, his red-rimmed eyes glaring about this place where there had been so little to take. He walked into the kitchen, on into the parlor. The glass of the china closet gleamed softly in the light from the windows, the spiderweb mark of the bullet hole in the center. He picked up a chair and threw it into the glass, shattering it and some of the dishes behind. Back in the kitchen, he threw open the cookstove door, and with an ash shovel he scooped out live coals and threw them into the center of the ripped mattress. He kicked over the kitchen table and strode across the room and out to his horse to follow the others, swearing and hungry.

The plume of dust lifted behind them as they rode across Ruddick's Field and slanted back to Wire Road, bearing always north toward the border. The hound watched them go, still growling deep in his throat, and then he trotted back into the yard, stiff-legged, reclaiming his domain. He lifted his nose and sniffed, and there was the odor of smoldering goose feathers, and soon the wisp of gray smoke coming from the kitchen doorway.

3   Spider Epp knew as soon as he rode near the Hasford farm-yard that no one was there. Else they would be out to challenge, bristling like mastiff dogs at the intrusion, either that hard-eyed woman or else her towheaded son. But no one came out, and he knew before he rode past the barn that the place was deserted.

He did not know at first why he reined the army stallion around and moved along the back side of the paddock in the rear of the barn, nor was he sure why he allowed the horse to find his own way into the timber along the slope east of the house. Then he recalled those days he had been here, hired out by Martin Hasford to work in the timber, and he remembered that the girl Calpurnia had always been going off to a little plum thicket along the ridge, going off to be alone in those safer times. He grinned under the pillowcase that covered his face. There was just a chance, a slight chance, but one he intended to take.

He was uncertain of where the plum trees grew. It had been a long time since he'd ridden here. He cut back and forth through the trees, his wolf eyes watching through the slitted pillowcase, casting through the dense green for a break in the woods where sunlight would be coming bright now in the growing morning. There was no haste in his movements. Unlike the shaggy crew with whom he rode, he felt no fear, no apprehension. The thing that had happened at Wolf Cove had somehow made him calm and confident, somehow made him powerful. There, in the dim mill, he had even pulled off the pillowcase mask at the last moment, before they lifted the old secesh trash Jew up, so he would know who it was doing such a thing to him.

Ahead, he saw the trees thinning, and the fresh sunlight made a dazzling glow, as though a curtain had been opened on a lighted stage. He moved more slowly, his eyes darting back and forth. Then he saw the plum trees, and beneath one of them a splash of gingham color. He drew in the army stallion and watched, beginning to pant. She was there, and it made his heart pound furiously against his ribs, just seeing her, sitting there with her sunbonnet tilted back.

Pull off the mask and let her see me, he thought. No, you'd have to kill her if you did that. Or maybe she won't care. Maybe she's just waiting for something like this.

He touched the army stallion's flanks with his rusty spurs

and the big horse moved ahead, out into the brightness of the plum-tree glade. He was close enough to see her face clearly before she realized he was there. Her head came up and her eyes grew wide, and that made his heart pound even harder. Her lips opened to speak, but no sound came, and then she was up, more quickly than he had thought she could move—so fast, he sat for a moment uncertainly as she ran back away from him and toward the deep woods. Then he laughed and kicked the army stallion and the horse leaped out after her.

She was still carrying the basket and the hickory stick when the stallion came up to her in a rush, shying at the last moment to avoid hitting her. Spider Epp swung out a stirrup and struck her in the back, and she went sprawling into the dead leaves of the oaks. He heard the breath go out of her and saw the wicker basket spinning through the underbrush. He wheeled the horse and stepped down, breathing hard and laughing, and as she rose he saw her eyes, terrified but defiant, and the hickory stick was still in her hand. She caught him alongside the jaw with her first swing, hitting him hard. He staggered back and grunted, and she swung again. But now he moved in close and caught the stick in both hands and wrenched it from her. She staggered and almost fell again, and he was at her, tearing her blouse down the front. He felt her fingernails clawing through the cloth of the pillowcase, sharp against his cheeks, and he threw her down and leaped onto her, turning her faceup, tearing at the gingham dress.

The fierce blue eyes were directly beneath him now, and the lips pulled back over clinched teeth, and the hard-set jaw. He wanted her to scream, but she made no sound, fighting him silently. He yanked off her bonnet and the hair fell around her face in a tangle.

As he lowered himself over her, she struck upward with a clinched fist, smashing his nose, still making no sound but with a fury in her face displacing any fright that was there before. She kicked him, bringing up her knees into his belly as he pawed over her on hands and knees, trying to hold her. She scrambled from beneath him, crablike, and kicked at his face, a glancing blow that almost tore the pillowcase from his head and ripped one ear so that he felt the hot blood running down his neck.

She was up then, and he made a grab for her ankles and missed, still on his knees. She kicked his head again and leaped away from him. Like a damned deer, he thought, as she disappeared into a tangled growth of sumacs. He got up and turned back to the horse, still laughing because he knew there was no place she could run where the big army stallion would not catch her.

"To hell with this damned thing," he panted, tearing the pillowcase from his face, his heat overcoming any caution that might remain. For one instant, he was blinded as he pulled the cloth over his eyes. And as it came clear, he ran solidly into the Indian, stepping from between two oaks, one hand reaching out to take Spider Epp's shirtfront, and in the other, the knife.

He felt the first thrust like a hot pinch in his belly, and his hands lifted to the Indian's shoulders. He stared into the black, flaming eyes, the flat, hard face. Spider Epp's hands seemed to scratch at the Indian's shoulders, just below the dangling earrings, trying to cling there like the claws of some sick, weakened bird, trying to find some purchase on the beaded jacket.

"Now just a minute, mister," he heard himself gasp, and then he saw the long blade again, and then again.

4   Calpurnia Hasford did not look back, even when she thought she heard him make some sound, some noise of frustration or despair. Only when she reached the paddock, was leaning against the peeled poles, did she turn to the dark woods behind her.

Nothing was there except the oaks, now beginning to move in a bright morning wind that had come up from the west. She clung to the fence for a long time, waiting to see any movement along the slope, but there was none, except among the leaves high up.

She heard the bluetick hound begin to bark, some note of frenzy in his voice, and she pushed away from the fence, her breath still coming hard, and ran around the barn. The dog was leaping and barking frantically, watching the smoke boil out of the kitchen doorway. She saw the scatter of debris across the yard, the empty pigpen, the trampled garden, the surface of the yard chopped with many steel shoes. Only then, even as she was running for the house, did she realize what had happened. The man who had clawed at her was part of this larger group, but now all of them were gone.

She ran past the bellowing dog, across the porch, and into the kitchen, and saw the flicker of fire through the smoke. She choked and staggered through the room, and saw the mattress in flames. She took it in both hands along the only edge that was not smoldering, and dragged it toward the door, moving backward, scattering flaming feathers and bits of cotton duck across the floor. There was a cold, hard fury in her, seeing what these people had done, remembering more and more vividly what one of them had tried to do to her. She yanked the flaming mattress through the door, over the porch and into the yard.

The dog yammered at her legs and she kicked at him.

"Shut up, you son of a bitch," she shrieked.

On the porch was a dark-stained cloth near a spot of color on the floorboards, and a bucket, half-filled. She took the bucket inside and splashed water over the smoldering bits and pieces spread across the kitchen. Beneath the bed was a spot of flame, but the water was gone by then and she ran out past the barking dog, kicked at him again in passing, and went to the well. But when Ora Hasford whipped the lathered team into the yard, standing in the wagon, the other two clinging desperately to the sideboards, the fire was extinguished inside the house. All that remained of it was the pungent smell of burnt feathers, and in the yard, the mattress, the last of it burning and sending smoke in a wisp of gray along the wind.

On the west side of the valley, near the base of Little Mountain, Roman Hasford had begun his rail splitting. In a small copse of oak, he found the debris of an army's passage. There were scattered canteens and haversacks and a leather belt and brass buckle with *US* engraved on it. There was also a bayonet, starting to rust now, and a number of cartridge boxes with the paper ammunition scattered across the ground, soggy with moisture and a few split open, the powder spilling out like coarse black pepper.

He marked off a number of the small trees here along the edge of the cleared fields, and began to fell them with sure, strong strokes of the ax. Then he trimmed the limbs and cut the trunks in eight-foot lengths before opening the grain with the ax blade, enough to drive in the steel wedge. Even after the saplings had been split along their entire length, the oak fibers clung together stubbornly, and it required another ten minutes with the ax to separate the two halves and trim them for fencing. Each tree yielded two fence railings, and left a litter of small limbs and twigs that he would come back for later with the wagon and haul home for kindling.

Even in the early morning, the work was hot, and he paused often to rest, wiping his face with a calico strip of cloth his mother had given him for a handkerchief. The split oak fencing was piling up before him when he saw a movement along Wire Road far to the east. Shading his eyes, he could make out horsemen riding into the road from Ruddick's Field and on toward the north, kicking up a plume of white dust, obviously in a hurry. He knew they were not soldiers, but from that distance he could see no details.

"What in hell's name?" he said aloud. He moved to a small rise of ground, under the shade of trees not yet touched by his ax, and continued to watch until the horsemen were out of sight.

Without thinking why, he gathered his tools and started back across the valley in a long lope. He was midway across the last field when he saw the wagon, his mother whipping the team, coming up the road from the south, then careening into the drive up the slope and into the trees where the house stood. Now he dropped the ax and heavy hammer and wedge and started to run hard, so that when he crossed the road and started up to the farmstead he was panting and soaked with sweat.

The horses, still hitched to the wagon, were blowing and lathered in the backyard, and Lark was trying to gentle them, rubbing their necks with a burlap bag, talking to them in a low voice when Roman burst around the corner of the house. He saw a cookpot overturned near the wagon, and there was a scatter of broken china and what was left of the burnt mattress. The bluetick hound ran up, barking with the excitement that Roman could still feel in the yard, dense as oil smoke.

"Your mama's in the house with that Yankee man, Mister Roman," Lark called, but Roman was already bounding across the porch and into the kitchen.

She was sitting in one of the ladder-backs, bent forward with her face in her hands, Allan Pay standing before her, his hand on her shoulder. She raised her face, and Roman could see she had been crying. But she was composed as she rose to meet her son, and he ran to her and they embraced for only a moment.

"I was about to come looking for you," Pay said. "To see if you were all right, and to bring you home. We've had some trouble."

Roman was still panting, his mother before him with her

hands fluttering across his shirtfront, trying to control her emotions after the strain of what had happened, and the struggle in her face terrified Roman because in all his life he had seldom seen her in such a state.

"What is it? What happened? Where's Cal?"

"She's all right," Ora said finally, patting his chest. "She's all right. Get a drink of water. You're all hot."

Pay's face was different, too—hard, and the muscles working along his angular jaw, the lips tight beneath the straw-colored mustache. His eyes were bright, and stared into Roman's with a penetrating intensity Roman had not noticed before. His good hand was clenched at his side into a fist, the knuckles standing hard and white.

"What's happened? Tell me what's happened!"

"Partisans," Pay said.

"But Calpurnia—"

"She's all right," Pay snapped. "She's upstairs changing her dress. She tore it."

"How did she—"

"They didn't harm her," Ora said, speaking more calmly than either of the other two. "One tried to catch her in the woods. She was at Plum Thicket Ridge, but no harm's come to her. They only passed through and did no harm here, except for some of this."

Ora looked around the room, littered with broken china and pans and other utensils. Roman's eyes had become accustomed to the dim kitchen after the sunlight outside, and he saw the bedstead, the bare leather lacings and wooden slats showing where the mattress had been. His first thought was, Goddamn, I've missed them again. He looked quickly to the corner, and the shotgun was still there, too old for the jayhawkers to bother carrying off, he supposed.

"What did they do?"

"They were only looking for grub," Ora said, and her lip

started to tremble until she set her mouth to prevent it. Allan Pay put his hand on Roman's shoulder, but he drew back.

"Your friend, Mr. Crozier, wasn't so lucky, Roman," he said.

"What do you mean, not lucky?"

"Honey, they killed your uncle Tulip."

"They did *what*?" He was unable to digest it at once, unable to understand what his mother was saying to him. He shook Pay's hand off his sleeve.

"From what Lark told us, he shot one of them, and they hanged him," Pay said. "We found blood on the back porch here, so they must have stopped to rest, and took what they could find, of course, and then went on, back toward Missouri from the looks of the tracks across the garden."

"I know that," Roman almost shouted. "I saw them riding up Wire Road. Bloodstains, you say?"

He turned and ran to the porch and saw the dark stain, still moist, and the bloodied rag and the empty water bucket. He kicked viciously at the floorboards, then struck the bucket out into the yard with his foot. Glaring once at the wide-eyed Lark, he wheeled back into the house.

"For God's sake," Roman cried. "For God's sweet sake!"

Ora was in the chair again, wiping her face with her fingertips. She sighed and looked at him and shook her head.

"It's over now. They've gone. But they came to your uncle Tulip's just before we were there. I imagine about daylight. Then they rode cross-country to here. But we're all right. Lark can tell you what happened at the mill better than we can."

"They rode in and started bullying Mr. Crozier and he shot the one and they hanged him," Pay said, almost impatiently. "Then they came here, like your mother said, and went off to Missouri."

"Of course they went off to Missouri," Roman said. "They're Yankees, aren't they?"

There was a sudden glint of anger in Pay's eyes, and his head came up and his back stiffened, as if he were about to come at Roman, but Ora waved her hand quickly to stop it.

"They're scum—that's all they are. No Yankees or hill people like we know or anything, but scum," she said.

"Uncle Tulip? Hell's name," Roman said helplessly.

"We'll need to go back and bury the poor man," Ora said softly.

"No. There's no reason for you and Calpurnia to be subjected to such a thing," Pay said.

"I guess you're right."

She's conceding to him, Roman thought. Goddamn, she's conceding to him, like she's all washed out and hasn't got any gumption left, like it's all faded out of her. But he knew Pay was probably right.

"As soon as the horses cool a bit, then we can go. Someone will have to notify the authorities," Pay said. Ora looked up at him as though he were delirious again.

"Authorities?" Ora laughed bitterly. "What authorities?"

"The army, then."

"We don't need the Yankee army," Roman flashed, his anger up again.

"You need something," Pay said.

"You Yankees brought it on us!"

"All right, I won't have this politics now," Ora said.

"The army! In hell's name!" And once more, she did not call Roman down, and it was some small triumph for him at least.

2   They left before Calpurnia was down from the loft, but Roman was thinking now only of Tulip Crozier, because his mother had said Cal was unharmed, and if she said so, it had to be so. At first, Ora had resisted Roman going, but only weakly.

Roman wanted to go, even though he dreaded what he would see at the mill. He wanted to go to help with it, now that he was sure the partisans were gone and, from the way they were fogging north, likely would not return. And Pay had insisted that he go.

"We'll need him, Mrs. Hasford. I'll not be much use digging."

Well, Roman thought, he's got some backbone all right, bucking against Mama's will.

"Besides, he needs to see it. To remember."

Roman drove the team, and his mother called from the back door as he turned them out of the yard.

"Go easy with those horses, Roman. They're almost blown now."

He said nothing, but he thought, I know about the horses as well as anybody does. And he remained silent along Wire Road, thinking about what they were coming to. Nor did Pay speak, respecting Roman's need for the resolution of this thing within himself. Lark sat at the tailgate with his own thoughts, staring out across the open valley as they drove along.

Roman almost cried once as he remembered the times he had watched his father and Tulip Crozier working together or sitting around a ridgeline fire above White River, listening to fox dogs running. Roman recalled Crozier laughing and pulling him over to rub his head, and him hardly old enough yet to hold a shotgun without help.

"Hear Old Jim? Hear that high keen, like a Comanche squaw at a burial? He's leading the pack now, over across that next ridge. Fox better watch out or Old Jim will have his teeth in that fox's tail."

And Roman's father had laughed, too, with the sheer joy of hearing the strange, high-pitched notes of the dogs in chase. They had sat there listening around the fire in the deep woods and, when the dogs finally lost the fox, remained until the east was growing light, telling stories of races they had known, and of dogs. And of the most famous foxhound that had ever run these hills, named Andy Jackson. Bred and trained to the trail by Tulip Crozier himself. Roman almost cried, but not quite, and Allan Pay could feel his torment and kept his eyes turned away.

When Roman saw the stiffened form hanging by baling wire from the mill rafter, he did cry. Not tears of sadness, but of furious anger, and both Pay and the black man elaborately avoided looking at his face, as though the tears were not there. They lifted Tulip Crozier's body, Roman and Pay with their arms around his legs while Lark went up a stepladder to unwind the wire from the swollen neck. Lark brought a blanket then, from the shack where Crozier had slept, and they wrapped the body quickly, but not before Pay had closed the old man's eyes with the fingers of his hand.

They buried him up the slope, near the elderberry bushes, overlooking the mill yard. Pay helped cover the body, scooping in the loose earth with his feet. By then Roman's tears were long finished, and he felt beat and drained out, like he did after a long summer afternoon swim in one of the White River deep holes. Before they were done, Lark spoke, the only words uttered since they had begun to dig.

"He'll like this, close to them bees," he said. "He liked them bees 'cause they never run off. He tole me his foxhounds run off, when there was all that shootin' in the valley. They never come back."

"We'd better get on," Pay said, as Roman stood beside the grave, looking out across the mill hollow to the ridge beyond.

"We ought to say something," he said.

"I didn't know him," Pay said. "Even though he helped save my life."

"We ought to say something. Mama and Papa would want us to say something."

Allan Pay pulled off the old hat of Martin Hasford's, and Roman bared his head, too, and the three of them stood around the mound of fresh earth for a long time, silently. Finally, Roman began to speak, softly, the words trembling off on the breeze that was coming up from the hollow and the sycamores where they could hear jays callings and the gurgle of water under the mill wheel.

"The Lord's my shepherd, I'll not want. He maketh me to lie down in green pastures. He leadeth me beside the still water. Though I walk through the shadow of the valley of death, I fear no evil, for Thou art with me. Thou preparest a table before me in the presence of mine enemies."

He stopped and looked at Allan Pay.

"I can't remember it."

"Surely goodness and mercy shall follow me all the days of my life, and I will dwell in the house of the Lord forever," Pay said, and pulled on the hat, quickly, almost savagely.

They went back down the hill, but at the wagon, Lark held back. Roman waited for him, reins in hand.

"Well?"

"I reckon I'll stay," Lark said.

"You'll be all right?" Pay asked.

"Somebody needs to stay. Ain't nobody gone hurt an ole nigger," Lark said, his eyes moving, taking in all the cluttered yard, and the hill behind with the white rows of hives. "Them bees, they might starve, Mister Tulip says. Durin' winter. Iffen somebody ain't here to sugar-water 'em. I needs to get acquainted with 'em 'twix now and then."

He did not mention that he was still afraid of them. He shook his head apologetically. Beads of sweat stood like ice pellets in his bushy hair.

"He tole me the bes' beekeeper man he ever seed was a black slave. I ain't no slave now, the Yankees say, but I still got the black part."

"Do what you want," Roman said impatiently, and clipped the horses with the line ends. They left Lark standing in the high sunlight before the mill, watching after them, the shovel still in his hands.

3   Calpurnia knew there were things not spoken of in this family. Or if they were, only in whispers between her mother and father before her father went away. Like the time one of the Taliferro girls had gone raving mad and dashed into the woods near Mudtown, stark-naked, and had to be run down with horses because nobody could catch her on foot, and was finally taken to some asylum in Missouri.

Or the time Henry Ruter, the youngest of that clan, had made trouble for a Bentonville girl. Her father had come with a shotgun and his daughter, already well swollen, in a spring wagon. In back of the wagon was a Baptist preacher with his marrying book.

Or the time a former schoolteacher in Leetown had caught a disease brought about by unusual lasciviousness and had to resign and go to Little Rock or some such place to find somebody who knew how to cure it.

Or all the times her uncle Tulip got spiffed up and rode off in one of the coaches to Fort Smith or Springfield to visit one of the wicked houses there.

These were simply forbidden subjects for conversation. Nobody was impolite enough to bring them up, not even Roman.

Beyond those unmentionable things, Martin Hasford had often been forthcoming with his thoughts, particularly with his daughter, who had the capacity to draw him out whenever she chose. Even when she had been a little girl, Martin would sometimes take her on his lap and answer her questions at such length and in such detail that she understood only a little of what he said.

But Ora Hasford was another matter. She often went into a brooding silence, quietly and furiously going about her chores with a frown, frequently raising her fingers to pursed lips.

The children never tried to invade their mother's thoughts. She had taught them, without their ever knowing how, that there were times when she needed to keep her own counsel, to be silent until she had made a determination of what the right words were—if any were needed at all.

Roman was like his father, blurting out anything as it came to mind. But Calpurnia followed the pattern of her mother, and Ora Hasford honored that.

And so it was with Calpurnia's experience in the woods, the man chasing her with the hooded head. She told her mother only the barest details of the encounter, and when she was through Ora knew there would be no more said about it, and she respected her daughter's wishes. Of course, she knew a great deal more than she was told. She knew that outside of fright—and perhaps not much of that—all Calpurnia had suffered was a scratch on her cheek caused by running through the brush. Nothing more, not even wounded pride. Had there been more, Ora would have seen the shame of it in Calpurnia's face, for at that time a young girl would have considered it so. But there was no shame, only the defiant and furious blue eyes and the satisfaction that she would take her body to a husband intact. Which was, among these people, a thing of considerable significance, too.

While the men were away to bury Tulip Crozier, Calpurnia and her mother worked silently, cleaning the house. Calpurnia waited, watching her mother for some sign that would tell what had passed between her and Allan Pay that very morning on their ride to Wolf Cove. But no sign came, and the only words spoken was a suppressed, violent oath when Ora looked at her shattered china closet.

When the men returned, without Lark and explaining that he had stayed on, they were quickly silent, too, sensing Ora's mood. Roman went back to splitting rails—after he finally found his tools where he had dropped them in the field—and Pay rubbed down the horses and then went to the garden to weed the potato patch.

Carrying an old straw tick from the barn to cover her mother's bed, Calpurnia thought about it. Everybody to his own little business, quiet as mice, everybody with his own thinking. As though nothing had happened this day. But something is about to happen. And I hope I know what.

It had to wait until after dark. None of them was hungry, and after Allan Pay had gone out to milk the goat, they ate corn bread and drank warm milk. There was little said at the table, but twice Calpurnia and Allan Pay looked at each other, and a great deal of conversation seemed to pass between them without words being spoken.

The tree frogs and cicadas had begun their nightly chorus when Ora called them around the lighted lamp on the kitchen table, Roman on one side, Allan on the other, and Calpurnia standing behind her. By now the girl was sure what was coming.

"After today, you can see why there can be none of this decent time for courting," Ora said bluntly. As she and Pay stared at each other, his head lifted as though he were standing before a commanding officer.

"Yes," he said. "I can see that."

"Then ask your question, now, before her and her family, and at least that part of it will be according to your form of things."

Pay's mouth opened for a moment and he licked his lips, but he was not surprised, and Calpurnia knew that perhaps he had come into this family more fully than any of them realized. He had known, more surely than she herself did, what was coming.

"Mrs. Hasford, in all respect, I ask your daughter's hand in marriage," he said. He said it quickly and firmly, stating the proposition that stood now between only himself and the older woman and concerned Calpurnia not at all.

"If my daughter agrees, then I give that consent, for myself and my husband."

"I agree," Calpurnia said, louder than she had intended, for she wanted to be an active part of this bargain now, not a passive one like a prize shoat being traded. She almost laughed aloud.

Ora turned to Roman, who was standing rigid, his face red and his mouth clamped tight shut. She looked at him with her piercing eyes, and after a moment he nodded abruptly, then stalked from the room to the back porch, where he sat down heavily and began to throw rocks at the bluetick hound until the dog tucked tail and ambled into the darkness, out of range, looking offended.

Ora had turned quickly from the table, but she paused at the parlor door without looking back.

"It's bedtime, Calpurnia," she said.

Allan Pay moved quickly around the table and took Calpurnia's hand in his own. He slipped the stump of his left arm from the sling and let it hang, holding it back from her, but she took it and pulled it around her waist, and he slipped his hand up her arm and drew her to him. She lifted her face, looking at him with bright eyes, and he kissed her, but very lightly as though she might melt away if he pressed too closely.

"You waited long enough to ask," she said.

"I didn't know how you would take it, nor her."

"It wouldn't have mattered. I'd have gone with you anyway."

He looked at her intently, and she was smiling.

"I doubt you would have," he said. "I'm glad I didn't have to find out. But now it's settled, and tomorrow I'll start back."

"You won't take long?"

"I won't take long."

She kissed him again, quickly, then slipped from his arms and ran to the parlor door, turned and smiled, and was gone. He knew Ora had been waiting at the ladder stairs because he heard them go up together, Calpurnia laughing and whispering. His heart was pounding so hard it sent little stabs of pain into the stump of his arm, and he lifted it back into the sling.

He walked to the back door and saw Roman sitting on the edge of the porch, in the lamplight from the kitchen, scooping up rocks from the yard and flinging them into the darkness. There was a rattle of metal as one of them struck the well-curb bucket.

"Roman?"

"Yeah," Roman said. He threw again, but missed the unseen bucket with this one.

"I promise you to take care of her. I'll be good to her so long as we live."

"I guess you will," Roman said. He threw another rock, this time at a larger target, and it thumped against the barn wall. "Wartime sure brings the damnedest things."

4 The morning was clear, and the dawn had come to turn the sky pale gray when Roman went out to saddle Bess. He did it carefully, patting her belly and whispering to her. He liked horses as well as anyone did, but each time he went through this with the mare, he remembered the mule, and he missed being nipped at with those long mule teeth.

He took his time, knowing it didn't matter because his

mother was in there with Allan Pay, inspecting him before his journey, Roman supposed. Giving him all kinds of advice.

"You know the way to Cassville, girl," he said aloud, throwing the blanket on her and smoothing it down tight. He lifted the saddle into place and threw the stirrup and fender up over the seat. It was a Texas saddle, with double cinches. The front one he pulled down tight against her belly, but the rear one he left loose.

"That second cinch is useless, isn't it, girl? You don't need it, do you? Listen, now, you don't pay any mind to how he talks. It's just that strange Yankee talk, is all. You just stay on Wire Road, all the way. And maybe he'll get you some oats in a livery barn at Cassville. You'd like oats, huh? But you'll carry him well. He's not very heavy. Skinny as a rake."

And inside, Allan Pay was ready, wearing Martin Hasford's clothes as he had since coming here, too large for him but at least freshly cleaned and brushed, and one of Martin Hasford's hats held under the stump of his left arm. Calpurnia stood well back from him, her eyes watching, bright and close to tears. Ora went to the fireplace and dug out the gold coin that had been so much a part of her own marriage, and placed it in his hand as dowry. As good-luck charm, too, perhaps. And as a means of providing for himself in Cassville or Springfield or wherever he might go until the Union army mustered him out.

Pay walked quickly to the back porch, anxious to be on his way, to have this part of it done so he could be back here. He paused at the step and turned back to the women, who had followed him.

"Soon," he said, smiling. "I'll be back soon."

"Ride carefully," Ora said. "And if your arm starts to hurt, stop and rest, and stay out of the wet in case it rains."

"I'll stable your horse somewhere along the line," he said.

"Wherever I can find coaches still running. They may send me to Saint Louis to pension me out, but most of that should be by railroad car, and shouldn't take long."

"Do what needs doing. You'll want to see your family, anyway. But be careful. You look like a healthy man now, not like that wet cat the Indian brought in."

"Yes, I'll be careful."

Suddenly he took her hand and kissed it, then with a flourish of his hat he bowed low toward Calpurnia, smiling.

"Miss Calpurnia, stay in good health."

Pay moved across the yard to the horse, pulling on the hat, a little rakishly, and Roman was waiting, the reins looped over the saddle pommel.

"She's gentle," Roman said. "You don't need to use the bit on her, just let her know with your knees where you want to go. I've fed her corn, and she'll take you a long way."

"I thank you, Roman," Pay said, and pulled himself up, holding the horn with his good hand.

"She's a little slow running flat-out."

"I doubt I'll need to run her," Pay said, looking down. He stretched out his hand and Roman stared at it as though he had never been offered a handshake, then took it, eyes averted.

At the porch, Ora said, "Go tell him good-bye."

Calpurnia ran across the yard and lifted her face and allowed him to kiss her forehead, and then he was pulling Bess around, waving with the hand that held the reins. Ora lifted her hand, too, looking anxious, afraid he might fall from the saddle. But he had no trouble as he moved the mare around the house and out of sight.

This may be the last time we'll ever see Bess and that saddle, Roman thought. But watching his sister's face, he had to force himself to think such a thing, and was ashamed for doing it.

———

5 Wild blackberries were growing along the south slope beyond the spring hollow. Calpurnia and Roman were there picking them late in the afternoon on the third day after Allan Pay's departure. And Ora had dough ready for a deep-dish pie. But she was in no hurry for that. It seemed her solitary moments were more precious now, and she cherished them.

She was at the kitchen table, sipping sassafras tea from one of the few china cups the partisans had left unbroken. There were tin cups, of course, not much the worse for wear after the raid, but she always enjoyed at least one cup a day from her chinaware. It was a touch of quality she needed now and again to remind her that the Hasfords were a quality family who prided themselves in being hardworking and honest but also understood the delicate things, like drinking from a cup with the Meissen mark on the bottom, a mark that went back to the early eighteenth century, almost a hundred years before Picture Grandpapa had gone off to fight Napoleon.

Before her was the small cedar box, repository for her private and prized possessions—a string of tiny pearls, given her as a girl by one of her uncles in Georgia, a cameo pin of the goddess Diana, a curved Spanish comb, and the letters Martin had written. The little box had escaped capture by the jayhawkers, hidden as it always was under a rafter in the loft.

As she read the letters once again, she kept thinking, Martin, I hope I did right about Allan Pay. I think he's a good man. Once, she said it aloud, as though Martin were there before her, instead of only his scribbles across the worn and dirty patches of paper. After a while she carefully folded them and replaced them in the box, and closed it gently.

The shock and misery of what had happened at Wolf Cove had worn off quickly because there were too many other things to think about. When she thought of it now, it was with some detachment. She felt regret that her last real meeting with Tulip Crozier, in this room the morning they had taken off the hand, had been filled with recriminations. And she regretted, too, that the old man had to be buried without proper services. But it was a thing brought on by the war, she thought, and the warm weather, when the dead could not be left lying about waiting for arrangements to be made. Besides, that strange old man would likely have willed it so. He had always seemed to seek unusual ways of doing things.

At any rate, there was nothing she could do about any of that. Nor about hastening Allan Pay's return, though she thought about it almost constantly.

Since he left, she had sensed a further blooming in Calpurnia's womanhood, with her expectation of Pay's return and a gladness at what lay ahead. And in Roman, too, since they had buried Tulip Crozier, a seriousness grown suddenly older. There was far less banter between the two of them now, and they treated one another with some new tenderness. Even Roman's flares of hot temper were less frequent.

Each day she saw more of Martin in the boy. Only now he was no longer a boy, she had to admit. The long, purposeful walk, the serious face suddenly breaking into the broad grin, the supple strength and sureness of his hands with tools or working with livestock. It was as though the years had slipped past in only a few weeks, her children new to her again, and no longer children.

She heard them then, Calpurnia's laughter coming rich and full up from the spring hollow. Thank God, Ora thought. Thank God that everything we've seen in this dismal year has changed them only for the better. A tough breed, she thought, and with considerable pride, but taking no credit to herself.

Well, soon it will begin again for her, when Allan Pay comes back from Saint Louis or wherever it is. I hope someday I can see their babies. Then, I'll know most certainly it has started again, all started again like the sun coming each day and the snow in winter and then gone with the spring. All started, never stopping, really, the family going on and on, never ceasing, like a turning wheel. I hope someday I can see their babies.

XVIII

And then the summer came, hot and humid and rainless, and they fought the drought with water from the well until that ran low. Slowly, the vegetable garden began to parch. The only showers came at night, sudden and furious out of the Indian Territory, with blinding lightning and thunder as crashing and violent as the second day's artillery bombardment during the battle of Pea Ridge. By morning the sky would be clear again.

After the human fury of the spring, it seemed of little consequence.

The corn came on strong, tough and enduring in the heat, good enough for milling and roasting, and more than good enough to crib for the livestock. Because it had been early planted, risking a late frost that never came, by August much had already been harvested and the stalks plowed up for fodder.

Cucumber vines crept across the garden patch like leafy snakes, and in the lower corner where the ground held more moisture above the slab slate below the surface, watermelons came on dark green and bulbous. There were carrots and squash and a few green beans, none of them so large and juicy as might be hoped, but good enough considering the dry spell. And from the woods they took wild plums and polk greens.

The roads turned to talcum powder, and whenever one set a foot on them, the gray dust rose and hung like cobwebs. A brassy sun, made larger than it should have been by the haze distortion, moved across the pale sky, taking an eternity to reach the western horizon. Sometimes then, a timid breeze skipped across the land from the west.

They heard nothing of marauders for week after week, even in southern Missouri, where the pickings were better, with more horses and mules remaining in barn and pasture. There were few horses left along Little Sugar Creek, fewer pigs, and even the people had thinned out so it was like the old days, almost like the times when Osage warriors still roamed here, making their bows from the Ozark orangewood and hunting the streams with fish spears.

When Allan Pay came he wore a new uniform, gold bars on yellow shoulder straps, a first lieutenant of cavalry, looking more grand and less dirty than he had that first day he had ridden into the yard for water. Except that now the left coat sleeve was folded up and pinned, giving him a lopsided appearance when he walked. He had not been mustered out after all, the Yankee army explaining to him that there were many things a man with one arm could do. He had been assigned—partly through his father's influence—to a supply depot in Saint Louis, even though he wore insignia of the line.

He drove a rented rig, drawn by matched bays. The Hasford saddle was under the seat, and Bess tied on behind.

Calpurnia ran out to meet him, and this time allowed him to kiss her lips, if only briefly. But afterward she stayed aloof from him, because it seemed proper for a bride-to-be. Even in the evenings, when Ora and Roman made themselves busy in the house while the two bespoken sat on the front porch in rockers, she would not allow him to touch her. She even teased him a little with her eyes about it, but he only laughed, willing to wait for this prize.

"He looks so good," Ora said to Roman. "There's color in his face, and he's put on ten pounds if he's put on an ounce."

"He ought to. He eats like a horse," Roman said, but there was no spite or truculence in his words.

From his mother, Allan Pay had brought a bolt of linen cloth, white and finely woven, and a lace veil. Ora began the wedding dress at once, completing it in the three days she had before the occasion. But the veil she put aside, for Calpurnia to take with her when they went away, explaining that she had not married with a veil, nor would her daughter.

"She'll be beautiful," she said. "But there will be no veil."

Roman began the rounds of the county, giving invitations to the wedding, even so far away as Bentonville to arrange with the Methodist minister there. Ora had conceded that duty to him as man of the house, and even though she did not express it in that way, Roman knew without any words that finally she was beginning to regard him as full-grown, no matter how reluctantly.

And once, Allan Pay, out of his uniform now and back in natty mufti he had brought from Saint Louis, insisted on going along. They saddled one of the bays and Roman rode Bess bareback. The first time Pay went up on the little red horse, he had to cling desperately to the horn through a violent fit of bucking. But it lasted only a minute, and he and Roman burst out laughing when it was finished.

"All it takes is one good hand and two good knees," Pay said.

"He's a spirited little horse."

"I may just buy the pair of them, for Calpurnia."

"She could sure in hell ride him—you can count on that."

"She won't have to ride him. I'll get her a surrey, too. With red wheels."

2   It was a large wedding for the time and place. There were more than two dozen people, the remaining southerners of the

valley, demonstrating their stubborn resistance to changing times and upset systems. Even the former sheriff of the county came, although he was no longer a law officer because that function had been taken over by the occupying army. They crowded into the parlor and watched Calpurnia, in the white linen dress, a cluster of scarlet wild verbena in her hair, standing beside the shattered china closet, Allan Pay beside her looking hot and embarrassed in his woolen uniform with the folded sleeve as the minister read words from a tattered black book.

At Allan Pay's insistence, Roman stood as best man. He looked more flustered than the groom, sweating almost as badly in a coat he had not worn since winter, a coat too short in the sleeves and tight across the middle when he tried to button it.

When Allan Pay slipped a golden band onto Calpurnia's finger, Ora had to hold her jaw clamped tight to keep from crying, but Maud Ruter and a few other ladies did the ceremonial sniffing.

Then it was over, and the party began. The guests were a little standoffish with Pay at first, because this Yankee was marrying one of their own. Not that any of them held against him and his army the partisan atrocities that had been committed against them, because by now they all realized that the night riders who came into the valley were no partisans at all, but bandits. Yet he was still a Yankee, with outlandish ideas and ways, and most of all, outlandish speech.

Old man Ruter, who had lost a son to these times, and therefore was as entitled as anyone to bitterness, brought a jug. He hid it in the barn and went to it from time to time throughout the afternoon on one pretext or another, and finally on no pretext at all. Before long, he was talking to Allan Pay as though he were a part of the valley, even patting his shoulder and winking and telling off-color stories when they were out of hearing of the women. Seeing this, and even knowing the old man had been making trips to the barn more and more frequently, the others lost their coolness. But even so, Allan Pay continued to sweat, anxious to be away.

When Ora and some of the other women went into the kitchen to cut cake and pour the elderberry wine the Methodist minister had brought from Bentonville, old man Ruter staggered in from his latest trip to the jug.

"Ora, that's a mighty fine girl you've got," he said, and tried to kiss her cheek.

Maud Ruter ran him out, screeching at him, her chin bristling with fine white hair.

"Get on outside, you old Lucifer," she yelled, waving a cake knife. "You stay away from that whiskey, now."

Somebody had a fiddle, and the former sheriff of Benton County had his French harp, and soon there was dancing on the wide front porch. Lark, who had walked over from Wolf Cove and had been only in the background until now, did a jig, and they all shouted and clapped hands. Allan Pay managed to bear it all in good grace, standing stiffly, and smiling. Calpurnia and her mother were in the loft, the girl changing clothes and packing, and the two of them saying their good-byes privately, away from the eyes of all the others. Roman started up once, and Ora sent him back to the dancing.

When Ora came down, Pay drew her aside away from the others, and pressed the gold coin into her hand.

"I want you to have it back. I know what it means to you. Calpurnia told me the story."

She looked at the shining disk in her hand, lifting her fingers to her lips to stop the trembling there.

"But it was her dowry."

"She needs none. This is the very same coin you gave me."

"How did you come not to spend it?"

"A good man in Cassville held it for me until I came back

and redeemed it. I'm afraid he charged me a little interest. Like a pawnbroker. But only a little."

Then he bent and kissed her cheek.

He carried Calpurnia off that afternoon, the sun lowering, the dancers still rocking the house with their stomping on the porch. Before they climbed into the rig, Ora hugged them both, and Calpurnia hugged Roman and Allan Pay shook his hand. Roman stood watching them drive off, around the house and toward Wire Road, solemn as an owl and a little unsteady on his feet because at least three times thus far he had accompanied old man Ruter to the barn.

Later, after Lark had helped old man Ruter into his wagon, and after the last of the carrot cake had been eaten and the last of the elderberry wine drunk, and all the people had gone off calling for Ora to come and visit, she sat in the shadows of the back porch, her shoes off and toes digging in the dust. Roman was aimlessly wandering in and out of the barn. When it was almost dark, she cried a little. And finally when Roman came over, staggering enough to embarrass himself, she patted the porch floor and he sat down beside her. For a long time, neither of them spoke.

"Well," Roman said, his speech slurred. "She may be a Yankee now. But she's still Calpurnia, isn't she?"

"Yes," Ora said, touching his shoulder. "She's still Calpurnia. She'll always be Calpurnia."

Then she rose, and leaving him there went into the kitchen and down into the root cellar and found the jug the partisans had missed in the dark. Back at the kitchen table, she poured two fingers of the clear liquid into a pair of tin cups and took them to the porch, where Roman still sagged against a post.

"Here. We can have a proper wedding sip, now. Elderberry wine was never to my taste."

Roman gave her one startled look, then took the cup of whiskey obediently and drank it down with one gulp. He gasped.

"Well. It's better than old man Ruter's, anyway."

"Of course it is. Your papa made it. I wish he could have been here today."

She watched the purple shadows running back from the oaks behind the barn, fading into the darkness that was already there in the heavy timber where the slope rose toward the east. The tops of the trees were flaming pink and gold in the sunset. Her arm ached, but only a little, and the whiskey seemed to help it. She'll always be Calpurnia, she thought, and then said aloud, "Now go and milk the goat."

3   It was a gray and blustering day, threatening a cold rain. Roman was still half sleeping as he left the house to draw fresh water for the horses. He walked around the barn first, as he had done all summer, looking for Spavinaw's sign. It had been a long time since he had seen anything, but on this morning the tracks were there.

There had been two horses. One was a small one, leaving the dainty prints that Roman recognized at once. The other horse had been a large one. The pony had been tethered along the rear fence of the paddock and then ridden off around the barn and toward the west. But the other tracks, those of the larger horse, led directly across the lot and into the barn. As soon as he walked into the dim and cool interior, Roman knew a strange horse was there.

He found the army stallion in one of the stalls, snorting and looking around walleyed as Roman moved in close to his flank, pushing him aside. There was a brand that had been reworked crudely with an iron of some sort, but the original was still clear. The *US* stood out as plainly as a written word. Roman felt a choking in his throat, not unlike the sensation he had suffered when he watched his father walk away off to war on just such a dark autumn morning.

He bolted out of the barn and across the yard, but stopped short at the porch. On the long wooden bench beside the grinding wheel he saw the two dressed squirrels, neatly wrapped in still-green walnut leaves. He knew even as he looked that this was the last time he would find game from the Indian's gun. Because beside the squirrels was a powder flash, a tin of percussion caps, a leather bullet pouch, and the brass and blue steel of a Navy Colt pistol.

Roman left the weapon and its accoutrements on the bench, but took the squirrels inside, where his mother was at the stove, frying potato cakes. She turned and saw the squirrels in his hand, and the expression on his face, and she knew then, too, that this would be the last.

"Mama, he's gone home," Roman said.

"I thought he would soon. I thought maybe he already had."

"He's gone. He left some presents."

"Besides the meat?"

"Yes. A horse and a revolving pistol."

She turned back to the stove, flipping the cakes with a long spatula. It came to her then who had run Calpurnia like a hound running fox along the slopes of Plum Thicket Ridge, and she knew where the horse and pistol came from, and knew, too, that she would never tell Roman because of the rage it would create in him. And she remembered a line from Jeremiah's Lamentations: "Persecute and destroy them in anger from under the heavens of the Lord."

So, sometimes, justice comes after all, she thought. But she said aloud, "I told you before, when you're decent to folks, it always comes home."

———

4   It would be a long time yet before hunters discovered the bones, scattered among scraps of clothing and an old slouch hat, far off to the east in White River country, unburied and left for the foxes and wolves to gnaw.

Other than the hat, there was little left to identify the remains, and before they were found, everybody in the valley except Ora Hasford had forgotten who had worn it. It was, to them all, only a vaguely familiar shape.

And Spavinaw Tom had kept the watch.

5   In September, they began to hear of the terrible battles in the east, of Shiloh and second Manassas and finally of bloody Sharpsburg, which the Yankees called Antietam. Ora Hasford waited for another letter, but none came, and they harvested all their corn and took some to the mill where Lark was well established by then. He spoke of it as his place, his hives, his Wolf Cove. Its tenure had passed from Osage to Jew to black man, and Ora accepted it as she did the passing generations of her own family, always changing, yet somehow solid and permanent, too.

The armies seemed far removed in that fall of 1862. The federals had abandoned Elkhorn Tavern as a supply depot. Now the scarred and mutilated building stood windowless and deserted at the eastern foot of Pea Ridge, and there was only the occasional passage of trains or cavalry patrols along Wire Road.

The men who had fought there on either side were widely scattered, the Union soldiers on occupation duty throughout much of Arkansas, the Confederates deployed as far away as Vicksburg or Tennessee.

Ora watched the time stretch out beyond belief. It seemed impossible that Martin had been gone a year, and yet each day she felt closer to him. Especially at dawn, with the sun still hidden behind the oaks of the eastern ridge. She could recall those times, the smell of her biscuits as she made them each morning, when they had had white flour, and the frying sausage and eggs, and then him coming from the barn with a pail, and walking in and bringing with him the sweet smell of hay and fresh, warm milk.

With Calpurnia safe away from this place, there was a great and deadly weight lifted from her, and already she was becoming accustomed to the girl being gone. But without that concern, her thoughts turned more and more to Martin.

She had never before permitted herself the thought that he might not return, might be buried even now in foreign soil, in Maryland or Virginia. But she began to think of that when the days grew short, and the nights cold, and she alone on the straw tick brought from the barn after they had burned her mattress. Lying in the dark, listening to the owls and the last of the year's chuck-will's-widows, she did not cry again. She had done that when the last letter came, and once was all she would allow herself.

And later still, after all the oaks and gum trees had turned gold and red before dropping their leaves, she was wakened in the night by some sound unheard, but only felt. She went to the front porch, a blanket about her shoulders against the chill. There was a rising glow from along Wire Road to the north, and soon she saw the licking flames. Elkhorn Tavern was burning.

She watched without surprise or apprehension, having long known that it was not yet finished. Instead of fear, there was the hard determination that no matter what else came, she and Roman would be among those who survived.

ABOUT THE AUTHOR

Douglas C. Jones was a three-time winner of the Western Writers of America's Golden Spur Award, as well as the recipient of their Owen Wister Award for Lifetime Achievement.

From Douglas C. Jones, recipient of the
Owen Wister Award for Lifetime Achievement,
comes a remarkable novel of the extraordinary bond
between soldiers in our nation's bloodiest war.

THE BAREFOOT
BRIGADE

"One of the best Civil War novels I have read."

—James M. McPherson, Pulitzer Prize–
winning author of *Battle Cry of Freedom*
and bestselling author of *Tried by War*

"Jones writes about some of the most haunting men in
the history of the American South—the dirt-farm infantry of the Confederate Army. . . . The strength and
heart of *The Barefoot Brigade* lie in small events, individual antagonisms, boredom, waiting, slogging, hunger.
One senses the men's growing mutual dependence, a
reflection of the families they have left behind, the cement that holds the Confederate Army together."

—*The New York Times*

**Coming in trade paperback from
New American Library in April 2011
Read on for a special preview.**

F ury was a constant state of being for His Honor Judge Guthrie Scaggs. He went about everything angrily, to include eating and sleeping, breathing and copulating. Those who knew him claimed that he had issued from the womb with a scowl on his face and, as the years advanced, never once observed anything that had the capacity to change it. On this May morning, as he guided the mule down the mountain to the small tributary of the Buffalo River, he was more furious than usual.

The larger part of it came from an upset stomach. Being a circuit-riding judge of Arkansas in this year of 1861 threw him on the mercy of tables set for him at the various farmsteads where he stopped the night during his rounds. On this particular morning he had breakfasted on hog jowl and gravy, a greasy mess he had wolfed down without regard for the consequences, and had been forced since on at least four occasions to take soothing drafts from the bottle of corn whiskey in his saddlebags.

And he had not slept well, having shared a bed with two gangling and bony sons of his host, neither of whom had yet consigned his winter underwear to the boiling pot, nor taken his annual spring bath. His Honor Judge Scaggs did not consider himself a fastidious man, but he had been cursed from birth with an extremely sensitive nose, designed by its breadth of nostril to pick up scents and odors lost on other men with less classic proboscises.

And still another part of it was this business of the convention in Little Rock that had procrastinated for so long before seceding from the damned Union. The governor himself had implored the convention to sign the articles of secession. But they had refused, voting down such a resolution again and again, bone-headed and stubborn as the mule that Judge Scaggs was now astride. Only when Sumter fell and Abe Lincoln called for volunteers had the convention voted the necessary document, taking it as insult and even threat to freedom that the Federal power would ask them to send soldiers for an invasion of sister states in the South.

Had His Honor Judge Scaggs been running things, the Union would have been dissolved back in Andy Jackson's time, when there was all that nullification business, four years before Arkansas became a state, when it was in fact still a territory peopled mostly by bottomland men along the rivers and by wild Indians. And Judge Scaggs himself a boy of only thirteen, learning the rudiments of cotton and hatred of strong central government while he worked alongside his grandfather's Negroes in the delta country west of Memphis.

There were other irritations, too. Here he was riding a circuit he had never ridden before because some idiot judge in these northern districts had run off to join Federal armies in Missouri or Illinois or some such place, leaving this area without the proper dispensation of justice. His Honor Judge Scaggs thus found himself in this mountain wilderness, attending to matters he had no desire to attend to, in a strange country and among people who had never seen his name on a ballot—a great many of whom, heaven forbid it, supported the Union. Dumb bastards, His Honor Judge Scaggs thought viciously, and pulled the amber-colored bottle from his saddlebag.

The woods that bordered the winding road were thick-leaved and gleaming green, and from among them came the calls of jays, the hammer strokes of woodpeckers on hardwood, the chattering of squirrels. As the road pitched down into the valley of the stream, the trees changed character, oaks and hickories thinning, their place taken by the redbud and sycamore and willow of lower elevations. The stream glistened in the sun, running fast and clear and cold. Looking ahead at the ford, His Honor Judge Scaggs pulled up and studied the proposition, glaring between the mule's ears.

It was impossible to gauge the depth of the water, for even though he could see the shine of gravel at the bottom of the stream, the dazzling sunlight on the surface could be deceptive as to what lay beneath. Judge Scaggs made a quick and unalterable decision, and dismounted.

He slipped off his frock coat, then the collarless gray shirt, and draped them over the saddle. He pulled down his doeskin pants—which were so short in the leg that they failed to reach the tops of his shoes—then the shoes, and there were no socks beneath. He stood now, glaring around, clad only in his stovepipe hat and flannel underwear that had once been red but had long ago washed out to a ghastly pink.

With only a moment's hesitation, he peeled off the underwear and, standing naked, took a copy of the Statutes of Arkansas from the saddlebag and wrapped that and the clothes in a large bundle resembling an army bedroll. Placing bare toe to stirrup, he swung up, his naked butt slapping against the saddle leather. He kicked the mule forward, holding the bundle high above his head in one hand.

The mule marched daintily into the water and toward the far shore. Soon, the water had risen to the mule's hocks. Judge Scaggs glanced down as they approached the center of the stream. The water was still at the mule's hocks. Farther into the stream the mule trod, but the water rose no higher up his legs. Judge Scaggs began to suspect a miscalculation.

With his nakedness shining in the bright sunlight, he glanced along the far shore. There, in a thicket of willows, were three young women wearing poke bonnets and calico dresses done up high-waisted with ribbon, like the ones their grandmothers might have worn during the Revolution. They stood with eyes popping and mouths agape, motionless as statues, watching the tall, naked figure now passing midstream on his mule.

When he saw the young women, Judge Scaggs did not flinch. He did not try to twist his body to hide his manliness behind the pommel. He did not lower the bundle from above his head. He looked at the young women for only an instant, and then observed the far bank directly ahead as the mule approached the gravel bar there.

He had always been a deliberate man, and he was now. As the mule came to a halt on dry ground, Judge Scaggs dismounted slowly and began to unravel his bundle of clothing, his naked back toward the women. After slipping the Statutes of Arkansas back into the saddlebags, he began to dress. As he pulled on the doeskin pants, he glanced over his shoulder, and where the women had stood was now only the salad green foliage of the willows. There was no movement there, not even the rustling of leaves marking their departure, and His Honor Judge Scaggs snorted and buttoned his pants.

He paused a moment, making another decision, or judgment as he would have called it, and finally pulled the bottle from the saddlebags and took a long swig.

"By the living God," he said aloud, "these hill people move quiet as wolves, even their bitches!"

And then he mounted the mule and with great dignity rode along the valley road toward the town.

They called it Town. Just that. There was never any mistaking the place to which they referred because it was the only town they had. There was a proper name, which could be seen on any map, but most of them had little use for maps, and many couldn't read any of the names on such a device anyway.

It was the only settlement of note within miles, boasting a population of well over five hundred. It was impressive, too, because it was a county seat and the home of the sheriff. Town lay in the valley of the Buffalo, its single street twisting alongside the bank of the river, with buildings on either side, most of them slab-side or shingle. But there was one sandstone edifice. The courthouse. It was not an imposing building to someone like Judge Guthrie Scaggs, who had seen such places as Little Rock, but to the hill people it was the symbol of government and power. And for most of them, such symbols were entirely negative.

The sheriff had his office there. The courtroom was there as well, a small room with a few chairs facing a table that had Queen Anne legs and served as bench. Across the hall from the courtroom was the single jail cell. It stood empty most of the time.

Except for the sheriff himself, there was no jailer. The only people locked up were murderers and highwaymen, and there were not many of these because most were never apprehended, and those who were seldom survived arrest. Sometimes there were casual shootings between members of families who disagreed on property boundaries or the ownership of milk cows, but not many of these affairs, even the lethal ones, came to trial, witnesses somehow becoming as scarce as hard money.

The hill people came down into Town to pay their taxes and discuss the news. They came from as far away as a day's ride on horseback because the county, like all others in the state, was laid out geographically so that no matter where a man might settle he could get to his seat of government on a single stretch of daylight.

Their school system was nonexistent as a state-supported institution. But Town had what they considered a good one, sustained by donations of hogs and chickens and free labor to repair roof and windows and siding.

Even so, most education was left to the scattered families, and that meant that a good many men, and even more of the women, could not read or write. Learning in the hills was usually taken at the knee of some ambitious mother who taught her children the verities of subject and verb from the Bible.

There were a sawmill, a blacksmith shop, a mercantile, and all the other things a town needed.

Everything worked pretty well. Boys and girls sparked and were coupled by mutual agreement between the heads of families. They wed and had their children, usually one each year for a time. There was plenty of wild land to be cleared; there were homesteads to be made, fields to be plowed, hogs and chickens to be raised. They were not close enough to any hostile Indian tribes to be worried about such things as sometimes troubled the western counties.

In all the hillside fields around the county seat, there was not a single black man working, and in Town there were only two, and they the property of the sawmill operator. The people of the county stayed well clear of the two blacks, for Negroes were as foreign to them as were solid black mastiffs among all their own mottled and varicolored hounds.

And there were no whores or beggars and only a couple of men who were habitually drunk. The townspeople recognized few diseases—although some could recall a smallpox outbreak a few years earlier—and they died of the usual maladies of the time: consumption or the vapors or measles. Or simply of old age when their time ran out.

Up to now they had felt themselves far removed from the hot whirlwinds of the nation. But now they could no more avoid those storms than control them, and for Noah and Zackery Fawley the whirlwind came in the form of His Honor Judge Guthrie Scaggs.

"Stand to the bar, Noah Fawley," Judge Scaggs rasped. He glared across the small room—empty now except for a cluster of Fawleys sitting along one wall and looking defiant, the prosecutor, and the complainant in the case, a small, weather-reddened man in homespun who from time to time cast an apprehensive glance in the direction of the Fawleys.

The youngest of the Fawleys, a tall, slender, hard-muscled man of seventeen years, rose as the prosecutor motioned to him. Stepping out to stand before the table with the Queen Anne legs, he glanced back once toward his family.

There were his mother and father, both tough looking and hard-faced with thin lips, and his four brothers, Tyne, Britt, Cadmus, and Zackery, all of the same stamp with thin blond hair and pale eyes that were more green than blue and, in certain light, almost yellow. The woman wore her hair pulled back to a bun; it was gray, matching a face etched like her husband's from exposure to sun and wind, although she was no older than forty-five.

"Charged with stealing a pig, on complaint of this gentleman," the prosecutor was saying, waving a hand in the direction of the small sun-bleached man without looking at him. To the younger man stepping forward he barked, "Take off your hat!"

Noah Fawley pulled the floppy, wide-brimmed hat from his head and stood with a spray of silky hair falling across his high forehead. He stared squarely into Judge Scaggs's eyes.

"Are you represented?" Judge Scaggs asked.

The young man stood uncertainly, but his gaze never wavered. One bony hand rubbed the seam of his homemade trousers, the other held the hat at his side.

"This here's my people," he said, looking back toward his family once more.

"I mean, have you an attorney? A lawyer?"

"What for?"

"I'll not dawdle with you, young man," Judge Scaggs snapped impatiently. "How do you plead?"

Once more Noah Fawley stared, uncomprehending.

"Did you steal the pig as alleged?"

"He was drinkin' that blackberry wine," the woman shouted from her side of the room, and the small man in homespun gave a violent start as though ready to bolt through the open door at the rear of the building. "It was Lucinda's weddin' day."

Judge Scaggs looked at Mrs. Fawley for a moment, but his curiosity soon overcame his sense of courtroom propriety.

"Who, may I ask, is Lucinda?"

"His older sister," the woman said. "She was married that day an' all the neighbors was in for dancin' an' my son sipped too much of that blackberry wine an' never knowed what he was about when he taken that pig."

"Your Honor," the prosecutor said, "it seems to me—"

"That'll be enough, sir," Judge Scaggs cut in sharply. He turned back to the woman. "Drinking blackberry wine has nothing whatsoever to do with the crime charged to this young man." And back to Noah Fawley. "Tell this court how you plead."

"I never plead with nobody," Noah said. Some color had begun to rise along his bony cheeks.

"All right, just tell me if you stole the pig."

"Well, me an' another boy taken it an' roasted it down on a gravel bar at the river an' et it."

"You ate the whole pig?" Judge Scaggs asked, his eyes bulging.

"We never et the hide ner the head," Noah Fawley said.

His Honor glanced from the boy's face to those of his family. The Fawley men were tight-lipped and hard-eyed, standing around the mother like a guard of wolves.

"And who was this other boy?"

"Ben Shackleford," Noah said. "He's gone off to Missouri to join some army he heerd about there."

"Noy," the boy's father said, pronouncing his son's name as all the family did, without any hint of the "ah" at the end, "you needn't tell about Ben."

"You keep quiet, sir," Judge Scaggs said, but once more his curiosity got the better of him. "Which army was it this Ben Shackleford joined with?"

"He never said which one. Just an army, he said."

Judge Scaggs reared back in his chair and tapped the fingers of both hands on the tabletop.

"Son, how do you stand on the separation of powers?"

Noah looked at him blankly. Judge Scaggs seemed to shake himself angrily.

"How old are you, sir?"

"Seventeen."

"Sound of limb and mind, it appears," Judge Scaggs said. He allowed his nervous hands to lie quietly on the tabletop and drew a deep breath.

"Sir, under the authority vested in me by the sovereign state of Arkansas, Confederate States of America, I sentence you to enlist in militia of said state, in one of the companies recruiting south of this place, and to remain loyal and true to your oath to said unit until the present war of aggression against the South has been brought to its glorious and successful conclusion, which it is the Lord's obvious will that such be done, and failing this on pain of arrest and sentence to a proper jail in aforesaid sovereign state for the duration of five years. Sir, do you have any statement to make before this court?"

Having little grasp of what had just been said, Noah Fawley shook his head. "I reckon not," he said. "Except the pig was no account. When me an' Ben Shackleford et it, we got sick as Old Nick."

"Forthwith," the judge had said. And forthwith it was, with only one more night spent at the hillside farm that sat among the small cleared fields and the hardwood timber.

These were a forthright and simple folk, of English origin. The old man's people had come from east of London, hers from Cornwall. Each counted among their ancestors men who had scouted for the British Army during the Revolution, men who were then and through all their following generations distrustful of the United States government for no apparent reason other than willful ignorance of any institution found in cities.

In fact, Old Man Fawley had immigrated to these hills to place as much distance as possible between himself and that government and such cities as might house any extension of it. The Fawleys had not come alone. Others of their kind had settled in the valley of the Buffalo, many also of old English stock, and their language was still colored with the strange sounds of other places. They called a sack a poke, and sassafras was termed grub hysin.

Twenty-six years ago they had come, Zack being born on the march and all the others born here in a house built with Fawley's own hands, surrounded by fields cleared by his own labor, among the woods that he hunted, for many years alone.

None of the five boys had ever been away from the farm except for a day or two from time to time when they helped some neighbor with his butchering or stump pulling or barn raising. None of them had ever been far outside the county. Thoughts of what lay beyond the distant blue mountains had seldom entered their thinking. Now, two of them would go, because of justice and because Pap had said it was to be.

"Zack, you taken this," he said, handing his eldest the family Dragoon revolver, the powder flash, the caps in their tin box, and the heavy lead balls. "You go an' look after your baby brother in this war you're a-goin' to be at."

And Noah, almost six feet tall, stood proudly by, knowing there was no stigma attached to his conviction for crime. In this family, as in most of the others in these hills, transgressions against outsiders were not considered transgressions at all. Pap had said nothing to that effect, but he didn't need to. He had just put substance to it by giving Noah his prized possession, a gold watch that Noah could feel now in his trouser pocket like a hot, heavy mule shoe.

They were on the front porch overlooking the lush valley of the Buffalo. The old man and Noah and Zack were on one side, making their arrangements; the mother and the other three brothers, Cadmus, Tyne, and Britt, stood near and watched, saying nothing. Now and again the boys looked out across the long valley to the far hills, making a great to-do about keeping all expression from their faces. The woman watched her youngest son with each move he made, and when he finally turned to her and they embraced, there was an added dampness in her eyes, which the other boys tried elaborately to ignore.

Noah turned to his brothers who would be staying, each in turn, and took their hands, still with no one saying a word. Then he and Zack lifted their blanket rolls and stepped down off the porch. Zack embraced none of them, nor shook their hands. He kept his eyes away, but along his beardless jaw the clamped muscles stood out like young hickory nuts.

"You, Noy, be a good boy," his mother called. "An' do what you're told by your elders. Mind your brother."

"Yes'm," he said, turning away down the yard.

"And you, Zack, watch out for your little brother and keep him clear of the Yankees," she said.

"Yes'm," Zack said, not looking back.

The father said nothing but watched his sons walk down to

the rocky road and turn south along it. They walked with backs straight, their feet clad in the new shoes bought on credit the day before, after the trial in Town. There was about their walk a certain awkwardness, yet also a distance-consuming grace. Their slouch hats cast a dark shadow across their heads and shoulders.

The family remained on the porch to watch the two boys come to the first bend in the road, beyond which their home would be lost from sight.

"Who are them Yankees, anyway?" Cadmus asked.

"Outlanders an' city scum," his father said. "They're a-comin'. They mean us harm. The preacher tole me so."

"It ain't Yankees I'm afeared of," the mother said. "It's all them no-accounts they got in armies that carry bad habits. God keep my boys," and she turned quickly and disappeared into the house.

Noah Fawley wished that he had never seen that damned pig. A young man of many regrets, he was always contrite for actions brought on by his impetuous nature. His brother, by contrast, never appeared to regret anything.

Noah was leaving more than family, too. There was the lovely Luanne Lacy, her family's farm only a mile up the hill from the Fawleys', with whom Noah had already tasted the sweet flavor of loving in an old, abandoned smokehouse. It had been in the afternoon, broad daylight, and neither of them brave enough to actually look at what was happening but bringing it to culmination just the same. There had been a gathering of the clans that day, for religious services and late supper on the ground. Those frantic moments in the smokehouse had been a delicious experience—away from all the others, secret. Now, as he walked down the road toward the Buffalo, Noah could see Luanne Lacy's face, the lips pouting, full, and inviting.

In a month or so, when this Yankee thing was finished, he'd

be back. And sweet Luanne Lacy ripe for marriage. Fourteen years old!

He was in this wise unlike any of his brothers, who kept emotion in check as a matter of pride. Many of the hill folk said the Fawley boys would all end bachelors unless their Pap made business arrangements for wives, which he had never shown any inclination to do. It had seemed important to him only that daughter Lucinda be married off to someone capable of impregnating her, which had happened now. As for the boys, if any of them ever longed for soft company on a permanent basis, they made a good job of concealing it.

Except Noah. He was growing from hot-blooded boy to hot-blooded man, given to quick temper, fistfights, and violent spasms of passion.

Beautiful Luanne Lacy! He would tell her grand stories as they lay together after more of the loving that had come but once so far, but that he knew was ready to be had at his taking. Tales to be spun of far places and of people he would see—even the Yankees, maybe. He was unclear in his mind what a Yankee was, with no definite idea of where they came from or what they intended. He wondered how they might look, and if they wore hats like other men and spoke in words he might understand.

"Where's this war at?" Noah asked.

"We're bound to find it, wherever it's at," Zack said in his flat voice with its sound of oak barrel staves clapping together.

"What's it about?"

"Pap says the Yankees aim to come make us live like them."

"How's that?"

"Hell's fire, I don't know," Zack snapped impatiently.

Anxious to end this conversation about things he did not understand, Zack moved off the road and sat on a fallen hickory log. He took out the Dragoon pistol and slowly began loading it. Noah stood still in the road, watching.

"You aim to use that right off?"

"It ain't worth a Gawddamn unloaded."

Zack charged all six cylinders but capped only five, letting the big hammer down on the empty nipple. He shoved the pistol back under his coat, rose, and moved back into the road.

By Gawd, thought Noah, he thinks there really is a war, don't he?

But to Zackery there was no thought of war. Rather, he saw little logic in hauling about an empty weapon, now or ever. All of this was a matter of the moment to him. He was taking this journey because Pap had said to go, but he did not concern himself with anything except tomorrow's dawn. Time enough then to consider the new day and what it might bring.

Although of the same blood, looking brothers every inch, they were as different as two men could be in all other aspects, as each was aware. Now they were going together up the valley of the Buffalo to its head, thence across the intervening ridges into the watershed of the Arkansas, and then along that river to someplace—they had no idea where—to offer their service. Going together in a cause neither of them understood, in total ignorance of why, except for the judgment of His Honor Guthrie Scaggs.